AF605085

THE CARETAKER OF SECRETS {FATE}

A Novel

A.T. Geiger

An imprint of Mountain Peak Press LLC
Bonney Lake, Washington.

Book Cover by Lynn Andreozzi
First Edition July 2023
Manufactured in the United States of America
Library of Congress Control Number: 2023912482
ISBN 978-1-961910-00-3 (paperback)
ISBN 978-1-961910-01-0 (ebook)
ISBN 978-1-961910-02-7 (hardback)

For Mother, the first of warriors

Someone once told me plans are fickle things. And yet long before we become women, we are told we can be anything we want, do anything we want, and dream big. But some plans and dreams are never monumental. They are the simplest of aspirations like many young adults have: Fall in love, find a dream job, and buy a car to drive anywhere but here. Maybe we all should dream bigger. Or yet, perhaps our plans and dreams are never ours to begin with. Because maybe, in some grand scheme of things, fate always plays its part, and we all end up exactly where we are meant to be.

Chapter 1

Sam 2003

"You are beyond incompetent, Samantha. How hard is it to water these plants?"

Oh, Lord. Here we go again.

Ignoring my employer's usual nagging tone, I finished watering the old lady's flowers before excusing myself to the restroom. My job—taking care of Jane Nelson—was an easy enough task, but most days, it took a toll—a mental beating at best. And on this day, there would be no exceptions. Hence why I desperately needed a bathroom break.

Down the hall, I passed by a framed picture of my state of Washington's most dangerous and famous volcanic mountain, Mount Rainier. It reminded me of Jane—an icy old-aged glacier with sharp, rough edges and an unseen boil simmering deep within. The majestic, active volcanic mountain packed yearly layers of ancient snow, just as Jane did—accumulating anger, burying happiness, and compressing whatever secrets held her hostage. I never knew why or what would set her off.

As Jane's caretaker, I had tried to figure out my employer the first few months. Like what made her tick, why she was so disagreeable and angry, and why she treated me like a child when I was eighteen—an adult by legal standards. But Jane didn't see me as an adult, not when I was still a junior in high school, which was no fault of mine. Thanks to my mother, who'd started me late to kindergarten and then held me back in first grade for being socially inept, her choices stretched my suffering in school a year longer than most had to endure.

My friends had suggested quitting my job, but the truth was, I desperately needed the money to buy a car. It was my only way to escape my small town of boring endless nothings that included too much fighting. My family was dysfunctional in epic proportions—often feeling like World War III at home. And add all the arguing with my boyfriend of four years, well, I was simply ready to escape. So, if I didn't want to feel like a hamster on a wheel going nowhere, I would have to endure my employer's mountainous eruptions.

As I made my way down the dark hall of Jane's small home to the bathroom, a sliver of morning light shone through the cracks of her bedroom door, diverting my attention. I was not someone who normally snooped around, but after six months of caring for Jane, I still knew nothing about her. She disclosed very little, and our relationship was awkward, to say the least. Plus, I was beyond bored with the mundane daily productions of work, school, chores, homework, repeat.

The door to the bedroom stood slightly ajar, and I pushed it open before slithering into the cold room of bins, boxes, and organizers lining the wall. Removing the nearest lid closest to the door for a quick peek, I found a stack of old black and white family photos lying haphazardly inside, which was a shock, since Jane was typically a well-organized woman who demanded perfection.

I nearly gave up on finding any insight into Jane's past after only finding more boxes containing the same array of haphazard collections of mementos. But when I opened the next bin in line, a burgundy, leather-covered notebook dated 1972 captured my attention. I skimmed my fingers over its weathered surface and opened to a random page filled with feminine handwriting. My curiosity took hold when the word 'naked' jumped out at me.

1972

How did it come to this, I thought, as I lay naked in the cold, windowless room with just a sheet covering my body. My wrists and ankles were raw from the restraints. My screams ignored. It smelled like a mix of urine and bleach. I wanted to throw up. No one would listen. No one cared. I am nothing.

I lost track of time on how long I had been lying there, trying to free myself from that horrible place—a place I knew I didn't belong. With fists stuck to my sides, I seethed in anger, knowing ***he*** *had lied to them all.*

When the door finally opened, three men in white coats approached me using calm, reassuring voices, telling me, 'This will all be over quickly.' But I could tell by their faces that they meant anything but.

I pleaded for them to listen, but the man stopped me mid-sentence, placing a rubber block into my mouth before holding my jaw shut. I was no longer cold as sweat pooled between my breast, and my heart raced when they wheeled in a small metal table with a wooden box—one with wires, knobs, and numbers.

Recognition hit me hard. And I knew exactly what would become of me.

My muffled screams seemed to come from someone else as I pleaded with my eyes to the man on my right, begging him not to do it. My body betrayed me as tears poured from my eyes and other places from my limbs that shook involuntarily.

I had failed.

I had lost control of this fight.

Something I was so good at.

They placed the device onto my temples as the other man held my jaw shut even tighter, as if preparing me for the worse. And when the sound of the machine came alive with the sound of static buzz and nightmares, I stared up at the ceiling, forcing myself to take long, drawn-out breaths through my nose, desperately searching for repose that I knew would not come. But just as cold paralyzing fear coursed through my entire body, there came with it an oncoming rush of pure, hot hate that brought me one calming thought;

'If I make it out alive, I will find a way to kill him. By God above, he will pay.'

The journal entry was like finding a wallet full of dirty money, and I knew I should have put it back without ever looking back. But I didn't. If the journal was Jane's, it was finally my chance to discover who and what she was all about. Quickly flipping the page over, I started to read the following sentence but nearly dropped the book when Jane bellowed, "Samantha Carey! How much longer are you gonna be in the bathroom? You've got work to do before leaving for school."

I begrudgingly slammed the diary shut before storing the mysterious book in its box and hurried to soothe my employer's impatience. "Coming, Jane!"

My mind went a mile a minute. What had I just stumbled upon in that diary? Who were those men? What were they doing to Jane? Was it Jane? Did Jane kill someone? Holy hell, did I work for a murderer?

I looked at my bedridden boss differently as she sat eagerly in her adjustable medical bed—a bed that happened to be located in the middle of her living room. When she'd first hired me as her caretaker, I'd wondered why someone had placed her bed in the middle of the family room. But it made sense after viewing the only bedroom where I found the journal. At least her great room offered more space and light, with a picture window to look out, which helped keep her mind off the pain.

At sixty-nine years old, Jane Nelson had been bedridden for over fifteen years due to an incurable disease called rheumatoid arthritis. Her immune system had been attacking her body's tissues and joints for so long, it had left her bones decaying, deformed, stiff, and frozen almost permanently. Any regular movements were not something her bones allowed. The disease also brought excruciating pain from osteoporosis, a brittle bone thinning that made her as fragile as a dry leaf. Even for one to hug Jane, which I doubted she permitted, one would need to squeeze her ever-so-gently, so as not to crack, snap or break her.

"What took you so long? We've got work to do," Jane griped.

Because Jane's living room was small, she never allowed clutter. She had a TV she never turned on, one mahogany nightstand to her left with an old picture and a small glass bowl filled with the little lemon candies that she loved so much, and across from her were two visitor chairs. But the only person who visited her was her son Charles, on the weekends. And finally, next to the middle of her bed, sat my arch-nemesis—the portable toilet.

But without the portable toilet, Jane could no longer call herself independent and would be sent to a nursing home, which she said would be her death. So, to avoid the nursing home and still have her dignity, Jane had hired me through the state to bathe her, cook, clean, empty the toilet, and listen to her endless scathing remarks.

"Samantha," Jane said, waving a frantic finger at her potted plants in the window, "hand me one. I want to see if you did what I told you. Like I told you, African Violets *cannot* have that much water in the soil. And you mustn't get any water on the leaves." She punctuated the following words as if explaining to a two-year-old, "They are *delicate*."

"I know. You've only told me a million times, and look, nothing has died." Patience had never been my specialty. I grabbed one of her precious plants from the window and handed it to her.

"*Yet.* Nothing has died yet," she said. "And don't get smart with me." Jane stuck a frail and bony finger inside the soil, and by the look on her face, I knew my boss's words before they came out of her mouth. If Jane ever said, '*oi, oi,*' in any sentence, she was not happy in North Dakotan terms, so I waited for the inevitable scorn to leak from her lips.

She clicked her tongue and shook her head. "*Oi, oi.* Look here, Sam. See? I said no water is to get on the leaves."

I glanced down at where her finger pointed to a ridiculously tiny bead of water resting on one velvety leaf. She would most likely add this incident to the long list of evidence of my incompetence. I let out an exasperated breath before wiping the water off that one measly insignificant leaf with my shirt. "There, all fixed."

"I can tell by your attitude you're thinking, 'This crazy little old lady caring about her dumb little plants.' Well, guess what? I am trying to teach you, Samantha, that even the smallest things deserve your attention and care. If you don't care about the little things in life, it will all spill over into the most important things. You gotta do it right from the beginning."

"Yes, Jane. I understand."

"Good. Now please go make breakfast before your ride comes. Oh, and try not to burn the toast this time."

My mother would say I needed to learn the art of patience, especially not taking everything too personally when Jane criticized me. So, it was good that a wall separated Jane's kitchen from the living room, where I cooked Jane's breakfast in sweet silence and out of sight from the old lady's critiquing eyes. Most people could leave their work troubles behind when their shift ended, but my shifts were unconventional. I had to see my boss twice a day. Once to make her breakfast early in the mornings, and a second time after returning after school, when I tackled chores, made her dinner and helped Jane wash and get ready for bed.

While I flipped a delicate egg over, trying hard not to split it, I thought of the woman's diary again. Maybe she did kill someone. I added Jane's pain meds onto her breakfast plate, a total of fifteen pills. If I ever left for school and forgot to give Jane her pain meds, it would be most cruel. I didn't envy Jane Nelson one bit.

With breakfast finally ready, I carried the tray to the living room to find a glow from the morning's sun ribboning its way through the window, illuminating Jane's petite form. I expected her face to be lifted to welcome the warm rarity, but instead, there seemed to be a cold gloominess that wrapped around her as she shivered.

"You cold, Jane? I can put that throw blanket over your legs?"

Jane sighed, "No. I'm fine."

I doubted anyone would be fine in her condition, and due to the mere fact that she was utterly alone each day, except when her son Charles visited or I helped her. I placed the tray gently on her lap. "Okay, here you go."

It took Jane a moment to securely maneuver the toast between her fingers, and I hated to see how she struggled to eat. But Jane was adamant that she fed herself. 'It's all the little dignity I have left,' she once said when I offered to help feed her.

"Samantha," she said, catching me watching her, "the sun's showing me all the dust on my nightstand."

"Yep. On it."

After polishing her nightstand, I picked up a framed photo and dusted that too. "I like this picture of you here, Jane." I somehow resonated with that black-and-white photo—hungry and starved for a life of color. "Is this your sister or friend?" I asked.

Both women were young and in their early twenties, though Jane towered over the other girl, who seemed plain in comparison. And even though the image was black and white, I imagined Jane in color—a vibrant redhead with bright, emerald-green eyes and full lips parted in a sultry look, going perfectly with her shapely body. Jane could have been a model for all I knew.

But now, Jane's hair hung limp, cropping short to her head with thin strips of salt and pepper, and her once-green eyes were glazed over with a milky white haze—a mist of clouded cataracts. As for her body? Only a bag of brittle bones. I suppose when you lost your health, you lost everything that once flourished—like a wilted flower left without sun or water. And there was no set date or time period one had before a disease like Jane's took over completely.

"The girl in the picture is my friend," she said without divulging more. An expression of disappointment etched her face as she bit into her eggs. She asserted with annoyance, "Samantha, these eggs are runny."

"They are?" It wasn't that I didn't believe her, as I still had much to learn, but I swore she looked for anything to gripe about.

She slid her fork across the egg yolk and away from its white body to prove her point. "See? The whites still have a watery, translucent wetness to them."

I set the framed photo down. "I guess I didn't keep it on the stove long enough. Sorry. I didn't want to overcook the yolks like I did yesterday."

"I told you how to do it. Why is it so hard for you to follow simple instructions? In my day, if you didn't get it right the *first* time, you'd be out of a job."

Jane wouldn't fire me over eggs, would she? I saw myself without a car and forever stuck and quickly offered, "I can try again?"

"No. I don't want you wasting more eggs."

"I'll try to get it right next time," I said. I knew Jane's annoyance was warranted, just as I knew I desperately needed a few cooking lessons, so I hurried to change the subject before she thought of firing me. I pointed to the picture again. "What was your friend's name?"

"Ruth. Which reminds me. Would you put a letter in the mail?"

"Sure. Did you meet Ruth in high school?"

"Yes."

"I bet the two of you made some heads turn back in the day."

"Maybe." I was tired of her one-liner replies and almost gave up, but Jane surprised me and added, "But that was when life was easy and carefree." She sat her fork down and sized me up. "You know, Samantha, there was a time I looked just as youthful as yourself. How tall are you?"

"Five-foot-six."

"I was about two inches taller with a body as skinny as yours. You should eat more and take advantage while you're still young."

My hands rested over my slim hips. "Well, I do eat a ton. I don't seem to gain the weight, is all."

"Seems we both struggle in that department." She pointed a finger at my head. "Is it hard to run a brush through those long, thick curls? I can only guess you need a ton of conditioning cream to do the job."

"Yes. It took me forever to brush it until I learned the life-changing hack of brushing my hair in the shower with conditioner still in it. I still have to apply enough curling foam to tame the beast before it dries though. Otherwise, it would look like I put my finger in a wall socket."

"Well, don't go cutting it short. I don't think your small-framed face could handle it. Long hair looks best with your big blue eyes." Jane took a small sip of her coffee. "And don't go coloring your natural brown hair. If

I could offer any advice, keep your hair free from chemicals. I dyed and curled my hair too many times to count, and now look at me. Not enough hair to crochet a mitten for even a thumb."

"If you'd like, I could dye it for you?"

She gave me a tired look through her thick bifocals. "Someone who can't cook an egg to save her life? I'll pass. Besides, there's no point changing my grey hair when it's deader than a possum. If I could change anything, it would be the ability to walk again."

Jane never spoke of wishes or dreams. Her one wish seemed understandable. "I wish that for you too, Jane," I said and meant it.

I grabbed my cleaning supplies. "Well, you are stunning in this picture. I bet you had lots of boyfriends back in the day."

I could have been mistaken, but a rare, small upward crease formed around Jane's lips. "I didn't have *many* boyfriends, but the two who captured my attention were handsome enough. I'm glad they don't have to see me now, wasting away. Unrecognizable."

I didn't know how to respond, so I tried to lighten the mood. "I would love to hear about some of these boyfriends."

Jane waited for a solid ten heartbeats before responding, "Best be going. You'll be late for school."

It was the best I'd get from Jane for the time being. But eventually, I hoped Jane would soften and open up to me. It didn't seem healthy for the woman to be trapped in her home alone with her thoughts and no one to talk to. Not only was she dying from her disease, but she also seemed to be dying from a permanent vacation of boredom. I could understand a little about how that felt—trapped, stuck with a foreboding sense that nothing would ever change.

"Here is your lunch for later," I said, setting a wrapped sandwich on top of her nightstand.

"You're excused to go. But mail this letter today, will you? It's for my friend Ruth."

Chapter 2

Sam 2003

I couldn't catch a ride back to Jane's after school, but I didn't mind the walk for once. Usually, walks to and from work and school in the Pacific Northwest were miserable, with the constant wet drizzle in springtime. But by that afternoon, even the birds in our small town of Puyallup, Washington, chattered at their luck of warmer weather. So, I decided to relish the moment and took my time admiring all the trees.

With their lime-green sprouted buds giving them a fuzzy look, like a newly hatched chick, spring trees were one of my favorite things, aside from sunsets and books. When I neared an ancient, massive maple that towered over our small town like a protector, I stopped and smiled at its glory. My favorite time of year in the PNW was the fall, when all the maples changed into a rainbow of rusted gold, mahogany, fire orange, and mossy oak.

Once I owned a car, I dreamed of driving around the country, finding the grandest trees of oak, maple and pine and willow, all of which I would sit under and read a book for hours, until the sun faded to black and the ink on the pages was but a blur. It was the one and only thing I looked forward to.

I was sad that my leisurely walk had ended, but my watch showed me I was five minutes late, which meant Jane would have a hissy fit. I stopped to pull out Jane's letter I'd forgotten to mail, and noticed it wasn't sealed.

The right thing to do was to lick and mail it, but as the morning breeze picked up, the wind took my rationality with it. It read:

Dear Ruthie,

I wish you were here. It's springtime, and the annual fair will be in full swing next week, perfect timing to smell the corn dogs a mile away. As you know, my son Charles is writing everything I say in this letter, as my hands can no longer tolerate writing. He says, hello, by the way.

I'm writing to wish you a happy birthday, my dear, sweet friend. Even though we share the same birthdays, I remind you that you are older than me by five hours! Don't worry, sixty-nine for you is probably a walk in the park, and for this, I am slightly envious. But I am grateful for your friendship throughout all these years, Ruth, and I only wish you the best.

I hope you all are doing well. As for myself, I have been feeling a little irritable lately. I might need to fire this young lady that takes care of me. She doesn't know a thing about anything, I swear. Three times I've already had to explain to her how to make a piece of toast without burning it to smithereens. And my poor African violets have suffered from her overwatering too.

Maybe I shouldn't have chosen a girl of only eighteen, a baby, I tell you. She still has a lot to learn, and it may be the end of me to try and show her the ways. Just as I say this, my son just informed me that I need to give this girl another chance and that maybe I'd be a good influence on the girl. Ha! Pray for me.

Well, my friend, enough of my rambling. I better go. Love to you all,
Janey

My mouth hung wide. Her words were like a knife squarely wedged between my shoulders. The nerve to fire me over a few lousy pieces of burnt toast! It sounded ridiculous. I tried to appease my boss, but the truth was, there was no appeasing, Jane Nelson. She had no idea how much I desperately needed my job to escape the never-ending void.

When I reached Jane's mailbox in front of her home, my fingers itched to rip the letter into tiny pieces. But like a good employee, I shoved the dumb letter into the mailbox. And when I walked through the door, I barely said hello to the woman as she pointed to the clock above my head. Instead, I ignored her and headed straight into the kitchen to cook dinner.

And even though she was my meal ticket out, I knew acting immaturely wouldn't help my cause. But I couldn't control myself as I cooked for an hour tossing pans into the sink, and slamming microwaves and fridges. "Here's your 'perfect' meatloaf, *madam*, and 'perfect' mashed potatoes and 'perfect' gravy, minus the runny," I muttered to myself.

I couldn't help my over-exaggerated smile when delivering the tray of food to her. "Hope this is up to your standards." I wanted to add 'Your Majesty,' but I skipped that part.

Jane carefully held a fork of meatloaf mid-air, as if she were about to say something, and I jutted my chin out, nearly hoping we would have words. But she said nothing and only shrugged before continuing to eat.

As I watched Jane struggle to steady her hands long enough to eat, guilt tore at my gut. Why did watching her eat always pull at my heartstrings? As much as my boss annoyed me, she didn't deserve any more misery from me, even if the letter hurt me. Because deep down, I knew if I were to be mad at anyone, it was myself for prying into the woman's business without her permission. It was true when they said some things were better left unknown.

"Jane," I said, letting go of some of my resentment, "do you want me to turn the TV on or anything?"

"No, I'm fine."

"If you don't mind me asking, but what do you do each day if you never turn the television on?"

She wiped her mouth with a napkin. "Lay here and think about this and that. I often look out the window, watching the birds. I've even named a few of them. Which reminds me, I'm almost out of bird feed."

"I'll put it on the grocery list for Charles this weekend." Most caretakers did the grocery shopping, but Jane had her son take on that responsibility because I did not have a vehicle. "Do you have any books you would like to read?" I looked around the room, realizing there were none. "Or I could have my mother take me to the library to get you some?" I didn't know why I offered extra services when she didn't even like me.

"Well, that is nice of you; if only I could open a book's spine. These worthless hands make reading impossible. And even if there are audiobooks, I find it more entertaining to allow my endless thoughts to run wild. Like playing a game of make-believe or What Could Have Beens. Sounds silly when I say it out loud."

"No, not at all," I said. "I do that too, sometimes. Like how I pretend what it would be like if I had been born into a family that never wanted to kill each other. That's why I need a car. My feet can only take me so far away from all the fighting."

"I always believed parents shouldn't fight in front of their children, but I also know first-hand how hard that can be when things get heated." Jane pushed her tray of food to the side. "I'm not hungry right now. The medication is making me sick and making my feet dry and itchy." She pointed to the bottle of Nivea lotion next to her bed. "It would feel better if you rubbed some of that on them."

Ugh; My other arch-nemesis—Jane's feet. "Jane," I said, clearing my throat, "Caleb has offered to take me home tonight. He will be here in twenty minutes to go to school. Is that enough time? I still have dishes."

"Dishes can wait until tomorrow. So, Caleb's picking you up tonight and not your mother?" Jane's question came with an upper lip curled, clearly displaying how much she disliked my boyfriend, even after only meeting him twice. It made me wonder if maybe he looked like someone she'd once known.

I positioned myself at the end of her bed. "Yes. Caleb's coming."

"Do you think you are in love with this Caleb character?"

I picked up the bottle of Nivea lotion next to her bed, squirting a good amount in my hands. I stared down at it, thinking it might not be enough. "I don't know anymore. I thought he was the one since we've been together for so long, but sometimes I wonder what I'm missing. What I want more of exactly? I don't know. Maybe love doesn't exist."

"When I was your age, I fell in love. I can tell you; it exists."

Looking up at Jane, I asked, "What did love look like, then?"

As I rubbed Jane's feet, she sighed, seeming a world away in What Could Have Beens. When she finally spoke, her voice came in as quiet as a whisper, yet full of clarity. "My love looked beautiful and bright as the sun."

Chapter 3

June 1952

It was the beginning of Summer 1952. I was young—just turned eighteen. Life was carefree, and I was adventurous, full of wonder, and likable, unlike the person I am now. It was a time when the world lay before me without shade, and dreams, hopes, and aspirations weren't yet known. But you just knew something bright and exciting awaited within reach. You could feel it. You could even taste it. That was the summer I sought and found love.

Working on a ranch as a cook for the ranch hands, aka cowboys, you'd think I would have met a young fellow, as there were plenty to choose from. But none had caught my eye. I was disinterested in the current selection of boys from my hometown of Church's Ferry, North Dakota. It was a small town with a dried-up lake that had once been big enough for ferry crossings. And being it a small town, where everyone knew everyone, and everyone's business became yours, I wanted to escape. I wanted new adventures. And I wanted to know that love existed like I'd seen on the big screens.

I may not have known much at that age, but I sure knew how to dance. And it was none of that dancing like all the kids do nowadays, where they rub off the threads of each other's clothing, doing the grind or whatnot. Nope, we had *real* dancing back then; The Jive, The Twist, and The Rock'n'roll. So, one particular Friday night, my friends and I drove two hours away to a town called Grafton to hear The Benny Goodman Quartet play with Peggy Lee as their lead singer.

It was a formal affair, and I knew if I wanted to snag a respectable fellow, I had to dress the part. Earlier that week I had just finished watching Rita Hayworth in the movie *Affair in Trinidad*, and I made it my mission to model myself after the actress herself. After putting my cherry red hair up in a pin-up do, I pulled out a long red silk dress that I already owned, but had been too big for me just two years prior. But now the dress clung snugly over my body, matching my red Revlon lipstick.

I had not expected, but rather hoped, to meet someone special that evening. But never did I expect love to hit me the moment I took my first step inside the building.

"Well, I never." I looked for the owner of that deep voice and found it belonged to a smile of dazzling white teeth. "If you don't mind me saying, miss, you sure look the part in that red dress. Ms. Rita Hayworth has nothing on you."

I had to laugh at his remark. "I'm so glad you approve," I said, smoothing my hands down my dress. "That was my master plan."

"If you planned to catch the eye of every man in this dance hall," he said, looking around with wide, bright blue eyes, "I'd say you've most definitely achieved that, Ms.—"

I offered my hand to the gentleman. "Jane Nelson."

"Clint. Clint Brian."

His eyes sparkled with an invitation, like two rare blue-grey stones in a fountain of youth, ready with a lifetime of purpose. His hand, I didn't want to let go of for an eternity. Whoever invented the word handsome must have met Clint for that word to exist. He was dreamy, with an ocean of wavy hair, somewhere between blond and brunette, caramel and yummy. Along with his hair, reaching just over his ears, came perfectly proportionate features, all which seemed unfair to the rest of the simpletons. I was sure every man was envious of his beautiful solid jawline, because I wanted to run my fingers across it.

I could barely find my voice. "Do you live here?" I asked him, still holding his hand. My friends gave me a quick wink before leaving me alone, which I didn't mind.

"Close. A couple of towns over, Edmore. I almost didn't come tonight. But now that I'm here, it has to be fate."

"You think so?" I asked playfully, but hoping it was true.

"Yes," he said with such certainty that my eyes suddenly found my toes interesting. It was conflicting how could he make me feel so bold and shy, all at once.

At the refreshment table, I found out that Clint was a few years older than me and had recently come home to heal from an injury after serving a year in the Korean War.

"I'm sorry you got hurt, Mr. Brian, but I am also not sorry that I had the chance to meet you tonight."

"I'd do it over again and again if it led me to the lady in red."

I didn't know if I felt light-headed from all the flirting, or if the room was overly warm, but I didn't want the feeling to ever go away. I wanted to feel like this for eternity.

Clint offered me his hand to dance. "Shall we go into this together?"

The crowd looked intimidating, but with Clint, I felt safe. "Yes," I said, taking his hand in mine again.

The band began to play an older song, "How Deep Is the Ocean," which was the perfect song for a slow dance and the ideal opportunity to find out who this gorgeous man was who held my attention longer than anyone ever had.

"So, Miss Nelson from Church's Ferry, what do you do back home?"

He pulled me closer to him, his hands settling delicately over my hips. For a moment, the heat from his hands was my only focus, and I forgot what he had asked. "What do I do with my time, you said?"

He pointed to his left ear. "You'll have to come closer and speak in my right ear. This left one lost some hearing from an artillery gun."

"Of course," I said, standing on my toes to bring my mouth closer to his good ear. His cologne was intoxicating. "And you can call me Jane if it pleases you." As I said this, my lips accidentally touched his good ear, and I could have sworn he jumped.

Our heads were close together, side-by-side when he said my name with a prolonged sigh between his beautiful lips. "*Jane*." He said my name as if it were a long-lost missing puzzle piece. "Such a simple name, but I feel nothing is simple about you."

"Did it hurt very much? The accident?" I said, nodding to his injury. "It must have been frightful."

"It was a little close for my liking, but as much as it hurt, it was more shocking than anything. They said my hearing should fully recover. Just hopefully the war will be over by then."

"That's wonderful news."

"Yes, I was very fortunate compared to some. But again, I find myself grateful for this injury, as it brought me here to you tonight. I am a believer that everything happens for a reason." He smiled. "So, back to my first question, Jane; what do you do back home?"

"As in work?"

"Work, play, anything." He laughed, "Sorry, I find myself eager to know everything there is about you."

"Not much ever happens in Church's Ferry. But there is a cattle farm nearby where I live. I cook for the ranch hands and help clean their sleeping quarters. Nothing exciting, I'm afraid."

"But the folks there must feel very fortunate to have such a beautiful lady as yourself. Any ranch hands you've grown sweet on?"

I shook my head. "No."

"Poor fellows. I do hope *I* don't disappoint you?"

I laughed. "I'm talking to you and dancing with you, aren't I? I'd say you've got a better chance than any."

"Then I am *more* than lucky." Clint stepped back and gave me a little twirl before bringing me back to him. "I like the sound of Church's Ferry. It so happens that I'm looking for a rental place. Do you like your town?"

If Clint Brian was looking for a place to land, I wanted him in Church's Ferry. I already knew the sounds and names of every cricket and the rocks they lived under. I was desperate for a new face in town and could live happily seeing Clint's face for the rest of my life.

"One can find themselves a bit restless with the confinements there," I said. "But if you like small towns, not far from me, my father's friend, Mr. Gleen, owns a rental that no one uses. After he lost his wife, he wanted to downsize. But now that I'm thinking about it, it might be too big for a bachelor like yourself, unless you find some roommates."

"With the military, I know quite a few like myself needing a place to recoup. I could go home to Mom and Dad, but I'm ready to stretch my wings at twenty-one."

"Well, good. I don't know Mr. Gleen's phone number off the top of my head, but before I leave tonight, give me your number so I can get the information you need."

"That is very kind of you. You sound like someone who could do anything she puts her mind to. So, tell me, what is it that makes your heart go pitter-patter?"

I wanted to say, 'you,' but didn't. "I'm not sure what you mean?"

"All right, I'll go first. For me, it's hiking the mountains no matter the season. It's my mother's cooking when I feel low, and it's the sound of rhythm and blues that make me want to dance till morning. But above all, it's writing poetry. I love creating a flow of words like a soothing melody that provides me with an outlet to express myself. I could sit and write ballads all day; if only poets were paid a decent living."

"I would love to hear one of your poems someday," I said, and meant every word. I imagined a summer breeze with the two of us lying beside each other in a field of swaying poppies with the wind carrying his singsong ballads straight into my heart.

"Now, what about you?" he asked me again.

"I'm not sure exactly how to answer that. No one has ever asked me such a pondering question."

"If I had to befall a thousand injuries just hear all the things that make your heart beat, I would, *Jane*."

There it was again, my name spoken between his lips as if the gods had chosen it, and all at once I wanted to share my whole life with him. "I love when I am warm in my bed, listening to the rhythmic way the rain falls from the heavens—letting me know I am not alone. Or when the sun splits the darkness after a long day of too many clouds; it reminds me there is always tomorrow. And when I'm feeling lost without directions, I love sitting at the piano, allowing the musical notes to flow through my fingertips, calming whatever depths of uncertainty remain. And I love to sing, even though I have never set foot in front of a crowd." I looked down at the sea of feet and whispered, "I ... it's all too silly, really."

The pressure of Clint's fingertips at my hips deepened with reassurance, and his lips grazed my ear with tenderness, "Silly is that I am only just now meeting a woman as incredible as yourself. And silly it is that I would want to kiss a woman after only one dance." My face turned the same shade as my dress, and he continued, "I'm generally not so bold, especially with a woman I've only barely met, but I feel if I walk away and danced with another, I would be walking away from maybe the most important moment in my life. Do you think now, and even after tonight, you'd want to continue this dance? Maybe even forever?" he laughed.

I didn't hesitate. "I'd like that very much."

Clint was so different from the other men I'd met. For the rest of that evening, there was something protective in how he held my back as we slowly danced, and how he didn't shy away from looking into my eyes. Clint's body, so close to mine, was like a familiar song that calmed and carried me to a new and exciting place with hope and new beginnings. So, it was only fitting that I waited by the phone the next day, eagerly hoping to hear from Clint. And even more fitting when he moved into Mr. Gleen's big house with a barn down the road just a week later.

~

"Jane," Clint said one afternoon as he placed a small sofa chair in the corner of his new living room, "I think I owe you for finding my roommates and me this grand place."

We both stood back and admired the yellow-flowered wallpaper that Clint had promised not to change out of respect for Mr. Gleen's late wife. I had talked to Mr. Gleen about lowering his rental costs, making excellent points that it was our duty to help our soldiers.

"I still can't believe our luck," Clint said. "Let me make it up to you for finding this place for me."

"You don't owe me anything. Besides, with Mr. Gleen's stipulations that you guys to keep up the yard, well, you all might be cursing me later. That hydrangea out front needs watering daily. And I can't imagine how long it will take to mow an acre of lawn out back."

"I have time. And I also have time to take you on a date if you would allow me the opportunity?"

If toes could zing, mine did. "What do you have in mind?" I asked, beaming ear to ear.

~

Our first date was a disaster. I think it's when everything fails and goes wrong that you have insight into the real person you're meant to be with. It's then that you decide if their flaws and reactions to unplanned disasters are worth pursuing.

Before Clint would introduce me to his poems, he said he wanted to cook for me when I mentioned I loved those silly little chicken pot pies that Swansons had just come out with. He told me there was nothing better than the real thing, and so he sent his roommates away for a night out while he attempted to cook me one of his mother's prized recipes.

I remember sitting at the small red and white enamel dinette table with matching chairs in his kitchen, drinking the iced tea Clint had made me, as he moved about the kitchen with ease. I almost believed he knew what he was doing. But since I had a lot of cooking experience at the farm myself, I noticed after twenty minutes that the man didn't know diddly about cooking. But I kept my mouth shut, and thought it best to eat anything he put before me if I wanted a second date.

His first rookie mistake was overworking the dough for the pie crust. Bless his heart, but the toughened pastry wouldn't stretch long enough to even cover the sides of the glass dish, which left the creamy insides of the pot pie exposed naked all around. Of course, when he overcooked our dinner in the oven, the sauce all but boiled out, spilling to the bottom of the stove because he also forgot to put a cookie sheet under the dish to catch the drippings.

After he opened all the windows to let out the smoke, I think he knew it was a disaster. But not once did he curse or make a fuss. He only looked on at me with a glowing smile, as if all was right in the world. And it did feel right, so I smiled back.

As we dug into our dinner with a room smelling of smoke and blackened gravy, his second mistake was the undercooked vegetables. The trick to potatoes and carrots is to soften them by boiling them first before baking, and Clint must have skipped this part, so every bite was of crunchy carrots and undercooked potatoes. The sauce and filling, however, tasted divine.

I looked up at this beautiful man, whose reddened face looked on for approval. He arched a sweated brow. "How... how do you like it, Jane?"

I nearly choked on the burnt crust he'd forgotten to cover with tinfoil halfway through baking and suppressed my laughter as long as I could. It was only when I saw Clint holding in a stomach full of chuckles that we both burst out laughing.

I slowly stood and made my way over to sit on his lap. It was a bold move, especially only knowing each other but a few weeks. But we seemed to become brave people the minute we laid eyes on each other that first night we met. So, while running my hand through his soft waves, still dewy from the stress of cooking in a hot kitchen, I kissed Clint Brian.

The man tasted of buttery burnt crust and savory peppered chicken, and I knew right then that I would eat anything he prepared, even if torched or charred or blackened and dead six feet under. "I think I'll keep you," I said after a long minute.

His eyes met mine in wonder. "Even if I'm a terrible cook?"

"Who says you have to cook? I've got two hands."

"Will you put them two hands right back through my hair?"

"Only if you promise to let me make dessert?"

~

We quickly became a pair, the two of us—he, my Cary Grant, and I, his Betsy Drake. And what came next was a blissful summer love—a heaven on earth. Not even a day would turn over without us seeing one another. That was the summer two lovers sat for hours, swinging on the porch next to the sweet smells of blooming wisteria, reading poems about a girl with red hair and green eyes and the boy who called her his forever.

God, I could have stayed in that town forever and been happy. Clint was mine and home all at once. You always remember your first love. Even today, if I close my eyes, I am back on that porch again, listening to his voice carry the night's breeze of crickets and cicadas making love.

And if I closed my eyes, going even further back—I am there at that dance hall long ago—a moment imprinted into my very existence—with Clint's woody leathered cologne on the collar of his shirt fused with the intoxicating scent of aftershave that always left my skin tingling. I would do anything to return to those nights of fated magic spells, first loves, and forevers written in the stars."

Chapter 4

Sam 2003

The enchanting era of 1952 came to a halt when a startling horn blasted through the living room. "I'm sorry, Jane," I said, my hands mid-stroke to Jane's left heel, "that's Caleb waiting for me."

Jane sat with a sour expression, and I didn't blame her. I would be disappointed if I had to be yanked out of such a beautiful memory and thrown back into such a sad reality.

But because I preferred this new Jane, who spoke of fond memories over the daily moaning and grumbling, I offered, "I'd like to hear more about this Clint character of yours, sometime." I was happy Jane was finally opening up to me. To hear her say she felt stuck in that small town until she met Clint confirmed what I already knew. I didn't feel the same with my boyfriend of four years. I wanted to leave and never look back. And I wanted to find home, or whatever that feeling meant.

~

Caleb picked me up the next morning to drive us to school after working for Jane. I zoned in and out as he talked about tonight's Friday baseball game, until I noticed the homes whizzing by in a blur. I glanced at his speedometer. "Caleb, *slow down*. Do you want a ticket?"

He grunted before letting off the gas just enough so I could see the houses more clearly, leaving me to wonder about the people living inside.

Were they married and still in love? Were some of them unhappily married and stuck? I always wondered if love faded over time, or if there was such a thing as love lasting an eternity. I wanted to believe that love lasted forever. But with my parents always fighting, I doubted it.

And after hearing about Jane's summer love, I was a little jealous. Sure, I didn't know if their love had lasted longer than a summer, but I hoped it had. It sounded exciting. I looked over at Caleb's determined face to get us to school on time and wondered if I'd ever loved him. At that moment, it scared me that I couldn't see our future. All I knew was that I wanted everything Jane had with Clint.

"Did you hear me?"

"Sorry, what?" I asked Caleb.

"My purple jersey. At the baseball game tonight? I want you to wear it. And I need the white one back."

"Oh, yeah, sure," I mumbled. "And I already gave the white one back. It's probably buried underneath the mountains of clothes in your room."

It always marveled me at how put-together Caleb looked. Most guys at our school looked like they had just crawled out of bed but not Caleb. He put a ton of effort into perfecting his clothes and hair just right, taking longer than most girls. He could never pick out an outfit in under ten minutes.

I reached out to touch his hair. "You cut your hair. I liked it longer."

He quickly whipped his head away from my touch. "Sam—"

"Sorry." I had forgotten the cardinal rule: never touch the locks. "God forbid I mess up the *pound* of gel holding that thick hair of yours."

"You said you liked how I did my hair."

"I do. I just wish you'd let me run my hands through it for once." I took notice of his solid black shirt, which looked crisp. "New shirt?"

He pointed to his shoes under the steering wheel. "New shirt to go with my new shoes. Like them?"

"Super nice. Must have cost you a pretty penny." I didn't mean to sound envious, but it came out that way. My family struggled financially, the source of one of their biggest arguments, so I never knew what it was like to shop and get anything you wanted that was brand new and not off the Goodwill racks.

Caleb was very handsome in a jock sort of way. But even with those big brown eyes and boyish charms that I'd found myself lost in at first, I now felt a new kind of lost. It was like playing hide and seek in a bright room where he couldn't ever see me. But Caleb was all I ever knew, and I'd never been good at making hard decisions. Especially decisions that could hurt someone I had cared for over the course of four years of all our youthfulness firsts: My first crush; my first kiss; my first blush; my first dance; my first fight; my first cry; my first make up. Caleb might have had all my firsts, but I wasn't sure I wanted him as my last.

We arrived outside the high school and noticed most students were already inside the building. Caleb barked in frustration, "Why can't I ever find a parking spot closer to our classroom?" He turned around to find another open spot but accidentally slammed the car into park when he meant to put it in reverse. "*Dammit.*"

"Calm down. It's not the end of the world."

"Speak for yourself. This will be my *second* detention. And we wouldn't be tardy all the time if you didn't take so long with that old lady. If I get another detention, my coach will rip me a new one."

He was partially correct. "Okay, I'm sorry I wasn't ready on time. But Jane is old-fashioned. She has to excuse me before I leave. Can I make a suggestion without you freaking out? If you came a few minutes earlier, it would give me time to wrap it up."

Caleb rolled his eyes. "Fine, if you think that will help."

"Also, try not to honk your horn at Jane's house anymore."

"Why? How else will you know I'm there to pick you up?"

"The horn bothers her." I didn't divulge the truth, that Jane didn't particularly like him. "Just knock on the door instead."

"So, now I'm supposed to come earlier *and* get out of the car?"

"You would think I was asking the world, Caleb. But if it's too much, I can always ask Matt to pick me up. He never cares."

When Caleb slammed his foot to the brake and snapped his head in my direction, I regretted my words. Matt was a sore subject. Caleb's face twisted in annoyance. "No, I don't need that guy coming to pick up *my* girlfriend." Caleb resumed driving erratically. "Seriously, he needs to find his own damn girlfriend."

"Caleb, Matt has been my best friend since the seventh grade, so again, he is not trying to steal me from you. If he were, he would have already tried."

"Whatever. I find it pathetic how he is always around you."

Caleb finally whipped us into a parking spot on a side street nearly a block away. With over sixteen hundred students attending the high school, the odds of us finding anything closer were impossible. So as

Caleb's agitation built, so did mine. I slammed my side of the door shut before facing him. "Caleb, again, there is nothing for you to worry about with Matt. But I am *not*, for the hundredth time, *not* going to stop hanging out with him just because you don't like him."

Caleb locked the doors and locked his eyes to mine. "Look. I'm sorry, Okay? I don't want to fight today."

"I agree. It's way too damn early in the morning for this. I already had to hear my parents argue all last night, and I really can't take it anymore."

With no time to make up, Caleb and I practically ran to our first-period class, but there was no use. Like always, we were late.

We'd almost reached the front door to the classroom when Caleb pulled me back. "Hey, quick, can you give me the answers to our computer assignment for fifth period later? I spaced last night. I'll just copy it on the library computer during lunch. That way, I won't get an F on it."

My hand hovered over the doorknob. "Really? No."

"*Sammy.*"

It's funny the different ways someone says your name, each with its own meaning. Caleb often pouted, saying the *y* in my name with a long-drawn-out E for when he wanted something. Or he whispered, 'Samantha' when he wanted more than just a kiss, and 'Sam' when I was in trouble. I knew deep down that there was a difference between someone wanting you as opposed to someone wanting *all* of you. And Caleb seemed only to want bits and pieces of me. And none of the important parts.

"Please?" he tried again. "Coach says I have to keep my grades up."

"Caleb, it is not my responsibility to keep you from failing." Just then, I spotted our teacher through the slender glass panel—his face speaking volumes about us receiving another detention. I gritted my teeth. "Dammit, Caleb. If you don't want the coach to kick you off the team, then do your homework like everyone else." I couldn't believe Caleb would ask such a thing when I had spent hours on that specific assignment the night before, all the while listening to my parents throw out words like divorce and separation. But because Caleb's large brown eyes were bugging out of his head, and because we were already running late again, and because I didn't have the energy to argue because I had started my period a week early that very morning, I surrendered my papers like an idiot.

~

It bothered me that Caleb was copying my homework during lunch hour. But at the same time, it kept him preoccupied, bringing me a little relief. At least he wasn't stuck at my hip or monitoring my every move. Usually, we ate at a table with a mix of Caleb's friends, along with my closest friends, Emily and Matt, but today, it was just me and my friends.

"Are you guys going to Caleb's baseball game tonight?" Emily asked.

"Yeah, if someone could give me a ride. Caleb has to take the bus with all the other jock heads, so he can't take me."

Emily frowned. "Sorry, I have to babysit. I won't get there until late."

"I can take you if you need a ride," Matt offered.

I hesitated, thinking about my argument with Caleb that morning. With Caleb already irritated with Matt, I didn't know if I would be reprimanded for accepting Matt's offer for another ride. But, in the end, I decided that if Caleb wanted me so badly to watch his game, it didn't matter who took me. "Okay, yeah, that would be fine, Matt. Thanks."

Emily looked over at me, moving a cascade of long strawberry-red curls off her slender shoulders. "Where is your sidekick? Not like Caleb to leave you alone." There was a sparkle in Emily's green eyes, and her petite freckled nose twitched playfully. As much as she joked, I knew quite well she often felt like a third wheel when around me and Caleb. I often wished she had a boyfriend so we could double date, but she was too smart for that, saying dating was the last of her priorities.

"I know," I said, "it's a rarity—just the three of us. I keep thinking I would get quality time alone with you guys, but with juggling work, school, and Caleb, I don't know what the word fun means. Anyway, Caleb is off somewhere copying my homework." By the look on their faces, I knew they disapproved. "I know. I know. I shouldn't have. Can we talk about something else to distract me from feeling lousy about it?"

Matt, already a straight-A student, would never say it out loud, but I knew he didn't think very highly of Caleb. He tilted his unruly dark head of thick curls towards the senior tables. "Did you hear Sam Johnson broke up with his girlfriend?"

"What? No. You know who he reminds me of?"

Matt rolled his bright blue eyes, "You've only ever told us like maybe ten times."

I continued as if it were my first time declaring it, "Jake, from the movie*Sixteen Candles*. And if Sam Johnson is finally single now, maybe the rest of us girls have a shot."

"*Uh*, you're taken? Practically married to Caleb, remember?"

"Say hypothetically, Caleb and I couldn't make it work. I am perfectly capable of coming up with a plan on how to marry and have eight kids with Sam Johnson." Matt choked on his sandwich, and I shrugged. "Okay, maybe I'm reading too many romance novels. Four kids?"

"Four kids with Sam Johnson? Yum. Perfect plan," Emily said.

"Anyway, let's talk about your love life, Matt," I said. He scrunched up his face and looked at the ceiling as if it were suddenly interesting for the first time. I laughed, "Maybe *you* need a plan. Single forever doesn't suit you."

Matt was cute, medium height, and built like a rugby player, with humor as his main attribute, but for some reason, he was perpetually in and out of relationships, with none sticking longer than a month or two.

He rubbed his full scruffy five o'clock shadow that most guys envied. "Enough about my amazing love life. Can we please talk about something of more value?"

"I think my boss might be a murderer," I offered.

"What?" Emily said. After I explained how I'd discovered Jane's journal, she gave me a perplexed look. "So, you pried into this poor woman's diary?"

"I don't feel proud of myself, but I was bored. I wanted to know more about the woman who likes to make my life miserable."

Matt pulled out a pencil that I didn't even know he had buried deep in his thick hair and tapped it on top of the table. "Maybe she just needs a friend. The older generations love talking about their past. My eighty-nine-year-old grandma never stops talking about the time she had to endure the Great Depression and the massive drought that caused these dust storms so thick, you couldn't see your hand in front of your face." After Matt talked about his grandma for a whole five minutes, with us staring at him in wonder, he asked, "What? Grams talks a lot. So I'm a good listener."

"Funny you mention being a good listener. My boss just started talking about her first love, and I'm all ears now. But I doubt she would ever admit to killing someone."

"Are you worried she will kill you?" Emily asked, joking.

"No. I'm sure she'd like to kill me at times, but no. Plus, I'm pretty safe unless she magically grows new legs."

"Well," Matt said, "It might do her good if you talked with her more. After I talk with my grandma, she always seems happier."

"Jane? Happy? Yeah, right." I packed up my lunch. "You know what, Matt? I thought I knew everything about you, and yet, here we find you have a soft spot for seniors?" I ruffled the top of his head, making his hair stick out every which way. "Why you are still single, I'll never know."

"Gosh, Sam, I've been holding out for your boss, didn't you know? I like them older, helpless, and in bed."

I threw a carrot at his head. "You are a sicko."

He picked the carrot from off the floor and ate it. "You have no idea."

With lunch finished, Caleb spied me from across the hall and caught up with me before we entered our fifth-period class together. He looked around sheepishly before discreetly slipping my homework back into my backpack. "Thanks," he said. "I love you and owe you *big* time."

He gave me sloppy peck on my cheek, and I mumbled, "*Uh-huh*. Don't ask me to do this for you again."

Fifth-period computer class was my favorite. And not because I loved computers, because I rather loathed technology, but because I adored my fifth-period teacher, Mrs. Jones, who at times took us with her to see the Seattle Mariners play baseball. I liked most of my teachers, but Mrs. Jones seemed more relatable—young, hip, fun, and newly married. I respected and looked up to her in many ways, that I often wondered if she could have been my real friendin high school if we didn't have a ten-year age gap.

"Hey, Sam. Hey Caleb," Mrs. Jones said with a genuine smile, as if she really loved her job *and* her students. She waved us into her classroom and pointed to my long-sleeved top. "That shade of green might be my favorite color on you. Where did you buy it? I feel like you should let me borrow that," she joked.

"Thanks. It's super old. One of my faves. You can borrow it."

Ten minutes before class was over, Mrs. Jones called Caleb and me over to her desk. We stood in front of her. "Caleb, Sam," she said with a look of concern on her face, "come sit for a second." She had two chairs waiting for us to sit, and my stomach instantly twisted in knots.

"Guys, I just finished correcting a couple of papers, and well, I have a question. This is hard for me to even ask, but did you two perhaps copy each other's assignments? I mean, I truly hope this is not the case, but I had to ask." I couldn't move or blink, and I was sure my silence would give us up. And when neither of us confessed, Mrs. Jones bit her bottom lip and began pointing out the multiple mistakes as she flipped page after page. "It's just that, well ... I noticed the two of you have the same exact mistakes on all ten pages. The same mistakes tell me only one thing; someone copied from the other."

The silence was deafening, except for the loud thrum of my heart beating out of my chest. My face immediately heated in a shade of hot and then hotter before coming to a boil. I looked at Caleb and silently prayed he would say something as the current horror movie played out before us, starring Idiot Number One and Idiot Number Two.

Caleb finally mumbled heavily, "Yes, Mrs. Jones I ..."

Please, Caleb, take the fall. Don't say I gave it to you. Say you took it without me knowing. Don't throw me under the bus with you.

"Sam gave me her paper to copy today. I'm sorry," he blurted.

If my head could have spun 360 degrees, it would have.

I looked down at the photo of Mrs. Jones and her husband. "I ... I shouldn't have given him my paper; that's ... that's on me."

When I finally forced myself to make eye contact with Mrs. Jones, she was chewing on a thumbnail. She finally dropped a heavy hand on top of our papers before letting out a long breath, "Look. I'm sorry, you two. I absolutely hate to do this, but both of you will have to take an F on this assignment. I think this is punishment enough since this project was a good percentage of your grade. I am really disappointed."

Oh, God. She was disappointed. And an F?

I looked at the ceiling blinking several times as Caleb spoke, "We understand, Mrs. Jones. We really—"

I didn't hear the next words from his mouth as I ran out of the room before I made a further fool of myself.

The waterworks didn't come until I reached the end of the hall, where I slid down against the wall, pulling my knees close against my chest. I didn't know if I was being extra emotional from my hormones being off, but I didn't know how to face my teacher after what had just happened. I was mostly mad at myself for letting Caleb twist my arm first place, but the worst part was the betrayal. With Caleb on multiple sports teams, he should know what 'taking one for the team' meant. But he didn't have my back. He didn't step up to the plate. And his curveball hurt more than I imagined.

Caleb found me and sat next to me. He tried patting my back, but I moved away from his touch. "Seriously, Sam, you're overreacting. Mrs. Jones will get over it. I mean, people cheat all the time. You're acting like this is the end of the world."

"Caleb, I worked really hard on that assignment. This is going to hurt my grade." I wiped the snot from my nose with my sleeve again before continuing. "How am I supposed to get a scholarship and get accepted into any decent college away from home if I don't bring up my GPA? And since my parents don't have the money to help me, I'll be stuck here forever, attending some lame community college down the road."

"I'm sorry, okay? If it makes you feel better, I might not get to play baseball now. My coach said if any of my grades drop, I'm out the rest of the season."

"Then you should have done your homework, Caleb. But don't worry your little head, because we all know you athletes have special privileges. I'm sure your coach will find a way to bump up your grade point."

"I'm sorry. What else do you want me to say?"

"Why couldn't you just tell her you took it? Why throw me under the bus when it was *me* doing *you* a favor? Couldn't you repay me that favor? Can you ever think of me before yourself?"

"Look, at that very moment, I didn't think to say I *stole* it rather than you gave it to me. Besides, that would have been a lie."

My tears magically disappeared. "Hold on. You can't lie for me, but you have no problem cheating off my homework? That makes *total* sense."

"Sam, please, I said, I'm sorry. Don't hold this over my head."

"Whatever," I said, standing. "The damage is done. The bell is going to ring, and I don't even want to go back in there to grab my things." I waited for Caleb to offer to grab everything for me, but when he didn't take the hint, I shook my head. He was clueless about what I needed from him.

I found Mrs. Jones at her desk after wiping my face dry. "I want to apologize and say I am sorry, Mrs. Jones. It was pretty immature of me to give Caleb my work. I don't know why I gave in to him, but either way, I take full responsibility and agree with your decision. I'm sorry."

She stood and walked around her desk before giving me a hug. "Thank you for the apology, Sam. It means a lot." She pulled away before giving my shoulders a motherly shake. "You are a smart girl, Samantha. Just promise me you won't ever let anyone take advantage of you again?'

"I promise."

Chapter 5
Sam 2003

Exhausted was an overstatement. After the episode with Mrs. Jones, working for Jane was the last thing I wanted to do. But calling out sick was out of the question since Jane's son, Charles, worked so late. And to top off my day, I had stubbornly declined Caleb's offer to drive me to Jane's, which left me with an uneventful walk in the rain to work.

A horn honked behind me, and after wiping the rain out of my eyes, I found Emily waving at me through wipers running on full blast. She rolled her window down an inch. "Hey! Why the heck are you walking in the rain?"

I yelled out over the thunder, "Oh, just washing away my tears of guilt and sorrows."

"Get in, already."

While Emily drove me to work, I caught her up on the day's turn of events.

"What an ass," she said, shaking her head. "I'm sorry but, *wow.*" We were only a few minutes from the school, and she pulled into Jane's driveway in no time. "Look, Sam. This is hard for me to say, but sometimes after you tell me about all the annoying crap Caleb pulls, it makes me wonder why you're still with him."

I traced a drop of rain cascading down her window. "You don't like him that much, do you."

"It's not that I don't like him, I just think you could do better."

"Why didn't you tell me any of this before?"

She turned her dry face towards my wet one. "I didn't want to hurt your feelings. You said you loved him, so it seemed a moot point. But can I be real with you now?"

"Always," I said, bracing for the worst.

"Well, I know when you're happy and when you're not. Also, we used to have fun together, and lately, you seem distant."

Emily was perhaps my most intuitive friend. I looked out the window aimlessly. "You're not wrong. And I'm sorry about not being a better friend, Em. I really want to work on that. As for the other issue, yeah, I'm trying to figure that out. I'm trying to find out what song it is that I want to sing."

"You know I'm always here if you need to talk."

"I know that. Thank you. And I would talk, but I'm late."

"We need a girl's night out or something. Or we can watch that movie, *How to Lose a Guy in Ten Days*?"

I laughed, "Sounds like the perfect movie for me."

~

The front door to Jane's house unlocked easily. "Hello," I said, dripping puddles on the floor of her small entryway.

Jane shook her head. "You are a swampy mess. Hurry and dry off with a kitchen towel and then wipe the floor up. I don't want anyone slipping."

After drying most of my hair in the bathroom, I came back to wipe up the puddles. Jane made a *tsking* sound that sounded like a squirrel sucking on a nut. "Hope you weren't neckin' with that boyfriend of yours after school and that's why you are late."

Great, Jane was in a mood, but so was I.

"No, I wasn't necking." I didn't tell Jane I was late because Caleb and I argued longer than anticipated after school. Instead, I focused on mopping the wet floor. When finished, I asked her, "Is there any particular chore you want me to start first?"

"I would very much appreciate it if you would start with this here toilet."

My day had already headed down the toilet, so why not start with the shitter.

If anyone had a gag reflex, they would know why cleaning out the porta-potty was the second-worst thing about my job, the first being Jane's nagging. After dumping the bucket of contents out into the toilet, I quickly flushed before rinsing the bucket in the bathtub. Finally, once everything was cleaned, I added fresh water to half the bucket along with a sanitizing solution of Pine-Sol.

Once everything sparkled clean, I set her bucket back onto its portable frame next to Jane before discreetly going to the kitchen for a fresh breath of air.

"Don't be lollygagging in the kitchen, Samantha. We've got to get a move on. Let's get some of these chores done."

I wanted to yell out, *I am not lollygagging, just gagging*, but I didn't.

"Samantha, since you already have the supplies out, let's finish mopping the dining room area."

"Yes, Jane."

My thoughts took over as I scrubbed the floors. Mrs. Jones's class. Caleb. Parents' talks of divorce. My grades. College. No car.

"Samantha, do you see that smudge by the entry?"

I looked around on all fours. "No. Not exactly."

"To the right there," she said, pointing.

When I still couldn't see anything, I got down on my elbows for a closer look. But not seeing anything, I frantically began scrubbing in every and all directions.

"No, no, no. You are missing it completely."

I sat on the heels of my feet, panting. "Sorry, where?"

Jane's voice came in a wave of agitation, "*Oi, oi*. Just *stop* and *look* at where I'm pointing. The smudge is on the linoleum floor *right there.* How can you not see? I would get up to do it myself if I could, you know."

My eyes followed to where Jane wagged her finger from across the room. "Jane. I already did that area."

"Well, *no*, you didn't. If you were standing where I'm sitting, then you'd see that smudge. It's right there in front of your eyes."

I looked every which way while pulling my jeans up.

"Sweet Jesus, child, look to the left where my finger is pointing, which would be to *your* left."

I didn't know if Jane was making up this so-called smudge, but the bones in my knees couldn't take it anymore. I stood with hands on my hips and lost my nerve. "Where? I literally cannot see what you're seeing, Jane." I raised my voice an octave higher. "It looks clean to me."

"It's clean to whose standards? Yours? It's as though you refuse to see what I'm seeing." She shook her head and looked past me as if she were speaking to someone else in the room, "I swear kids nowadays don't take any pride in their work. They all wanna rush to get things done and then expect to get paid for a half-asked job." Jane gave me a severe look. "And by the way, I did not say half-assed; I said half-*asked*. I *asked* you to do a specific job, but it looks like you have only done *half* of what I'm asking."

I didn't know where Jane was coming from or why she felt the need to berate me for no reason. Maybe her meds had worn off, but I continued to hold my tongue while she kept wagging hers. "It's a hard lesson to learn, but there's a whole nasty world out there, and it isn't going to hand you a thing. So, it's best you learn that now."

Maybe because I had already had a crappy day at school and a more than crappy night at home last night, but I had reached my limit. "You know what, Jane? I scrubbed everything here, and I'm sorry I don't see this *so-called* tiny smudge you're talking about. And I don't do anything 'half-asked.' Quite frankly, I think I do a pretty good job most of the time. But your demand for perfection sometimes feels like an impossible task. And not just for me, but I bet for anyone who sets foot in here." My chest heaved five whole beats before I stopped myself from saying anything worse.

Jane adjusted her glasses. "Why on earth are you yelling at me?"

I didn't know how much more I could take from being unhappy at work, unhappy at home, and now, unhappy in love, but apparently not much. I looked up to the ceiling while patting my eyes, trying hard to stop the crack in the damn."

"All right, All right. Let's just calm down," Jane said.

I knew I was overly sensitive from everything building, so I tried to smooth things over so I wouldn't lose my job too, "I'm sorry, Jane. I guess I'm just not having a good day, or a week, or a good month."

My nose dripped onto the floor, which technically created a smudge worth noting, but Jane said nothing about it. She pointed to the roll of toilet paper next to her. "Come sit and wipe your face." I did as she asked while she looked out the window. "It's not my intention to be so hard on you at times, but I guess I'm frustrated that I can't just clean my own messes and do it my damn self." Jane's gaze turned away from the window and settled in on me. "Now you know why I'm mad, so how about you tell me what's gotten *you* so upset, because I know it's not about me poking you. After six months of knowing my ways, you should be used to that by now."

I didn't tell Jane about school. I didn't need her disappointed too. "I got into a fight with my boyfriend. I guess I'm just tired of fighting, is all."

"Well, you can't talk common sense into most men. It's useless. They don't get us women, because we are a different kind of breed. So, that would be your first problem. Secondly, I did not get the feeling your boyfriend was the gentleman kind, not like your other friend, Matt."

"I know Matt's a charmer," I said. "He has a great sense of humor. But *really* Jane, our relationship isn't like that. We're just friends."

"Well, I know a thing or two about gentlemen—how they look and act and how some *pretend* to be gentlemen. Either way, the fight with your boyfriend will all wash over. Besides, you're too young to worry about silly little arguments, and I'm almost certain your argument wasn't of a serious nature?"

I knew she was fishing, so I hurried to curb her curiosity. "Did you ever fight with your boyfriend, the boy named Clint?"

She paused before answering, "We only had one disagreement."

Chapter 6

Jane 1952

Clint was the epitome of a gentleman. Back then, men held doors open for women and stood up at the dinner table when you excused yourself to powder your nose. It was a time when men wouldn't dare hoot or holler at you when you walked by on the streets. But my Clint was more a gentleman than I was a lady, I hate to admit. That entire summer, he never once brought me to his bedroom, if that said anything about the man.

But by October, my bottled-up hormones were like a shaken can of soda pop, and all the late-night necking just wasn't cutting it for me anymore. As we lay in the back of Clint's blue Chevy pickup truck covered in thick blankets, gazing at a starless night, with clouds so thick a plane couldn't push through, we had our first disagreement.

While he was trying to be honorable, I, on the other hand, was trying to talk him out of a good conscience. I didn't take it lightly when Clint kept turning me down or that he had yet to say those three little words. I had my pride, you know. But I kept wondering,

Why isn't he acting like a complete fool like myself?

How can he so easily control his emotions?

Why doesn't he want to rip my clothes off like I wanted with him?

Could Clint possibly not love me?

Maybe I wasn't enough.

Finally, with all my insecure thoughts jumbling around in my head and wanting more than what he was offering, I pushed him away after another one of his meager kisses. "What is wrong with you, Clint? I feel like you're just not that interested. Do you like someone else? Do you got yourself a sweet girl on the side? Is that it?"

The dimly lit porch light across the lawn was enough to see his bemused expression. He sat upright and threw his head back into a deep laugh that echoed into the night, "You ... you woman are something; something else, I tell you." I glared at him in the dark as he held his stomach, laughing deeper. "There is no other woman, Janey. You know you're the only one for me. Besides, how would I have time for someone else when I have been with you this summer? Heck, my roommates don't even know me because I'm with you every waking moment."

He had a point, but I was not too fond of being made fun of. "Stop laughing. This isn't funny," I said, crossing my arms.

"I beg to differ. This is *quite* funny."

When he leaned back against the truck's bed with a daring smirk, I glared at him. "No, it is not funny. These are my feelings, and every time we kiss, you ... you act as if I've got the plague or something."

Clint gently grabbed hold of my angered fists and caressed his thumbs over the top of my knuckles. "Don't be ridiculous. *YOU* are far from any plague. Janey, you are the most beautiful woman I have ever seen. How could there ever possibly be another?"

"Well then, what is it? Our age differences? Am I too immature for you? You can tell me."

"Three years is nothing. You are eighteen going on thirty. Well, with the exception of tonight. Tonight, you are acting your age."

I punched him lightly in the stomach. "Then what? Do I stink? I shower every day after working the farm's kitchens." I looked at our hands. "I'm starting to think you don't like me, or maybe I'm no longer enough for you."

"*Oh,* I like you *just fine*. Can't you see?" He laughed again, "You're killing me here."

His amusement at my expense and not getting the answers I wanted fueled the fire more. I threw the blanket off me and jumped down from the bed of the truck. "I'm not sticking around for whatever game you're playing. If you don't want me, well then, maybe someone else will."

He didn't like that last comment, and his grin flatlined. I knew I was acting like a bratty two-year-old throwing a tantrum and storming off for not getting her way, but my emotions, hormones, and pride took over.

It seemed Clint had just about had enough of me when, like a parent chasing after their child, he grabbed my arms and twirled me around to face him. "Where do you think you're running off, and what has gotten into you?" A soft warning followed, "*Janey*, you're *my* girl. I want no one else, nor do I want you with another. Now, just ... just knock this off, please? You're ruining a perfectly good evening."

I couldn't just flat-out tell the man I had loved him since the very first night at the dance hall, and that I wanted him to make love to me. So, I did the only rational thing; I made up things to argue about.

But even God sometimes gets tired of senseless arguments.

We didn't even notice when the air grew thick as a woven quilt or hear the thundering noises above. Nor did we care when the man upstairs sent down a cloudburst of raindrops as fat as Granny's prized blueberries. Instead, we stood in stubbornness and withstood the drownings to see who would fold first.

It wasn't until the rain's downpour came like stinging pellets that I remembered what Momma always said, 'Pride comes before the fall.' 'One's pride is the ultimate catalyst.' As her words pecked away at my spine fitted with rods, my anger finally dissolved into a puddle around my feet, and the fire all but dampened out. "I'm... I'm sorry, Clint. I don't know what's wrong with me."

He pulled me to his chest, folding me into his arms, and finally whispered the three words I had long waited to hear, "I love *you*, *Janey*." His warm breath against my ears gave me goosebumps. "I love *you* and one else, you silly, silly girl."

It wasn't so much what was under a man's clothes I needed, but those three simple words. And right then and there, I melted under a sky of tears—happy tears that told me I was enough for Clint Brian. "Say it again," I asked, hoping I didn't just imagine the angels singing.

Clint held me back at arm's length and offered his face to night sky, "Jane Nelson, I love you!" His smoldering eyes found mine before he spoke with what sounded like a solemn oath. "There is no one else, *Janey*. Forever only you. If only you knew how much you mean to me and how badly the very thought of ever losing you hurts..." His nose brushed over my wet nose. "I had *hoped* to profess my love to you in a more romantic way. Not with all this rain and not with all this screaming at each other. But here you've gone and ruined it with all this nonsense of yours, thinking I had another girl on the side."

I snuggled into his wet embrace and finally said my piece. "Well, then, you should know I love you too, Clint Brian. I think I've loved you before you ever loved me."

"Impossible."

We folded into one, kissing passionately as the rain washed over us, sizzling out any anger that had burned just minutes ago. No more doubts were left, wondering if Clint was crazy in love with me because I felt his love for me; his whole body shook with passion and desire for me.

The tenderness of his kisses moved to my throat, leaving me faint. And as much as his declaration of love gave me relief, I now wanted the man more than ever before. The frustration of wanting and needing someone burned within me like an intense fire sweeping through a thirsty forest that no amount of rain could extinguish.

I broke from his spell and shamelessly asked, "Clint, if we both love each other, then why should we wait? I know you're a gentleman, no matter what we decide."

He grabbed my hand and pulled me along to follow him as he headed for cover. We ran to the big barn next to his rental house and swiftly sought shelter, although I didn't know what the point was since we were drenched through.

Once inside and out of the shivering downpour, Clint turned to look at me through the dark. "Now listen, Jane, my love. I want to do things the *right* way when I ask your daddy for permission for your hand in marriage. How can I honestly look your father in his eyes and ask for your hand if I have dishonored you in any way? What kind of man would that make me?"

My hand flew to my mouth. "You ... you mean to marry me?"

His laugh was as deep as the ocean. "Yes, you vixen! But I want to walk down that aisle with the new Mrs. Brian on my arm, *knowing* I've earned my spot beside you. I need to know I did everything right in the books because you deserve the world and more. I wouldn't feel right if I dishonored you, Janey. So, now quit all this nonsense and help a poor guy out by cutting me a break already."

"Oh, Clint, I am sorry for acting out. I am just terrible, aren't I."

"Incorrigible."

Filled with joy and excitement for what the future held for us, I couldn't contain myself and squealed like a schoolgirl before I jumped up into Clint's arms with such force that we fell into a fresh pile of hay.

Clint, having a good sense of where our fevered kisses could lead us, struggled for composure before saying in a husky voice, "Janey, this is not helping me *one bit.*"

I let out an exasperated breath, "Fine. I will try and be a good girl, Mr. Brian. You have my word until the wedding."

"Then maybe just a few more kisses would be all right, Mrs. Brian."

~

When you're young, no one really tells you what life's purpose is. Maybe it's because that notion is different for everyone. Through my mother's eyes, it may have seemed her children were the motivation, reason, and purpose. As for my father, he might have said his worth came from proving himself a hard-working man that provided means to his family. But for me, it was as if my worth, my motivation, my sole purpose, my reason to live, my existence, and all of life's true meanings lay in this one man's hands. And I saw everything different after that.

The next day, with Clint's hand in mine, we walked with purpose. We walked down the streets and storefronts, all looking different, and more vibrant than before. The sounds of merchant chatter seized, and in its place were birds of song and rejoice. Even on a chilly fall Saturday, all bundled in our coats, the air smelled of honey, and I suddenly craved something sweet.

"Clint. What do you say we stop in here," I said, pointing to a little store called Sworley's Sweets. It was no bigger than a chicken's coop. Still, once inside, they made use of the space by lining the walls from floor to ceiling, carrying various buckets of candies—Black Jack Taffy, BB Bats, Candy Buttons on paper tape, Caramel Creams, and my favorite, hard lemon candies coated in confectioner's sugar.

"Most girls love chocolate," Clint said after buying me a whole scoop of lemon drops. He popped one into my mouth. "But not you. You are everything sweet and sour, and it suits you. I don't think I could ever look at another lemon candy without thinking of you." I offered him one of my candies from the bag, but he shook his head no. "Gives me an excuse to kiss your sweet lips if I want a taste." I was disappointed when the kiss lasted only a minute, but he pulled away and gave me a toothy grin. "What do you say we make this day even sweeter?"

"How could it be sweeter than it already is?" I smiled.

"Follow me."

I didn't let go of his hand as we headed south, weaving in and out of apple trees that lined the streets. "Where are you taking me?" I asked, while snagging an October apple straight off a tree.

"You'll see."

Just as I was about to bite into the apple, Clint snatched it from me. He rubbed it across his trousers and polished it clean before taking a big bite for himself. "All right. It's okay for you to eat."

"Well, I know it's okay to eat; that's why I picked it, you goof."

"I just had to make sure it wasn't poisoned. I would rather die first before I let anything happen to you."

I shook my head as we walked on. "If you aren't careful, Clint Brian, I may have to marry you tomorrow."

"That's exactly what I'm thinking," he said as he stopped in front of a store that supplied and stockpiled various household goods. He pulled me inside, passing by the furniture, the dishes, the books, art displays, the clothing, and accessories, before finally stopping in front of a long glass counter. "Okay. Have a gander."

"What are we doing here?" I asked, looking around. I knew the owner of the store, Mr. Beasley, who stood behind the counter polishing a silver necklace. He smiled as I looked up at Clint in utter confusion.

Clint pointed to the array of sparkling new and used jewelry that was displayed elegantly in each case. "I can't marry you tomorrow if you don't pick out a ring first."

I looked at Mr. Beasley, wide-eyed. "I—"

"Now, I know you are probably wondering what the budget is," Clint said, "but I'm sure they have layaway. Is that right, sir?"

"That we do," Mr. Beasley said. He set aside his polishing rag and held a hand out to Clint first and then to me. "Congratulations! Your parents must be thrilled, Ms. Nelson."

Before I could stutter a word out, Clint came to my aid. "Well, we might be doing everything backward, but we should keep this under wraps until I speak to her father first. Then I'll come back and buy the ring, and then I'll ask Ms. Nelson for her hand. A Christmas wedding sounds about right."

"Well, then go ahead," Mr. Beasley said, "take a look, Jane. Once you pick out a ring, I'll size your finger and keep it on hold until your special friend here returns for it."

My hand found my cheek overly warm, even with the fans overhead on full blast. "Really? Right now?" I asked Clint, looking at him in wonder.

"I can't waste another day. Not when knowing you ... you were made for me."

I brought my shaking hand down and ran it over the top of the glass case. Before Clint, I didn't know exactly what my dreams were or what my purpose in life was, but as I said, in a blink of an eye, everything became clearer. My life and everything in it meant nothing without Clint Brian. "You're right, Clint," I said as my eyes locked onto a simple gold band, "this day just became sweeter."

~

The next day after I had chosen the perfect ring, the sun had been shining down upon me just before the eclipse and just before everything turned my world black. They said not to look directly at the sun or your eyes would burn out of your head, and maybe that was what I did. Maybe I looked too closely at the sun, my Clint; forgetting that dreams could change on a dime and good news often accompanied the bad.

Our family woke to an early morning knock on our front door. Momma answered the door in her robe as I hid. I was still in my morning clothes, and it would be improper to be seen half-dressed.

It was like an exciting jolt to my heart when I heard Clint's deep voice from the other side of that door. "Hello, Mrs. Nelson. I'm sorry for coming unannounced and for it being so early in the morning and all, but you see, I'm a bit short on time and need to speak to Janey as soon as possible. May I?"

I did not want to come out from behind the door as my hair wasn't even curled, and I looked a wreck, but there was something urgent in Clint's tone that made me put aside my vanity. "Good morning, sunshine," he said with a rasp to his voice. "Could we sit on the porch?"

I nodded as he led me to the swing under the eaves with the wisteria, now without its bloom. A horrible feeling scratched at my neck.

"*Janey.* I ... I had an appointment for a follow-up on my ear a week back, and with it being nearly healed, just last night they deemed me suitable to ship out. I've been called back to duty to join the fight in Korea again."

We'd known it was a possibility he would have to continue his duties across the world, but I didn't think it would come so soon. Not when we were to start our lives fresh and new. "But Clint, why now? Why do they need you when *I* need you here."

"Janey, sweetheart, it just doesn't work like that. But, God, I wish I could stay. But I gave my word. I have to follow through."

"But you gave *me* your word."

"I know. I know. I'm so sorry, but I have no choice. Trust me, I want to stay here and make a life with you. But that all has to wait until I come back."

While he held me in his arms and let me cry for both of us, it was the only time I wished to hell he wasn't a gentleman who swore oaths and gave his word. To hell with the war. I wanted him to take me and run far far away.

He handed me a tissue from his jacket. "It will only be for a short time. I'll be back. Please be brave, Janey. Can you do that? For me?"

"I don't know, but I will try." I wiped my nose before asking, "When do you have to go? Maybe before you leave, we can get married? I don't need a big wedding, Clint; honest, I don't."

The news just kept getting worse. "I leave tomorrow."

"*No*," I sobbed.

He took hold of my face in his big warm hands, kissing away my tears. "I love you so much, *Janey*. Promise you'll wait for me?"

"I promise."

Chapter 7

June 1953

Christmas had come and gone. Keeping busy to avoid thinking about Clint off and fighting for his life somewhere, I decided to get a second job in the evening at Café Rose as a part-time waitress. But even with my days cooking at the ranch and my nights occupied at the restaurant, the poems and letters Clint sent every week were hardly enough to dull the ache in my heart. I missed him terribly. To have an entire summer of love with Clint and then to find myself alone for months with nothing to look forward to but the cooking and cleaning ... I was a mere hollow shell.

Ruthie, my very close friend, was my rock during that time. Without her to confide in, I was sure I wouldn't have been able to get out of bed each morning. I placed a large slice of rhubarb pie down in front of her after serving her dinner at the café. "Here's the last slice."

"How about we share it, Jane? You need to eat something. You work at the best restaurant in town and never eat. And I hate to say this, but I wouldn't be a real friend if I weren't honest with you; you look like a stick bug without a leg to stand on. You have to eat more, hun."

"I can't. Honest to God, Ruth, I'm losing my mind. I get so sick thinking about what Clint's doing and if he's hurt or not. Food just doesn't sound so appealing with how I feel."

"Believe me, Jane, I truly understand, but listen, you gotta take good care of yourself. You don't want Clint coming home to a bag of bones, do you?"

I wiped a few crumbs off the table. "I suppose not."

"Good, then come sit down right here next to me and help me finish this here pie. We gotta fatten you up."

But I could not eat when days turned into weeks, and weeks turned into months. And by the time I had attended three spring weddings, around the same time Clint had stopped responding to my letters, well, I was beginning to feel like the jilted bride. It wasn't his fault he had been gone six months already, but I soon took the absence of his letters personally. There were days I was angry with Clint and days I cried 'til my eyes were swollen shut, as if my tears would will him back to me. And because time has a way of blurring things, I wondered if I'd only imagined the man, as if our love was just a forgotten dream.

~

One evening, just before closing at the café, a fight broke out between some high school seniors. I nearly welcomed it out of pure boredom as I stood between the two tables and asked the obnoxious group to calm down, but my words barely resonated when the argument boiled into an obscene mess. When one of them threw a punch at the other, I found myself caught in the line of fire and stumbled backward. Just before my head hit the ground, strong hands caught me, and I found myself staring into a pair of intense dark brown eyes belonging to a strikingly handsome young man to whom I had just served coffee—black, no cream, no sugar.

He thrust me behind his tall form just in time before another punch whizzed through the air, missing my face by inches—but unfortunately, the flying fist caught my savior square in the mouth.

I gasped, "Oh, mister, I—"

His eyes widened ablaze in a murderous glare just before he roughly grabbed the culprit by the collar, picking him up, and slamming him hard to the floor. I couldn't help but notice his thick arms when he turned an angry face to the others involved. The room was quiet for only a second before they all raised their hands high—the fight over as fast as it started.

As everyone slowly milled out of the restaurant, leaving me alone with the man and his bloodied lip, I went about to find the first aid kit. I came back, pointing to the nearest booth. "I am terribly sorry you got hit on my behalf, mister. But for what it's worth, thank you."

He had hair the color of black walnuts—glossy black ones freshly opened, still in their husk and mysterious. He held out his hand across the table. "Daniel Foley. And there's nothing to be sorry for. Those halfwits should have never chosen to fight inside an establishment, or worse, in front of a lady."

"Well, no, they shouldn't have," I said, shaking his large warm hand in mine. "Nonetheless, thank you, Mr. Foley."

"Just Daniel will do. And what may I have the honor of calling you, Miss—?"

My with hand still nestled inside his, the sultry stare he gave me was too good for any breathing female. I noted his olive skin, and sensual smile of full lips that accompanied an even fuller head of thick, dark hair that matched the smolder in his eyes. I swallowed before pulling my hand away. "It's Jane."

"Does Jane have a last name?"

I reached for a cotton ball and soaked it with alcohol before reaching across the table to wipe the red wetness that dripped from his mouth. My hand slightly shook at the intimate contact—need, want, and guilt all layered into one. And I thought of Clint.

"*Ouch*." He winced.

"Oh, so sorry, Mr. Foley. It's just a bit of antiseptic."

"I'm teasing," he smirked. "Again, you can call me Daniel; no, this Mr. Foley business. *That* would be my father. And being that I may be close in age with yourself, well, calling me Mr. Foley sure doesn't sound right; it's like having my father in the room, and I'm hoping I won't be seeing him anytime soon."

As curious as I was, I didn't question why Mr. Foley seemed to be running from his pa. "All right. Daniel it is."

"You didn't answer *my* question?"

"Oh, sorry, yes, last name Nelson."

"English?"

"Yes, my grandmother was full English."

"Foley is an Irish name." He laughed. "I would have thought you'd have a little Irish in you with all that red," he said, pointing to my curls, which hung close to his face as I leaned in to dab some ointment on him.

"I get the red from my Norwegian grandmother." I looked closely at my handiwork. "There. It's the best I could do," I said.

He touched his mouth. "Thank you."

"I must say, it looks positively swollen." I wanted him to leave, but yet, a perplexing need for him to stay nearly nullified any rationality. How could someone look so alluring after a fight? I got ahold of myself. "Best be going home in a hurry and put a cloth with ice on that."

"No worries. This is not my first split lip. Hence why I'm not too fond of my father."

"I'm sorry to hear that." As I hurried to clean up and place everything back into the first aid kit, I could feel Mr. Foley's eyes watching my every move, as if I were the first woman he had ever seen. His attention on me unsettled my nerves, so I broke the silence with a question that only kept him there longer. "You're not from around here, are you?"

"No. Just passing through. Looking for some odd jobs, enough to save up to get to my next destination."

"And where is your next destination?"

"Not sure yet. But this *here* place seems like a nice town."

His observation of our town after what had just happened made me laugh. "You think this town is nice, *huh*? After a split lip and all?"

"I see the irony, so let me rephrase that; *you* seem nice enough, so maybe I will stick around?" It was a question, but the words were more like a statement.

I stood up, nearly dropping the bloodied cotton balls. "Well, I've got to be closing up the café. The cook is nearly finished in back."

"Yes. It looks like it's closing time. Thank you again, Jane. It was indeed nice to meet you, even under the circumstances."

"Good luck finding a job, Mr. Foley. I mean, Daniel."

He walked to the door, and before exiting, he tipped his head toward me. "I *do* hope to see you around."

I didn't reply, because it seemed unholy to want such a man to stick around. I needed him to leave as fast as he'd breezed on in. Because the truth was, Daniel Foley was like a strong windstorm passing through, bringing anticipation and danger, and along with it came an uneasy thrill that only meant trouble. No, it was best he left. But as my luck would have it, Daniel found a job right next door at the mechanic shop next to the café.

~

He was a charmer, no doubt about it. Daniel Foley made friends with the townsfolk real quick, becoming all the rave in a short amount of time. All the curious girlies around—being full of gossip and lust—would try to get a quick peek at the unbearably handsome Mr. Foley, who ate three meals a day at the café. He was a bachelor, and not one single girl in town wasn't trying to snag Daniel for a husband.

Each day, when he came to eat, of course, I chatted politely with Mr. Foley. It was my job, after all. But so as not to confuse flirting with kindness, I made a quick mention that I was waiting for my soldier to return.

But then, a couple of days later, Daniel showed up at the ranch where I held my second job. I stood on the house's main porch with my hands on my hips. "What is he doing here?" I asked my super as Daniel made his way to the sheds holding a toolbox.

"So, you know that beautiful dark creature by the shed?"

"Well, I'm not talking about the horses."

"My guess is he's here to fill the mechanical job, which suits me just fine. This one has a nice front side to go with the back. I've never been more jealous of a pair of jeans. Do you know him? Is he taken? Does he do any tricks?"

"Marleen! You're nearly twice his age and married with kids."

Her laugh stretched out across the ranch. "So? I may need a serious upgrade. Ronald snores and farts in his sleep, and I feel as if that one out by the shed can do a lot more interesting things under the sheets."

I gave Marleen a look before I found Daniel's eyes on mine. I waved an awkward hand from across the yard.

"*Oh,* so you *do* know him?"

"Marleen, don't you have somewhere to be or someone to boss around?" I said as Daniel made his way over to us.

Marlene excused herself, but not before saying, "God, what I wouldn't give to be you for a day. "

"Jane, what a nice surprise to see you here," Daniel said, taking wide strides past the grinning Marleen.

"Daniel. What brings you out this way?" I asked.

He climbed up the last few steps to the porch and dusted his hat, banging it on his tightly fitted jeans. "I'm here to make a little extra cash by helping the big boss with some mechanical issues on the larger rigs. Figure I gotta get it where the money is calling."

"Oh, I see."

"You live here or something?" he asked.

"No, this is my day job; I cook breakfast and lunch for the boys. I live not far from here with my parents."

"I must say, you are one hard-working woman. You may perhaps work more than I do."

"I don't know about that, but it keeps me busy well enough."

"Well, I respect a woman who can work just as hard as a man."

As he pulled a plucked blade of grass from behind his ear and chewed at its end ever so slowly, my eyes found themselves lingering too longingly at his mouth. "Shouldn't you get back to work?" I asked.

I caught a twinkle in his eyes just before he reached a hand out to my hair. "Sorry," he laughed, "but you have a thick layer of wet flour or dough on that one strand there." He grasped ahold of my thick braid and gently slid his fingertips down toward its end before showing me his cupped palm full of white crusted powder—evidence of my messy cooking.

I ran an unsure hand down my braid. "Thank you. I'm making drop biscuits for lunch."

"You might want to save some of that flour for the baking," he said with a playful wink.

I shuffled my feet impatiently, not wanting to prolong our visit. Because any more time spent in this man's presence made me feel things I didn't want to feel. I blurted out, "Which reminds me, I have better get back inside. Things could turn sour if lunch isn't ready on time."

"I suppose nothing worse than a bunch of cowhands on an empty stomach," he said, patting his flat stomach.

I blamed Marleen for putting any thoughts into my head as my eyes followed that hand up to his chest, noticing how well his muscles filled his shirt. I cleared my throat. "Yep, gotta keep these men's bellies full."

Daniel must have smelled the biscuits browning in the oven, because his stomach gave off a low growl. With anyone else, I would have laughed, fetching him a fresh sample like I would any other ranch hand that came drooling at my door. But by the way Daniel looked at me, with so much hunger, my stomach betrayed me, giving an unnerved flutter, and not the kind from wanting baked bread. And that confused me.

With the tilt of his hat, Daniel finally took a clue when I offered nothing else to say. "I'll let you get back to cooking, Jane." Before he made it down to the last step on the porch, he turned around to face me with an alluring grin. "Til next time?"

"Sure," I said before swiftly turning on my heel.

I struggled to finish lunch that day. The man was like a stray dog without a home. I couldn't get him out of my mind. Only after I caught myself twirling my fingertips around those few flour-dusted strands of hair that he had touched earlier, did I want him gone. And I especially wanted him gone when the fog in my mind cleared and presented itself with an even clearer image. Clint. But instead of feeling guilty that my body naturally lusted for attention, I only resented the soldier who'd left and forgotten me.

Chapter 8
June 1953

I honestly did try to avoid the man. But as much as I tried to ignore the fact that Mr. Foley was single and desired by all the women, even the married ones, we started an unexpected friendship. And how could we not? We only saw each other multiple times every single day. Also, I was lonely and depressed and had not heard from Clint for months, so I allowed myself this friendship. It was harmless, I told myself.

Daniel had a great sense of humor and a way of making me laugh. Quick-witted, too. Every time he came to the café to eat, he would tell me stories of himself growing up and all his plans of one day moving to California. And the more I got to know him over the course of four whole months that summer, the more light-hearted I felt.

It was late that one hot August night, just before I closed the café, that the word friendship held a different meaning. Daniel approached me just as I was mopping. "Jane?"

"*Daniel!*" I said, turning around, clutching my chest. "You gave me a fright. I thought everyone left and didn't hear anyone else come in."

"Sorry to scare you," he said, sitting down on the same swiveled chair he always sat. "You look like you've seen a ghost."

I looked toward the front door with apprehension. "There was a drifter here just before you arrived and—"

He stood up suddenly, looking around. "Did he bother you?"

"No. No."

"Where's the cook?" he quizzed, peering through the open kitchen window. "He shouldn't leave you in here all alone."

"The cook left to take the garbage out back. I'm normally okay in here by myself for a bit, but this was the first time someone gave me the heebie-jeebies. I didn't know if he wanted money or if—"

"If what?"

"Or if he wanted more than just money."

The look that crossed Daniel's face looked murderous. He made an attempt to find the man, but I came around the counter and stopped him. "It's fine. Please, Daniel," I said with my hand on his shoulder, easing his back to his chair. "Sit."

He hesitated before sitting. "Did he hurt you? Did he touch you? I swear I'll—"

"No, no. I was only a little scared being alone. The cook came back the minute you walked in. He's probably washing dishes now. Really, Daniel, I'm okay." I laughed. "You really looked as though you wanted to kill the man."

"Maybe. But it would have been worth a lifetime in hell if he had hurt you in any way."

I didn't know what to say to that, so I went back behind the counter and resumed mopping.

"Well, let me know if this guy comes back tomorrow."

"He was a drifter. Probably long gone. Coffee? Soda? Sorry, the kitchen's closed."

"Do you have more of those cherry-filled powdered donuts?"

I laughed. "I knew you would want one, so I saved you this last one. Extra powder-coated to put you in a coma." I reached under the counter to retrieve it, but my arm bumped the mop I had left out, and the donut slid off the plate and onto the floor. "That's just great," I said, taking an exasperated breath. "So be it. It's been one of those nights anyway," I bent down to pick it up off the ground and stood up. "Sorry, it's ruined. I—"

I didn't get to finish my sentence as Daniel leaned over the counter with an outstretched hand. "Here. Give it to me. It's not a total loss."

We were nearly face-to-face. "But it fell on the floor," I said.

"When I was five, my father once made me eat an entire plate of mashed potatoes straight off the floor. Said if I didn't want to eat finish my dinner at the table, then I had to eat it off the ground. It's a powdered donut. I'll blow off the powdered parts that touched the floor."

"Suit yourself," I said, handing over the donut.

By the time I realized what Daniel was about to do, it was too late to stop him. He blew a large breath over the top of the powdered donut, releasing a billowing white cloud of powder across my face. My mouth hung open, and I had to blink several times to relieve the sugary snow that coated my eyelashes.

Daniel's eyes widened. "Oops. That's not what I intended," he laughed. He then ran a finger over the tip of my nose before placing it in his mouth. "*Hmm,*" he said in a pondering way. "Not as sweet as I thought you'd be."

With lips pursed, I quickly grabbed that donut from his hand and returned the favor. His gaping expression left me satisfied. "Why, Daniel," I said poking fun, "you look as if you've seen a ghost?" I held in my laughter but not until after I tasted my finger that I had just run across *his* powdered nose. "Nope," I said, making a bitter face. "Just as I thought; unpalatable."

I had never heard him laugh so hard. He was so unaware of those noises deep within him—noises that made him even more masculine and even more intriguing and indisputably irresistible. I grabbed a clean towel and threw it at him. "Stop your laughing and clean your face before I have to charge you double for making all this mess."

"If I didn't know it before, I do now."

"Know what?" I said, wiping my face clean with a dish towel.

"What they say about reds."

I threw my hands on my hips. "And what's that?"

"Fiery when mad."

"I'm never *really* mad."

"Well good then. I've seen enough mad in my life."

"I've got chores to do, but you're welcome to sit a while," I said, wiping the chairs beside him. "I forgot to ask, but what brought you in here so late?"

He was the same height as me standing when he was sitting, and he swiveled his chair to face me. "I've been thinking. You once said you were waiting for someone to return from the war. Who is he, if you don't mind me asking?"

We had never spoken of Clint—it was almost as if he knew my hurt wasn't ready for the sharing, just like I knew he didn't like to talk about why he'd left home. I was silent, thinking of how to formulate my words, when Daniel sensed my hesitation. "You don't have to tell me, Jane."

I thought by now, with all the small talk the town folks did, Daniel would have known the reason there was no ring on my finger. So, feeling the full weight of his question on my shoulders, I sat with a thud opposite him. "His name is Clint Brian. He promised not to be gone too long, but it looks like the war needed him longer than expected. It's been ten months since he left."

It took Daniel a minute to let it sink in. "Must be hard waiting."

"Yes. Yes, it is."

"Does he write to you?"

I did not want to disclose the truth that Clint had stopped writing six months ago or that Ruth's father, who had ties in the military, had informed us that Clint was indeed alive and well. I tried to focus on the positives, that Clint was at least not hurt, or worse, dead. But it hurt to know I was so disposable. And with Daniel acting as if he had all the time in the world for me, I spoke my truth for the first time. "Clint used to write, but that's all stopped. And I'm not sure why."

"I'm sorry, Jane."

It hurt to speak the truth aloud, but I didn't let on to how devastated I was. Instead, anger took precedence, and I straightened my back. "I just don't get why they've got him fighting anymore when I heard there were peace talks with Korea. I mean, why they don't just send our men back home already?"

Daniel twirled a silver bracelet on his wrist. "Wars are temperamental. They can keep you for months or keep you for years. For me, they didn't want to keep me one day; flat-footed, they said. Of *all* the things to keep a man from fighting for his own country. But it's just as well, since I've been fighting a war in my house for as long as I could remember."

"I'm sorry to hear that. I hate the war and what it does to those who are left waiting and wondering. It's an endless, tiresome job."

"And depressing, I bet."

"That too."

Daniel looked at me and tilted his head in a curious notion. "Jane, how long do you think you can wait for this boy of yours? What if they keep him another year or two or more?"

His bluntness threw me. "Well, that's a silly question."

"I say this because I know what it feels like waiting for someone you care for and maybe even love."

"What do you mean you've been waiting? You have someone you've been waiting for too?"

"You could say that."

"Who? A friend back home? Or is she a nurse in the service?" I didn't mean to sound so eager to know his business, but I wondered why he never spoke of this woman.

His eyes honed in on mine, and I felt it before he spoke it. "She is *you*."

When he reached across the space between us and touched the top of my hand that lay resting on the counter, I stared down at its meaning. I would be lying if I said I didn't long for affection—one touch—anything to know I was still desirable to someone. The notion, the suggestion, brought an elated feeling, but only for a mere second before the guilt.

Clint.

Guilt gripped me, leaving me breathless. I panicked, snatching my hand away from Daniel's hot touch. "I don't know what to say to this."

"Say you feel it too. I mean, how could you not have noticed, Jane? It's been you since the moment I stepped inside this café five months ago. You are all I can think about. And as much as I love the chase, I have patiently waited for you to give me a clue or a sign that you are tired of waiting too. I don't know much about this man you find yourself attached to, but what kind of man stops writing to the most incredible woman? I would kill a thousand enemies just to make sure my letters reached you."

The world tilted at his last sentence. Why didn't Clint write? "Daniel," I said, fidgeting with my hands under the counter, "I don't know what to say. I mean, you have plenty of girls to catch your attention."

Daniel leaned forward. "And what if I don't want anyone else's attention? What if this feeling I have is what I've been waiting for my whole life? Are you saying I'm supposed to ignore these feelings and walk away? I would be an idiot to walk away, now or ever."

If anyone was the idiot, it was me for feeling torn. I still loved a man out there in the war, and even though Clint had stopped writing, what we had together was something I wasn't willing to throw away. I couldn't betray Clint. "I am spoken for, Daniel. I love Clint, and yes, it feels like forever that I have waited for him to come home, but I made promises."

Daniel lifted an eyebrow and cocked his head to one side. "Tell me this, Jane, and be honest; is there any part of you that may feel the same as I do for you? Because lying would just hurt the both of us."

I stood and turned my back to him, unable to speak the forbidden words out loud. I'd never been good at hiding truths, and he knew that.

Daniel's voice came close behind me, "Look, I don't want to upset you. It's the last thing I want to do, but I said what's on my heart, and I can't take it back, nor do I want to. If waiting is what you want, then I'll wait. I'm not going anywhere anytime soon. And I won't lose sight of what I want."

Don't give in, Jane, I told myself. Without turning to face him, I held onto a chair beside me. "I think you should go."

Only when I heard the sound of the front door shutting did I let myself slide into a chair. I stared at the back wall with a red-framed poster with the words, 'Come Hungry. Leave Happy.' And that was the truth; Daniel was hungry, and I was hungry; there was no denying that. But could Daniel Foley make me happy? I craved happiness once again, because, for a solid year, I had slowly been starving from the happiness I'd been promised. And yet, instead of facing the decisions head-on, I all but shoved the what-ifs away and out of my heart and out of my mind the best I could. For Clint's sake.

~

It was hard to forget someone like Daniel Foley. And let me tell you, when a gorgeous man set his eyes on you and refused to give up the chase for the next two full months, it ignited every part of you. Because when you couldn't have what you desperately wanted, it only made the wanting worse. It ached like no other. Each time I saw him at the café or the ranch and our eyes met, I wasn't fooling anybody—no matter how hard I pretended, sparks flew.

Like the night I caught him watching me walk home after work to ensure I got home safely, I wanted him. Or the time he brushed his hand across mine after picking up the generous tip he'd left for me at the table, I wanted him. And the time at the ranch when he helped me haul a box of provisions inside the kitchen, and his leg rubbed against mine, I ached for him then too. He was everywhere, and I couldn't get away. I naturally wanted the man, and he had to have known it too.

"You can't ignore me for long, Jane," he said one afternoon as I stormed up the front porch to the ranch's kitchens.

I had been trying to ignore him, but his presence alone burned me in places that brought me shame. "I can do whatever I need that it is for what I need to be done." The nervous words coming out of my mouth made no sense, but he had that effect on me.

"I have a good mind to run up those stairs right now and make you see that this charade of yours is just wasting precious time."

"You take one more step up those stairs, and I will—"

"You'll what?" he said, taking a daring step up.

"I'll scream."

We stood unmoving, facing each other on that hot August day full of heat waves consisting of need and want, but I didn't melt just yet.

"Fine. Have it your way for now. But I've got time," he said, turning around. He walked away while whistling a tune, which only infuriated me even more. The man was wearing me thin.

It only came naturally, when after Daniel's never-ending relentlessness and persuasiveness, I started to truly feel confused about what I exactly wanted. Doubts of choosing Clint over Daniel became like a coin toss that never landed heads or tails—a gamble that I clearly couldn't leave to the fates. But it became nearly impossible to run from his determination to win me over, which all but left me in a terrible avalanche of emotions: angry, intrigued, worried, hopeful, anxious, and annoyed.

A few days later, I found myself exhausted, snapping at Daniel, telling him to leave me alone and that I never wanted to see him again. He sat on top of a magnificent coal-colored quarter horse that matched his shining black hair, and everything that embodied a perfect specimen was this man and his stupid horse. "Please just leave me be," I begged.

"No. That won't do," he flat-out said. "You are going to see me every day and every day I will see you. Eventually, you will see it all clearly. Why fight it?"

"You don't get to choose for me. I get to choose. My mind is set and I can see perfectly clear. I know what I want." I had no clue what I wanted. The penny was still high in the air with no sign of coming down just yet. I still held out hope there was a good reason why Clint had stopped writing. I couldn't deny how much I still missed him.

Daniel suddenly ran his horse in circles around me, causing a dust storm, and when he finally stopped to let the smoke settle, I questioned him. "What is that about?" I said, coughing and waving off the cloud of dirt from around me.

"Just trying to clear all the confusion from your mind. Can you see me more clearly now? I'm here, and no one else is."

I indeed saw him more clearly after the dust settled. But because I wanted the upper hand, I slapped the rear of his mare with my heavy hand and didn't mind when the dumb thing took off running for its life.

"Good riddance!" Marleen said behind me.

I spun around to find my super watching Daniel curse as he tried to control his horse, who ran clear past the barns and past the creek beyond.

"He is too much, right?" I said in disgust.

Marleen crossed her arms. "Jane, why don't you just screw him and get it over with?"

"What?" I said, mortified. "No!"

"Look. The staff around here can only handle so much of this so-called sexual tension you two have going on. Get on with it, or get off the pot. If you can't handle him, let someone else have your stallion in heat."

I gave her my best death stare. "You can have him! Heck," I yelled to the gathering crowd, "please have at the man. Anyone feel free to take him off my hands!" At that, I stormed inside and slammed the door shut.

I went to work that night and barely made it through the dinner rush as my mind compared the two people I loved. And did I love them both, even if they were polar opposites. Daniel was night to Clint's day.

So, how could I choose the sun over the moon?

Daniel had olive skin, sharp features, and dark black hair, along with eyes so rich and brown they made you hungry for some of Ruthie's grandma's chocolate pie. Whereas Clint—with his fair skin, caramel wavy locks, and bright blue eyes—made me feel as whole as the day God created the earth.

And looks aside, the two also had distinctly different characteristics. Daniel, with his intense charm, held a fearlessness and an unknown mystery that created a compelling combination. He had this determination to know *precisely* what he wanted, which made me feel like the most desirable woman. He brought out a side in me that left me feeling high on the most expensive drug you could buy. No one had ever pursued me like that. But Clint, Clint didn't need to pursue me. Not with his soft-spoken, gentle ways and warm, sweet disposition. He was what calmed my storms and pushed the clouds far and wide. He was the air I breathed. And the sun to warm me.

So, it seemed I loved both the sun and the moon, and would die having to choose.

After I locked and closed the café with my mind completely mush, I almost didn't hear Daniel's voice push through the dark. "Tough night?" I turned around just as he lifted me high and up off the ground. "Let me fix it all, Jane," he said, holding me tightly to him. "Just one kiss."

I was too tired to wiggle free but not too tired to glare. "People might see us. Put me down, will you"

A gleaming dose of mischief took over his dark features. "Fine. If you say so."

When he slid my body down his, *ever so slowly*, making me more than aware of how his body sparked fireworks inside me, I was no longer tired. I was alive and awake as if I had slept a full week straight. And when my toes finally touched the ground, and his hands still gripped firmly to my waist, I had no more fight in me. The kiss was unavoidable.

I gasped when he crushed his lips to mine. Everything that had been building for months exploded, leaving me forever into a million colorful pieces. I was floating high above myself in a weightless galaxy full of wonder and awe. And while his hands roamed the sides of my hips, I found mine too, in half-want and half-protest as I walked my hand across his chest that led straight to his thundering heart.

At that exact moment, I knew I could not keep Clint's heart close to mine. Not when I couldn't resist Daniel's bewitching charms. I was human, after all. I would learn to live with the guilt, along with the desire, the excitement, and the confusion. I didn't know how else to exist. I was irrevocably Daniel's after that.

Chapter 9

Jane 1953

A kiss could change everything.

A few days after our first kiss, Daniel showed up at the ranch. He stood leaning so handsomely against his car and held a squirmy blond thing—a sweet cocker spaniel puppy with a red bow tied to her neck.

"*Oi, Oi,*" I said, laughing and shaking my head. "Now, why the heck are ya holding that sweet baby?"

He set the dog on the ground. "Take a look for yourself."

I squatted down and called, "Here, sweet girl, come here." She happy-danced her way to me with ears flopping every which way, and when my hands reached to pet the neck of her soft fur, it was there that I found something hanging from her bow. Thunder pounded in my chest as I reluctantly peered closer, wary of Daniel's obvious snare of a gift. The coin had landed, it seemed.

I was still crouched down on the ground, holding the dog, when I looked up to find Daniel in front of me. He bent down and untied the ring from the bow and smiled. "Jane, would you do this little lady and me the honor of being my beautiful princess? I would move the hottest of suns to make you the happiest woman alive. I love you, Jane. Please say yes?"

If I could warn anyone about the woes of love and the pain that came with that four-letter word, it would be that the heart and brain were often two separate energies that sometimes worked against each other.

When making a decision, in the end, one of those organs was supposed to be stronger than the other. But, in my case, I still didn't know if it was my heart exactly or my mind that said *yes* to Daniel Foley. I could only say that maybe I said *yes* because the man made it too hard for me to say no. And also, for the sheer fact that there was no one else there to claim me.

In November, almost a year and a month to the day from when Clint had left for the war, I found my soldier standing at my door as if no time had passed. In fact, time stood still. Nothing had prepared me for that moment as I looked up at his beautiful face—a forgotten face that I'd once called mine. And every possible emotion slammed into me all at once.

With a wavering, thin smile, his eyes searched mine, almost in question. Was it a sparkle of hope? An apology asking for forgiveness? I didn't know. But if it weren't for Clint stepping forward and wrapping his arms around me in a loving embrace, I might have fallen straight to the floor. My feet lifted off the ground as his voice seemed to catch at the whisper of my name, "*Janey.* Hello again."

"*Oh, sweet Jesus, help me*," I said, muffling into the folds of his arms. I inhaled his familiar scent that carried all the memories that made him *him*.

"I didn't think I'd ever make it home to you," he said, looking strikingly handsome in his uniform. He pulled me back after several moments to take a good look at me, and I couldn't help but shy away, wondering if he could see through me, revealing my devastating secret.

His wavy hair was shaven nice and short, making him look trim and clean, but his cleanliness somehow made me feel dirty with shame. "You're home," I said, swallowing.

Clint softly caressed his hands down the length of my arms before holding my wrists in his hands—his thumbs circling the frantic pulse there. "You're shaking like a leaf."

"Am I?" I was not cold, and if anything, a pool of sweat collected between my breast. I forced my knees to lock into place and prayed to God for guidance.

"Let's get you inside and out from the cold," Clint suggested. My feet were heavy and weighted down with concrete shackles as he motioned a hand toward the sofa. "Here, let's sit down, and I'll warm you up. It seems you are in a bit of shock, perhaps?"

"Perhaps."

Once seated, Clint inched closer and took my hands in his, and there it was; I didn't have to tell him as we both looked down at our entangled hands. It was hard not to note the pain in his voice. "What a pretty ring."

I pulled my hand away from his and covered it with my other hand, trying to hide the truth. "Clint, I—"

"You deserve happiness, Jane."

I didn't want to look up into those bright blue eyes. I didn't want to see the hurt in them. But when I did, I knew I deserved every bit of the way his eyes pierced my soul. My words came pained, tangled and unsure, "What could I have done, Clint? You ... *you* left me. I waited, but you stopped writing after only four months; you stopped caring." My eyes cast down to the ring that burned a hole through my skin, and I choked out, "I waited as long as I could. I have not married *yet*, but yes, I am engaged to another."

Saying those words made me sick, and I doubled over as a sob raked through me. But then I braved a look into his sorrowful eyes and explained. "I was confused and hurt. You must understand. I promise I did try to write and tell you, but what was the point? You stopped writing and I had not heard from you for eight painful months. You stopped answering my letters. Did you even get any of my letters?"

Clint's face took on a ghostly look, and he hunched over as if someone had slugged him in the gut. "I received them, yes. They meant the world to me, Janey, and I thank you for that. But out there ..." he said, suddenly raising his head to gaze out past the living room window, "out where the world is not like this one. Everything becomes meaningless and tiresome. And when I had to do things ... unimaginable things, it changed me. I wasn't the person you met. How could you still want that?" He shut his eyes and swallowed. "Out there, I ... I began to lose hope. Hell, most of us lost hope. Most days, it seemed I'd never make my way back to you. And what good am I to you without hope?

"I'm sorry I stopped writing. But I decided it was only fair not to hold you back from any opportunities that could bring you happiness. It wasn't fair to make you wait for me." Clint hesitated before stating, "Maybe I didn't make the right choice by not writing back, and maybe I will always hate myself for the choices I made, but if anyone should be sorry, Jane, it's me. I'm sorry I hurt you. But it seems I was partially right in making that decision, as here you are, happy, like I only ever wanted for you."

Of course, Clint would always put me first before himself. I shook my head, not wanting to hear his reasons, reasons that would only make it harder for him. For me. For all of us. I wanted to hold onto that anger I had for him for not writing, because it gave me an excuse for choosing Daniel over him. But I couldn't stay mad, not after Clint's selfless reasoning. So instead, my anger turned into a labyrinth of emotions that replaced all prior decisions, and there I sat with the brutal truth.

I only complicated things more. I know that. But I couldn't lie. "I am happy, Clint, and yet, at the same time, now that you are home, how do I live without you?"

Clint paused, but for only a moment, and there, in his eyes, I could see the slightest sparkle of hope. "Then say it's not over for us just yet?"

I shook my head with dread and held up my hand, showing I was Daniel's. "How?"

"But that's just it. You're not married yet." I watched Clint's Adam's apple bob with uncertainty. "There is still hope for us. I came home just in time. Say you will give me a chance to change your mind. Give me a chance to remind you of what *we* had."

"And what did we have? It seems so long ago."

"*This*. This is what we had, Janey."

Clint pulled me to him, melding our lips into a timeless trajectory that instantly unlocked and threw open the door of lost memories. It's as if what we once had all came crashing forward; the times he made me safe in his arms; the first time he made me laugh; the time I couldn't imagine a life without him; the time we said we were made for each other. His lips smothered the gasped cries that I had held in for so long, and a mix of tears with old memories washed over me like a rising tide of regrets.

My feverish hands found his sweet face, pulling him closer as if he had never left me at all. And there it was—I was still somehow Clint's girl. But it was a guilty conscience that gently pulled me away. "Clint, I ... I need time—time to think this all over." I nearly groaned in pain, "I'm more than confused now than ever before. This ... this is a lot to take in."

"I understand, Jane. This time, it needs to be *me* who waits. And I can wait for you."

~

What an utter mess I'd made. Sickening really. Because time to think gave Clint all the motivation he needed. But while Clint came around daily to win back what was his, the problem was, Daniel wasn't going to let Clint win if he could help it. After Daniel learned Clint was home and discovered my 'yes' was now a mere 'maybe,' well, he too tried many tactics to show me that Clint was nothing but the past, and that my future was with him and only him. And so, I found myself in a fairytale of nightmares with these two men clamoring to find ways to win over my love.

And the courting started with Clint.

I woke one Friday morning and found a trail of red rose petals. I followed them to the barn where Clint had professed his love only a year and a half ago. I expected to find Clint inside the barn, but instead, I caught a glimpse of something red dangling from the top of the lowest beams. A red dress was hanging with an attached note—a poem that ended with, 'Be ready after work. Love Clint.' I was hesitant to even go forward with the whole charade, but I was like a zombie—moving to whatever drum and beat these two men had planned for me. What else was I to do?

So, there I was, dressed and ready at the door after working at the ranch when Clint picked me up. "Where are we going?" I asked him as he tenderly held my hand, leading me to his car.

"To where it all began."

"Of course. Now I understand the red dress," I said.

It was a two-hour drive to Grafton, which led our conversation to many places; my second job at the café and how hard I worked feeding the ranch hands. "Two jobs kept me busy while you were gone," I said with a note of resentment.

"I can't tell you how many times I thought about coming home and finding you in the kitchen making me a blueberry pie," he said. "Especially when my team got stuck behind enemy lines for six solid days, and we found ourselves almost to the point of starvation when no relief came. I thought of your pies, then. Not one day went by that I didn't think of you."

I wanted to point out that he could have written me and told me all this, but I didn't want to ruin the evening. "What was the first thing you ate after those six long days?" I asked, rubbing my arms from the chill.

"We call it slop—a watery soup made out a potato or two. We sure could have used a cook like you out there. Clint jerked his chin upward. "Could you come sit closer to me? I hate that there is even a foot between us."

I did as he asked and instantly felt his body radiate with heat as I sided up against him. I sighed at the warmth. "I bet your mother was happy you were finally home safe and sound," I said.

"You have no idea. I stopped in for a few days to see her, and that's when the force-feeding began. I had to tell Pops to make her stop. I want to keep my figure," Clint said, patting his flat stomach.

"You look amazing. I doubt you have anything to worry."

"It's not my figure I'm so concerned about now." Clint picked up my hand and kissed the back of it while staring straight ahead. "My worries are no longer about something as silly as a hole in my stomach from lack of food. Now, I worry about a hole in my heart if I am to lose you forever, Janey."

It was such a matter-of-fact statement, but I couldn't comment, nor could I promise him a future where his heart would remain full. Not when my heart was torn in two. "So, what band is playing tonight?" I asked him, changing the subject.

"I wish it were The Benny Goodman Quartet and Peggy Lee duo again. I don't think anything will beat that night."

"No, nothing can beat that night."

And he was right; nothing could beat our first night of magical spells and first loves, but we made do. When I set foot inside that building, I set out with determination to put aside any thoughts that I still had to choose. I wanted to remember everything we'd once had. So, we danced until our feet ached. We laughed until it hurt. We drank our worries away. And as he held me in his arms all night, it was like the first time that I'd laid eyes on Clint Brown.

"Here, something for the tastebuds," Clint said, pulling out a lemon candy from his pocket after he pulled me aside at the end of the night.

I laughed, popping the sugary goodness into my mouth. "You didn't forget. Want one?"

We were both perspiring when he maneuvered a wet strand of my matted hair behind my ears. "No. Your lips are the only thing I have ever needed, Jane."

I understood how much Clint wanted me to remember. That lemon-candied kiss was a perfect reminder of the day he'd taken me ring shopping. And so, we kissed those memories to life again as if no one was in the room. We kissed as if it were our first time. All over again, and again. I wished that night wouldn't have ended.

~

In the wee morning hours, after Clint dropped me off, I fell asleep wearing that red dress. I was dreaming of his lips that left me aching for a lifetime, until I heard a faint knock at the door.

"Daniel?" I said, holding the door open wide while still wearing my red dress. "It's five in the morning on a Saturday. I only get two days to sleep in."

He gave me a look over. "Well, your attire won't do for what we've got planned." He came inside the house and dragged me to my room. "We've gotta bundle you up real nice and cozy."

Whatever he had planned, I wanted to protest from lack of sleep. There should have been a law about courting someone just hours after courting another, but I didn't want to hurt his feelings. "What is it that you've lined up for us?"

"That would ruin the surprise." He pulled out winter clothes from my closet and a pair of thick socks from my drawer. "These should do," he said, tossing it all onto the bed. "Get dressed. Meet me and Lucy outside."

"The dog is coming?"

"She's our baby. Family sticks together."

I stood alone in the room and looked at the clothes begrudgingly. I wanted to sleep. And I wanted go back to dreaming of Clint.

~

The horses carried us on their backs, unfazed that the sun had yet to rise. I watched in a daze as their noses let out misty clouds into the chilled November air while listening to the sounds of their hooves crunching down upon the frosted blades of grass.

"Don't look too enthused, Jane," Daniel laughed.

I looked up. "Sorry. I ..." I couldn't admit I was tired from being out all night with the one man who threatened his claim on a future wife, so I forced a smile and tried to appear chirpy. It was only fair that I gave my best to each one of these men as they moved the heavens and earth to prove they were the chosen ones. "I was just thinking of what it is that you have planned."

Daniel turned the reins, prompting the horses in a new direction. "Well, think no further." We had just passed the ranch where we both worked and began a climb up to the top of a steep hill. "We're here."

Once at the top, we came upon a picturesque scene of a roaring fire lighting up the night and two chairs looking out beyond a dark valley below. Daniel jumped down from his horse before helping Lucy and me down from ours.

"This is a beautiful set-up," I said, spying a picnic basket.

"Ever seen a sunrise and the moon all at once?" he asked. He was carrying Lucy in a carefully wrapped blanket, and if I didn't know better, I was sure he was trying to prove to me how he would become a stellar father one day.

"No. Can't say I have."

Lucy wiggled out of her blanket and out of Daniel's arms, ready to adventure her new surroundings. And as she explored, Daniel bundled a pile of blankets around me before setting me into one of the chairs. "Then you're in for a treat in about an hour. I looked up the sun and moon occurrence in the *Farmer's Almanac*." He stoked the fire with a stick, allowing the flames to thaw the tip of my nose while his other hand reached out for mine. "Are you hungry?"

I took a skeptical peek down at the basket. "I'm afraid to ask. I know you don't cook because you come to the café daily."

"You're right. But I was smart enough to have the cook at the café prepare us this breakfast late last night. We've got biscuits with butter and jelly, cheese, ham slices, and hot chocolate. I was informed there is cinnamon added to the hot chocolate too."

My stomach growled. "You are so thoughtful. Thank you."

As we talked, ate, and drank from heated thermos cups, Daniel spoke of our plans as if I had already decided. "Lucy and I thought a honeymoon out to California would be perfect. I've never seen an ocean before. My cousin out there said it's the closest thing to heaven, if you can believe that."

"Is that so?" I watched Lucy sniff under a rock before squatting to pee. "So, Lucy the dog is making all our future plans now? I can't wait to hear what she thinks about where we would live afterward," I joked.

"We could live here or there or on the moon, or anywhere you wanted. As long as I had my girl by my side, I would be the happiest—the luckiest."

His words generally made me melt like the marshmallows in my cup, but for some reason, they also made my heart squeeze in such a way that I couldn't breathe. "Whose cabin is that over there?" I was getting good at changing the subject.

Daniel looked to his right. "It's the boss's. Pretty nice setup in there, I must say. I hope you don't mind, but he has offered it to us to use today." I gave him a sideways glance, and he threw his hands up. "No pressure. I thought Lucy should be indoors and out of the cold at some point. Maybe watch the sunrise, then start a fire inside before we cozy up and talk."

"Talk? Oh, *sure*. I know you like the butter to my bread. You want to slather me with kisses in hopes it leads to something toasty, don't you."

"A man can only dream." Daniel tossed his blanket aside and patted the top of his thigh. "I'm a bit chilly over here by myself. Come toast me up before the sun rises." The irresistible grin he gave me propelled me forward, and I found myself moving to his open arms. "There. See?" he said, pulling my back close to his chest. "No point of us being apart. We fit, you and me."

He nuzzled his nose to my neck, and my laughter echoed out and beyond. "Stop, *you*," I said, suppressing the bubbles building.

"Why? No one can hear you but me."

"I don't like hearing my voice so out in the open."

"Your laughter is music to my ears, and besides, I'm sure the creatures are already awake. Look, even our Lucy isn't fazed." Daniel's hand slipped beneath my thick jacket, and I nearly screamed at the cold air that snuck in.

"Look there!" I pointed, starving him of any further caresses, "The sun's making its way through just now."

Beyond the valley and over the jagged tips of the mountain plains, the sun peeked its presence into existence. A sliver of the moon hung to its right, blending in with the salmon-pink hue of the morning dawn. The duo fighting it out amongst the stars seemed fitting; Clint my sun, and Daniel, the moon—both beautiful and mysteriously breathtaking.

How could I ever choose one over the other?

"It's beautiful," I said, achingly.

"*Nah*. Nothing compares to the beauty sitting right here on my lap. You really are all I need, Jane."

We watched the sunrise in silence while the moon faded into the background. And once there was nothing else to eat and nothing else to say, we made our way inside the quaint little cabin.

While Daniel tended a fire at the smallest of hearths, I sat down heavily on a twin bed with Lucy jumping up onto my lap. "Daniel? Could I just shut my eyes for only a moment? I think all that food has made me drowsy." I'm sure he knew I had been out late all night with Clint and hadn't had have a wink of shut-eye, so we both skirted around the truth.

"Sure. But not before I tuck you in with a kiss."

He covered me with a blanket before proceeding with a trail of kisses from my lips to my neck. I never could resist the man's touches, and yet I didn't want to confuse them with choices I needed to make. Luckily, I didn't need an excuse to stop him because somewhere between his kisses to my neck and down to my clavicle, I inevitably fell into a deep sleep.

~

"Good afternoon, sleepyhead."

I jolted upright, forgetting where I was. While Lucy looked at me from the end of the bed, I looked out the one window outside to see it was indeed past morning. "What time is it?" I asked, tearing off my jacket, hot from the amount of heat the fire gave off in such a tiny room. Daniel, too, must have felt the sweltering temperature rise as he lay beside me, wearing only an undershirt.

"Quite past lunchtime," he said, stretching. "But unfortunately, I didn't pack anything else for us to eat."

"I'm so embarrassed. I've ruined the date, and you must be starving at this hour."

Daniel slowly ran a finger down my thin-shirted stomach, before pushing me back into the soft folds of the pillow. "You didn't ruin anything. And who says we need food? I've got the tastiest of snacks right here in front of me." He picked up off from where he'd left off before I fell asleep. "Just give me the word that you want me to continue," he said, gently biting my ear. "I hear there are other ways to ward off hunger."

I returned a few kisses but pulled away shortly after, feeling that familiar pull my body had toward him. "I want nothing more than to continue this, Daniel, but I'm thinking I want to wait until ..."

He stopped his teeth mid-graze across my shoulder before looking up. "You want to wait until what? Until you've decided?" Those eyes of his held a mix of heat, irritation, and hurt all blended into one.

Yes, I wanted to say, *until I've decided*, but instead, I spoke only half the truth to calm him, "No. It's not that. I just think people in love should wait until they are married. I know where your kisses lead, and

I'm not sure I can stop myself." I held his face in my hands and kissed his nose. "You are almost too irresistible."

My words must have worked their magic as I watched his irises change from dark brown to an accepting amber. He let out a long breath. "You are such a good girl, Jane. It's why I love you so much." He gave me a small peck on the lips. "I'm glad you said that, because I don't think I could handle knowing you were with another man in that way. It would kill me."

I sat up again, quickly turning toward him. "You would think I would do that? With two people?"

"Don't get upset. It's just how I feel. You have to know how much it's killing me to see you with *him*, especially after I've already put a ring on your finger." He looked down at my left hand. "Which by the way, I've noticed you've taken it off. Everyone is talking and I feel like a fool."

The back of my head hit the pillow in defeat and I hugged my arms to my body. "I'm sorry," I said, staring bitterly at the ceiling. "I didn't ask for any of this. And I can't help that I'm confused, and I certainly hate knowing you feel the way you do. Please believe this. I don't want to hurt you or anyone."

Daniel laid his head next to mine. "I'm not going to lie, but today, I was hoping to give you something more than just my heart and soul. I wanted you to have all of me before he did." He laughed in a sad way, "To think I could make you fully mine in one day seems silly now."

I turned to face him, nose to nose. "In another lifetime, I would have laid with you in a heartbeat. But I'm trying so hard not to mess everything up like I already have. Just please know I *do* love you. I need more time."

"Okay," he said. "But in the end, I know you'll choose me. It's the only sure thing I've ever known."

I didn't have the heart to tell him or Clint that with all the lines drawn in the sand, I still stood directly in the middle. It was no easier than picking which parent to live with after a divorce. Because I loved them equally. If only there were an alternate universe with two of me. Clint on one side shining bright and warm for one me, and the other me in another universe where I had the moon too. But instead, we were running out of time. All of the looming decisions orbited all too rapidly, and only discord remained. I knew I had to decide which universe our reality would become, and if we could at all co-exist on one planet.

~

Stupid, stupid me.

It was only inevitable that the two loves of my life would eventually collide. For nearly two weeks, with all the love poems and late-night walks, and enough flowers to grace all the gravestones in North Dakota, the three of us lived in a love triangle of hell—fully aware that, in the end, someone's whole universe would burn to ash, and I was the fire.

How I wished there were two cafés to separate the two when both men nearly came to blows at the café one day. But there they both sat, Daniel at the counter with Clint sitting behind him in a booth. My back burned as I took each of their orders, fully aware the other could hear every word.

I had just finished taking Daniel's order, and now I had to face Clint, acting like it was just any other regular night. "So? What will it be?"

"I'll just have whatever you think is best, Janey," Clint said, handing me back the menu with a smile.

I was glad I didn't have to write his order down. Otherwise, he would have seen my hands shake. "You sure?"

"Yes. I trust your decision."

"She's already decided," we heard Daniel mumble under his breath behind us, loud enough for all to hear.

We both ignored the comment, but it had its effect when I noticed Clint's worried look. I shook my head no, to assure Clint I hadn't decided.

Clint winked, seeming to believe me, and handed me a folded note. "I wrote this for you this morning."

Daniel laughed. "You should have written to her when you had the chance," he mumbled again.

At this, Clint stood and faced the counter. "You know what? Daniel, is it? This isn't easy for any of us. So, let's not make this any harder than it is."

Daniel rose from his stool and took a step forward, his arms crossing before he spoke. "I'm just thinking a guy like you should know the facts."

I stood uncomfortably between these two men while Clint asked, "Since you are *so* keen on telling me the facts, let's hear it."

It was clear to me that Daniel wasn't so sure of himself as the clear winner. It was written all over his face. His chin jutted out defiantly. "You, Clint Brian, are a coward."

I hurried to put my hand over Clint's chest to hold him back. "Please? Please don't."

Clint looked down at me with a hurtful look on his face. "I'm not going to do anything. I'm not going to lower myself to his level. If he wants to talk out of his ass, let him."

"See?" Daniel laughed. "You can't even be a man right now and admit you're a coward. You should just let her go, like you did once before."

While the patrons in the café grew quiet with inclined ears, I grew scared at the way Daniel had provoked Clint. I turned to face Daniel. "Stop it. Right now. Do not do this."

Daniel wasn't even looking at me when his eyes glared threateningly at Clint. "Okay, let's do this outside. Let's see who's the bigger man."

"You look like a fool. Just let it go and—"

Clint didn't finish his sentence as Daniel reached around me and grabbed Clint by the collar. "Buddy, you were the fool the moment you forgot about her and left her wondering. I'm the one who's never once given up. You don't deserve her."

Clint didn't budge a muscle, not when my eyes bore into his, begging him to remain calm. The only emotion I saw from him was the slight twitch of his clenched hands that he miraculously controlled at his sides.

When Daniel didn't get the reaction he sought, he finally dropped his hands and stepped back. "Like I thought. You can't even fight for her."

At this, Daniel walked out of the café.

~

As Clint sat back down in the booth, looking bitterly out the window, I wished I could have consoled him. I knew Daniel's words had hit a nerve, but I had to leave him with his thoughts, along with the many customers waiting.

I ran outside to make sure Daniel didn't do anything rash. I had never seen Daniel so angry. "Daniel! Wait!" I yelled after him.

He turned around before climbing into his car. "What?" he said, not fully facing me.

"Daniel, please look at me."

Under the lit parking lot, his face seemed to crumble before me. "Why? So, you can see the real me?"

"I understand why you snapped. I've prolonged this agony for us all, far too long."

"Then why do you still allow this charade to continue when you know damn well he's no good for you? Are you really that confused?"

Daniel didn't know the real Clint. He had it in his head that Clint was worthless, whereas I knew Clint to be just as the most selfless person possible. But it was clear to me that Daniel was scared. Plain and simple.

"I can't just throw away what I once had with Clint. I need to be sure that what you and I have is just as remarkable. This is my life. I'm so afraid of choosing wrong and living with regrets. But my biggest fear, above all, is knowing I will hurt one of you. But that man in there that you're so angry with, it's not his fault. It's me who you should be mad at.

"And the terrible thing about all of this, Daniel, is that I had the best intentions to do the right thing. But right now, since I am *that* confused, maybe I shouldn't choose anyone at all. Maybe it's better if we all just go our separate ways, because I can't see a way out of this hell. It's too hard."

"Well, it's not hard for me. I love you as easily as the air enters and leaves my chest. It's the most natural thing in the world to love you. It kills me that you don't feel the same."

"That's just it. I do love you. I just ... I just—"

"You just love him too."

We stood silent, letting his words sink in, and it came as a relief when Daniel finally let out what sounded like a long pent-up breath of air. "I'm sorry I embarrassed you in there. But I don't think you should let us both go. I have faith that your heart will choose the right one."

"Can I see you tomorrow?" I asked him. "I have to go back inside. I'm sure the cook is having a fit with all the food sitting in the window."

"Yeah. I'll see you tomorrow. Save me a powdered donut?"

"Of course."

I stood on my toes and gave Daniel an apologetic kiss before running back inside to smooth over the other mess I had made.

After I took care of everyone, serving them their dinners and trying my best to evade the customer's nosy inquiries, I returned to Clint and placed his dinner in front of him. "You're probably not hungry now."

"Not really."

"I'm sorry Daniel said those things."

Clint looked up at me standing there, twisting my apron. "Do you believe him?"

"Believe what?"

"That I'm a coward? And that I didn't fight for you?"

As an employee, you weren't supposed to sit with the customers, but I didn't care. I sat next to Clint before placing my head on his shoulder. "No. You are not a coward, Clint. You explained why you stopped writing. The fact that you put my happiness first before yours makes you the opposite of a coward. And you did fight. You fought for so many out there. You made us all safe. You fought your way back to me." I took his fork and stabbed a green bean covered in butter. "Don't think about what he said, okay? Daniel is ... I don't know, I suppose he's anxious and scared, like we all are. Guess we just tend to hold our fears a little differently."

"I couldn't live with myself if you thought I was a coward."

"You're not. So, stop it already. Now, how about you eat your vegetables like a good boy," I said, shoving the fork in his mouth.

He slowly chewed his green beans. "Why did you give me that look when he grabbed me by the collar?"

"Because I didn't want anyone killing each other. And thank you for being smart enough to take my hint and not his bait."

"But that's the thing. I wasn't gonna clobber the guy like you thought. I've done enough fighting. I wouldn't do that to you. I'd rather die for you, Janey. I'd die for you a thousand times and over again before letting anything happen to you."

And that was just it. Clint would die for me and Daniel would kill for me. But no amount of poems or horseback rides or dances or picnics could sway me one way or the other, and even though the sun and the moon were at a total eclipse, where I couldn't see my own hand in front of me, I had to make the final choice of whom couldn't live without. Even if it killed me.

When lost, we are often told to listen to our inner voice to seek the answers. That inner voice is supposed to provide some subconscious guidance that pinpoints and directs us precisely where to land successfully on the map. And so, it seemed my overly beaten subconscious mind heard one name more than the other. I don't know why Daniel's name kept pulling at me with the slightest sliver more than Clint's. Maybe it was because Clint had been gone for such a spell that it left our love and passion with a minuscule gap of uncertainty—a space in time of faltering particles of doubt. And with Daniel, we had no space or gaps to fill. We simply were.

It was a bone-chilling December day in North Dakota. The winds blew over the flat plains without a second thought while I wished it would carry me away to the ends of the earth. I sat down next to Clint on his sofa. My eyes blurred, filling with tears as I looked around at the place where we had so many fond memories—a summer's love of poems and ballads that I would have to pretend never happened. But he knew. Clint knew the moment he looked into my sorrowful red swollen eyes that silently said a million times, and over, that I was sorry.

And I was sorry. Sorry I ever existed.

Too chicken to meet his stare, I focused elsewhere and found a small yellow flower on the wallpaper across the room. "Clint. I ... I will always remember you as my first love. The summer before you left meant the world to me." I looked down at my nails, bitten down to raw stumps with my words falling on deaf ears before I finally plucked up the courage to meet his eyes—eyes that were once my forever. "I cannot explain this decision because I still love you something fierce. But maybe it's because too much time has passed, and things have changed in that time. And maybe I will always regret this choice." I choked, "But I'm all out of time."

For a long moment, Clint sat there, appearing numb, like in a daze, as if a bomb had descended onto his lap. And after a while, when he finally came to, I thought I sensed in his eyes a silent acceptance. I almost changed my mind at that very moment, but I had already come this far. And even though I didn't want to hurt Clint, or anyone for that matter, I'd promised myself I wouldn't change my mind.

Clint sighed with a nod as if that was it, and before placing his hands on his knees to stand before me, he bent over and picked up my limp hands from my lap. "Janey? Could I have one last dance?"

I silently nodded yes, and cried into his arms as we danced to an unsung tune with his lips across my cheek whispering, "You will always be my forever, Janey. Always."

After I left Clint's, I went home and cried myself to sleep and dreamed in a fitful way. I dreamt that I married Daniel and cried the whole way down the aisle. I kept turning around, looking for someone not there, and I dreamt that I was forgetting something with immense importance. I dreamt I was drowning too. And when I woke with a jolt, a few hours after dinner time, my mind raced in circles with his name.

Clint. Clint. Clint.

My eyes zeroed in on a poem across the room that I had pinned to my wall. Clint had written it to me recently, and it had become my favorite of his thus far. Swinging my feet over the bed, my hands shook as I took it off the wall and reread it.

WITHOUT YOU

What if I'd chosen another, and what would I have missed without you?

Without you, I would have missed the upward curve and grin of your mole. It always smiles at my touch, a mischievous smirk in all ways.

Without you, I would have missed the perfume of your essence that somehow mixes with every emotion. It grips a depth within me, leaving an immediate languished response.

Without you, I would have missed the tiny hairs on your neck that reach up to brush my lips, like how the fluff of a dandelion stretches toward the sun with an eminent need and want.

Without you, I would have missed the content in your sigh when you burrow deep within the folds of my arms, the sound of finality to life's meaning, and the only reason for our existence.

Without you, I would have missed the familiar sweetness of your kiss that always seems to linger intuitively as if we've already tasted each other in another lifetime. I am certain we have loved in another past life.

Silly I ever thought it, the 'what if.' That question alone frightens me now and causes a permanent ache. No. I would never question it again. Because without you would only mean,

I don't exist.

I didn't even have time to fix myself as I rushed back over to his house. I needed to tell Clint I could never live without him, and I made a mistake. I loved him for as long as eternity existed.

I knew I looked disheveled with the crumpling of my clothes and hair in disarray this way and that, and with bloodshot eyes like red lightning bolts, but I didn't care. I knocked and pounded on his door screaming, "Clint! I choose you. Open the door!"

"Jane?" Clint's roommate stood before me. "He's not here."

"What? But I have to tell him something."

"I'm sorry. He left without a word or where he was going. But Jane, the guy looked wrecked."

My chin dropped to my chest in guilt. "I ... I feel awful about that. But I can make him happy once I speak to him. Can you tell him to come to my house as soon as he gets back?"

"Sure."

"Even if it's late, tell him to wake me, okay?"

I went back home and waited for Clint. I chose Clint to be my forever. But that's the thing about life and our forevers. We do not know tomorrow's destiny but only that today's choices determine our fate. So, all my choices that led up to that very moment in my life, came with unforeseen consequences, especially when I chose too late.

If I had known what the future held out for all of us, I would have said and done what I hadpromised Clint from the very beginning—I would have fought a lot harder to keep his heart close to mine until he returned from the war. And I would have waited for my first love as if time held no meaning.

But no. My choices sent us on down a spiraling path of mistakes and regrets that would last me a lifetime.

Because after I left Clint that cold December day, they said he had gone to a bar a couple of towns over—a little place called Jack's. Some swore on their lives he seemed okay to drive home, but they found his car wrapped around a tree at two in the morning. I remember getting the call the next day, my screams not my own, yet somehow mine never to forget. So yes, my choices impacted the fate of my future forever and thereafter. It has never been easy knowing I killed two people. Because part of me died along with him that night.

Chapter 10
Sam 2003

I tried not to cry for Jane, as my hand hovered over my mouth. Instead, I sat frozen in disbelief—shocked to hear Jane's beautiful love story end in such a tragic way. I allowed Jane a moment of silence as she stared motionless up at her ceiling, swallowing several times to regain her composure.

Jane glanced down at my hand on top of hers before finally looking up at me. Wetness on the rim of her eyes stayed put, threatening to fall, but it didn't. Her voice struggled unsteadily. "That was the past, almost forty-some-odd years ago. I try not to talk about my mistakes, but I often think of Clint and the love we once had. In my heart, he still is *my* Clint."

I wanted to tell her the accident was not her fault, but my voice caught in the back of my throat too. After forty years, one would hope Jane would somehow know the accident, although tragic, had been an unfortunate incident and not her fault, yet questions of what had happened afterward swirled in my head. Did she marry Daniel?

"I'm sorry, Jane," was all I could come up with.

"You mentioned before how you weren't sure if you believed love existed? Is that still the case?"

"Yes," I said.

"Well, that's the thing about love; no one ever tells you it's utterly beautiful and thrilling, but at the same time it's ugly and heartbreaking.

So, let me be the first to tell you that yes, love exists, but so does the never-ending heartaches that follow after. Nothing stays beautiful forever."

After a few moments passed I asked, feeling a bit helpless, "Would you like any coffee or tea? It's almost dinner time. I could start dinner if you are hungry?"

Jane shook her head. "No. But thank you. You can call your mom to come to get you, now. Besides, it looks like you had a bad day yourself, and well, I'm not feeling up to eating anything right now. Let's call it an early night."

"Sure. I understand. I'll just leave a couple of snacks here by your bedside in case you get hungry later. You'll need something to eat when you take your pills."

"That's fine."

After calling my mother, I worried about Jane as I made her a quick snack of Ritz crackers topped with peanut butter and jelly, along with sliced apples on the side. I didn't particularly like seeing my boss in such a way. And actually, maybe I preferred her anger over sadness.

I added pills to her plate of snacks, then I set the items beside her nightstand before looking around the room. "Well, guess that's it, then?" I said, hesitant to leave.

"Yep."

It was clear Jane Nelson was ready to be alone. With Jane's story ending and hanging woefully about the room, the air was cold with such thick loneliness that even I shivered. I lifted a throw blanket off her chair and draped it over her legs. "Jane, do you want the TV on?"

"No, thank you."

"Okay." I grabbed my backpack by the front door and turned around to face Jane. "Your story about Clint was truly heartbreaking, but there were so many parts to your story that were beautiful too. I guess what I'm trying to say is that I feel honored you chose me to share it. I'll see you tomorrow morning."

I left Jane with a sympathetic smile before locking up. And as I sat outside Jane's porch until my mother arrived, the chilled air accompanied my thoughts of what all had transpired that day. With new insight on life and how fast things could change for the worse, I learned what I'd considered a horrible day at school just a few hours beforehand was not such an enormous tragedy after all.

~

Hours had passed since I'd called Matt and Emily to tell them I was skipping Caleb's game. When the phone rang on the wall in the kitchen, my mother didn't even scoff that the clock read nearly ten o'clock at night. We all knew Saturdays were for sleeping in.

My fourteen-year-old sister, Stephanie, jumped up to answer the phone before I did, which irked me to no end. We only had one phone in the house, but she seemed to think she was the only one with a social life. Which was mainly true. She smoothed down her dirty blond hair as if whoever was on the other line might see her through the phone. "Hello?" When Stephanie realized the call wasn't for her, her large baby-blue eyes thinned into two small slits. "It's for you, *loser.*"

Feeling smug, I took my time getting up off the couch before yanking the phone from her hand. I batted my eyes. "Did your boyfriend forget to call you tonight? So sad."

When Stephanie shoved past me and mumbled some obscenity that sounded like the word 'itch,' I decided I would talk to whoever was on the line for as long as possible to make her suffer.

"Hell—"

I hadn't even finished my greeting when Caleb's gruff tone scratched through the line with a hiss, "Sam," he said, "wanna ask me how my game went?"

The heavy sarcasm wasn't lost on me, and even though I wasn't in the mood for his attitude, I couldn't help myself and played along with a mocking-clipped tone of my own. "By the sound of it, I assume horribly? So, tell me what happened."

"Oh gosh, where do I begin? Okay, well ... *hmmm*, let's see ... I'm pretty sure the x-ray shows I fractured my fibula. I won't get to play on the team for the rest of the year. So, if that tells you anything about tonight's game, then there you have it. But you'd know this if you would have been there."

"Caleb, I—"

"Really, where were you? I needed you tonight."

"Caleb, I am truly sorry you got hurt, really, but it's not like I would have known this *one* game would end the way it did. I didn't know, okay? And, for your information, I didn't go because I was exhausted from a long day."

It was as if Caleb didn't even hear me. "I happened to notice that Matt wasn't at the game either. What a coincidence."

I pinched the bridge of my nose. "You know, if you're implying what I think you're implying, you better think again. Look, I am sorry you got hurt, Caleb. And I'm especially sorry you won't get to finish the season."

"Just tell me where you were then."

"Are you serious? I was home by myself! I don't need this from you right now." Before I slammed the phone down, I added, "How about you call me when you're done acting like a jerk?"

It took me a full minute to stabilize my blood pressure and before the phone rang again.

"What!" I answered in a low growl.

"Sam, I'm sorry," Caleb said. "Don't hang up."

"I'm listening."

"I guess I'm just mostly mad I got hurt, okay? And yes, I may have thought you were with Matt, and well, that was just where my head went at the time. Sorry for acting like a jerk." When I remained silent, Caleb proceeded, "Will you please just come over tomorrow? I *really* need you."

At this, I knew I couldn't break up with Caleb. Not when he was already down in the dumps and feeling low.

I couldn't handle Caleb anymore after a week of sitting on the couch watching baseball game after baseball game. So, when our current spring weather went from reasonably warm and beautiful to temperatures dropping into the lower forties, I accepted Matt's invitation to go skiing, even if Caleb didn't approve. Just a forty-five-minute drive away, Crystal Mountain Resort had gotten a surprising three inches of snow, and we didn't want to miss out before they closed for the season.

On Fridays, I usually took extra care after school tidying up at Jane's because her son Charles took over for me on the weekends, but I needed to rush before Matt came to grab me for our nighttime session. Jane wasn't too thrilled that I was rushing about making dinner until I told her I had plans with Matt. That seemed to shut her up. She gave me her blessing as long as I came back in the morning to plant flowers to make up for the time I owed her.

So, with chores miraculously finished in record-breaking time, I locked Jane's door behind me to find Matt waiting for me. I joked with him, "Why didn't you come in and say hello to your girlfriend, Jane? Did I tell you she likes you over Caleb?"

He opened the truck door for me and gave me a little shove inside. "Sam, everyone prefers me over Caleb. You're a little late on that one."

"Very funny."

After driving for several minutes with Matt talking the whole time, he said, "You're quiet tonight."

I glanced over at my best friend who knew me all too well. He turned onto the highway, his dark curls poking out from his wool beanie hat, and I nearly laughed at how he had a good day's worth of stumble. He looked like a grown man but never acted his age. Which suited me just fine, because I hated the thought of us now as adults. I knew damn well nothing fun would come of this adulting thing, especially after seeing how that had turned out for my parents.

"Sorry. I should be super excited about tonight, being it's the first time in a long time that I've done anything remotely exciting at all," I said. "I guess it just dawned on me that I literally can't remember the last time I was happy or looked forward to something."

"Well, now you're making me sad."

"Sorry." I took my sleeve across Matt's glass window to clean a smudge. "You ever feel stuck inside yourself, Matt?"

"No, I have never stuck anything up inside myself."

"You're so gross. What I mean is, do you ever feel like you're going nowhere and there's nothing to look forward to?"

"Are you depressed? Do I need to give you the crisis hotline or something?"

"No. But I'll let you know if that becomes the case. What I'm saying is, I'm stuck. I have yet to experience this thing called life, Matt. LIFE."

Matt adjusted his rearview mirror. "Okay. Let me ask you this then; what would make you feel unstuck?"

"That's the thing, I don't really know. Well, a car would help. I could finally go and do things. But do what exactly?" I gave out a puffed laughed, "I don't even have the gas money to go anywhere. And without a car, I have to save up for a local college, which means I'm stuck here while everyone else gets to go off into the world and have fun."

"We're going skiing right now together? That's fun, no?"

"Sorry, yes loads of fun. But I mean *besides* this one moment in time that rarely ever happens due to the fact that skiing is super expensive and I can really only afford to go twice a year, the fact remains; there is nothing to do here. I'm bored out of my mind. I'm fearful that I'm headed nowhere. My sister has more of a social life than me. What if I get stuck here forever? What if nothing ever exciting ever happens for me? What if I'm stuck marrying Caleb and turn out just like my parents because I'm not even likable?"

Matt laughed. "Holy mother, where is all this coming from?"

"I'm an adult with zero life experiences. That makes me so freaking boring. You answer this; why am I your friend? What can I remotely offer you as your extremely boring friend? Do I even make you laugh?"

"You have zero filters. That's funny. Like the time that I wore striped shirts all throughout the eighth grade and you told me we couldn't be friends if I wore another striped shirt again—"

"I was just kidding."

"I know but I thought it was funny, until I finally got Becky Rogers to notice me. I think it's because I switched to solids, thanks to you."

"You did look much better in solids."

"And Sam, you always make me laugh with how gullible you are. I can almost tell you anything and you'd believe it. I could say, 'Hey, there's a monkey outside,' and you'd most likely believe it."

"No, I wouldn't. Well, maybe for a few seconds."

"Exactly."

When Matt slammed on his brakes, I cried out, "What the heck, Matt? Why are we stopping?"

He pointed out my window at the Safeway parking lot. "That guy running just stole that lady's purse!"

"What? Where?" I said looking out the window.

Matt laughed and sped away. "See? You'd believe anything. And that's funny to me."

"Very funny, *haha*."

"And besides laughing, there are other things about you that make you anything but boring. You're always helping people who are struggling. Remember Gerald Bussle?"

"How could I not? He still calls me once a week to say hello."

"That's just it. New, dorky eighth-grade kid comes to our school and you quickly befriend him when no one else would. For God's sake, Sam, he smelled terrible. I don't know how you could stand it."

"That's because he was super poor. I don't think his parents had a washing machine."

"Hold up. Is that why you asked me to hand over all my stupid striped shirts when I stopped wearing them?"

"Maybe."

"Seriously? Sam, I thought I had a clone for entire year." Matt shook his head. "Look, your problem isn't that you're boring, it's that you're more bored than anything."

"That's exactly it."

"Does this have anything to do with Caleb? I'm only saying this because it seems all the arrows are pointing in that direction."

I shifted in my seat. "Forget it. I'm being a complete Debbie downer. We are finally doing something fun, and I'm ruining it."

"Well, for what it's worth, you are not boring. Just bored. And if you don't think this has something to do with Caleb, then I'll move on. But I might be the one to ruin the night for you."

"How's that?"

"Because I have badass snowboarding tricks that'll make you look like a terrible skier."

I ripped off his beanie hat and threw it at his head. "I ski just fine, but I would feel better if you lied and told me how amazing I am all night."

~

We arrived at the lodge and quickly jumped out of his truck and into our ski gear before heading to the lifts. Matt walked ahead of me a few feet and called back, "I wish you'd let me finally teach you how to snowboard. That would be something new and exciting for you. Plus, skis are for wussies."

"I like having control over both my feet, Matt. Spending the entire time flat on my backside doesn't seem exactly enticing."

"Then you might be boring after all."

I picked up a handful of snow and threw it at him. "Maybe my problem is I don't like change, nor do I want to sacrifice comfort."

"But if you want anything new and exciting to happen to you, you might have to embrace change and comfort. You can't always experience life without those two things."

"Well, aren't you just full of insight," I said as we hopped onto the lift in one big whoosh together.

Once situated on the ski lift and on our way up the mountain, we admired what little was left of the sunset's afterglow, leaving behind a stunning silhouetted valley of snow-covered pines.

"Do you think—"

"Matt," I put my finger to my lips. "You know the rules."

"Sorry. Carry on," Matt said, leaving me to marvel at the majestic mountains of trees as far as the eye could see. I had a slight obsession with trees, and Matt knew the rules: no talking the first minute up the majestic mountain.

A full minute had passed before Matt pointed below us. "Looks like someone lost their glove."

I looked down at the bright red lone mitten without its owner. "Someone is going to be sorry. There is no way I could ski without gloves. I'm freezing as we speak."

"Maybe we could grab it on our way down. If we notice someone without a glove, we have our owner."

"What if it belongs to a blond bombshell who rewards you with a mind blowing kiss?"

"Then let's get this glove to her fast." We reached the end of the line at top. "How about the first one to reach it wins?" Matt proposed.

"Are you kidding?" I said, fully aware he would win.

"Hey, anything is possible."

"Okay then, let's go, Casanova."

We hopped off in a mad race down the fresh white powder, with Matt already yards ahead. After he'd captured the glove and we'd skied at least six more runs down the mountain, we were still unsuccessful in finding the rightful owner of that red glove.

Matt shrugged, dangling the glove in sad defeat. "Guess my hot blondie left already."

We were at the bottom of the mountain, and I was adjusting my boot after a fall I had. "*Aww*, don't look so morose. Maybe it's a good sign. Like maybe we didn't find her because it saved you from a terrible fate."

"But you said she was a blond bombshell."

"She could have had chronic fish breath."

Matt threw the glove on the ground in disgust. "*Ew*. Then no, thank you very much."

I laughed. "See? Saved you from making a huge mistake." The lights came on above us, and the lamps made the snowy slopes glow from white to a warm yellow hue. "I'm hungry. Let's get a quick bite inside."

~

Matt looked at me funny after I ordered three slices of pizza, and I shrugged. "What? I'm hungry, especially after almost dying up there on that last run you took me on. Side note; no side trails for me."

"You did kind of biff it hard back there," he joked, before following suit and ordering three slices for himself. "You sure you're okay? Your mascara is running from your face eating all that snow."

With hot plates in hand, we found a wooden picnic table and sat down to devour our dinner. "Then don't take me on back trails again," I said, taking a napkin under my eyes.

"So, Sam," Matt said, taking a mouthful, "you never really answered my question in the truck. So, I'll ask it in a different way. How's your love life going with that husband of yours?"

I nearly choked. "Caleb's not my husband. And if I really told you how we were doing, you'd just make a joke of it like always."

"Try me."

"All jokes aside?" I said, giving him a quizzical look. "Because I haven't been able to talk to anyone about what's really going on, and for once, I wish you could try to carry on a serious adult conversation."

"Okay, okay. Go. All jokes aside."

"Sorry. Just the mention of Caleb gives me a massive heart attack. Anyway, I don't know if it's this mountain that always puts things into perspective or if it's the lady that I care for and her stories, but I'm just gonna say it; I have to break up with Caleb."

"What?!"

"I know. I'm a terrible person. Four years together, but I have to, Matt. I'm more depressed with him than not with him. I'm not sure exactly what love looks like, but I now know this isn't it. He's not ... he's not my forever."

"Good. I've always said you could do better than Caleb."

"Wha?! You never told me that."

"Not to your face, I haven't. But you've known for the longest time he's not my favorite person. And, if someone's not my favorite person, Sam, then how can they be *your* favorite? Everyone knows I have really good taste in whom I spend my time with, so what's that say about your taste, huh?"

"Wow."

Matt shrugged, "Either way, you could do better, is all I'm saying. And that's not a joke; that is a four-year serious and factual observation."

I looked down at the pizza I had covered with too many red-pepper flakes. "I guess you could say the fire is gone between us, or for me it is anyway. But Matt, telling Caleb it's over is going to hurt him. And I don't want to hurt him. This is going to come as a big shock to him."

"You only have two choices. You break up with him and he's the one that hurts, or you stay with him forever and you're the one that hurts." Matt took a long swig of his Coke. "Or ..."

"Or what?"

"I guess there's a third option."

"What's the third option?"

"How about this; since you can't break up with him like a mature person, just do something stupid to piss him off. That way, Caleb would be more *pissed* at you rather than be *hurt* by you."

"What could I do to make Caleb mad at me? He seems mad at me all the time anyway, and vice versa. But I think I get what you're saying; it would be nice if he broke up with me rather than the other way around?"

"Yeah, exactly. I mean, the mature thing to do is just flat-out break the guy's heart. But it seems," Matt inserted air quotes, "Samantha Carey doesn't like hurting people."

I took a drink from his Coke and swallowed. "But I'm not gonna lie; I'd rather *not* be the bad guy, but ..." I blinked ten times before finally admitting, "I don't know; maybe you're onto something."

"Say it."

"Say what?"

"My idea is genius."

Matt sucked the last of his drink dry before I finally caved. "Fine. It's pretty genius. You amaze me sometimes."

"Well then, this will blow your mind. I got the whole idea from that movie, *How to Lose a Guy in 10 Days*."

"How is it that everyone has seen this movie but me? See? Caleb doesn't ever take me to see movies anymore."

"Sad, considering you love movies so much."

"Whatever. But who would have ever thought Kate Hudson and Matthew McConaughey would be the ones to help me with a breakup?"

~

The air had a bite to it, more than there had been an hour earlier, so for each nip that came scratching at our cheeks, we inched closer together on the ski lift to block the winds that seemed to pick up unexpectedly.

We noticed quite a few people had left for the night. "Guess we'll never know whom that red glove belonged to," Matt said with a sad note in his voice.

"You still bummed about that?"

"*Nah*. Come to think of it, it would have been weird having that blond bombshell tagging along with us since you'll be single soon."

"I could be a third wheel."

"I would never let you be the third wheel. I would have to tell my girlfriend to stay in the car while you and I ate dinner at McDonald's, and then I'd call you a cab before I took her inside for her turn to eat."

I laughed, "Wow, so thoughtful. But if you're taking girls to McDonald's for dinner, that explains why you're still single."

Matt joked, "Fine. Taco Bell it is."

"Good boy. You can never go wrong with tacos."

The lift dropped us off at the top of the mountain for the last run down, and while Matt stopped to adjust his coat, I decided to take full advantage of his preoccupied state. I yelled out behind me, "First one down wins!"

Matt, being the better athlete who had been snowboarding since infancy, had nearly caught up with me in no time. Determined to win, I crouched lower and leaned forward in a skier's racing stance, as I had seen them do in the Olympics. The strained move did me no justice when something in my knee pinched, throwing me off balance. It didn't help that I hit a divot underfoot, and I screamed out for dear life, "For the love of—"

I tried to catch myself from falling, but I made the mistake of thrusting my pole too far out into the snow, and I landed with a jarring thud. My right side immediately throbbed in pain, but I didn't have time to assess, not when two seconds later, Matt's face came into full view—flailing frantically like a blurred blob with a long trail of sorries attached to his screaming lips. Even with his expertise, it was too late. We collided like two spinning pretzels, rolling downhill in a tangled mess before coming to a complete dead stop.

Our heads nearly touched as we lay motionless—staring up at the night sky, trying to catch our breath. Matt grunted and rolled over to his side and face me, "Samantha?"

I didn't answer him right away as I mentally tallied all my body parts; My leg and hip slightly throbbed from all the tumbling, but miraculously, nothing too damaging stood out—no broken bones. Perhaps a slightly pulled groin muscle, but I would live. Matt's snowboard was wedged under my right hip, and both my skis had flown off sometime during our spectacular 'Olympics Freestyle Competition."

"Dear God," I laughed, still in shock. "Trying exciting things is *way* overrated. It seems I fail at everything, new and old." I turned to face Matt whose serious stare fully tipped me over. I burst out laughing, "If you could see your face right now." I finally wiped the tears from my eyes but Matt still stared at me. "Matt, they almost had to helicopter us out of here. Say something. I just had yet, *another* heart attack tonight, and I'm only eighteen. Maybe it is time I retire from skiing. I may be prone to too many accidents."

When Matt remained quiet and didn't comment in return, my heart skipped a beat. "Wait," I said. "Are *you* okay? Oh, my God, are *you* hurt?" When his face remained zeroed in on mine, I scooted closer to him and gently touched his shoulder. "Matt? What is it? Just tell me."

An odd and mischievous glimmer in his eyes brightened his face back to life again. He seemed to want to say something. But instead, my best friend placed his gloved hands on the sides of my flushed cheeks and pulled me to him.

Chapter 11
Sam 2003

I was not prepared for his kiss.

My eyes widened as if someone had thrown a wrench in the spinning gears of my mind.

This is my best friend.

This is my best friend.

To stop my brain from further malfunctioning, I hesitantly nudged Matt away. "*Uh*," was all I could utter.

I waited, expecting Matt to say the kiss was only a silly joke, but instead, his baby blue eyes seemed to speak a different language. A jolting charge of curiosity sparked in me. Was that for real? If anyone had borne witness, there was no question that our heavy breathing—coming in thick clouded puffs—wasn't from the fall just a minute before. In fact, such heavy breathing seemed to come from two people who were no longer certain the world had ever been round to begin with.

"That ... that wasn't my best," Matt said, "So I'm gonna try that one more time."

My eyes flew wider, and I couldn't speak as he placed a forefinger under my chin and pulled me to him yet again. But this time, I closed my eyes and let him.

His lips were soft with a hint of sweetness—remnants of his soda pop from earlier.

And I liked it more than I should have.

When he turned his head and angled his lips more fitting to mine, it was like meeting him for the first time.

And I wondered all of a sudden if I'd ever really known my best friend.

Finally, the spell broke, and we pulled apart. I tried to recollect my brain cells—or what was left. "What was that?" I asked.

Matt's forefinger still held my chin, and he ran a thumb over my bottom lip, giving a shaky laugh, "*That* was what I meant when I said you could do something to piss Caleb off."

His statement didn't match his voice. In fact, I could have sworn there was something meaningful in that kiss. The way he looked at me, all reasoning left me to believe my intuition. "What are we doing here?" I finally asked again. "That felt real."

"I don't know?" he said, in almost a question. Matt averted his attention to the ground and picked up a handful of white powder. We both watch the delicate snow fall between his splayed fingers just as his words slid delicately from his mouth. "I have wanted to piss Caleb off since the seventh grade, Samantha; for him getting to you first, before I could. I guess I finally had enough guts to do it this time."

With his bold and naked truth laid out so plainly, I sucked in a breath before quietly blurting, "*Oh.*"

Had I always known?

I had heard how so many friendships ended when best friends crossed the line, and I didn't want to lose my best friend. But a line as thick as a massive tree now lay like a roadblock between us. There was no ignoring or denying the line. For the first time in our relationship, that kiss presented itself as serious and real and everything we had ever known before it had altered into the *now* and *what next.*

As we lay there for what seemed like ions of time contemplating the newness—*our* newness, the sky before us darkened thickly with tiny beads of moisture-turned snowflakes. While it sprinkled down like the fluttering of dwarfed fairies, we watched in part wonder and part worry.

Where do we go from this?

I thought about that the whole drive home. I wanted to talk about what happened but couldn't. I couldn't just come out and say, 'So, you like me, *huh*?'

When Matt pulled into my driveway, he turned to face me, finally breaking the silence, "Sam, I didn't plan for that kiss, but now that it has happened, well, I hope you're not ... disappointed?"

"Disappointed?"

"Just tell me what you were thinking when it happened or, moreover, what are you feeling now? Like are you mad?"

It was so unlike Matt to ask such serious questions, making him look nervous and unsure of himself. I almost wanted him to crack a joke to have the old goofy, confident Matt back. I slid my weighted head into my hands, suddenly tired. "I'm not mad, no. And the kiss was ... well ... it was surprisingly sweet. So, yeah, part of me did like it." My hands found my gloves in my lap, and I picked them up, twisting them together. "But Matt, I can't lie. It scared me. And honestly, with everything I'm trying to figure out with Caleb right now, I don't even know what to think. It's a lot to digest?"

"Guess I just made a mountain of more problems for you. But, listen. I see your mind running a mile a minute. I understand this is all entirely out of the norm, but did you feel anything? Wait, no, don't answer. Just promise me one thing. After you figure out Caleb, think about it."

I coughed out an uneven laugh, "Matt, I don't think I will be able to think about anything other than what has happened tonight."

~

The following morning, I pretended it was just like any other Saturday morning—*normal*. Without thinking about the night before and what hearts I would have to break, I dressed in a pair of old tattered jeans and a white NSYNC t-shirt before making my way over to Jane's.

Jane appeared in happy spirits when I arrived. "You ready to plant?" I asked.

I laid down a few old newspapers and prepared her bed as our make-shift working area, while Jane used the closed lid of her porta-potty as a chair for herself. She joked, "You know Sam ... we could use what's under this lid I sit on as a little fertilizer?"

I looked up wide-eyed. "What? You're kidding. Right?"

"Yes. I'm kidding."

I liked this new Jane and asked, "Do you want me to fill the pots with soil, and you can just put the seeds in the holes?"

"Good idea."

After cutting a small empty milk carton in half, I scooped dirt into it, careful not to spill any over the sides before pouring it into a flowering pot. Handing Jane the pot of freshly filled soil, she held it in her lap and then carefully poked her fingers into the dry, loose dirt, making tiny holes. "I think it's the smell of fresh soil I like the most," she said. "The earthiness reminds me of home when Momma used to have a garden."

"I don't like the smell of our flower beds along the sides of our home. My cat uses it as its own personal toilet. Kind of takes the fun out of weeding." I held up a clear zipped-locked baggy of micro-sized shiny black seeds. "So, what kind of seeds are we planting? With no labels on any of these bags, how will you know what flowers will grow?"

"I told Charles to buy whatever was on sale and not to tell me what they were; that way, when they bloom, it'll be a surprise."

"I like that," I said, handing Jane the seeds.

Because Jane's fingers were bent in permanent shape like that of an open-lettered C, she found herself struggling to grasp and pinch onto the baby seeds. "Damn these fingers," Jane complained.

"Here, I'll do that part," I said, taking the bag off Jane's lap. "Seeds are slippery suckers anyway." I reached inside the bag to place a few seeds into each hole, and when done, I watched Jane take the time and care to cover each seed using her hand's back-side to smooth over the dirt. I knew life wasn't fair sometimes, but it sucked to helplessly see it so front and center.

"You went quiet on me. You okay?" Jane asked, looking up after she finished.

"I'm fine."

"I raised two kids. I know when something is up. What's on your mind?"

"I don't know. Just stuff, I guess."

There was a time I thought Jane could never relate to any of my problems or that she would judge me for having such silly relationship problems, especially with her real-life struggles that existed in the now. But that was before Jane had opened up to me with her story about the two men she'd loved and the choices she had made. Jane and I had more in common than I thought—a sort of duality of experiences, except in different time periods. So, all at once, I found myself blabbing on about everything that had been weighing me down.

Jane cleared her throat while wiping her hands with a towel. "Told you love is complicated."

"Exactly," I said while looking down at the pots we'd just planted. "But Jane," I said, "I just don't want to hurt anyone."

"I know. But it's part of the process."

I nodded my head in understanding and asked, "Did you end up with Daniel? I mean, did you end up marrying him?"

Jane looked out the window for a minute before lacing her words with what sounded like a tinge of regret, "Yes. Yes, I did Marry Daniel Foley."

Chapter 12

Jane 1954-1966

Guilt has its own grief of festering wounds. After what happened to Clint, I went weeks and even months in a state of anguish from the guilt that ate me up from the inside out. Sleep ceased to exist, food was forced and then upheaved, and darkness welcomed my thoughts wholly. No one could help me through the pain that consumed my entire soul.

I never did tell Daniel that I chose Clint over him. I didn't want to be the reason for any more pain. I had done enough damage. And having no one to blame but myself, I found myself lashing out at anyone who tried to help me.

"Jane, this too shall pass. I know it hurts," Ruth said, trying to console the inconsolable.

"You don't know this pain I feel. And you can't help me. Not one person can ease the hurt that seems to be thickly weeping out of every single one of my pores. I wish I had died with him." At that, I told Ruth to leave me be. It was pointless for her to waste her energy on a lost soul.

After she drove away with her head hanging low, I sat outside in the cold, crying by the leafless wisteria tree next to my parent's porch swing. That's how Daniel found me.

"Jane," he said, sitting down next to me. The swing creaked and groaned at the extra weight it bore. "Listen, you can't continue to carry on like this."

"And why can't I?" I said defiantly. "It's not like you could understand. You've never lost anyone. I ... I can't breathe. It's crushing my—"

When I let out a massive wave of sobs, I think Daniel was at his own breaking point. He took me by the shoulders, trying to shake some sense into me before a panic attack took hold. "Jane. Look at me. Enough. You have to stop this. I know you miss him, and what's happened is hard to grasp, but you have to stop. This isn't healthy to go on like this."

"You don't understand," I cried, throwing an angry gesturing hand out in front of us. "Look at my surroundings. Everything reminds me of *him*. This silly little porch swing may not mean a thing to *you*, but it is a constant reminder of what was." I didn't divulge to Daniel how my first summer with Clint, he would read his favorite poems to me on that very swing. And how that creaky old porch took the feet of two lovers dancing barefoot under the moonlight. Or how I knew once spring arrived, the pale purple wisteria hanging over the porch swing would bring a full bloom of sweet fragrance that spoke volumes of memories and now regrets. "How can I move on?"

Daniel wrapped his arms around me. "Let me take you away from all of this then? We could find happiness again by making a fresh start. I have a cousin somewhere over in California who needs help with his mechanic shop, and I bet it pays decent. We could get a cute place of our own. Doesn't that sound nice? Maybe even have a garden in the backyard a few chickens roaming. Don't you think Lucy would love that? I think a change of scenery would be nice, and it would help. Let me do this for you. Let me make it better."

I looked down at the dog at my feet, and she barked, as if to agree with his plan. "Besides, Jane, aren't you sick of this cold weather? California will be warm, and we won't need to find ourselves stuck indoors anymore. We can explore a new state with new opportunities. Wouldn't that be fun? Let me try and make you happy. Marry me. Let us leave these memories behind and start a new life."

Promises of a new beginning swirled in my mind that whole night after Daniel left me to myself. I wanted to grasp onto anything that would help me escape the heartache that was slowly drowning me. And so, when Daniel offered me a life preserver within reach, I grabbed ahold and said yes to a life with Daniel Foley.

~

We got married on a cold February day in 1954. I was twenty years old and borrowed my mother's wedding dress, made of silky satin with a lace train that billowed at the bottom. Even though it was a little too large for my small figure, since I had lost a lot of grieving weight, I wore it anyway. Ma pinned it in the back and asked if it was too tight, but even if it was too tight, I couldn't feel.

My bridesmaid Ruthie cried for me, and my father said I looked like a princess as he walked me down the aisle of our small church. Only Ruth and my parents attended because no one could stomach celebrating, not when the memory of a funeral remained fresh in our minds. And I'm sure everyone questioned if my tears were from Daniel's spoken vows or from wishing Clint stood in front of me instead. Maybe it was both.

Even so, when I looked up to the man before me as he finished saying, 'I do,' I chose to believe Daniel would go to the ends of the earth to make me happy. I had to trust in that. I had to remind myself that I loved Daniel almost as much as I loved Clint, and I owed it to Daniel to give him that love in return.

That night when we made love for the first time, Daniel tried his hardest to make me remember all the reasons he loved me. "You're nervous, aren't you?" he asked when I crawled into the bed of the hotel we'd rented for just one night.

"A little," I said with a shiver.

He laid beside me, fully dressed. "We don't have to do anything. We could just cuddle."

I took shook my head in the dark. "No. I want to. Make me forget I'm nervous. Make me forget everything."

He drew my body close to his warm one and began to kiss all the curves and dips and soft parts of my ear before whispering all the reasons he loved me. "I love you for the strong woman you are, even when I know you don't feel so." He kissed my temple. "I love you for the way your vows reached my heart, letting me know this means forever." He kissed my neck. "I love you for all the times you can't remember why we should be together, because it only means I'll have to try harder to remind you." He kissed my shoulder. "You make me want to be a better person, and you make me want you and only you for as long as I live."

When Daniel's lips found mine, I tried to force Clint out of my mind so that for once, I could love Daniel and only Daniel. He deserved that in a wife. But married or not, forgetting Clint was like forgetting my own name.

~

It wasn't more than two weeks after our wedding when we packed up Daniel's 1946 black Plymouth De Luxe with what little we had and drove to a town called Rancho Santa Fe, California. Daniel's cousin and his wife said we could stay in their spare bedroom until we saved up and found a place of our own. Which wasn't long because, after much hard work with his cousin, Daniel's job as a mechanic allowed him to make sufficient money for a down payment on a little run-down distressed grey rental.

I was grateful for our meager home. It was an ideal distraction at a critical time in our lives—a fresh start, like Daniel had promised me. I didn't mind its drabness at first, and it became a decent home after adding a few feminine touches. Most importantly, we finally had the privacy we needed as newlyweds.

But Daniel was mainly thrilled to see a small, joyful change in me. I found myself pleased at how happy he was when he would come home every day after work to find the house spotless, dinner in the oven, a cold refreshing drink ready for him, and all the chores finished. He was the sole provider, so it was up to me to show him how much I appreciated his hard work, and in return, his happiness made me happy.

But there were plenty of times I thought of Clint. I would imagine Clint sitting in the very same sofa chair Daniel sat in, wondering what life would have been like with Clint. Would it be any better, or the same? Would Clint have hummed a tune when he showered? Would he have wanted milk with dinner? Would he have loved my meatloaf? Would Clint have laughed when I screamed in fright upon finding a mouse in our kitchen?

These questions seemed endless, even amid my new happiness, but I forged on because that was how you continued to live while gone were the dead. But even on my best days, eventually, I became bored playing house.

"Daniel, what if I got a job? You're working nearly twelve-hour shifts. I'm lonely here by myself."

"Jane, coming home to see your beautiful face is all a man needs. I don't want you to have to go to work like some of those other wives."

"Well, I'm just wondering what to do all day while you're gone," I said as we ate a late dinner once again. "I miss Ruthie and my Ma and Pa. I write to Ruth almost every day."

"Where did Ruth move to again?"

"Washington State, and yes, we have a lot to share with both of us in new territories, but soon the letters won't be enough."

Daniel stood and came around the table. "Do you know what they say about lonely wives?"

"No."

He picked me up and twirled me around. "Fill a home with busy little feet running around, and loneliness won't be an issue."

~

It doesn't take long to conceive when a woman's husband is an amorous lover. I could have sworn it was only a month later when I found out we were expecting. But when pregnancy did not agree with me; I had lost a lot of weight.

"Jane, you have to force yourself to eat something."

I stared down at my bowl of untouched oatmeal and swallowed the bile I already tasted. "I try, Daniel, but nothing stays down."

"Well, our baby needs nutrients to grow. Did you know I was born a whopping fifteen and a half pounds?"

My mouth hung slack and wide in disbelief. "*Nooo*."

Daniel chewed off a big piece of his bacon and I tried not to gag. "I kid you not," he said.

"Well, now I don't want to have this child at all. I'll rip down there if our baby gets that big!"

Daniel laughed again, "I should mention my mother was over three hundred pounds when she delivered me. She was a month overdue, which was why I had grown so large inside her. But you have nothing to worry about. You're just a tiny little thing. That's why we've got to fatten you up. Please try to eat."

I took the slightest bite of my breakfast. "What happened to your mother after the birth? And why are you not so—"

"Fat? I must have had my father's genes. As for my mother? Well, my mother needed hospitalization for two months after having me."

"I bet she ripped from North Dakota to South Dakota. That poor woman."

"More like she ripped from North Dakota to Texas."

"Well, I'm telling you right here, Mr. Daniel Foley, if I have a fifteen-pound baby, you and me are divorcing."

"You will never divorce me," he said, "not when I love you so much. I can never let you go."

We didn't have a fifteen-pound baby, thank the good Lord. I was twenty-one years old when our baby girl came early one sunny morning, weighing only six pounds and three ounces. We named her Kathleen Elizabeth Foley, after my grandmother. Kathleen was as cute as a baby kitten on a warm summer day.

Daniel's smile was as long as the Nile when he held his daughter for the first time. "She looks just like you, Jane. I might have to nickname her Red."

My yawn was a wide as a dinner plate. "She does look a lot like me, right?"

"Maybe my son will take after me. What do you think, Jane?"

I threw a hand over my eyes as I laid on the hospital bed. "Can we talk about the second one some other day? I just had the first."

"What? Can't a guy have it all?"

Daniel was used to having whatever he wanted. And so, I became pregnant again with our second child, Charles, a year later. It didn't come as a surprise when Charles looked just like his father—all tan skin, a head full of black hair, and dark brown eyes.

As I looked down at my newborn son, I couldn't help but wonder what my baby boy would have looked like if I had married Clint. Not one stage in my life went by without me thinking of the what-ifs. But luckily, those children kept me busy enough to dampen the guilt that so often had blanketed me. My children were my saving grace more times than not when it came to Clint.

And when both of our workloads increased around 1960, when we were able to buy our first home—a beautiful farmhouse—I was too busy to think of Clint. Daniel found a better-paying mechanic job working for the Pacific Southwest Airlines at Lindbergh Field, where he loved working on the aircraft. Kathleen was four and Charles three at that time, so living on a farm was a perfect time to get ourselves chickens, goats, horses, dogs, and cats. I even had a nice-sized vegetable garden—growing some of the most enormous zucchini around.

I was so busy keeping everything perfect that Clint no longer haunted me. It was how I survived for so many years, that eventually, with all the hustle and bustle, Clint naturally became a distant dream. It was as if I'd tucked him into bed for a peaceful slumber and everything became the 'now' and not 'back when'.

~

For the first ten years of our marriage, our lives resumed without any major snags. But everything changed in 1965, when Daniel started working night shifts and weekends at the airline. With him coming home at such odd hours each day, that's when the shift in our relationship began.

It soon became the norm that he slept on the sofa, so as not to wake or disturb my sleep, and at first, I didn't mind. But because Daniel slept during the day and worked all night, eventually, we all missed him.

"Daniel," I said one night as we laid side by side. I held onto his arm tightly, knowing he would be leaving soon for his nightly shift. "We only see you a meager few hours before your shifts. It gives us little time together as a family. Would it be terrible to ask your manager to trade shifts with someone without a family?"

If Daniel ever felt a longing to have back what we all used to have as a family, he never complained. "It is what it is, Jane. Nothing I can do."

"It's just that Charles seems to miss you the most. He wished the other day that you two could play catch or ride horses on the weekends like you used to do with him. Remember when you and him would tinker with the engine parts from discarded planes? Wouldn't it be nice to have that time together again?"

"I miss them too. Trust me, Jane. Some early mornings, before the sun even rises, I make my way to the kids' room and kiss them goodnight. I watch their sleeping faces and realize they're growing up all too fast. But a father sometimes has to sacrifice time away to ensure his family is well provided for. I love you and you'll just have to trust I have everyone's best interest at heart. Have I ever steered you wrong?"

"No."

"Good. Then trust me. We will be okay."

It's funny the things we think we know about our spouses. Like how I believed what we had was good and something beautiful. Or how I thought I knew all there was to know about the man who'd promised to love me. Trust was something I never thought I had to question with Daniel. And us, being okay? I was never okay after the year 1966.

~

Clint came to me more than ever that year. Guilt and regrets that once slumbered, suddenly awakened, and there was only one man to blame for dredging up the past. On a sunny day, while the children attended school and Daniel slept, my world tipped.

I thought it was the perfect time to freshen up my perm that day, and so while I sat in a chair under the heating lamp with my hair in rods tightly wrapped under a plastic cap of heavily fumed chemicals, I vaguely heard the chatter of customers around me.

A fashionable blonde next to me conversed with her stylist, her hands waving in the air excitedly. "No, no, no. I don't quite live here exactly. Just a visitor from out of town. I'm a stewardess at the airport, so I come and go."

"What a fun job!" said her stylist.

"It is. You meet new people every day." She laughed, "Actually, I've met someone here just recently. It's become a little serious. I might have to visit your town more often."

I barely listened with one ear and wasn't particularly paying much attention until I heard the stylist ask, "Honey, I know just about everyone locally. Maybe I know your gentleman caller?"

"*Oh?* Maybe you do know him. He's a mechanic for the airlines. He just got out of a relationship with one of the other stewardesses, and quite frankly, she didn't deserve him."

My ears perked up, wondering if Daniel worked with this woman's fella. Daniel knew just about everyone in his department.

The woman blushed before she spoke, "I call him Danny. He's the most *gorgeous* creature. I'm meeting him again later tonight."

"Danny what, hon?"

"Well, actually it's Daniel. Last name Foley. He says it's Irish."

The stylist gasped and looked to me, but I couldn't hear what was said next, not when my ears thrummed with the sound of my hammering heart. The room moved in a sudden blur. The chair I sat in seemed to swallow me whole, and for a delusional moment, I wondered if the chemicals engulfing my head had caused me to mishear his name.

But I'd heard her correctly. It was highly unlikely it was another

Daniel Foley. I *knew* in my gut I heard right when she said his name so flippantly, as if he didn't just live a mile down the road with a wife and two children, a cow, a horse, and ten chickens.

I don't even remember how I ended up in the bathroom. I gripped the rim of the bathroom sink while an unrecognizable, stunned and tearless woman stood ashen in the mirror before me. A million questions came slamming into me all at once. I couldn't catch my breath.

Could it be true?

Was everything I knew a lie?

Was this why he was never home at night?

Did he even work nights?

After throwing up, I quickly unwrapped the curling rods from my permed hair and exited the building as fast as I could. Only when I entered my vehicle did I lose all composure. "Damn you, Daniel Foley!" I cried out, hitting the steering wheel with the soft heels of my palms. There were so many questions, but the biggest one hurt the most: Why? Why me?

I drove around town aimlessly for over an hour, broken and lost in a fog. And when I nearly hit an oncoming vehicle, that was when I saw a flash of him. My Clint. It was as if he was telling me himself, he was with me no matter what hurts came my way. He was with me always. Forever.

I cried even harder as I pulled over to a payphone and called my only friend in the world. I cried out, "Ruth. *Oh, God*, Ruth."

"Jane? Jane, is that you?"

"I don't know what to do. How ... how could he? To me?"

"Jane, you are making no sense."

"Ruth, he's cheated." I sobbed, "Daniel is having an affair."

"Oh, my sweet, *sweet* friend. Jane dear, where are you now?"

I wiped the liquid pouring from my nose with the back of my hand. "I'm at a phone booth."

"How did you find out?"

"I overheard this woman at the salon say he and her are ..."

"She could be lying, you know? Women are ruthless. Maybe they just wanted to gossip. You know how those salons are."

"The woman said his full name, Ruth! There is only one man named Daniel Foley who is a mechanic at the airport. Please, please, just tell me what I should do. I can't go home and see him." I almost vomited inside the phone booth with the following words: "He's even seeing her tonight!"

The quick intake of Ruth's breath wasn't hard to miss. "Jane. Listen, take a deep breath. When does Daniel go to work?"

"Eight o'clock tonight. And the kids don't get home for another two hours."

"Okay. That's fine. Here's what you're going to do—"

Chapter 13

June 1966

With a plan in place, I went back to the car and drove to the closest gas station like Ruth instructed. I shoved the gas nozzle into the car's fuel tank and watched the numbers rising on the meter's face before me.

$4.06; *When did it start?*

$5.28; *How many women are there?*

$6.92; *How could he look into my eyes every day and lie?*

$8.53; *Why am I not enough?*

$9.44; *Did he think I would never find out?*

No longer did grief exist when anger and rage became my fuel. Ruth was right; I needed to get far away to think about what to do next; because I was not ready to face my husband with all the emotions consuming me.

I ran inside the convenience store to grab a few snacks for the long road trip to Washington State, where Ruth resided. And when the clerk at the register gave me the foulest look and covered her nose, it took me a moment to register why she'd responded in such a way. To my horror, I'd forgotten my hair reeked from the perm's chemicals still left in my hair.

I knew I couldn't go back to the parlor, nor could I go home, so after quickly paying for the snacks, I used the gas station's bathroom sink to rinse all the chemicals out as best I could. But to further my horror, my red hair that Daniel loved so much broke off in bits and pieces from sitting in such a harsh solution for too long. I thought of the pretty blond woman at the parlor, sitting in her chair, beautifying herself for *my* husband, and I wanted to scream at Daniel for ruining my life.

Arriving at the children's school to sign them out wasn't my best moment. The secretary looked at me peculiarly, and I could only imagine how I looked—wild, swollen eyes with makeup running off my face and wet, choppy hair missing in parts. While I waited for my children, I wondered who all knew of my husband's infidelity. Did the secretary know? The principal? My neighbors? Was I the only one?

Kathleen, being almost eleven years old, and Charles, nine at that time, knew something was amiss the moment they saw me. I gave them a halfway laugh. "Bad day at the salon. I'm fine. Let's go." I know I looked a fright, but I was sure as hell not prepared to tell the children what had taken place. That conversation wasn't something I could mentally tackle. So, I rushed the children out of the building as they fired out questions.

"Where are we going?"

"We're driving to see my friend Ruth. She lives in Washington. I have lots of snacks for the long trip."

Kathleen asked, "Right now? Why? What's wrong, Mother?"

"Yes, right now," I said with determination and without explanation.

"What about Dad? Is he coming too?" Charles asked.

"Mom, I don't have my suitcase or clothes. And I'll need to get my homework from my teachers if I'm gone for more than a few days."

The questions came a mile a minute, and I couldn't take it. "Don't worry, you two!" I yelled as I shoved them into the car. "Charles, no, your father is not coming. Kathleen, when we get there, my friend Ruth will have everything we need, and I'll call your teachers later. No more questions, PLEASE, children."

Slamming the car doors shut, I peeled out of the school's parking lot and swerved around the corner to jump onto the main highway. I didn't care how far I had to drive to put distance between myself and the man I'd thought was good. Tears no longer blocked my view ahead, and it was anger and revenge that kept me moving forward.

~

June in Washington State was almost ten degrees cooler than California, and I immediately welcomed the change to cool off from my seventeen-hour drive full of fevered thoughts of wanting to kill my husband.

While Ruth's children showed my kids their vast property on the river, her wide-open arms closed around me and I wept. "I don't know what to do, Ruth. Maybe some folks would immediately confront their spouse, but for the last twelve years, my marriage has been a fraud, and I can't bear to see my husband's face when he tells me the truth. Maybe we can live here with you?"

"Jane, I would love that more than anything. But you can't just run to another state and upheave your children away from their father forever. There are custody laws. But the law says nothing about you taking a small vacation. Either way, we have to have a plan in place, Jane. Things like this have to be handled delicately."

"I can't even think straight."

"This might be a foreboding question, but how would you support the children on your own if you do leave Daniel?"

I squeezed my eyes shut. At fourteen, my family had needed help financially, so I had dropped out of school and become a cook for a ranch. "I don't know, Ruth. I don't know."

"Maybe you could find a waitressing job again?"

"Would it pay enough for me to take care of the kids?"

"I don't know, Jane."

With a mix of pain and anger, I rubbed my eye sockets. "Now that you mention the law, can you call Daniel so he won't send the search dogs looking for us? I can only imagine him calling in reinforcements for our sudden disappearance, and that's something I want to avoid."

"Okay. Good idea before Ray picks the kids up from school."

After Ruth sent Charles and Kathleen to pick strawberries out back, I held my breath while she called Daniel.

I put my ear next to Ruth's while her hands twisted the phone's cord. "Daniel? This is Ruth. Jane—"

"Ruth! Do you know where my family went?"

I nodded for Ruth to continue. "Well ... yes. Jane and the kids stopped by to visit us here for a while."

"In Washington? Ruth, put her on the phone, please."

Ruth swallowed and looked to her husband, Ray, who sat at the table with a solemn look. "I'm sorry, Daniel, Jane doesn't want to speak to you."

"And why the hell not? What is going on, Ruth?"

"Look, I'm only calling because Jane wanted me to let you know they all made it here safe."

"Ruth, you are making no sense. My wife left without a word, and took the kids. Put her on the phone. I need to talk to her."

"Well, that's the thing, Daniel—" Ruth looked to me for permission to explain, and I nodded in approval. "It's just that, she came upon some devastating news."

"What news?"

"*Uh* ... well," Ruth cleared her throat, "that you have been unfaithful in the marriage? It seems that Jane feels she needs time to process this news. She's very hurt by it all, Daniel."

There was a long pause on the other end, and for a minute, we all thought Daniel had hung up. But then his voice boomed as if he were in the room with us. "You tell Jane to get herself and my kids back into that car and drive home *right now!* I want to speak to her. Put her on the phone this instant!"

Ruthie stared wide-eyed into the phone as I pulled my face away, appalled. No man had ever talked to Ruth in such a manner, nor did Daniel ever speak to me in such a way. The last time I'd ever heard Daniel that angry was when he'd wanted to fight with Clint so many years ago.

Ruth pressed on. "*Now, now*, I understand you are upset, Daniel. But maybe it's best you two have some time to reflect. Emotions are high right now and—"

"Don't tell me what you think is best for us. I don't want to hear any more nonsense. Whatever Jane said or thought she heard is false. Put my damn wife on the phone, Ruth!"

I didn't blame Ruth when she hung up on Daniel in a panic, nor did I blame Ruth's husband for the disdainful look on his face as he sat at the table shaking his head.

"I am so sorry," I whispered. "I am utterly embarrassed for the way he spoke. I should have never involved you two."

"Don't be embarrassed, Jane," Ruth said while pulling me into a hug. "His reaction nearly proves his guilt. It's the defensiveness in him speaking. It will take him a moment to calm down."

"Well, I'm not going home for a good spell. Let him sit on it."

After a good thirteen days away from my husband, I'd had a good enough time to reflect on my future. I knew I was not one of those women who could live with their husband's mistakes. His mistakes would eat at me for a lifetime, and I didn't want to live that way.

"You know what, Ruth?" I said one afternoon while looking down by the river at my two children. Charles looked so much like his father—olive skin, dark brown eyes, and a full head of black hair. The image of him alone gave me a stitch in my side. "I wish I could figure out where to live before I face Daniel. And the kids need to know what's going on too, and I want them to have a say in where we live. There's just so much to do."

"I can't get over how wrong he did—"

Ruth paused at the sound of tires crunching gravel behind us, and we both turned to look. I thought maybe Ruth's husband Ray had returned from the store, but I realized it wasn't him when a familiar car whipped to a stop.

I gripped Ruth's wrists. "He probably found your letters you wrote to me with your address on them."

He stepped out of the car and held a hand above his eyes, blocking the sun's glare before turning towards the back of the house when he heard his name called.

"Dad!" Charles yelled, racing to his father.

After Daniel gave his son a bear hug, he made his way towards us down by the river, greeting everyone as if it were any normal summer day. "Looks like a nice set-up here, Ruth," he said.

My stomach coiled inside itself as Ruth replied, "Thank you, Daniel. We like it here very much." She stood from her chair. "Kids, why don't we let these two have a moment, and let's see what's biting down there," she said, nodding toward the river.

While Ruth occupied our children, I walked to the back porch, under the shade and away from ears. Daniel followed.

I had shed so many tears for all kinds of anger in those last two weeks, there were no more to shed. I had come to a resolution that nothing could change my mind about going home. No matter what Daniel said, I *refused* to let someone embarrass me. I was no fool. Plus, it seemed impossible to go back to a healthy life without anger, hurt, and resentment. Some couples may have found that they could work through such things, but for me? No. No, I was undeniably done with Daniel Foley. The trust was gone and unforgivable. There was no going back.

Leaning against the stair's post in a relaxed posture, Daniel lit a cigarette and took a long drag from it. His quietness made me feel small, but I stood firm and held my ground. "So, you think you're here to take us home, *huh*?" I asked.

"Yep," he said.

The indifference in his tone shocked me. "Don't you have something you want to say? Like an explanation as to why you would do this to our family? Why would you do this to *me*?"

"And what exactly *did* I do, Jane?" His head bent down in a suggestive way that said I was stupid to even suggest a thing.

"Enough, Daniel. *Please*, don't play games."

"Look. I think you heard some silly town rumors that have gotten the better of you, and it messed with your head. It simply isn't true. I'm here to take my family home. I don't have time to entertain this, especially since I have to get back to work tomorrow night. The drive here was long, and I'm not playing games. You are my wife, so pack up, and let's go home."

For the first time in my marriage, I wanted to raise my voice to shake him out of whatever calm, subdued mood he'd brought with him, but then I thought better of it after looking down at the river where the kids played. "Those weren't rumors, Daniel. I heard it straight from the horse's mouth. I didn't quite catch the blonde's name, but she sure as hell knew yours. I deserve an explanation. So please, don't just stand here like I'm making this all up."

He was silent for what seemed like forever as he watched my chest heave up and down. Daniel flicked the cigarette's ashes where he stood and finally said, "Don't you think you're acting a little rash? You can't go around believing everything you hear. I didn't do anything. Whatever you heard is false, *Janey*."

My eyes grew like saucers. "Don't you *ever* call me Janey," I hissed. Daniel knew Clint was the only one who'd ever called me that. The fact that he chose to use Clint's nickname for me nearly confirmed my husband was lying. I stood firm. "I don't believe a word coming out of your mouth. I find it hard to believe there could be another mechanic working for PSA, one who's cheating on his wife, with the same name as yours. If you mean to tell me what I heard was all just a pack of lies, well, don't! Don't start lying to me now. I beg you, after all these years of marriage, I deserve the truth, Daniel."

"Fine. You want to know the truth?" He threw his cigarette onto the ground, grinding it into pieces just as he did to my heart.

I tried not to cry. "Yes, the truth."

He took a step toward me. "If you think I don't love you, *you're wrong*. I love you and always have. Nothing has changed, Jane. I am not lying when I tell you those women don't mean a thing to me. I'm a man. Men have needs and urges from time to time. That's all there is to it. There is no harm in giving pieces of myself away, not when my heart is yours."

My ears stung when no apology came from his lips and my ears bled when he admitted to cheating on me with *multiple* women. I was so stupid for not knowing. "You're a man with needs, Daniel? What about *my* needs?" I wiped the unstoppable tears with the back of my hand. "When I said my vows to you, I meant what I said. I thought I was enough for you. I thought what we had was *good*. I believed you when you said you loved me, and I damn well don't ever remember our vows stating I had to share you with other women. For God's sake, do you have any values or morals or even any decency for yourself? For us? For our children?"

"A man can love his wife and his family, all the while still satisfying his needs. I'm not the only one. Hell, all men do this, Jane. We just don't make it public. Besides, we *are* married, and there's no need for this to get all bent out of shape. I understand you are mad. I do. But after a few weeks in your own home with our lives back to normal, we need to put this to rest. It's what's best for us all. Now, go and grab the children, and let's go home. We can talk about this later in private."

I took a faltering step back. "I don't even know who you are right now. I am NOT going home with you. There's nothing to discuss. If you think we can pick up where we left off, think again. I can't be that kind of wife. I can't, and I won't. Not ever." I finally whispered the words I thought I would never say. "I ... I want a divorce, Daniel."

Daniel's posture no longer seemed relaxed at the word 'divorce,' and he took a step forward. "Well, good luck with the courts," he said. "Because whatever you *heard, Jane*, it's all hearsay. If you think you can paint me in this terrible light that I'm this terrible husband, and you want to try and take my kids away from me, well, think again. Those kids are my kids, too. I have rights as a man that say so. Don't make this any harder on yourself or the kids. So, do as I tell you, and pack your bags. *Right now.*"

Even though a warm breeze ruffled my hair, a chill crept its way over my skin. I contemplated whether or not my husband was bluffing. I had never seen him in such a harsh light, but he had painted himself ugly in it and he'd done so all by himself. "You're a *fool* to think I'll just do whatever it is you bid me. I don't think you understand the severity of your actions. I *do not* want to be with someone who cheats. We are *not* going back with you. You made me look like a fool, Daniel, and I won't tolerate it. You are nothing but a fake and a phony. You don't love me. You never did."

Maybe I shouldn't have said what came out of my mouth next, but I did. "Clint would have never done this to me."

My words had their intended effect, and Daniel lunged at me like an animal pushed in a corner with nowhere else to go. His face came an inch from mine while his sneering voice belonged to someone else entirely. "Well, he isn't here is he, Jane? You think the courts will side with a woman who only has the education of a ninth-grader? One with no job and one who would rather believe in small-town gossip over her loving husband who has done nothing but provide for his family? No one will believe you. I'll tell them you're abandoning your family on the grounds of insanity, and the children will hate you for ruining our family over a bunch of lies."

"Who the hell are you? *You* are the liar, not me. This divorce is a result of *your* doing, not mine." I stood motionless, wondering who or what evil had replaced my husband with a counterfeit. Where was the Daniel I knew? I wanted to believe my husband was merely grasping at anything to keep me from leaving, but I couldn't handle this dark shadow before me. "I don't even know this man standing in front of me right now. It's over, Daniel. Just leave."

If I happened to be surprised by his true colors that afternoon, it came as a more devastating shock when he grabbed me roughly by my shoulders and spun me around to face the river where our children played. He spat closely in my ear, "YOU belong to me. You *will* do what I tell you, or I will take those kids away from you, and there will be *nothing* you can do about it. We can do this the easy way or the hard way." Daniel's firm grip around my arms squeezed harder, forming a bruise already. "I didn't want to do this, but you're only making it harder on yourself. So. Get. Your. Bags." At that, he roughly shoved me away from him while I stood, panting in terror.

I glanced down at the river's edge, toying with the idea of yelling for Ruth to call the authorities. But just before I called out, the image of a dramatic scene with the officials wasn't the memory I wanted for my children. And Daniel was right; what would I say? That my husband was forcing me to go home so he could provide for us? I didn't know for sure if he was bluffing or if he meant every word that he would turn the courts against me. But I knew then and there that I couldn't chance losing my babies, or worse, have them hate me after Daniel told them it was all my fault.

In those first ten years of marriage, you could say I lived in total ignorant bliss. But how could I have known that the one person I'd trusted with my life was a fake—a phony? If I had known what life had in store for me after finding the truths of my marriage, I would have never married Daniel Foley. Not when the next five years would be a more devastating nightmare than I ever could imagine.

Chapter 14

Sam 2003

The events of Jane's story ended in a way I had not expected, and left me heartbroken. I watched her eyes take a curious glance down at the pot of soil still on her lap as if almost forgetting why it was there in the first place, and I, too, stared at the container in silence. I didn't think Jane meant to tell me all the details of her marriage, but maybe she needed that heavy burden to take flight as a way to release some pent-up aggression. Or maybe Jane had told me this particular story as a way to ensure I didn't make the same mistakes in life.

Jane's voice pulled me out of my thoughts. "You must think I'm a silly woman to have stayed with my husband, but I thought I was doing what I *had* to do and what was best for the kids. I believed I had no other choice. You are still so young, Samantha, and you don't know anything about the word 'hard' yet."

Jane's last statement carried a defiant tone, and she may have taken my silence as judgment. I hurried to clear the air. "I don't judge you for staying with him, Jane, really, I don't. I think what Daniel did was wrong. *More* than wrong. If anything, I'm angry about what happened to you. I feel sad you had to stay with a man you didn't really know at all."

Jane shook her head dismissively. "It doesn't matter now. Can't change or undo the past."

I wanted to ask Jane why the next five years of her life had been such a nightmare, but quickly opted not to inquire. From the look of it, her memories had clearly put her in a sad funk.

"Well, I think we're finished planting," she said. I had the feeling she was ready for me to leave, and I didn't blame her. I was getting the drift that after her sad stories, she needed time alone.

Awkwardly, I began to clear away our mess. "Yep. Guess that's it for today. I'll just water these seeds before going." I wiped a few crumbs of dirt off her leg onto an old newspaper. "Is there anything else you might need done today?"

Jane looked around. "No. There's nothing else here."

"All right."

After I cleaned up and watered the newly seeded pots, Jane called out my name before I left. "Samantha?"

"Yes?" I said, turning around.

"Whatever you decide in the near future, just know this; you don't have to choose anyone right now. You don't have to settle. Your life is just starting, and you should be having fun, not worrying about who to spend the rest of your life with at this very given moment. You have all the time in the world to explore. Just focus on staying in school; that way, you'll be too smart to ever let a man tell you what to do."

"I needed to hear that, Jane. Thank you. I'll see you Monday."

Just as I walked through the front door and shut it behind me, my father called out from the kitchen, "Samantha. Is that you?"

"Yeah," I said, tossing my purse onto a loveseat before making my way into our overly warm kitchen.

My father stood at the counter hunched over the bills. "Caleb called. He said to call him as soon as you can."

There was a thud in my chest. "*Oh*. Okay. Thanks."

I wasn't ready to call Caleb, or Matt for that matter, but it wasn't like I could ignore them or pretend I didn't play the leading part in which way our futures bent. So, I groaned and threw myself onto my bed to contemplate my life choices—choices that had to come sooner than later. I didn't want to wait a lifetime to find out my mistakes were now regrets like Jane's, but it didn't make the task any easier.

I stared at the ceiling for over an hour, experiencing a rollercoaster of emotions. I knew what I had to do, but I hurt knowing I would lose the best parts of someone with whom I had spent nearly all my teenage years. And I hurt knowing he would be hurt by my choices. I especially hurt knowing there was no other way around all the damn hurting.

"Samantha, did you not hear me call you to dinner?" I felt my bed dip beside me. "*Oh, Sam, honey,*" my mother said, sitting beside me and rubbing my back.

I dissolved at my mother's touch, and it took me a full minute before I could sit up to face her to tell her my troubles. Her concerned green eyes never left my wet ones as she listened and never once interrupted me.

My mother, Julie, was beautiful. There was a time that she'd worried cutting her long straight brown hair would age her, but her new haircut above her shoulders somehow made her large green eyes and petite nose look even more striking than ever before. The love in her eyes seemed to say she could fix any heartbreak, and I secretly hoped she had all the answers to healing mine.

When I finally finished explaining all that had transpired, I watched my mother's features soften. She offered a small smile while sweeping away the strands of wet hair stuck to my tear-streaked cheeks. "I'm so sorry, Sammy girl. Love sucks, sometimes. Hurting people is never easy."

"I still love him. That's what makes it hard," I said, wiping my eyes with my fuzzy sleeve to my pjs.

"I know you do. And having feelings for more than one person doesn't make you a terrible person; it just means you have that much more room in your heart to give. Think of it this way; there are a million amazing people out there in this world, and with so many beautiful souls wandering about, well, sure, it can be tough to pick only one to love forever. And you are right; we can't ever know for sure who is the right one. We can only hope. But it sounds like you already know Caleb isn't the one."

"Relationships shouldn't be this hard. With Caleb, we fight all the time. And I'm sorry to say this, but my biggest fear is ending up like you and Dad. You two are miserable. I couldn't live like that."

"I'm so sorry you have these fears because of us. I'm ashamed you girls have to hear your father and me fight so much."

"Are ... you two getting a divorce?" I asked.

"When I met your father, we were crazy about each other. But after kids, full-time jobs, financial struggles, and other things that I don't think you girls need to worry about, well, we definitely have things to work on. I don't know, maybe it's time we see a counselor, because I don't want a divorce. I still think what we have is worth saving. I still think my fate is with your father. But as for you and Caleb, if you don't think your relationship is worth saving, then you need to come clean with him. As for Matt, why not take some time for yourself before seeing where your heart leads you? Just do *you* for a while."

I dug into a small hole in my pajamas that frayed just above my knee. "Jane practically said the same thing."

"She sounds like a wise woman."

"A *bitter* and *sad* wise woman."

"Either way, what I'm hearing from you is that you are trying to avoid heartache." My mother squeezed my leg. "And you know what, Sam?"

"What."

"You can't go through life untouched or without heartache. When it comes to love, we have to suffer the good and bad, the extraordinary and the ugly. It's part of life and what makes us all so unique."

I looked around my room at all the photos of me and Caleb. Not one single picture in the last four years was of me by myself. "It's going to be hard, being alone," I said.

"You will be just fine." My mother stood and held out her hand to help me up. "I bet you're starving."

"Famished," I said. "But Mom, I can't eat dinner just yet."

Twenty minutes later, my stomach growled—angry that I'd made it wait as I now sat in my bedroom facing Caleb.

"You hungry or something?" Caleb asked, sitting next to me.

"No," I lied, folding my arms around my abdomen.

"You're making me nervous. What's going on that I needed to come over so badly?"

Here it goes.

"We've been together for four years, right?"

"*Uh, yeah.*"

"And although we have had our ups and downs, some downs more recently, well, don't you ever, I don't know, have these weird feelings?"

"What feelings?"

"Like, uncertainty and doubt?"

"About our relationship?"

"Yeah."

He took a moment's pause, as if to really contemplate such a question. "To answer your question, no. Why? Are *you* feeling doubtful about us?"

I picked at my lip. "It's just that ... well, there is this feeling sometimes that I have, that we, um ... I don't know, that we may be going down a dead-end road."

"A dead-end road? Are you serious?"

"*Sorry. Sorry.* Wrong choice of words. Let me finish." I shook my head to clear the jumbled words banging around in my mind. "Look, we fight all the time. We don't laugh with each other as much anymore." I swallowed. "It's, well ... well, it's not as fun anymore. I'm not sure what's changed, but lately, you've been inconsiderate of any of my feelings, and it feels like you sometimes take our relationship for granted. It's like you expect me to be here forever."

"*Whoa.* Back up. Yeah, we've been fighting a lot, but it's only because of my leg and how baseball's been stressing me out. I sure as hell don't think we're headed for a dead end like you're making it sound. I'm sorry it hasn't been fun lately, but *geez*, give me a break. I have a lot going on."

"Caleb, it's not about everything going on just recently. I've been having these feelings for almost a year. I'm trying to be honest here when I say that I'm just not happy."

"For a year? You've not been happy for a year?"

I picked my lip harder when Caleb's eyes widened in disbelief. "Yes," I said. "Yes. And I don't want to do this to you but, I think we need a break."

Caleb's head whipped back as if I'd slapped him. "What? I ... but for like for how long?"

"How long? I don't know the answer. I mean, we've been together longer than anyone at our school, and, well, I want to see what it might be like outside of you and me." I smoothed out all the imaginary creases on my pajama bottoms to avoid his eyes.

He repeated himself, "How long, Sam?"

I couldn't lie. "Perhaps, infinitely?" His mouth dropped open with a silence that left me feeling terrible.

His question came soft and broken. "Are you saying you don't love me anymore, Sam, and you want to see other people?"

I finally looked up into his eyes and wished I hadn't. His stare seemed to carry the weight of everything I'd said, and I immediately wanted to take his pain away. "*Caleb*. I will always love you. But the question I struggle with the most is if I'm really, and I mean, *really*, in love with you?"

"And?"

My words came out like a tumbleweed without direction. "I don't know anymore. I love you; I do. Just maybe not *fully?* Or maybe I don't particularly love how things have been going lately, so I feel like I've fallen out of love. I'm sorry, I don't quite know how to say it, but my feelings have changed."

"When did this all start happening? Because *I* am still in love with you. I feel like this is all coming out of left field, and you're side-blinding me here."

"You mean 'blind-siding," I corrected him. Seeing the look on his face, I immediately wanted to take it back.

"*Whatever*," he said, clearly irritated. "Don't correct me right now and just answer the stupid question. *When* did you start feeling this way?"

I threw my hands up. "*Okay*. So, I guess it probably started last year? And then this year, a whole lot more."

Caleb took a long pause—maybe to mull over our past year together, recollecting flawed data on where and when our relationship had gone haywire. He swallowed. "Sam, listen. We can make it work. I can try harder, you know, be nicer and more considerate. I'll do whatever it is you need me to do. Just tell me what that is. I promise it will work out. And I don't want to see other people." He squeezed my hands tightly in his as he barely got the next words out. "I only want you."

It wasn't easy to hear the hurt in those last four words. I knew he would try and convince me to rethink my decision, and for a moment, I almost backed down. Because having someone say they wanted you and no one else was what every woman wanted to hear, except it only worked if the other person felt the same. And, I couldn't stay with Caleb knowing I wanted more. I didn't know when exactly it had all changed, but he wasn't enough for me anymore.

As much as it hurt, I held firm to what I needed to do for myself. "Thank you for saying you would try to make the relationship better, but, even if you did, I know in my heart what I want. My feelings have changed."

I could barely stand watching as his heart beat so fast through his shirt as he choked out, "Sam, *please?* Please don't say that. Don't do this to us. We are good together. Can't you see that?"

His pleads made me feel so damn horrible.

"*Please,* Caleb. Try to understand and listen to me. I hate to see you so hurt, but understand this is hard for me too."

Caleb wiped a heavy teardrop away from his cheek. "I don't want to lose you. I actually see us married one day. Please don't do this. I am begging you. I love you *so much* it hurts."

Dammit, dammit, dammit.

The tears had arrived.

I couldn't take it, and Matt was right. I would rather Caleb be mad at me over his crocodile tears that rained on like a raging flood. So, I urgently carried out the only stupid strategic plan I could pathetically muster because I was too chicken shit. "Caleb, there's something else I need to tell you." I swallowed and ran the top of my teeth over my bottom lip multiple times before finally blurting out, "Matt and I kissed."

Chapter 15

Sam 2003

I watched in amazement at how fast Caleb's tears dried up.

He sprung off the bed and loomed over me. "Are you freaking kidding me?"

"It was an accident," I said, crouching away from his intense glare that suggested he wanted to throttle me.

"An accident? *Oh, give me a break.* There's no such thing as *accidental* kissing!"

"What I meant was that we didn't plan the kiss. It just, I don't know, it just happened."

"When?"

I squeezed my eyes shut. "Last night."

"When you went skiing? Wow." He shook his head. "I *knew* I couldn't trust you two. I find the timing a little funny that you are breaking up with me right after this *so-called kiss*."

"Caleb. I'm sorry. It was unexpected."

"So. Who kissed who, Sam?"

I grabbed a matted fur pillow beside me and feverishly began to untangle its mess. "Well, I think Matt was joking around and accidentally kissed me. Then I kissed him back, and then, well, it got weird."

"Really? You kissed him back? *Perfect!* I told you Matt had the hots for you, Samantha, but no, *you*," he said, jabbing a finger into my shoulder, "*you* never listen to me."

"Caleb, listen," I said, rubbing my shoulder, "I already wanted to take a break before kissing Matt, I swear. It's just really terrible timing—a coincidence."

"Wait. When you mentioned you might want to see other people, are you talking about seeing Matt?"

"No," I said. It was partially true, but still, I tried to explain. "I don't know. Maybe? I'm sorta confused right now. I don't know what I want or if I want anyone at all."

"I deserve answers, Samantha," he said in a low deep voice.

I threw my pillow off my lap. "I don't *have* all the answers. There were no premeditated plans to see anyone else, if that's what you're wondering. I swear to you. Before all this, my feelings were solely on the grounds of not being happy anymore, okay?"

Caleb squinted as if he didn't believe me. "Four years together, but now it's all too confusing for you just when Matt kisses you?"

"No, you're not listening. My doubts about us were before Matt ever kissed me."

Caleb shook his head before sulking over to my bedroom door. He roughly grabbed the handle before looking back. "I'm sorry you are so damn confused, Samantha. But let's just get one thing straight. *I* am not confused. I love you. I always will. You're making a mistake." At that, my ex walked out and shut the door behind him.

~

I took a three-hour nap before making my way to the kitchen to eat dinner. Eating cold spaghetti straight from the Tupperware, I picked up the phone. I wanted to call Caleb to check in on him, but I knew it would only confuse him and stretch out the hurt even more. So, I dialed the other thing I needed to tackle.

"Hey, Sam." Matt said, answering the phone. "What's up?"

"Just eating."

"I wondered if you were ever going to speak to me again after the other night."

"Yeah, about that. That was crazy," I said, placing the cold spaghetti in the microwave.

"Crazy good or crazy bad?"

"That's the thing. It was, well, I don't know ... both?"

"I'll take that."

"You were right though, Matt; about making someone angry so the sting wouldn't hurt as bad."

"Wait, so you did talk to Caleb about what happened?"

Anytime there was a crisis biting at my heels, Matt was always the first person I'd reach out to. I tried to pretend it was the old Matt on the other end of the line instead of the new one, whose Coca-Cola lips still remained fresh in my mind.

"Yeah," I said. "That's why I'm calling. It didn't go well."

"This is all my fault."

I watched my spaghetti go round and round in the microwave. Matt was the one who'd started that kiss, but it was just as much my fault for not stopping it the second time. Thinking of that kiss, a tinge of heat reached my cheeks, and I tried to ignore how complicated we were now.

"It's not all your fault," I said. "But you were right about making Caleb mad. He was so pissed when I told him everything that he actually forgot how sad he was for a hot minute."

"Well, I guess I'd be pretty pissed too. I suppose he wants to kill me now. But what's new."

The timer went off, and I pulled my food out. "Possibly. But don't worry. Eventually, Caleb will get over all this. I hope."

"I highly doubt he will get over it anytime soon."

"Well, I'm just thinking come Monday, when people find out we broke up, that I might skip that day."

"You guys really broke up?" he said, sounding shocked.

"Yes. Also, *please* don't tell anyone about our kiss."

"I would never."

"I know, but I'm just worried. People won't understand I wanted to call it off way before the kiss."

"I won't say a word. Promise. And I'm really sorry you had to deal with all this. Are you okay?"

"I think I'm still in shock. It was the hardest thing I've ever had to do, but, I'm okay, I think. Anyway, I only hope Caleb still wants to be friends. I never thought about how leaving on a bad note would affect our friendship."

After a long silent minute, Matt finally broke the spell, though I could barely hear him. "Have you figured out what you feel about us yet?"

I took a large bite of my steaming noodles. "Dammit!"

"I knew it. It's too soon to talk about the other night."

"No. Sorry, just burnt my mouth." I took an ice cube out of the freezer. "I meant to say, no. No, I have not figured that out yet."

"*Oh*. Gotcha."

I placed my fork down and pushed my food away. "It's just that I have had zero time to think it over. Maybe everything's just happening too fast, you know? My brain actually hurts thinking about what I'm supposed to do or how I'm supposed to feel." My mother's advice about being honest came to the forefront of my mind, and I delicately continued, "If I'm completely honest, Matt, the timing doesn't feel right."

"*Oh*. Sure, I get it. But can I ask you something? Just tell me if there's any hope for me someday. I know I'm acting impatient, but I need to know how to act around you going forward."

"What? Matt! This is exactly what I *don't* want to happen. I like the way you were before the kiss. I want you to always act yourself around me. Why would you change?"

"I'm not necessarily going to change. It's something new that I would add to the table."

"What the heck are you talking about?"

"If there's the slightest hope for you and me, well, then maybe I wouldn't have to suppress or hold back my more flirtatious side? I would show you my—" he coughed, "my undeniable and irresistible charms, you know, to woo the girl?"

"Woo what?" I laughed. I cleared my throat the moment I realized Matt wasn't joking. "Sorry. You're ... you're serious."

The truth was, wooing or not, it was almost too much. Too soon. Way not ready. I already wanted the old Matt back. The thought of seeing this other side of Matt, well, it scared me. I had to put the brakes on.

Matt, "I wish ... I wish I could answer your question right now, but I can't. It's like the most complicated math equation and you know how much I hate math. For the time being, I just need a friend right now. Can you stay *you* for now? I don't know if I'm ready for the other *you* just yet."

"Okay. We can come back to all this when you feel you're ready. There's no rush. *Ever*. I mean I've waited seven years for you, so what's another seven?" he joked.

"There's the Matt I like," I laughed.

"And Sam?"

"Yeah?"

"I'm always going to be here for you, no matter what you decide. That will never change about me. I just want you happy."

I was so relieved that Matt was still in my corner, unlike Caleb, who didn't really care if I was happy as long as he got what he wanted. "Thanks, Matt. And ditto. So, I guess I'll talk to you later or see you at school on Monday?"

Matt laughed. "I can't wait. If you're unable to locate me, I'll be inside my locker, hiding from Caleb."

"Same," I said.

~

Monday morning came all too fast.

I shook off my wet umbrella before walking into my first class and found I was on time for once. I sat down and avoided the eyes of my peers, just in case they'd heard about the breakup, but I couldn't help but scan a look to my right. Relief flooded me to find Caleb's chair empty. I wasn't ready to face him.

My pen rolled to the floor, and as I bent to pick it up, I felt a tap on my shoulder. When turning around, I met a pair of intense brown eyes with dark, bushy eyebrows that followed further up to a mane of medium-length dirty blond hair—all belonging to the one and only, Sarah Hansen. I had tried, to no avail, to become Sarah's friend, being that she lived only a few streets over for as long as I could remember. But I gave up after too many snubs.

I never could figure out why she had it out for me, like some vendetta for breathing the same air as her. It was just as well. She was all gossip and drama anyway. She reminded me of a lemon meringue pie—pretty on the outside and sour in the middle. If she had any sugar in her blood, it was the artificial kind.

"Hey, Sarah," I said.

She whispered like a child who'd just found secret buried treasure. "I just heard you broke up with Caleb. What happened? I mean, like, *everyone* thought you guys would get married one day."

"Wow, news travels fast."

"So? What happened?"

She was like a pestering gnat, and I knew it was pointless to ignore her. "I just needed a break. Plain and simple."

"How long is this break? Are you guys going to see other people?"

"Sarah, *geez*. I don't know yet. It just happened yesterday."

"Well, I heard Caleb's pissed; I mean, I'd be pissed, too, if my girlfriend of a hundred years kissed someone else."

I looked around the room for the first time and found others intently looking at me. Dear God. By the end of the day, everyone would think that the reason Caleb and I had broken up was solely because of Matt.

As cold as it was in the classroom, my upper lip began to sweat.

Calm down, Samantha, and think.

I tried begging first. "Sarah, *please,* please tell me you are *not* going around blabbing this stuff."

"I only told like maybe two people." She shrugged. "I can't help if it goes around. That's on you."

If my eyes could have fired missiles, I would have aimed true. "What is your deal? It would have been nice if you had come to me first before making assumptions. You don't know the whole story." I shook my head. "Whatever. It doesn't matter. But for your information, it's not like how it sounds. You don't get it. And, quite frankly, it's none of your business."

"Okay, *chill*. Don't go all postal on me. Listen, I won't tell anyone else, okay? Pinky swear."

As Sarah held her pinky in the air and I debated offering her my middle finger, but Caleb walked in. He didn't look mad. Instead, his overall façade had taken on what appeared to be a sad, puppy-dog look. A quick glance at Sarah's sympathetic look confirmed where I stood. People would take sides, and I was already at the losing end without ever being heard.

Fabulous.

The small chatter throughout the classroom stopped, followed by awkward silence when Caleb took his seat beside me. The bell rang and he barely looked my way before offering a quick 'hello.'

"Hey," was all I could reply before our teacher took roll call.

As the next forty-five minutes dragged on, I didn't hear a word the teacher spoke. I was too worried about what the hell a person was supposed to say after a breakup, and how the hell I was supposed to act with a million eyes glaring at me. With Sarah's eyes burning a hole in the back of my head and with Caleb's sad and depressing vibes that could melt an entire continent, the bell couldn't ring fast enough. And when it did, I grabbed my stuff and ran out the door to my next class.

I didn't even make it even to the next building before a hand grabbed my arm and pulled me to the side of the building. "Sam, wait! I want to talk to you."

"Caleb, what the—" I pulled my arm out of his grip. "Why would you tell people that I kissed Matt, knowing perfectly well what it would do to my reputation?"

"I only told *one person*. I mean, come on, Sam, I needed to vent to someone. I told my best friend. Is that all right with you?"

"Well, maybe you forgot to tell him to keep it under wraps? Because it seems he probably told his girlfriend, and of course, she told Sarah, and now the whole world knows." My hair began to take a beating from the rain, so I flipped open my umbrella with vigor. "I don't blame you for talking to your brother, Caleb, but now I look like a horrible person in everyone's eyes. To refresh your memory, before that kiss with Matt ever happened, I needed a break and *wanted* a break from you. And now everyone will only focus on how awful Samantha Carey is for breaking Caleb's heart."

"Sam, I can't help what everyone else thinks, except that I still love you." Caleb gave me his best 'I'm dying' look before adding, "*Sammy*, I am miserable without you. It doesn't have to be this way. Just come back to me, and everyone will stop talking."

My eyes went as wide as my umbrella. "No, Caleb, you're not listening to me. If you care at all for me, you will give me this without guilt or something to hold over my head."

"Okay, calm down. But I'm not going to wait around forever."

"Then don't. I don't need you to harass me. And please don't make Matt out to be the bad guy in all this. We had issues *before* Matt. Just remember that. Promise me you won't do anything stupid?"

"I promise I won't pummel him to the ground if that's what you mean. But I'm not promising that people won't judge him for kissing *my* girlfriend. What did you expect?"

"Please let me by," I said, sorely irritated, almost enough to cry. "I'm going to be late for class."

I raced to my next class but showed up forty seconds late because of Caleb. It was my fifth tardy and with that came an automatic detention

—my second detention of the year. Seated in my chair, I hugged my backpack for comfort and prayed the day would be over soon.

~

Lunch period was for the tortured. I was sure of that.

I didn't know why I'd even bothered to show up, knowing my peers would survey my every move and have conspiracy theories hanging on their tongues in genuine excitement. It was expected, since Caleb was somewhat a popular jock and well-liked by most. I suppose in everyone's mind, hurting Caleb was like kicking a puppy, so I was somewhat surprised that no one had stabbed me with a fork just yet.

Matt stood at the end of my table with a food tray in hand, seemingly debating whether to sit next to me. I knew his hesitation wasn't out of embarrassment to be seen with me, but probably because he worried that us sitting together would only make things worse for me. The look on his face said he wasn't having the greatest of days either, and even though it was a tad awkward between us, I needed a friend to lean on. My friend Emily was home sick, so that left me with Matt.

Our eyes met, and I asked him, "You wanna eat lunch in your truck with me?" I half-heartedly laughed but hoped to God he would say yes.

We both took in the scene around us: The cafeteria growing noisier by the minute; a girl shrieking out when someone threw an orange at her chest; the sound of someone's food tray dropping, kids laughing at whoever dropped their tray; the room smelling of old beef and tuna, with a splash of bleach.

Matt didn't hesitate. "Let's get the hell out of here."

We exited the building like two escapees minutes before our hanging, and I didn't care that our classmates looked in our direction suspiciously. Either A; they assumed we are guilty, or B; they were questioning it. Either way, I hated Monday and wished I had skipped it altogether.

The rain had finally let off, and while I stared out Matt's truck window at the baseball field where we parked, I took an aggravated bite of my sandwich and talked with a mouth full. "I know I shouldn't care about what people think of me or how they judge me. I mean, most of these people will forget about all of this by next week, right? So why do I care so much?"

"Okay, here's my theory," he said, attempting to wipe a drop of mustard from his grey Star Wars t-shirt. "For starters, you're a nice person, and you don't want people to think you're a jerk. And two, well, you care about what people think of you because you're human, plain and simple. All humans want to be accepted, and if people think you're a jerk, you won't feel accepted."

"*Wow*. That's some good insight there. And here I thought you didn't have a serious bone in you."

He popped a Dorito in his mouth. "Who knew, huh? Look, eventually, people will forget today's paper and move on to the next juicy news article. You stop caring when you realize that."

"I think it would be easier if I just went to another school or just moved to another town. Don't you think? I mean, this is all the more reason why I hate it here. I just wanna buy a car and move far away."

Matt placed his hands on the steering wheel and looked out the window. "You think running will help solve everything?"

"Maybe."

"Don't be ridiculous. You know you've always had a problem running away from conflict, right? Remember that time you got that huge zit on your forehead in the seventh grade, and instead of dealing with it like every other normal hormonal teenager, you didn't come to school for a week? And then you fell behind on studies and nearly had to go to summer school to catch up."

"Yeah. So?"

"Just pointing out your obvious flaws. You want me to be straight with you right?"

I sighed before answering, "Yes."

"Okay then, don't run away because you're scared. Sam, people break up all the time. Big deal. You're reading too much into it. And if you leave me to go to another school, I'll kill you."

"Fine. I won't go," I said, crossing my arms. He was right, but I didn't want to hear it. "You know what, Matt? As much as your words have an uber amount of truth and wisdom and all, I kind of like the old jokester Matt. Can I have him back?"

"You want a good joke? I got tripped today by one of Caleb's so-called 'jock' friends. You're not the only one who's dealing with all this. You and me, kid, we've just got to stick together. We'll get through it. Eventually."

"Wait. What? Who tripped you? Was it Bryce?" I glared through the window and balled up my paper bag. "I swear to God, I will find him and—"

Matt laughed, "Okay, calm down there, Bulldog! *Heel. Heel!*"

"What? I'm serious. Who was it?"

"What are you going to do anyway? Go around beating up everyone for me? I can handle them myself, *thank you very much.*"

"Fine. But if you need backup, I got you."

"I don't doubt that."

Before we climbed out of the truck, I had a profound urge to tell Matt how much I appreciated him. If I didn't have him to talk to, I probably would have eaten my lunch in the bathroom. I squeezed his arm with as much sincerity as possible because, jokes aside, I wanted him to believe me. "As much as this situation sucks, I'm glad we are in this together."

"Same," he said, looking down at my hand resting on his arm. He could have taken the gesture to mean one of two things; an innocent indication or me making a move. He gave me a playful wink following his reply, and I had my answer. My once-platonic gesture wasn't platonic for him. And in that moment I wasn't sure if I wanted anything to change between us. I knew he was waiting for me to decide our fate, but I wasn't ready yet. Plain and simple.

With a heavy heart, I pulled my hand away from his shoulder, cementing Monday as a total loss.

"Oh no, I don't like that look," Matt said, sensing my somberness.

"Matt?" I said, forcing myself to look up at him.

"Do I want to know?"

"Look, I still don't have an answer to your question."

"What question?" he asked, but I had a feeling he knew what I was about to say.

"The question of whether I have feelings for you other than being friends?" I bit the inside of my cheek too hard and didn't mind the metallic taste that followed. I deserved every nasty thing that came my way for hurting everyone I loved.

"*Oh. That* question." He took hold of the steering wheel again as if it was his turn to drive away from what he didn't want to face.

I picked up my balled-up paper lunch bag and smoothed it over. "The thing is ... my biggest fear is losing what we have. Part of me wants this to work because what better person to love than your own best friend, right? You make me laugh. You've always been there for me. I don't think I was even shocked that you liked me or even loved me for all these years because, in some small way, I think I have always known how you've felt. But maybe I didn't *want* to recognize it because you are literally the only person I have who keeps me sane. If we dated, and somehow turned into my parents or just like me and Caleb, the risk is too great. I would die to lose you as my best friend."

I cleared my throat. "But that kiss you gave me the other night, it was well ... *epic*. And although epic, it confused me. What it comes down to this is this; you are an amazing kisser, Matt, but kissing my best friend just, well, it scares me too much."

Matt's hands suddenly fell slack, sliding off the steering wheel to his lap in a thud. And when he continued to stare out the window in silence, I panicked. "Say something."

"Hold on. I'm thinking here," he said before resuming his grasp on the wheel. He tapped his thumbs over the top of the worn-out leather as if contemplating something important. Finally, he turned to me and clapped his hands, just once. "Okay, I got it! *So,* I'm a good kisser, right?"

"Yeah, but what does that have to do with what I just said?"

"You said I was a good kisser, *but* this 'best friend' thing is too complicated for you, right?"

"I'm not sure where you are going with this, but yes, it's way the hell too complicated to pursue whatever this is."

"So, how about we move our status from being 'best' friends to 'just' friends. The 'just' kind-of-friends with the benefits of kissing sometimes. *Boom*. It's that easy. No more of this 'best' friends pressure. And if it doesn't work out being two regular friends kissing, then we can easily go back to being 'best' friends with zero kissing."

"Am I living in the twilight zone? Because I feel like I'm living in the twilight zone." Of course, Matt would joke at something so detrimental to his heart. It was his only way to protect himself. "What is it with you in your ideas? Where the heck does your brain go sometimes?"

Matt crossed his arms and pouted theatrically. "So, you're saying no to my genius solution all because you are a scared rabbit who likes to run?"

"You are killing me, Matt."

"Don't think too much into this. I promise our friendship will never change no matter which way you split it. You never have to worry about losing your best friend with me."

I was suddenly tired. "Fine. It's not a for-sure, yes, but it's not a for-sure no either. That will have to do for now."

"Well, at least you didn't say no and break my heart like you did Caleb's. You'd be two for two."

"Matt!" I said defensively.

"I'm just kidding. But no, seriously, I think this may be the best day of my life."

"I didn't say yes or no. How is this the best day of your life?"

"Because hope is a beautiful thing. You haven't broken my heart just yet, Sam Carey." When I gave him a long scowl, he laughed. "Look, kid. I think as long as we stay 'just' friends, and you don't get all awkward on me just because we had one epic kiss, then what's the harm in any of it?"

"Trust me; there is harm in everything new I try. So, for now, because I'm not ready to venture further, I have to listen to this," I said, pointing to my heart.

"Wait, you have to listen to your boobs? How can you even hear those little things?"

"I swear to God, Matt—" I reached over and grabbed two of his fingers and threatened to pull them back.

"*Uncle*!" he faked.

I let go of his hand and laughed. "You're too much sometimes."

He grabbed hold of the rear-view mirror and angled his jawline—tilting it left and right as if checking himself out. "It's a good thing you didn't flat-out say no. You'd be missing out on a killer stud here. You'd be a complete moron, not wanting all this hunk of meat."

"*Oh, boy*. Here we go."

He sat back in his seat and shrugged. "It's not like you could get someone hotter."

"Is that so? I'm glad you're taking this so well. But if you're looking for a girlfriend, you may need some pointers. Let's start with your cheesy sarcasm."

"Well, at least I have the kissing thing going for me."

"*That* you do, sir."

Matt took a deep breath. "Now that we have established some kissing possibilities in the near future, can I at least get a hug?"

I couldn't resist his pout. "Sure, you dope. But don't try anything. I'm not ready, remember?"

"Scout's honor," he said, raising three fingers up.

With his strong bear hug, everything between us righted itself. Until he pulled away, and I saw out of my peripheral vision we had guests. I jumped. "Crap. Matt."

It dawned on us that our innocent hug had happened at the most inopportune time. Matt groaned. "Great."

As Caleb's jock friends opened Matt's door for him, Caleb was right there to greet me as soon as I opened mine. "*Wow*, that was quick, Sam. I thought you said you needed time to be by yourself?"

"Caleb, you have to trust me when I tell you this is all wrong. You are taking this little scene here at face value."

"Trust you? That's a joke."

Matt got out of the truck and casually leaned against the hood, as if all the drama was beneath him. One of the jocks named Donny closed in on his personal space. "Geez, Matt, can't you give a guy a break before moving in on his girl? Pretty low, don't you think?"

When Matt ignored him and Donny didn't get the reaction he had hoped for, it only antagonized Donny more. He flipped Matt's hat off his head, taunting him. "What? Got nothing to say? Not even a sorry? Because I think you owe Caleb a sorry."

Matt didn't take the bait, and instead, he crossed his arms coolly. "*Darn it, Donny*, that was my *special* hat."

Matt's sarcasm only made it worse. Donny and came at him again, "*Oh*, I am *so sorry*, *Matt.* How about your shoes? Are these special too?" Donny crushed his heel on Matt's foot, but Matt surprisingly remained unaffected.

"Caleb, stop this," I said while trying to stand next to Matt. Caleb pinned me to the truck and I looked up at him in shock. "What the hell are you doing, Caleb?"

"What? I'm not doing anything," he said innocently.

"Let go of me," I said through clenched teeth.

When Donny's heel grounded down harder, crushing Matt's toes, Matt lost his composure and pushed Donny hard. "Touch me again, *asswipe*, and your face will look like last week's lunch."

Donny laughed, "Okay, tough guy. Let's see you give me your best shot." Matt may have been shorter than Donny, but he was built like a brick, so I didn't doubt for a minute that Matt could flatten him. But cocky Donny had two more friends with him, making it unfair.

"STOP. Stop all this right now!" I tried to take a step around Caleb's large frame to get over to Matt, but Caleb grabbed my arm again to prevent me. I yanked my arm away. "Caleb, listen. Knock it off. It isn't what it looks like. I'm telling the truth! I never thought you would stoop this low. This pathetic side of you doesn't look good on you."

When Caleb pushed me against the truck in anger, Matt chimed in, "Caleb, leave her alone already. If you must know, Sam just finished telling me in the truck that she only wants to be *friends*, nothing more. That hug was a 'let's be friends' hug, all right? It seems neither of us will get the girl anytime soon."

Caleb's grip loosened around me. "Is this true, Sam?"

I pushed Caleb out of my face. "If you would just listen to me, yes! Okay? There is nothing between Matt and me right now." It wasn't a total lie, because I was really no one's girl. "And, Caleb, you don't get to tell me who I can hang out with anymore. The sad part is, I was hoping you and I could remain friends, but you're out of control."

I saw the guilt in his eyes. "Whatever. You know what, Matt?" Caleb said, facing him, "I knew all along you had the hots for Sam. Maybe she wouldn't be feeling so damn confused if you wouldn't have tried to make a move on *my* girlfriend."

I interrupted Caleb. "I am *not* your girlfriend anymore."

It looked as though someone had punched Caleb in the stomach when my words finally hit home, and as much as his overreaction to everything pissed me off, I still cared enough to know he was acting out from hurt. I reached out to touch him. "Caleb—"

My ex backed away as if my touch burned him, and in a way, I guess I did. "Let's go, guys," he said. "There's nothing here."

As Caleb and his crew headed back inside, my legs shook as I walked over to Matt. I picked his hat up off the ground. "Here. Sorry about those idiots."

Matt flicked the water off his hat before placing it on his head backward. "It's fine. But I was kind of looking forward to a fight. I hear fights make you manly."

"It would have been an unfair fight. You against four?"

"Who cares? At least it would have helped me feel like a winner right here," he said, pointing to his heart.

"What, your boobs?" I snorted.

"No, my heart. *Duh.*"

"Well, I don't want you in any fights. Especially for me," I said, giving him a playful thwack to his arm.

"Your hits are weak, you know that?" He ran a hand over his cheeks. "Just make sure you don't hit me in my beautiful, chiseled face. This masterpiece has to stay pretty for all the ladies if you decide to pass me up. And what a shame that would be."

"You will be the absolute end of me," I laughed. "Let's go, *Fabio*."

As we walked back inside the school to an unrelenting atmosphere of talk and judgment, I took Matt's advice and concluded that maybe I didn't care what people thought. Because not knowing what would happen today or tomorrow wouldn't be the end of the world. I'd survive it one way or another.

Or maybe not.

Chapter 16

Sam 2003

The rest of the school week passed as planned—*crappy*, with a capital C. I didn't know that breakups could feel like a divorce, where people took sides. Apparently, kissing your best friend when you still had a boyfriend classified me as breaking a social boundary. The fun games of 'Whose Side Are You On' pitched me all the way to the left side, meaning there was no one on the left to claim me. Well, except for Matt and Emily, of course. Either way, if I hadn't already hated school, I did now.

Lunch hour was the worst. I had to skip it altogether and eat in the library when Matt came up with the idea that maybe it was best we didn't hang out together for only a while, at least until the masses found their next victims to prey upon.

"I heard Jerod and Lacey might break up," I said to Emily at a corner table furthest back the library. "Maybe their gossip will be wild enough to take some of this heat off of me."

Emily had been listening to me whine about the injustices of my situation for days and, for the umpteenth time, she tried to change the negative narrative, to no avail. "What book you reading now?" she asked me.

"It's called, *A Girl Named Disaster*. Seems fitting, no?"

Emily put down her romance novel. "What's the book about?"

"It's about this young twenty-year-old who escapes her village in Zimbabwe because her arranged marriage turned abusive. On the run, she spends months fighting off starvation, dehydration, and various animals attacking her. That's as far as I've gotten."

"Maybe you should read something, I don't know, less depressing?"

"No, actually it's helping. I realize my problems are nothing compared to hers."

"If you say so. I just think you need something positive to focus on."

"Actually, I do have something positive to look forward to. Do you remember my friend Heidi, from third-grade summer camp? She invited me to a party tonight after I filled her in on my woes. And being that this is her school and not ours, where everyone hates me, it's a perfect much-needed break—kind of crucial to my survival at having any social life. You're invited."

"Wish I could, but I'm babysitting again. But you'll have to tell me all about the party afterward."

"I will. Can you believe this will be my first function without Caleb watching my every move? However, I do have another slight problem to tackle. My mother grounded me for getting another stupid detention."

"How do you plan to get out of that one?"

"If my plan of sneaking out works, I'll be enjoying myself in—" I grabbed Emily's wrist and looked at her watch, "eleven hours. That's when my parents are fast asleep."

"This is a new side of you. Have fun tonight, you rebel, you."

"Hey, if people are going to depict me as some rule-breaker, I might as well play the part."

~

I could barely contain my excitement when my father's snoring confirmed my parents were fast asleep. I checked off numbers one through three from my to-do list.

Sam's Friday To-Do List

1. 10:30 Check to see if parents are asleep
2. Get ready
3. Stuff bed
4. 11:00 Sneak out
5. 11:15 Meet Heidi down the road
6. Have fun for once in your damn life

7. Be back by 4:30 a.m.

By eleven o'clock, I'd checked off numbers three and four and hurried out the front door, shutting it softly behind me without making a peep. While I crouched behind a bush and waited for Heidi at the end of my road, I reflected on our friendship.

At nine years old, bunking in a cabin at Camp Seymore with Heidi had been a godsend. It was our first time away from home and away from our parents. When we couldn't handle the stories of the one-eyed bogeyman who lived under the floorboards and hairy spiders that crawled into sleeping bags, we found ourselves clinging together that first sleepless night. We especially had to draw strength from each other to ward off a pair of mean girls who called us crybabies the rest of that terrifying weekend. But after Heidi stuck up for us and told those girls she would tell everyone they'd peed the bed, you could say we became pen pals.

When I saw Heidi's little red Beamer pull up near the stop sign at the end of my street, I snuck up and slapped my hand on her driver's side window. The look of fright on her face was priceless.

She killed the engine. "Dammit, Sam," she hissed while rolling down her window. "You scared the *crap* out of me!"

"Didn't anyone tell you it's dangerous to be out so late at night all alone?"

"Well, I'm not alone anymore, so hurry up and get in the car before you get caught and ruin our whole night of fun."

"No worries. My parents are dead to the world and out cold." I slid into the passenger seat. "Smells good in here. Is that tea tree oil and a hint of trouble I smell?"

She slapped the car freshener hanging from her rear-view mirror. "They done run out of Bitch Boss scent, so this had to do." Heidi used her best 'mom' voice as she smoothed back her straight raven hair just below her shoulders. "Seatbelt, darling."

"*Ooh*, you got new bangs," I said. "Love it."

"My stylist said it would go well with my cat eyes and heart-shaped face. I even extended my black eyeliner. You like?" Heidi turned the interior lights on and showed me the elaborate artwork. "See? My eyes have wings to fly."

"Love it. Very Cleopatra of you. I just went simple tonight."

"Ripped jeans and a crop top? Your simple classy girl-next-door look never disappoints."

Heidi started the car and it purred to life. "You know, Heidi," I said, caressing the top of the dashboard with envy, "I'm not gonna lie, you don't know how much I need a getaway car right now."

"I'm sorry it's been bad at school. If I went to the same school as you, I'd set some people straight for you. Especially that Sarah Hansen chick."

"Thanks. I'm staying clear of her. Although, I might ask Jane if she knows a hitman."

"How is your murdering boss doing?" Heidi laughed. "Any more clues?"

"She told me her husband cheated, so maybe she killed him?"

"Let's say you did find some evidence that insinuates she killed this guy? Could you still work for her?"

"I don't have a choice. Like I said, I need this job if I'm ever going to get a car. My happiness depends on escaping this stupid town. And even though I want to quit at times when she's super rude, the job is easy enough. But I can't quit. I need this job like a prisoner needs freedom."

"You could turn her in to the police when you finally leave."

"What's the point? She's already living in prison—alone and bedridden in that house. Plus, she's been oddly chill lately. For once, my job hasn't been my biggest problem."

"Bet your job is better than mine."

"I thought you loved being a veterinary assistant."

"Try cleaning up after a veterinarian when he finishes his surgeries; I'm talking blood, fur, and guts. It's sick."

"I clean human poop out of a bucket."

"You win."

I laughed, "Seriously, Heidi, it's been too long."

She knocked my elbow off the middle console playfully. "Agree. Glad you have a little freedom without 'you know who.' How are you doing about that anyway?"

I mulled and inhaled her question in one long draw before letting it all out. "I feel weirdly ... great? I know I should feel a mess, but I don't."

"It sounds like the decision was a long time coming."

"Maybe," I said, flipping the visor down to apply lip gloss. "But either way, tonight couldn't have come at a better time."

She looked at me as I blotted my lips with the back of my hand. "Single looks good on you. You're glowing."

"That glow might be because of this light," I said, closing the visor shut.

"Well, it's nice to have you back, Sam."

"What do you mean? I never left, silly."

Heidi merged onto the freeway. "How do I put this? I guess Caleb had a way of making it seem like you were off-limits. I didn't call you to hang out as much because I knew he would insist on coming with us. It's like he saw me as some bad influence, so he kept you to himself."

"Well, you *do* party more than anyone I know." I smiled. "But it's no longer a problem who I hang out with. Plus, I don't think I'll be invited to any parties at my school anytime soon. You'll have to adopt me for all your Friday parties." One of my favorite songs by No Doubt, "Underneath It All," played on the stereo, and I bounced in my seat. "Sister, turn this song up!" Windows down, we sang to the lyrics as my fingers danced to the ripples of the wind and my hair flapped, sticking to my lip gloss.

Heidi turned down the music twenty minutes later when we pulled up to a massive brick house. "I think this is it, but I have to turn around. There's no parking left."

"There's like a million people here. I rarely got to venture out when I was with Caleb, so what city are we in again?"

"Enumclaw. The house is some guy's grandparents' house. I guess they're out of town, staying in their second home in Arizona. Lucky them *and* lucky us."

After Heidi parked a block away, she pulled on her black leather coat. "Do I look too goth?"

"No. Far from it. But I sort of feel like the new kid in town. Do you think someone might recognize me from my school?"

"So what if they did?" she said, running a finger under her eyes to ensure her mascara didn't fleck.

"Shall I remind you? Our two schools hate each other."

"Fine. How about you're my cousin visiting from out of town?"

"That would work. But cousin from where? We should get the story straight before we go inside."

"Right. Okay. You came from Missouri?"

"I haven't a clue about the state of Missouri. Idaho?"

"Ida-*ho* it is."

We passed nearly twenty cars parked along the dead-end street, and as we got closer to the house, the music's bass grew loud enough to feel vibrations under our feet. I chewed the inside of my cheek when the windows of the cars closest rattled in protest.

Heidi grabbed my hand, squeezing it. "You need to get out of your head."

"What?" I said, pretending to like my newly found freedom.

"I *know* you. You're biting your cheek again. So listen up, when we walk through these front doors, I order you to have fun for once in your life. Is that clear?"

"Crystal."

"That's my girl."

We walked into a blast of music that came at us in a deafening assault. I covered my ears. "Heidi! We need earplugs!"

"Beer jugs?"

"No! My ears are bleeding. I need *earplugs*!" Heidi cocked her head as my dog did sometimes, and I mouthed, *I. Need. Ear. Plugs.*

Heidi shouted, "You'll get used to it. Drinks should help!"

If someone had asked me to describe the inside of the home, I couldn't have even said if it was contemporary or modern, or if the owners collected Hummel figurines or went with a shaggy beige or grey carpet. I could only make out the sea of heads, moving to and fro to the music from the Black-Eyed Peas while we squeezed past the masses to find the drink station.

I wanted to go back to the comforts of the car with the wind blowing in my hair while No Doubt took away all my doubts, but as I looked over at Heidi with her new haircut, cute outfit, and her wide smile plastered across her pretty face, I knew I couldn't do that to her. So, I braved the mob of drunks, keeping my head low to avoid someone recognizing me. It was bad enough to have one school hate you, let alone two.

The kitchen wasn't nearly as loud when I heard Heidi squeal, "Brian! This is my cousin, *uh* ..." We both realized we forgot to give me a fake name, but Heidi quickly blurted out, "Ida! This is Ida." My eyes widened at the hideous name, and I elbow-jabbed her. She rolled her eyes and tried again, "Ida here likes to go by her middle name, Samantha, or Sam for short."

I shook my head and went with it. "How's it going, Brian?"

He poured a cup of beer from a keg before giving it to Heidi. "Good, thanks. What's your poison? Beer or shots?"

I hated the taste of all alcohol, but I promised Heidi I'd have a good time. "Beer is fine."

With two red plastic cups in hand, we headed over to a few people Heidi knew. I tried my hardest not to gag on the first sip. "Why does this have to taste like rotten dirt?" I asked Heidi. But she couldn't hear me over the noise.

Not knowing anyone, I became a nervous drinker, drinking my beer faster than her, and within ten minutes, we had to make our way back over to the drink station.

Brian looked at me oddly when I handed him my empty cup. "All right," he said, "you really are Heidi's cousin."

~

If there were any nerves or doubts or trepidations, they all but flew out the window by one in the morning, after both Heidi and myself had gotten a nice buzz. We sauntered over to the crowded dance floor, where I found myself lucky the room was dark. No one needed to see my wonky dance moves. When a guy came behind me and rubbed against me, I looked at Heidi and made a hideous face, like one of her dead pets on her vet's table.

She laughed but understood my silent cry for help before trading spots with me.

"Good Ol' Heidi," I laughed and kissed her on her cheek.

"I told you this would be fun! Remember when we used to have dance-offs in my living room?"

I nodded happily, my hair matted with sweat. "Oh, you mean, like this one?" In our drunken state, we were past caring what we looked like dancing as we pulled out all the iconic dance moves—the running man, the Roger Rabbit, the sprinkler, and the cabbage patch. Heidi didn't miss a beat and copied my every move for the next few hours.

We were drunk and out of breath from laughing when Heidi mouthed, *Fresh air?*

I nodded feverishly.

Once outside, the refreshingly cool night air washed over us, and I lifted my hair off my neck. "For the love of God, why didn't we come out here sooner?"

"Agree. We should have been dancing out here all along."

"Did you say dance?" I asked her with a telepathic look.

We both busted out a few MC Hammer moves before ending in a fit of giggles. I was still bent over, holding my stomach in stitches, when I noticed two Nike'd feet standing across from mine. My gaze moved up to a pair of blue jeans and then up to a stark white t-shirt before ending on a full mouth that slowly turned upward into an attractive smile. I couldn't help but notice his teeth matched his t-shirt, and wondered how he kept them so white. And whatever his cologne was, I wanted to bathe in it.

"Liam," Heidi laughed while bumping into me, "this is my cousin from out of town, Samantha, *uh* ... Samantha Ida?"

Samantha Ida? Lord.

"Hey," I simply said with a slight wave.

His features were sharp in all the right places, and his soft smile reached hazel and gold-speckled eyes that seemed to hold in a chuckle. It could have been the alcohol or even all the dancing, but I held in a giggle when he replied, "Hey yourself."

"Want us to teach you these moves, Liam?" Heidi joked.

"I think I'll pass," he laughed.

I held my chin up higher than I meant to. "You don't like our timeless dance moves?"

"Oh, I do. But I only thought people danced like this alone in their rooms and when no one was watching."

My hands found my hips, and I tried not to sound too drunk. "In my opinion, *Liam*, is it? To hide these gems from the world would be a disservice. Almost tragic."

Heidi placed her elbow on my shoulder and let her hand dangle in challenge. "Maybe Liam needs a lesson?"

"I guess I wouldn't want the fate of our humanity at stake here, so fine. Why don't you show me what it should look like again?"

Liam waved a theatrical hand over the patio, waiting for us to teach him, but I wasn't keen on having an audience—a cute one at that. "Well... now I feel put on the spot. Next time?"

"Oh, yes, *please*. I can't wait," he joked.

When Heidi turned to flirt with someone she knew behind her, I couldn't help but laugh. She practically came out of the womb batting her eyes. And even though Liam was cute, and I was drunk enough to flirt on my first time out as a free woman, Matt came to mind. I cupped my hand over my mouth and whispered in Liam's ear, "Have you ever dated your best friend?"

He laughed. "I can't say I have. But I have a girlfriend I'd consider a great friend."

"So she's not your best friend? I'm only saying this because I am recently single, and I might like my best friend, and I'm sorta freaking out. I don't know why I'm even talking about this," I laughed. "It might be the alcohol speaking. It's like truth serum or something. Just ignore me as if I'm not here."

"First of all, I couldn't ignore you if I tried. You're pretty entertaining, unlike some of these other drunks."

"Wait, so I'm considered a drunk now?" I place my hands on my hips. "Just so you know, I haven't gotten this drunk since junior high. I'm quite the sober individual."

"Sorry. Poor choice of words. I just meant you're an entertaining person when you're, let's say, feeling good?"

I smiled lazily. "I *am* feeling pretty good."

"Tell me about this girlfriend or best friend you may or may not like?"

"No. My best friend is a *he*." I squeezed my head with my hands. "It's so complicated it hurts my head. Can we talk about anything else?"

"What should we talk about then?"

"Cars?" When Liam cocked his head, I waved my answer away. "Scratch that. That's a sore subject too." I turned around to see where Heidi went, but she was MIA. "Do you know what time it is?" I asked Liam.

"My guess is it's threeish."

I looked at Liam as though I had another secret. "Technically, I'm not supposed to be here. I'm grounded. But my trusty friend Heidi snuck me out of my house."

"Oh? Then a few questions for you, Samantha. Why are you grounded, and I thought you said Heidi was your cousin?"

"Oh, that yes," I said, resting my hand on his shoulder while giving him a sheepish grin. "Don't tell anybody, but Heidi's not my cousin. And yeah, I'm grounded over a few lousy detentions. I mean, I'm eighteen. Who actually gets grounded at that age?" I pointed to myself. "Me, right here. And to clarify, Heidi and I lied that we were cousins. My name is Samantha Carey, not Samantha Ida. I'm actually from your rival school you all hate so much."

Liam raised an eyebrow. "Oh really?"

"Guilty."

"Wow, you really are quite the rebel showing up here. I better stay near you tonight so no one gives you any crap," he joked.

"I can hold my own. But, speaking of people from your school, is your girlfriend here? We've been talking forever, and I don't need any more enemies."

"No. She doesn't really come to these parties. And actually, she goes to your school. You might know her."

"What? No way. What's her name?"

"Trisena Madden."

I scratched my chin. "I'm not sure who that is. With sixteen hundred kids at my school, it's hard to know everyone. Plus, I've been a hermit for a few years." I looked around me again. "I wish I could talk with you more, Liam, but I have to find Heidi. Also, did anyone ever tell you your name sounds like a baby lamb?"

He burst out laughing, "No. That would be a first. You are an interesting one, Samantha Carey. Anyway, go find Heidi. But if you need my help, I'll be right over there," he said, pointing to a group loudly playing beer pong.

I nodded with a wink. "Thanks," I said before stumbling away.

I wanted to smack myself for my eye having a mind of its own. I reminded my eye that even though it found Liam attractive, he had a girlfriend, and we had a best friend to think about.

Stupid eye.

Heidi was nowhere as I surveyed the backyard full of people. When I turned my head too quickly, my big feet stumbled over each other, and I caught myself in time before falling. I told the two random girls standing near me, "Is it just me, but are these floors irregularly shaped?"

When they looked at me oddly, I continued to move on to find Heidi.

I nearly tipped over the flagstone patio again, but someone's hand steadied me. "*Whoa,*" Liam said. "You may need to rethink the assistance I offered."

"It's these floors that need refurbishing, Liam. I mean, the owners of this house only cared about showing off these expensive stones and didn't think about the safety of others."

"Or, it's the alcohol," he laughed. "But if you really think it's the patio's fault, we could leave a note for the homeowners to reconsider changing them."

"That's a great idea. Let's go find some pen and paper," I said.

"Yes, and some smoother ground inside too. Plus, I think Heidi may be in the kitchen."

"Okay, sounds good. Will people think it bad that I'm holding onto you?"

"You can hold on to my arm. And people are used to me helping them at parties."

"So, I'm a charity case?" I said with a pout.

"No. Just the most memorable case so far."

"You're funny."

"You're funnier."

Once inside, we found that more than half the people had left the party, and someone had turned on the lights. "I *can't* believe I'm this drunk. You must think I'm a total lightweight."

"You're what, like a hundred and fifteen pounds? Alcohol always hits girls harder."

"It seems not to affect you," I said.

"That's because I'm sober. Also, I wouldn't know what drunk would feel like. I don't drink."

"Like ever?"

"Nope." Liam handed me an unopened bottle of water that he'd found on a coffee table. "Here. Drink this."

"Not that I'm judging; I mean, the more power to you, but if you don't mind me asking, why?"

"I had a friend in junior high who died from a drunk driver. I guess after that, I've never really been interested in the stuff."

"I ... I'm so sorry. That had to be hard."

"Thanks. It was. He was a cool guy. I also don't drink because I'm focused on sports right now. Plus, I can't stand the taste."

"Me too! Tonight's kind of my first time letting loose from my over-protective ex-boyfriend." I took a long drink of water before looking up at him. "So, why do you come to parties if you don't drink? Are you one of those guys looking for drunk girls to take advantage of?"

He looked hurt. "Do you think I'm that guy?"

"No."

"Good. I'm definitely not that guy. Since I don't have siblings, my friends have become my brothers. I watch out that they don't do anything stupid, and I'm always the DD, making sure they get home safely." Liam leaned forward close to my face. "So you're safe with me."

"Sorry I insulated anything else. You seem like a nice guy."

"You mean insinuated?"

"Tomatoe, tomato."

He laughed and then peered more closely at me. "I just noticed your eyes are two different colors. Stunning."

It was the first time someone had noticed. Not even Caleb or Matt saw the slight difference—how only one blue eye had a speck of burnt orange, making it look more green than blue. I didn't know how to take the compliment, so I hurried to change the subject. "So, you're not bored at parties being the only one not drinking?" I asked.

"You forget how good the entertainment is—just think about the free dancing lessons I saw tonight."

"Well, that one time was on the house. I may start charging you." I looked around again. "I need to find Heidi."

"Yeah, where is that cousin of yours?" He winked.

We found Heidi in the kitchen. "Heidi! Your *cousin* ..." Liam said, using air quotes with his one hand that wasn't holding me up, "seems to have lost her walking feet. She thinks it's time to go. Tell her to stay."

Heidi looked at the clock on the microwave, and I followed her gaze, squinting to read the glowing green numbers that seemed to dance before my eyes. "Wait. Does that say it's forty minutes past four? Heidi, we have to go *now*."

"Shoot. Okay, but someone will have to drive us in my car because I am beyond sloshed."

Liam questioned us, "You guys didn't designate a DD?"

We looked at each other like two twits. "Guess we forgot to discuss that," I said, feeling guilty.

Heidi and I both looked at Liam with a hopeful look.

"Yeah, I can drive you guys. But I'll need someone to follow me with my car so I can drive back here to get my friends." Liam placed me gently onto a kitchen stool. "I'll try to find someone. Don't go anywhere."

~

It was twenty-five *slow,* agonizing minutes before Liam finally found someone capable enough to follow us home. In my panicked and stressed state, I seemed to sober almost immediately.

We made our way out to the parked cars, and with the music muffled in the background, I could finally hear my thoughts. "Thank you for helping us, Liam. You really are a knight in shining armor."

"Glad to help."

"If we didn't have a ride home, my life would officially be over."

"Which would be tragic, since your life has only just begun without that lug holding you down," Heidi said.

When we finally got to my street, I pointed out the window. "My house is on the left, four houses down." When I peered more closely at my house and saw that a small living room light was on, I screamed out loud, scaring everyone. "*Oh my God.* Don't stop! Hurry, drive past the house. *Goooo!*"

"I thought you said that this was your house?" Liam said, swerving recklessly past my father's truck.

Heidi dug her fingers into the shoulders of the front seats and popped her head between Liam and me. "Have you lost your mind, Sam? What's the problem?"

"*Heidi,*" I wanted to cry. "The house was *dark* when I left!"

She slowly eased back into her seat. "*Oh.*"

"*I'm dead. I'm dead; I'm dead;* I'm so freaking dead."

She popped her head forward again. "Hold on; are you positive *all* the lights were off?"

"Heidi, yes!"

Liam pulled off to the side of the road and parked in front of my favorite neighbors, eighty-year-old Walt and Betty. They always gave us apples in the fall for being good little girls, but after tonight, I didn't feel like I deserved any more apples—not even the rotten ones.

Liam's friend, who had followed us, parked behind us. No one moved or got out. Instead, we sat in knowing silence.

This was the worst predicament.

A full minute passed before I succumbed to my fate. "Okay, well, it's been real. I'll see you guys in ten years after my sentence is served."

"*Oh, Sam*. I'm so sorry. We should have left earlier."

"It's fine, Heidi," I said, glancing back to where she sat with a sympathetic frown. My eyes couldn't meet Liam's, but my voice found him just the same. "Thank you, again—" I hiccupped, "Liam, for driving us all the way here. It was nice meeting you."

"Wait." Liam rummaged through his pockets before pulling out a silver-wrapped gift. "Here," he said, "take a piece of gum and chew it. They may go easier on you if you don't smell like you've been drinking all night."

Grateful for his departing gift, I took it. "Thanks," I said as my face burned, wondering if my breath had smelled like a drunken sailor the whole night while we'd talked. But it didn't matter, not when my life was over, and I'd never see him again. And, like a sailor whose ship was about to capsize, I waved a brave goodbye without looking back and walked the long plank home toward my imminent death.

Before I reached the front door, I prayed for a thing called luck. I turned the knob ever so slowly and pushed the door gently open while holding my breath.

Here goes nothing.

As my heart clawed rapidly at my chest, I heard, "Look at what the cat dragged in."

My father's deep, calm voice hit me full force, and I tripped over the threshold.

Busted.

He coolly continued, "Wanna tell me what the hell is happening?"

"Oh, just a little night-walking is all," I said casually. "I couldn't sleep." The lie sounded so pathetic, but it was worth a shot.

My mother came out of nowhere and chimed in from an unlit, dark corner of our living room. "Lies. But a nice try, though. Maybe you could have gotten away with your little escapade if you hadn't left the front door wide open."

"Wait, what? I did shut the front door."

My father crossed his arms. "Maybe you *tried* to shut it, but your cat must have pushed it open the rest of the way. The dang thing came meowing into our bedroom, where he kindly alerted us to your cold and empty bed."

"*Death by cat*," I muttered.

"Of course, at three in the morning, we were forced to call a couple of your friends." My mother shook her head. "Even Caleb didn't know where you were." My face must have shown a mortified look of shock because she raised a hand. "What did you expect us to do when our sweet adult-like child vanished? We were worried. We couldn't just assume you were safe. What if someone came into the house and kidnapped you?"

"But you called Caleb, Mom?"

"Do you have any idea the stress you put us through?" My father interrupted.

"No. Well, maybe," I said, looking down at his slippers.

He placed his hands on his knees and pushed himself to stand. "Well, if you weren't already grounded, you most certainly are now. Welcome to a month of house arrest."

And just like that, my life was officially over.

Chapter 17

Sam 2003

After two weeks of boredom and staring at the same four walls in my room, minus my days at school where everyone viewed me as an outcast, I finally found something else to keep me occupied.

Jane.

Usually, hanging out at work was the last place I wanted to spend my free time, but it was better than staying home and hearing my parents bicker and fight. It helped that Jane seemed in better spirits each time I stayed past my employment hours without charging her. And after a week with her, she was surprisingly tolerable and even enjoyable. I hardly recognized the woman who'd first hired me.

I couldn't figure out if the change in Jane came from the new and stronger dosage of meds that the doctor had recently prescribed her, or if she simply felt lighter knowing her evenings didn't have to be spent alone. Maybe it came down to both reasons. Either way, we both found an unlikely friendship blooming. One I'd never thought would exist.

"Jane, do you want me to do anything else today?" I said after checking the walls for cobwebs. There wasn't anything to do but visit.

"Everything looks good. I can't think of anything else. Thank you."

"I told my mom not to pick me up till later, so I have time to hang out." I pointed to the book beside her nightstand, *How to Murder a Millionaire* by Nancy Martin. "Should we read where we left off?"

"Maybe tomorrow," Jane said. "Come sit down and look what's

inside this box my son dropped off yesterday. I can't lift it." I grabbed the box she pointed to near the end of her bed and gently placed it beside her. "Go ahead. Open it," she said.

I pulled out a weathered cream-colored photo album with worn-out edges, giving me déjà vu of Jane's red journal I had read. The dark secret I knew about her was something I now regretted, and yet, at the same time, I was still tempted to go back into that musty room to read what had happened to her, just like I itched to read the rest of our mystery novel together.

Jane nodded. "Go ahead. Open the first page."

A black and white photo of Jane as a young mother with her children greeted us at first glance. "How old were you here?" I asked.

"About twenty-three or twenty-four?"

"These are your children?"

Jane sighed. "That was my Kathleen. And that there is little Charles."

The little boy looked nothing like her, with hair the color of molasses and skin so tanned he looked like an island native. And then there was little Kathleen, the spitting image of her mother—red strawberry hair and white porcelain skin.

"You have a beautiful family. You said she *was* your daughter? Is Kathleen no longer here?"

"No. Sadly she did not get to live a full life."

"I'm so sorry."

Jane ran a crooked finger over the picture of her daughter's face. "It's not supposed to be that way; parents outliving their children. It wasn't her time, and I regret so many things that happened to her."

"That must have been hard to lose a child."

"It was. But I tell you what, Sam. When I get to heaven," Jane said, glaring and wagging her finger at the ceiling, "I got a bone to pick with the Big Guy upstairs. Need to ask him why the bad ones get to stay and the good ones He takes. Kathleen deserved a longer life than what she was given."

Jane didn't disclose what happened to her daughter, so I didn't ask. With her being so perky lately, I didn't want her to return to her bitter self, so I hurried to flip to the next page in the album.

"Oh, my goodness," Jane said with a smug grin. "I don't know why this picture makes me happy." In the picture, Jane looked to be in her thirties, leaning against a new-looking car from an older era. "It's probably because my husband wanted to skin me alive when I destroyed his dream car—a 1947 Hudson Commodore. We had that thing for less than a month before I crashed it. Not proud of that. But looking back now, who really cares?"

"How did you wreck it?" I asked.

"Well, I am a little embarrassed to say, but back then, my life underwent a little change, or maybe some would call it a midlife crisis, if you will. More or less, I ended up taking the dumb thing for a drive when I shouldn't have."

"Like you were drinking and driving?"

"After what happened to Clint, I could *never* drink and drive. I wrecked Daniel's car after accidentally mistaking a sleeping pill for my morning wake-up pills before driving."

"Yikes."

"Exactly."

"Were you hurt?"

"Luckily, no. Just a bruised forehead and a bruised ego."

"I bet your husband was pretty mad."

"That's an understatement. I didn't drive for a long time after that. The lesson of the story is *not* to take drugs. Promise, Samantha. Because they will destroy your life, I know this firsthand."

Jane didn't promise me not to drink, so I complied with her wishes. "I promise," I said. "Well, at least you weren't hurt terribly in the wreck."

"No, the crash didn't hurt me physically. I was a wreck on the inside."

"What do you mean?"

"Looking at us in all these pictures, one would see a happy-go-lucky family. But if you look closely, my smile is a façade—an act. I was not a happy person."

"Because of your husband? What happened after you left Ruth's house?" I looked down at the pictures. "Sorry. You don't have to answer any of those questions if it makes you sad talking about it."

"No. I think it's time to share the rest of the story with you. Maybe if I tell you a little about my world, you could learn from these things too. I'd hate for you to make the same mistakes. I wish I had someone tell *me* a thing or two about how to avoid a lifetime of regrets."

Chapter 18

Jane 1967-1972

As much as it was Daniel's fault that started the mess, it was me who destroyed the rest. After leaving Ruth's in Washington, we went home, pretending to play the loving couple we were not. We did not want the children to suffer the woes of our broken lives, nor allow them to know anything was amiss, so we acted like nothing had ever happened. Everyone went back to normal—well, that is, except for me.

To find out my husband cheated was enough to break me, but to learn he was a serial cheater was something I couldn't fathom. I was shocked, hurt, mad, and beyond embarrassed—a fool for not knowing. And with such news, I tried everything to push Daniel away. It made me sick to even look at a man.

At first, I resolved that I wouldn't speak to him or allow him to touch me as punishment, but that didn't go over too well. I was beginning to learn that my husband was an unobtainable force who couldn't be tamed. Each time I tried to resist his advances, he threatened me with his power to take the children from me again. So, it became the norm that my wifely duties were more forced than given freely. I was no longer a person, but someone's property, and I hated myself for being so powerless. So weak. So pathetic.

Some days, I just ignored the truth of how pathetic my life had become, and yet some days, when he had no right to my body but took it anyway, I tried to fight back. I swear I did. That was until I learned that sticking up for myself came at a price.

"You are disgusting," I said, pushing him off me one night after smelling another woman's perfume. I didn't have anywhere to go, but I ran to the living room to put as much distance between myself and whomever he still wore on his clothes. "Why do you torment me this way? Just go and be with someone else and leave me alone."

Daniel followed and stood aloof in the hallway. "There's no use fighting me. You are still my wife, are you not? What I do outside this home is beside the point."

I shook my head. "You've become sloppy. Not an ounce of couth or a lick of morals to stand you straight. You were probably with her just hours before coming home." When Daniel didn't even flinch at the accusation, I asked, "After taking your fill elsewhere, why do you still want me?"

"Want? That's just it. I *want* other girls, which doesn't mean anything. But with you, Jane, I *need* you. But you wouldn't understand this. We would have a beautiful thing if you'd stop fighting me. So, I need you to go back to the bedroom, where your husband needs you. It's that simple."

I gritted my teeth, nearly chipping one in the process. "Nothing about your possessiveness is beautiful. And I hate you. It should have never been you." While I stood glaring at the man, I couldn't stop myself. I wanted him to hurt as much as I did. "Did you know?" I said, standing center of the living room with my fists balled to the sides of my legs. "Did you know I chose Clint and not you?"

Daniel stepped forward. "Don't say anything you will regret, Jane."

I laughed at the way Daniel's eyes became two small slits. "Oh, but regrets are all we have now. And don't think you were the only one with secrets in this marriage. You should know that it was Clint I chose. You were only an afterthought the minute I chose him, and I only married you to forget him."

"You were never a good liar, Jane," Daniel said, almost in warning.

"I'm not lying. As God is my witness, it was always him. It still is. He's the one I think about every day, and it's his face I see when I'm in bed with you."

I'll never know how someone could be jealous of a dead man. That was the day when the coffee table broke two of my ribs.

I also never understood why Daniel couldn't let go of a wife who hated him. Or how he still loved and desired me each time I lay there pretending to be anywhere but home. It left me to wonder if he was wholly out of touch with reality, or if he hurt me out of spite. Or maybe the chase fueled his fire for the one thing he couldn't have—my adoration and love, like he'd once had. I'm sure he was used to women flocking to him, but I wasn't one of them anymore. And how could he possibly think I could forget his deceitfulness and still be that loving woman he'd fallen in love with? That woman no longer existed. And in some way, she was dead.

Because that was the thing—when someone feeds you lies and broken promises, you become starved of all joy and happiness. Looking beyond California's gold-orange and pink horizon, the joy and hope I had once felt now looked bleak and colorless. I could only pretend that all the mascara streaks down my face weren't from broken dreams. But pretending only lasted for only so long. And even though my husband's nightly visits to my room stopped after a year, I thought I could find a little light and fight my way out of the dark. But I couldn't. Not when bitterness and anger, loneliness, and depression took hold, pulling me further under.

Enter prescription pills.

My three-year-long relationship with pills started when sleep would not come, and the dark circles underneath my eyes were no longer from the running of mascara caused by heartache and misery. I hated the anxious feeling at night when I'd close my eyes, thinking I'd finally get the rest I needed, only to be awakened in a cold sweat by my heart pounding out of my chest. Without sleep, I became a zombie. I found myself snapping at the kids more and more each day, and I couldn't even function to tackle the simplest of chores.

So as I fell deeper and deeper into depression and even contemplated killing myself many times over, my doctor provided me with anti-depressants and sleeping pills. But the only problem with sleeping pills is that it made it harder to wake up, and soon, I was asking the doctors to prescribe a counter-medication to help solve that problem too. At the time, I thought all the pills were helping me, but they undoubtedly worsened everything. They only masked the real issues at hand. I probably needed counseling, but when you take so many damn drugs, you are oblivious and unaware of the damage it causes.

But I will say, when the sleeping pills worked their magic, I had the most vivid dreams about him—about Clint. Seeing his face as clear as day was the sweetest of tortures, as my fingertips were aways short of touching his sweet smile just before I woke. Those were the most challenging times, when my mind sought out comfort from the man I'd buried deep in the ground, and those were the times I prayed never to wake up.

~

By 1971, all of reality ceased to exist.

You could say the pills were like nails to my coffin. I was so lost back then that even my children had become lost to me. I had fought so hard not to lose them, but I wasn't with them mentally anymore. With Kathleen fifteen and Charles fourteen, the children were no longer naïve or clueless about our family's issues. They knew their mother and father no longer loved each other, but they never knew why. That was something I decided not to disclose to them, because I truly did not want my children to hate their father. I tried to protect them as long as possible from our secrets. But I could not protect them from a mother who had begun the long downward spiral into oblivion.

Kathleen became the most awful teenager at that time. I'd heard such things were expected of girls that age, and who was to say I didn't have a part in it all? But if mood swings could kill a small army, hers could. The days I was coherent enough, I'd find her hateful eyes shooting bullets at me from across the room. Instinctively I'd flinch, but I no longer had it in me to fix whatever hurt I'd caused or whatever hurt others had caused her. Most days, I was immune to everything and aware of nothing at all.

I could no longer handle another person's look of disappointment, so when my son Charles never came home, relief replaced my child. But with the ease of him gone came a fit of unhealthy resentfulness. I was beyond jealous that Charles had places to escape to, and that his friends became his new family. It was so easy for him to run away while I remained stuck. More than ever, *I* wanted to be the one to run from the emptiness where the heart of our home no longer beat. Instead, brick and mortar became haunted, hollow reminders of what could have been.

But that had me thinking; the 'what could have beens.' If I was no longer wanted by my children, because it was clear I was no good for them in my state of depression, then maybe I *had* to leave them all. Maybe if I left my children, then in time, I could finally find myself whole again. And maybe, if the kids saw their once-deranged mother in a different ray of light, one where I found myself healed from all the hurt, then perhaps the 'what could have beens' would simply become the 'what could be?'

I could move to Washington to be near Ruth, and maybe the kids could visit once they saw their mother in a happier place. It was funny how that one sobering thought, that one thread of hope, provided me with enough willpower that I stopped taking all the drugs, all the pills, and all my medications. Cold. Turkey.

I did it for my sanity. Because if I was leaving my family to salvage what was left of me, of *us*, then I needed a clear mind to do the next thing: secretly pack my bags and drive far away.

I had been clean and sober for two weeks when I secretly packed. Daniel had just gotten home from his night shift when he found me sitting in the living room folding the laundry for the very last time. He didn't even acknowledge me or say hello before he closed his eyes on the couch and fell asleep. As I folded his underwear and stared at his face one last time, a face that I'd once marveled and fawned over, I almost relished the fact that I'd be walking away in less than an hour. My family probably wouldn't have noticed if I had left anyway, because by then, I had become a ghost to all of them.

I had already said an encrypted goodbye to Charles with a kiss on his cheek that morning before he'd left for school. When I told him how proud I was of him, he gave me an odd look and carried on with tying his shoes. It wounded me to know that such a simple motherly gesture wasn't something my boy was used to. But it was my fault. And he deserved better from me. But there was no way I could be a good mother to anyone, not when Daniel held me hostage in my own home.

My next goodbye would be tougher. Kathleen. While taking the basket of folded laundry into Kathleen's room before she left for school, I had practiced all the ways to say goodbye to my firstborn. I decided to lead with a final word of how sorry I was to have caused her any hurt or pain. I also had planned to tell her I should have been a better mother, and maybe, one day, she could understand how our battles within ourselves take time to conquer.

Holding back the tears the best I could, I forgot to knock when walking into her room. When I glanced up to find her changing, I dropped the basket and stopped dead in my tracks. I gasped at the sight of my daughter before me. "*NO*."

She looked mortified to see me in the doorway before quickly turning around to cover herself with an oversized shirt. And when she turned to face me again, she acted as if I didn't see it.

But I did see it.

I saw her rounded porcelain belly—a belly that should have been flat as a board and tanned for a fifteen-year-old girl who loved sunbathing. A mother knows these things, and that girl was at least five months along. For a split second, I wondered if my mind was playing tricks on me, but it couldn't be possible, not when my system was absent of all the medication that caused such hallucinations. No. I was on a new path, a new me, and I had gotten rid of all those pills. I swallowed the fear rising up from the depths of my chest and clenched my throat with both hands. There was no leaving now. How could I?

I was angry as I rushed forward and grabbed her arm sternly. "Don't pretend I didn't see what I just saw, Kathleen."

She jerked her arm from my firm grip and gathered her school books on her desk. "It's nothing. Please, just get out of my way."

"It's nothing?" I came close to her face and questioned again, "It's nothing that your belly is holding a living human being? You can't hide that." I crossed my arms over my stomach, as if it were me holding a child inside me—a child that had changed my entire future. "You judge me for taking pills when it should have been you taking the pill all along." Kathleen grabbed her things and tried to pass me, but I quickly blocked her exit. "You are not going anywhere." I turned my head over my shoulder and yelled out, "Daniel! Wake up and come in here right now."

Kathleen looked panicked at the mention of her father. "I have to go. I'm gonna be late for school. Please," she begged.

"You think you can continue schooling once you have this baby?"

When Daniel entered the room, I forced the bottom of Kathleen's shirt up to show proof of what had become of our daughter. "This is a problem."

Daniel froze as he watched Kathleen shamefully try to cover herself again. His eyes darted back and forth from her to me, and I waited for him to say something, but he didn't. It was the first time my husband had had no words.

"Who's the father, Kathleen? What boy have you been messing around with? Is it that boy down the road? Well, is it?"

When she didn't answer and kept her head down, I wanted to shake her so hard to get her to tell me who caused this, but I didn't get anywhere with her. I threw my arms up in the air and gave up. "Fine. Don't tell me. Go to school and act as if nothing is amiss," I said, storming out of her room. The Gods had handed me my fate, and I had no choice but to stay.

~

It's incredible what your mind can think of when you aren't muddled by prescription pills. And it is amazing what a good cry could do for you. When I woke up the next day, I decided I was sick of feeling sorry for myself. If I wanted my children to trust me again, then change began with me. There were no more excuses, not when I was sober enough to change for the better.

And so what if Daniel resided with us? Whether I hated my husband or not, I had to try one more time to find a way to show my children we could live happily. And if I couldn't sleep from all the anxiety, well, I would sleep when I was dead. Either way, I had to put aside my personal needs, because there was no getting around it; Kathleen needed my help. Everything changed the minute a new kind of hope presented itself.

A grandchild.

He or she could be the one good thing in our lives and the one thing to redeem all my past mistakes.

After the kids left for school the next day, my mood was like a light switch, and even Daniel took notice.

"What's gotten into you?" he asked me as I poured myself a cup of coffee, feeling lighter than ever before.

"Nothing. I've only decided that maybe a baby around here is exactly what we all need. My attention and focus have been gone far too long, and now, now that I have been off all my meds for two weeks, I finally have something to look forward to."

"You're letting her keep it?"

Daniel sounded shocked, and I turned around to look at him. I assumed he was talking about giving the baby up for adoption, since abortion was illegal. "What else would you have me do? I'm not letting a stranger take and raise my grandchild if that's what you're assuming."

"Don't be ridiculous. How the hell can you care for a baby? You're not even a fit mother now!"

I tried not to let his words affect me—words that came from a man who'd single-handedly caused all my turmoil in the first place. I grabbed a few sugar cubes next to all the bottles of pills in the cupboard that I had yet to throw out before slamming the door shut. "Our grandchild will be just fine. As I said, I will *not* be taking any more of those damn pills. But I'm not the only one who needs to change. If I'm to be stuck here with you, then you might as well get used to the notion that all the extra time you spend messing around with women must end. Because if you seem to think I'm so unfit, then you will have to help me raise this baby while Kathleen finishes school."

"We'll see about that."

That was the last thing I heard Daniel say.

Before I woke up in the hospital.

~

The incident that happened next, I couldn't understand. Nor could I ever forget. The last thing I remembered was leaving my cup of coffee to cool on the counter while I went to the bathroom. And when I came back to drink it, that was it. Nothing. No memory. Even as the doctors hovered over me and explained to me how they had to pump my stomach, I still didn't understand.

"Lucky for you, Mrs. Foley, it wasn't enough to kill you. But since we couldn't wake you up to ask how many pills you overdosed on, we had to take precautions. But don't worry. Now that you're awake, we have some work to do before sending you home."

As Daniel stood behind the window to my hospital room, I looked down in confusion at the restraints around my wrists attached to the hospital bed rails. I wanted to rub my sleepy, heavy eyes but couldn't. "I don't understand," I said, feeling loopy. "Why am I tied up, and what is this about an overdose?"

"The prescribed medication you took; for attempted suicide? I'm told this isn't the first time you've abused your dosages. Our records show that you were here for a head injury after crashing your car one day after taking sleeping pills?"

"That was almost three years ago. But I have never overdosed. I mixed up my waking pills with sleeping pills. It was an accident."

"Have you ever thought of suicide before?"

"Well, I—"

"I'm told you have been under tremendous stress at home and have had severe depression for the past four years?"

"I mean, yes, I haven't been myself, but I stopped taking my pills a few weeks ago. I didn't take any pills this time. I swear."

"Mrs. Foley, you don't have to worry anymore. We understand what is happening. And with your husband's help, we have made some executive decisions on your behalf. It is important you get the help you need before it's too late."

"What help? I don't want help."

"In just a few minutes, some very nice people will help you overcome your mental disabilities."

"Mental disabilities?"

"Yes, a specialized facility just outside of town awaits you. They specialize in depression and suicide, along with other mental struggles."

They didn't need to pump my stomach, not when I wanted to throw up right then and there. "This is all a terrible mistake. *Please*. Please just go get my husband. He can tell you I've been good," I said, trying not to cry.

"I'm sorry, Mrs. Foley, but it's best you try and not make this worse for everyone."

No matter how much I tried to reason with the doctor, no one believed me. They had given Daniel full rights over my health care when he'd told them about my erratic behavior at home, making it seem like I was a lunatic. And when the social workers wheeled me away minutes later, I did not go peacefully. I fought, kicked, and screamed profanities at my husband as he disappeared down the hall without even one concerned look back.

I knew it then. Daniel had poisoned not only me but all of them with his lies. And what happened next will forever burn into memory.

~

I couldn't tell you if the blue California skies gave way to black hours ago or if it was another day twice turned over. But I awoke to find myself naked under a cold sheet in a windowless room that smelled sickly in the worst of ways. I tried sitting up, but my wrists and ankles were tied in leather cuffs chained to a medical bed of some sort. "*Please!* Someone, please help me," I cried out.

Even past the hour when the rawness of my throat told me no one would save me, I cried out. I was a ghost, no matter where I resided. Daniel had made it sound as if I needed help fighting the demons that controlled my mind, but he'd left out the part where *he* was the devil and the puppeteer himself. I didn't belong there. He did.

I wasn't sure how long I lay there, shaking and seething from within. But when the door finally opened, revealing three men in white coats wearing smiles that didn't quite reach their eyes, I nearly cried out for my own mother.

They spoke to me as if I were a child lost, and maybe I was, because something in their demeanor told me I couldn't trust them. I panicked and begged them to listen.

"This is all a mistake. *Please*. Listen to me. You have to believe me! He lied to you all."

When they wheeled a small metal table carrying a device into the room, it was then that it dawned on me—what was precisely at stake.

They would steal my thoughts.

They would kill whatever was left in my mind.

They would make me forget it all.

Even with that tempting thought that they could wipe my mind clean of all the bad, I still begged, "Wait. No. Stop. You can't do this! This ... this isn't right."

They silenced my sobs by placing a rubber block into my mouth and tightly shutting my jaw. I didn't even care that one man bruised my jaw with his crushing fingertips, not when the other man placed two pads over my temples, just before powering up the machine that whimpered as loud as I did.

I could only stare up at the ceiling to prepare myself for the worst. And although fear coursed through every branching nerve in my body, my mind searched erratically to find one ounce of peace to bear the inevitable. It came then, the one last remaining thought—a thought that I could call my own before they took everything from me:

If I survive, I will kill Daniel Foley.

The electrical shock was so powerful it lit my world white, black, and then blue. Giving birth to two children naturally didn't compare to this type of torment, and I wished for death right then and there. I couldn't even scream out to God to help me as my thoughts slowly melted away as they repeatedly tortured me over and over again. God must have answered my prayers, because I had no more memories after that.

~

When I came to, my mind felt jumbled in parts. I couldn't connect the dotted thoughts that danced euphorically about the room. Even my speech was affected, which lasted many days after. If I hadn't already felt stupid with only having the education of an eighth-grader, not being able to say the alphabet scared me. Sure, I was an avid reader and learned most of what I knew from books, but if one had asked me what my favorite book was, I couldn't have even said. They left me with a memory wiped so clean and stripped so bare that I was surprised I knew my name at all.

For weeks, I could only lay there in a state of confusion.

Who am I?

What am I forgetting?

Where am I?

Why am I here?

And although it came in bits and pieces, little by little, the bigger picture became more apparent. I looked around the room where they'd placed me, along with other patients who remained in a state of nothingness.

Would I ever get out?

It became apparent that if I wanted to get out of that crazy place, I needed to act the part of a model patient. And that's what I did.

If the nurses and doctors wanted me to do or say something, I said and did exactly what they wanted. If they wanted me to take prescription pills to keep me in a state of blur, I did, only to immediately run to the bathroom after and throw them up. My life depended on having a sharp mind. And when they gave me a red journal to write in, to be honest with my thoughts and overall experience, I wrote what they wanted to hear.

However, I left one page blank in the middle. I left that for if and when I got home, I could write the truth. Because if they knew the voracious thoughts inside my head, they would have locked me up and thrown the key away forever. I wanted to murder every single one of them, along with another person I called my husband.

They released me from the cuckoo's nest a month later on the grounds of good behavior. When Daniel picked me up from the hospital that day, he seemed *more* than nervous. "How are you feeling, Jane? I hope you got the care you needed," he asked me as he drove me home.

I kept my calm and played the sweet, dumb, and brainwashed wife like he'd always wanted. "I'm so good. *Really* good, Daniel. Thank you for asking."

He smiled as if happy with himself, but I smiled too.

I had a plan in place.

Chapter 19

Sam 2003

I wanted to hear the rest of Jane's story, but she looked at the clock above my head. "Your ride will be here any minute. Besides, I got carried away. I only meant to tell you that drugs and pills will ruin your life, and that when you seek love, make certain he's the right one. Part of me wonders if I still have purpose by telling you my story, but maybe this is too much for your young mind. Even for me, it's, well, it's a lot."

I sat at the edge of my seat with my hands clenched in my lap after Jane explained her torture. I wanted to know the rest, like if she killed her husband, how Kathleen had died at a young age, and how it all went raising a baby with a man Jane hated.

"No. It's not too much for me," I said. "And you can always talk to me about what happened in your life. As much as it pains me to know your fate with men didn't have a pleasant outcome, I'm happy to hear you tell your story. And you do have a purpose. Who knows what my future will bring, but who's to say your story won't help me in some way? Maybe it will?"

"Samantha, I have only told one other person ever about what happened to me in my past."

"Was it Ruth?" I asked.

"Yes. But, I think, for now, I've said too much. Talking about my ex-husband tends to leave me exhausted. Just saying his name, even now, makes me feel angry and sick all over again."

"Okay. I understand. But for the record, what happened to you was wrong on so many levels. And also scary. I'm so sorry. And I would want to kill my husband too if he sent me away to a loony bin."

"Yes, well, make sure you never take pills or drugs that could mess you up in the first place. That was my mistake—losing sight of reality and all that was important."

"It wasn't your fault. Your doctor gave you all those prescriptions. You trusted him that he could help you, but it backfired."

"Maybe it was partially the doctor's fault for prescribing me so much, and yes, my ruthless husband didn't help my sanity, but everyone is ultimately responsible for themselves. At some point, when things were circling out of control, the moment I gave up on myself *and* my children, it became my fault. The aftermath of my choices is something I can't forget. So yes, it was my fault."

"It doesn't sound so black and white. Still, I can't believe you had to go through so much. So horrible. I'm glad you still have your memory after what happened to you at that facility."

"I don't know about that. Sometimes I wish I didn't have *any* of these memories to haunt me every day." Whatever Jane was about to say next, she could barely get it out. "And ... and I can never forgive myself for what happened next—with Kathleen and the baby."

A knock on Jane's front door interrupted her, and I apologized. "I'm so sorry, Jane, but I think that's my mother to pick me up."

I opened the door to find my mother smiling with a plate full of cookies. She popped her head in past the threshold and waved at Jane. "Hello, Jane? Hope you don't mind me popping in. I brought you some cookies. Hope you like peanut butter—my mother's recipe."

The solemn mood in the room shifted the minute my mother's cheerfulness entered through the door, and I snatched a cookie from under the plastic over the plate, knowing they were still warm. "Don't mind if I do."

Jane's overly cheerful voice floated over to us, sounding too foreign to me, especially since she'd been about to reveal something. "What an absolute doll you are, Mrs. Carey. *Please*, please come in, come in. And I've never shied away from sweets. And, I could use a little sugar high right now."

"Oh good, because if I don't get rid of some of these cookies, I'll eat them all! I'm trying my hardest to watch my figure."

"Don't be absurd. You look fantastic."

"Why, thank you, Jane. And please call me Julie?" My mother placed the plate of cookies on top of Jane's nightstand before nodding at me. "Now, I hope Sam here is doing a good job working for you?"

"We have our moments," Jane said, giving me a sly look. "But yes, Samantha is doing *just* fine. You've done a great job raising this young lady here."

My mother looked at me quizzically as I shimmied my way over to the plate again and shoved another cookie in my mouth. "Well, that's good to hear," she said. "You know, this is Sam's first job. We were a little worried it would be quite an adjustment, with juggling school and all."

They talked about me as if I wasn't in the room, and after twenty minutes of eye-rolling, I ended my torture. "Mom. I'm an adult. I think I'm handling this adulting just fine. Are you ready to go?"

"Yes. I suppose you have homework. Well, Jane, so very nice to finally meet you. And thank you for having Sam."

"My pleasure, Julie."

Before we left, I threw a blanket over Jane's legs. It was becoming my only way of comforting her after her stories. "Thank you for showing me the pictures of your family, Jane." I leaned in for an awkward hug and whispered, "And thank you for telling me your story."

It looked as if Jane didn't know what to do with such affection—she diverted my attention to the nightstand. "Here, take another cookie home before you float away. I'll see you tomorrow."

~

As my mother drove us home, I clued her in on Jane's horrible experiences after finding her daughter pregnant. "I mean, Mom, wouldn't you want to murder Dad if he did that to you?"

"I would come damn close; excuse my language. That poor woman."

"Jane said she was telling me everything to warn me. I don't take pills, so nobody needs to worry about that, but as for picking the wrong guy? After hearing Jane's story, I'd rather be single for the rest of my life. I'm almost too scared to ever fall in love, even if it is with my best friend. And if I'm being honest, look at you and Dad. You both talk about divorce all the time. And look at Caleb and me. We fought all the time too. I don't want that with Matt. My biggest fear is losing what we have. But at the same time, I don't want to close that door with Matt just yet."

"So, no new feelings about Matt yet?"

"How can I explore any feelings when I never see him? I'm grounded, remember? And at school, with all the Caleb drama, we barely hang out."

"Gotcha."

"And speaking of which, how much longer am I grounded?"

"You're lucky we didn't ground you for life. You only have a couple more weeks left."

I crossed my arms and sulked deeper into my seat. "It's as if you guys think I did the unthinkable. I'm literally a normal teenager. Don't tell me you didn't do anything crazy when you were younger."

My mother parked in our driveway before looking at me. "Sure, I did a lot of things I shouldn't have. That's why I want to steer you toward a better road than I chose for myself."

"But answer my question; what was the worst thing *you* did as a teenager?"

"I plead the fifth. Only for now."

"Are you serious? Why can't you tell me?"

"Because some people don't want to tell their story until they feel good and ready," she huffed.

"Why are you getting all upset? Jane had no problem telling me all the crazy stuff she went through. And how bad can it be? I won't judge you or do whatever you are worried about." My mother rested her head on the steering wheel, and I sensed it wasn't good. "*Mom.* What?"

"I know you won't judge me, Sam. I just ... I don't talk about it because I am ashamed."

"Ashamed? Mom, people make mistakes. It's life. And also, maybe if you got whatever it is off your chest, you'd feel lighter. Trust me; Look how unhealthy it is for Jane to bottle up all her regrets. She's just now opening up, which is a good thing, in my opinion."

There were tears in my mother's eyes when she finally looked up. "When you were talking about Jane's daughter, that hit a note for me."

"Why?"

"Because Sam, I was Jane's daughter once."

"Wait. What? Jane's my grandmother?"

"No. No. I, too, had a baby when I was fourteen, *like* Jane's daughter. But my parents made me give my baby up, which has always eaten at me. I wanted to keep her desperately."

"Her?"

"Yes."

I couldn't speak for a moment as it all sunk in. "So ... so I have an older sister?"

"Half-sister."

"Does Dad know?"

"That's what we've been fighting about, besides other things. He's hurt I kept it a secret from him for so long. I only told him a few months ago, because I had signed up with an adoptive match agency who might have found her."

"When were you even going to tell me?"

"I'm sorry I didn't tell you sooner, Sweetheart. But please don't be mad. Like I said, I didn't want to tell any of you because I am so ashamed of my past."

"So Stephanie doesn't know?"

"I'll have to tell her soon, now that I have found her. I'll find out for sure in a few weeks."

We talked for over an hour in the car before I shook my head.

"I'm totally floored. If I'm being honest, Mom, I will need to process all this. I don't judge you at all, and I'm happy you might have some closure on something that obviously has meant a great deal to you. I'm just in shock right now."

"Understandable. Thank you for listening and for not judging."

"Between you and Jane, I should be a counselor."

It totally sucked. By the third week of no phone, no friends, and no life, and watching my mother pace the floors each night, stressed about finding her long-lost daughter, I had just about had it. And because Jane went no further with her stories and the mystery novel we were reading had a predictable ending, I could no longer contain my boredom at home and risked sneaking a phone call.

Heidi answered the phone. "Hey! You finally out of prison?"

"No. But I wish." I leaned my head against the wall where our ancient phone base hung, an antique my mother couldn't let go. "I'm stilling calling from jail."

"Bummer."

"I can't talk very long because my parents will be back from errands, but I just needed to hear your spunky voice. It's been tense over here."

"They fighting again?"

"Them *and* me and my sister. If I have to hear Stephanie ask me what my plans are again, when she knows quite well I don't have any, I might choke her. Oh, speaking of sisters, I have another one."

"Another what?"

I explained to Heidi all that had transpired in a week, and she cleared her throat. "Oh, wow. That's crazy."

"I know. I'm still processing. But you know what kind of irks me about this whole thing? My mother had a full-on baby at fourteen, yet I'm still grounded for sneaking out.

"I'm sorry, Sam. That's no fun."

"It's whatever. Look, enough about all my problems. Just tell me anything to cheer me up. What parties did you go to? Anything new? I'm dying over here from boredom. TALK. TO. ME."

"I'm sorry you're still grounded. We all couldn't stop thinking about you that night. Remember the guy who drove us home?"

"Liam?"

"His name came out of your mouth *real* quick."

"Oh, stop. I'm just completely embarrassed about that whole night."

"Yeah, well, he asked if you were okay."

"That was nice of him. But really, I acted like a complete idiot. I was really drunk."

"We *all* were."

"Liam wasn't. And that's what makes it so embarrassing."

"That guy wouldn't judge his worst enemy. He is super chill. But hey, I really do wish you'd come with me to the next party. It's an outdoor, woodsy party far out into the Pacific forests. Everyone is going, and you know how much you love trees."

"I wish, Heidi, but what part don't you get? I. AM. STUCK. HERE. FOREVER."

"You know what your problem is? You're going to one day look back when you're eighty and regret being so boring. You have to take risks if you ever want to experience new things. By the way, how did you get caught in the first place? I thought you said your parents were dead to the world when they slept?"

"Heidi, get this: my stupid cat ratted me out."

"*Say what?*"

"Never mind. It's a long story, and I can't talk much longer. The fact is, I can't come with you."

"Look, girl, hear me out; You obviously *suck* at sneaking out. But what are the odds of getting caught twice?"

"Wait. Are you serious? If a cat can snitch on me, my odds are probably not good."

"Fine. Whatever, but you're going to miss out BIG time."

I chewed and peeled off coral peach nail polish from two of my fingers before answering, "You're killing me, Heidi. Let me think about it. If you don't hear back from me by Saturday morning, count me out."

"Okay. In the meantime, remember you only live once."

"Gotta go, Heidi."

Chapter 20

Sam 2003

There would be no more cat-snitching for me. After shutting my front door *again*, giving it a solid push this time around, I threw the cat in the garage for safekeeping. And for an added bonus, I fed the dang thing a package of lunch meat to put it into a long and deep kitty coma.

"*Boo*," Heidi whispered, jumping out from the hedges.

"Dammit, Heidi." I clutched at my chest. "You said to meet you at the stop sign."

"Payback, baby. Plus, you were taking forever. I thought you might need some help."

"*Shhh!*" I hissed. "No more talking until we get to the car."

We stealth-walked down the road until I saw a sleek red Mustang. "Wait. Did you get a new car? Whose car is that?"

"It's Liam's."

"Why didn't you tell me he was coming?"

"And remind me how I could have forewarned you? You're grounded, remember? I had no way of calling you. I asked him to drive us since he's the best DD around."

"Sorry. It's a good call. I'm just nervous about sneaking out again. Also, I guess I just thought you were trying to hook me up with this guy or something. I can't focus on anyone right now. Well, except possibly

Matt. He thinks there's a chance." I groaned. "God, I don't even know what to do about him."

"We aren't even in the car yet, and you're freaking out. Listen, I'm *not* setting you up with Liam. He has a girlfriend. Liam's been a cool friend to me this last year, and since he drove us home last time, I thought he was the perfect fit. Plus, he was already going to the party anyway."

"Okay. Like I said, I'm super stressed."

Heidi gripped my shoulders. "About this whole Matt thing. How about you have fun being single and live your dang life before you get married and have babies? Just stop overthinking and let loose tonight, because you are wound the heck up. Also, I should mention; you're just Samantha Carey tonight, not my fake cousin. You realize people from my school already know who you are."

"*Oh*, right."

Liam stepped out of his car and saluted us. "Ladies." He bowed. "Chauffeur at your service."

"Hey," I said.

He was tall, even with him leaning an elbow across the top of his shiny car. "Hey yourself."

"Thanks for doing this again."

"No problem. Hopefully, it won't be so chaotic this time?" he joked.

"Can't promise you anything."

Liam's passenger door opened, and out popped a head of red. My mouth dropped open, "Emily?"

She stepped out of the car with her curls bopping along to her bubbly giggles and yelled, "Surprise!"

"*Shhh*," we all said in unison while laughing.

Emily covered her mouth and whispered, "Sorry, I forgot."

I gave Emily a massive hug. "I can't believe you're here."

"Heidi told me everything going on at home for you and thought you needed a girl's night out."

I held a hand over my heart and glanced back at Heidi, whose eyes batted sheepishly. "What's a girl's night out without a trio of trouble?"

"Okay, troublemakers," Liam said, "let's get you all in the car before the neighbors get suspicious. Don't want Samantha here to miss out on the fun before the night even begins."

I half-listened to Heidi and Liam chit-chat about some drama at their school, allowing me to take an inconspicuous, sober glance at Liam's profile from the back seat. I'd been so drunk the last time that I hadn't remembered his perfect jawline or how his hair was the color of caramel coffee and matched the gold in his eyes. He almost passed for a pretty boy. He wore a long-sleeve shirt that looked tight on him, and I wondered how often he had to work out to look that fit or if it was from playing sports. I also wondered why his girlfriend would be okay with him driving a bunch of girls around town.

Emily asked everyone, "So, any bucket lists this summer? We have less than a month left of school, you guys."

"I don't do bucket lists," Heidi said. "Lists are not spontaneous or whimsical. I'm more of a free-spirit kind of girl."

"Mine's dumb," Liam said. "I want to get a basketball team together and drive to Spokane for something called Hoopfest. Sometimes NBA players show up."

Emily chimed in, "I've always wanted to donate blood. Since I'll be a nurse one day, I figured I should get over my fears of needles."

"I have the same fears, Em," I said. "Maybe I'll go with you this summer to do it."

Liam asked, "What's on your bucket list, Samantha?"

"It may be a stretch, but I'd like to buy a car and drive all around looking for the largest weeping willow."

"To just look at it?" Heidi quizzed.

"No. Well, yes, but to also sit under and read a book all day. Maybe watch a sunset too?"

"So Jane Eyre of you, Sam," Heidi said, sounding disappointed.

"What? I said a car too. That's a pretty big. Whatever. There's just something about trees, books, and sunsets."

"Since you love trees, here's a tree joke for you, then," Liam said. "What's a tree's favorite drink?"

"I want to say water, but I have a feeling that's not it," I answered.

"Nope. Root beer."

No one laughed, and yet Liam continued, "Okay, here's another—"

"Save it while you're NOT ahead, Liam," Heidi joked.

"Wait, I have one more," he said, laughing.

I encouraged him, "Go for it. One more since I like trees so much."

"How do you know when a tree has had too much root beer?"

"What?" we all asked.

"He won't stop texting his ax."

Laughing at how stupid it was, I added, "What did the momma tree give her baby to eat?" I didn't wait for them to guess. "A treee-t."

Heidi shook her head. "It amazes me you both are that good looking and yet you have the worst of jokes. I can't be seen with you two if you keep this up."

~

Forty minutes later and far out into the boonies, the road began to twist and turn. Liam saved me from hurling when he came to a complete stop. "We're here. This is Alder Lake," he said. "You can't see the lake from here, but it's out there."

The fresh scent of sappy pines greeted us like Christmas morning, and I smiled, soaking it up. A hint of smoke came from somewhere, and I hoped there was a bonfire.

Liam turned on a miniature flashlight. "This way, guys," he said, leading the way.

We followed him blindly through the thickly wooded forest. It was almost too dark to see the moon under the blanket of trees, and after a few minutes of walking, I asked him, "How exactly do you know where you're going?"

I nearly tripped over a tiny stump, and Liam righted me. "I see you tend to lose your walking feet not only drunk, but sober too?"

"*Haha*," I said.

He laughed before letting go of my arm and continued, "To answer your question, we come out here mostly at night because no one can hear us party all the way out here. But the daytime is better for hiking and fishing. The water is the most aqua blue color around."

"I'll have to come in the daytime then."

"You should. No weeping willows, but tons of trails through trees."

Liam rounded a corner, and we all followed him up and over a large hill that looked down into a hollowed opening. The roaring fire was the size of a small car, and I smiled big-like. "I hope someone brought marshmallows for the s'mores."

The bright fire gave some of our features back, and Heidi's sparkly iridescent lips, painted a shade of crimson, moved upward into a sarcastic smirk. "S'mores, Sam?"

"What? I like s'mores. What's the big deal?"

"You sound like a five-year-old," she said jokingly.

I crossed my arms like a child. "*Pfff.* No, I don't."

"Sam, I love s'mores," Liam said.

"Me three," Emily added.

"Well, good. See? The world needs *s'more* people like us," I said, elbowing Heidi. "You saw what I did there, *huh*."

"Yes, Sam," Heidi said, "we all heard your pun. Now can we go down there and start this thing? We only have two hours since it took so long to get here, and also, I need a shot if I'm going to hear any more of these terrible jokes."

We navigated through the narrow trees before climbing down the steep hill to a group of thirty or more people, all scattered in various social conversations. Some smiled and waved while a few danced to a country pop song that echoed in and out between the trees.

"Hey," Liam said, pointing to a giant portable speaker. "You and Heidi gonna show us your dance moves again tonight?"

"Yeah—*no*," I said.

His full bottom lip jutted out. "*Aww*, why not?"

"One, I need a fat drink to attempt that again." We passed two people head-locked together in a full-on make-out session, and I added, "And two, they're playing country music. I think I'll pass. I'm more an '80s and '90s kinda-gal."

"I'll remember that for the car ride home. No country music."

"Thanks. That's a point for you."

"Oh?" he said, caulking his head. "We're tallying points for how cool I am?"

"Maybe."

"Guess I need to bring my A-game."

"Perhaps."

We didn't make it to the bonfire before a guy rudely slurred to his friends loud enough for us to hear, "Wrong, party *bitches*."

My step faltered, knowing his comment was for Emily and me.

Liam slapped a comment back, "Shut up, Ronnie, or I'll show you and your friends the exit."

"Yeah, Ronnie," Heidi said, "shut it."

Once by the fire, I couldn't hide my worried look as I stood warming my hands. The glow from the fire revealed Emily's worried face too, and Liam nudged our shoulders. "Really, you two. don't worry. Ignore him. I always do."

Heidi threw a stick into the fire, "Who invited them, anyway? He's always causing issues." She leaned her head closer to Emily and me. "He's a bigot and bully at our school, and we hear he hits his girlfriend."

"Really?" I looked over at the girl who stood next to him. She was a small thing. "So he hits girls, and no one stops him?"

Liam shrugged his shoulders. "No one's seen it, so we can't do anything. Besides, making enemies with a guy like Ronnie would be like having a permanent cockroach chase you; his infestations always come with diseases. So my advice is to stay clear of him and closer to me." Liam saw how I chewed the inside of my cheek, and he threw his face in front of mine, giving me the biggest smile. "Don't tell me this idiot has already ruined your night."

I smiled back. "Another point for the straight white teeth."

He ran his tongue over his teeth. "Remind me to send a thank you note to my orthodontist. You would have given me ten negative points if you saw me in the seventh grade." He clapped his hands. "Alright, ladies, you have two hours, so have fun." He left us girls but stood nearby as he hung out with some friends.

We found the drinks, and Heidi handed me a pink wine cooler. "This should help you with all your stress lately."

Emily shivered. "And hopefully, these will make us warmer."

Heidi popped the lid off her drink. "Or we could go straight to shots with a drinking game? You know, make the most out of our two hours."

"Why not?" I said. "Carpe diem."

For the next thirty minutes, Heidi was our shots sergeant. We had already taken three shots of something brown and bitter that burned my throat, and I closed my eyes. "I've nearly forgotten all my problems. Let's make three shots might be my limit, Heidi. NO MORE. My legs are feeling numb and tingly."

"Me too," Emily said. "This is what patients must feel like when they get an IV of morphine."

Heidi whined, "Those were baby shots, you guys. Two more!"

"*Oh Lord, help me*," I said. "I'm going to regret ever meeting you at camp, Heidi. Remember, Emily and I aren't professionals like you."

Liam walked over just in time to hear Heidi say, "Oh come on. If we can't live and have a bit of fun, what's the point?"

"Fine." I toasted them, hoping it was the last shot. "To no regrets!" I plugged my nose and took it like a champ before chasing it with a Sprite.

Liam looked at me funny. "Can I just point out the elephant in the room without losing a point? Do you always plug your nose when you drink alcohol?"

"I know I look ridiculous," I coughed, "but I have to plug and chug. It helps mask the gross and bitter."

"Shameful, Sam," Heidi said while wiping a drip of her drink off her chin. "Just try drinking one time without plugging your nose. You look like a damn fool."

"Fine," I caved. "Give me one more shot. But make it a tiny one."

It took everything in me not to make the ugly gagging face as I shot back the thick slimy drink that tasted like pure acid. I thought I was in the clear until I took a full breath. The scent and taste collided all at once —hitting me hard, and I made a face as if I had swallowed a slug. To my embarrassment, I gagged and coughed.

At this, Heidi nearly spat out a mouthful of pop and doubled over in tears. "I can't take you anywhere!"

"I think you should plug your nose from now on," Liam said after giving me a cringeworthy look. "No shame in that."

I looked up at him as my eyes watered and coughed again. "Really? Ya think so?"

Emily kindly patted me on my back. "I'm with you, Sam. This stuff *is* gross. I wish we had a blender out here to make some piña coladas, and a nice warm beach would be nice too." At this, Emily closed her eyes as if she were fantasizing about a beach, and teetered on her heels and toes before losing her balance.

Liam steadied her and escorted her to a camping chair behind her. "Here. Sit while I grab water for you all."

Emily smiled lazily as he walked away. "He sure is nice. And his butt is too."

I leaned heavily onto the back of Emily's chair and watched Liam walk away. "You know, it's actually a good thing this stuff tastes like butt, because if it tasted like piña coladas or even chocolate cake, I'm pretty sure I'd become an alcoholic."

Heidi laughed. "You guys are wussies. Everyone loves the taste of butt."

Emily giggled. "I can honestly say I have never had butt before."

"Speaking of butts, if you could choose any guy here, which one would it be?" I asked them.

Emily looked around. "Well, Liam's is the obvious one, but I'm more into the nerdy type."

I looked at Heidi and joked, "That leaves you with that Ronnie guy."

"Oh hell, no. If that's how you're playing this, then you get Ronnie's friend standing to his right."

I looked to where she pointed. "No way! I can't have someone who looks like the character from that movie *Joe Dirt*."

"What? With your beautiful long hair and his mullet, your babies would be stellar."

I threw a bottle cap at her head, laughing, "Minus ten points for you."

The alcohol had done its job. It was evident that no matter the direction of our stupid conversation, we had developed a case of the laughing fits.

Liam appeared with a couple of beers, "Sorry, ladies. This is all they have left."

"Beer? Minus two points," I said.

"Or hey, you can have your two measly points back, Liam, if you go over to Ronnie's friend there and give him Sam's number. She has the hots for him."

Liam looked at me wide-eyed. "You must be feeling *real* good, or you need your eyes checked."

Chapter 21

Sam 2003

Two things were lost: the time and why I suddenly didn't hate country music so much.

We swayed complacently, linking arms and singing to Shania Twain's "Any Man of Mine" while Liam stood a few feet away with his friends. It was clear we had become everyone's entertainment for the night.

The song ended, and I announced to my girls with a smidgen of a slur, and loud enough for all to hear, "I have to pee, y'all."

"Me too," Emily said.

We passed and overheard Ronnie in what sounded like an argument with his girlfriend. "Fine, I'm sorry, Ronnie," we heard the brunette say.

I whispered to my girls, and out of earshot from the jerk, "I wonder what they're arguing about?"

"She's probably sorry he's so ugly, and she just now told him," Heidi said laughing.

"Yeah, I feel sorry for her, especially if he hits her," Emily added.

I thought of Jane for some reason. "He sounds like a douchebag," I said in disgust. "Someone should teach him a lesson before he becomes a full-grown man wreaking havoc on society and ruining families."

Emily led us blindly to the right to find us a spot to pee. "Let's forget about that creep. Come on. I think the lake is over here. I can hear it."

"Wait, is it a lake or a river?" I asked, stumbling over a divot on the rugged pathway.

Emily whispered into the wind, "It is whatever you want it to be."

Moisture clung in the air from the rainfall we'd had hours earlier, leaving the ground damp, and my walking feet made a slight squishy noise in the dark. A low-hanging branch scratched my arm, and I hit it away before it slapped me in the face. "I hope we can find our way back."

After weaving in and out of trees for a few minutes, following the sound of water lapping against a shore, the trees finally thinned out, revealing the lake's vastness. The quietness of the lake gave a peaceful yet eerie feeling to the night, as the half-moon illuminated the water's surface. The only sound besides the distant murmurs of the party behind us was the gentle splashing of water on the shore.

"Oh, *wow*. Pretty," I gasped.

"So pretty," Emily added, with Heidi agreeing.

And as we stood arms linked, I asked, "Do you ever imagine yourself as a tiny grain of sand?"

Emily's jaw dropped as she looked at me. "Like all the time. I thought I was the only one who thought that."

"Right? I said. "Like we are nothing compared to the great big universe out there."

"Exactly."

"And yet, even though we are small, we can't be insignificant. I mean, whatever the rhyme, don't you think we must be the reason? Like we have to be the reason for something greater?"

"Do you think this greater can hear us out here?" Emily asked us.

"I don't even know what you two freaks are talking about," Heidi laughed. "But I'd say we are totally faded."

"Yes, definitely faded," I added, laughing.

The noise of a stick snapped somewhere behind us, cutting through the silence of the night, and we jumped.

"What was that?" I said, turning around. My voice was barely audible when I asked again, "Seriously, what was that?"

Another branch snapped, and we could barely make out the movement of something in the bushes. We huddled close and stood alert as something, or someone, closed in on us.

"What is making that noise?" Emily squeaked.

I whispered, "I don't know. I hope it's not a bear. My mother always took us camping and took drastic measures to ensure the bears didn't come into the camp. I don't have any bear spray with me."

Emily's death grip on my arm increased. "Please don't talk about bears right now."

"Whatever it is, rest assured. I know karate," Heidi said.

As scared as I was, I couldn't help but ask her, "Since when do you know karate?"

"I took like six months of it when I was ten. After those mean girls at camp terrorized us."

"If it's a bear, your karate won't help us, Heidi."

We heard another noise, and Emily let out a small yelp of fear.

I urged my friends, "Hurry, pick up a large rock or stick for survival measures. We can hit or stab whatever it is."

A dark figure jumped out from the thick bushes, and yelled, "*Boo!*" making us all scream.

Heidi punched the air. "Dammit, Ronnie! What's wrong with you? You nearly gave us a heart attack."

An ugly laugh oozed out from Ronnie's wide mouth, and I could almost smell him from where I stood. "Bunch of *babies*," he said.

His girlfriend timidly walked out from behind him. "Sorry. I told him not to scare you guys."

I could barely see her face, but her quiet apology seemed genuine.

Ronnie spat out what sounded like juice from his chew, and the wet splat landed near my feet somewhere. "God, you're boring, Nikki," he whined. "Just having a bit of fun."

The moon's light revealed our guests' faces more clearly as they came closer, and with Nikki standing a few feet from me, I had to look down at her. She was miniature-sized, with a plain and forgettable face, like that of a house mouse. So, when she offered us an apologetic smile as if she was sorry for everything that came out of her boyfriend's mouth, I had the instinct to pick her up and put her in my pocket for safekeeping.

On the other hand, Ronnie was an excellent example of a redneck—baggy pants that he washed maybe once a month, along with a plaid shirt holding an already protruding gut. One could gauge that his adolescent years had already been his golden years, and anything after would be downhill. But it was his scary, overly greasy face that made me take pause and take a step back. It looked like an overused backroad—potholed deep with an expression of arrogance that suggested he hated anything and everything on earth that held a heartbeat.

Ronnie laid a heavy arm holding a six-pack on top of Nikki's shoulder. "You girls are a bunch of wussies—scare too easily." He threw an empty bottle into the lake behind us, barely missing our heads. "What are you three doing over here by yourselves anyway? You three amigos a bunch of disgusting dikes? Is that it?"

Emily had an older brother who was gay and had killed himself in junior high after he'd come out to the world. The bigots and bullies were too many, compared to the few understanding people. She let go of my arm. "So what if we were, *huh*?" Her voice cracked. "There's nothing wrong with being different."

"Well, fine then. If you three want to put on a little three-way action ..." Ronnie made grotesque hip thrusts, "then my girl and I would love to watch. Would you like that, Nikki? Want to watch these three hags put on a show for us?"

Nikki pleaded softly, clearly embarrassed by the immaturity of her two-year-old boyfriend, "Stop, Ronnie. Let's just go."

"Yeah, get lost, Ronnie," Heidi said. "Go find someone else to annoy."

"*You* girls leave. You don't own this lake. Besides, I want to show my Nikki here how pretty the lake is at night. Unfortunately, you three are ruining it for me with your skanky faces."

I'd already wanted to throttle this low-life for calling us bitches earlier, but now my irritation simmered to a boil.

I listened to Heidi take charge. "You're an ass, Ronnie. We'll leave, but only because you've already ruined our experience here."

Ronnie took two beers out of the six-pack. "Good. Then *git* going. But you're the ass who brought this trash here tonight." At his last statement, he nudged passed me before throwing the entire box of empty bottles into the lake.

"*Uh*, excuse you?" I said. I wasn't sure what irritated me more; that he drunkenly bumped into me on purpose or that he threw litter into the lake, along with all its packaging. In hindsight, it was probably both the former and latter.

"Come on, Nikki, let's go," Ronnie said, suddenly changing his mind. "This lake is stupid anyway. And these heifers are giving me hives." Ronnie didn't wait for Nikki to follow and instead yanked her arm in the direction they'd come from.

I wasn't even shocked that Ronnie called us cows or how he embarrassed his girlfriend by yanking her around like a dog on a leash. I did, however, see red the minute he littered our great mother earth.

There was a reason why they called the disgusting alcohol we'd drank liquid courage. "Hey, Ronnie," I called out, "wait up."

He stopped and turned around as I approached him with long, purposeful strides, mostly because walking like a gorilla lessened my chances of tripping over myself. I grabbed him by his chin, forcing him to face me head-on. "Didn't your momma ever teach you not to litter?" Even as I did such a thing, a warning bell rang loudly in my mind, but I wasn't in the right mindset when I squeezed his chin even harder. "Answer me, you little twit."

He slapped my hand away before inching his face close to mine. "Screw you, you dumb whore."

I jerked my head back as if he had slapped me.

"Go ahead; you got something else you wanna say?" he challenged.

Completely embracing the new me, I tested the waters, "Sure. Your breath reeks, and you should also know that hitting girls is unacceptable." My last word sounded more like *uneseptible*, but he got my drift. And because I was on a roll, I snuck in, "You're a terrible excuse for a human being. Go get some counseling, *you moron*."

For a split second, I wondered if I had gone too far when Ronnie's eyes narrowed. But when a grisly grin full of crooked yellow teeth formed across his evil face, yep—I *knew* I'd had gone too far.

I didn't have time to rethink my actions before Ronnie slammed his palms into my shoulders with such force that I flew a good ten feet in the air. I landed flat on my backside and stared at the moon, baffled that I felt no pain.

"You son of a bitch!" I heard Heidi screech behind me just before she and Emily ran past me.

When Ronnie grunted and a scuffle pursued, I tried to stand.

But the struggle was real.

The combination of alcohol and this thing called gravity made me a five-hundred-pound gorilla with no feet.

I finally stood, steadying myself, before my eyes adjusted to the combat scene before me—arms swinging, legs kicking, grunts, and yelling from all, minus Nikki, who hid behind a tree. The battle between two brave cats versus the dirty stray dog showed my feline friends in the lead, and I couldn't have been more proud.

"Get 'em, girls," I yelled, running over to help. But I didn't make it in time before Ronnie roughly pushed Emily down to the ground and swung his foot back. I gasped and rushed forward, but it was too late.

Even with Heidi on his back, it only threw him off balance for a second before his pointy cowboy boot made contact with Emily's beautiful face.

I cringed when she yelped—the blow left her in a helpless heap on the ground. And while she held her hand over her eye, I knew there was no time to think of a plan of action. I screamed a battle cry and ran full force like a linebacker, catching Ronnie off guard. He hit the ground with a thud, and I felt Heidi pounce on him to help me lay him flat.

Maybe I had watched too much Animal Planet when I was grounded. But I bit down over Ronnie's shirt and into the flesh of his soft belly of mush. And even though his stomach hardened and he roared in pain, leaving me to hold onto a thin piece of muscle that he had hidden under his fat folds, I vigorously shook my head back and forth, trying to rip off his stomach. When I couldn't rip off his stupid stomach like I had seen on TV, I assumed my teeth had dulled from all the grinding I did at night or that Ronnie had the toughest skin known to man.

Either way, Ronnie somehow pushed us off him and stood holding his stomach in a tiring huff. He reached down and grabbed Heidi's hair. "You crazy bit—"

I quickly head-butted him in his stomach like a ram, only to bounce off him like a rabbit, and once again found myself sprawled on the dampened forest floor. But my eyes never left Heidi. I was amazed and perplexed at how bizarrely she fought like a Mexican fighter.

Heidi had him on all fours when I finally stood behind him and took the perfect opportunity of my own. My foot never made contact between his knees as someone grabbed me from behind. "Let go of me!" I yelled. I turned around to find Liam with half the party holding flashlights.

His eyes were as wide as the moon when he asked us, "What the hell is happening?"

My answer didn't come because I was out of breath, and I was too focused on watching three of Liam's friends struggle to detain Ronnie, who was still yelling obscene profanities at us.

Someone yelled at him, "Dude, calm the hell down, man."

Emily was still holding her injured eye when Heidi helped her stand. Mud covered both of them, and their hair stuck up in the air, filled with twigs, branches, and pine needles. Heidi's lip looked wet and shiny, and her legs looked bloody with scratches.

I wondered what I looked like as Liam's eyes took me in again.

Still breathing hard and out of breath, I bent down and rested my hands on my knees. "We had a disagreement," I finally answered him.

Ronnie interrupted me, and his gaze fell upon Liam. "What happened is that you brought these half-crazed whores here, and they've lost their *freakin* minds."

Two things were a lie: Ronnie didn't say freakin, and we weren't whores. As for us losing our minds, well, that was the thing about perception. I happened to think *he* was the one who'd lost his mind the moment he'd thrown garbage into that lake, which *then* gave me the right to carry out my civic duty. And maybe it was the alcohol in me that encouraged such primitive behavior in an attempt to right in the world from all the Ronnies and Daniel Foleys, but either way, for the first time, the nothingness inside me disappeared, and boring Sam Carey was more a badass B than a crazy one, like Ronnie had suggested.

I tried to defend myself. "That son of a bitch littered!" Even as I said it, I knew I sounded deranged. When Liam's mouth hung open, and he looked at me like I had two heads, I was too drunk to explain my need to protect mother earth and how invincible I felt when drinking. I looked down at my shoes, covered in mud. "Someone had to show that guy a thing or two about manners."

"So, the three of you just started attacking him?" Liam gawked.

My chin came up defiantly until I saw Liam hide a half-smirk. "No, he pushed me. He started it." I left out the part where I'd grabbed Ronnie by the chin, which I guess you could consider it the moment everything had gone haywire.

Liam's head whipped over to look at Ronnie. "You pushed her?"

Even as Ronnie mouthed off his excuses, including saying how we'd deserved it, the look in Liam's eyes and how he leaned forward, suggesting he wanted to kill Ronnie, worried me.

I didn't want to cause any more messes, so I gently squeezed Liam's arm just before he stepped forward. "Hey. I think we have to get Emily home, Liam."

He turned back around to look at Emily again and winced. "Are you going to be alright?"

"I think so," she stuttered. We knew she was bluffing. Even in the dark, her eye looked considerably swollen and red.

Liam's shoulders came down a notch. "Honestly, it doesn't matter how it started. I just need to get you girls out of here before this escalates again. Let's go." Liam said to his friends, who were holding Ronnie, "Can you move that idiot aside so we can get through the path?"

Ronnie seemed to get fired up again as he was manhandled.

Liam took hold of my hand as he led us all away, but Heidi couldn't resist as we inched closer to Ronnie. "Woman beater," she whispered.

Liam panicked and turned his head around. "Heidi. Enough."

It was too late. Heidi's words hit home, and Ronnie's arms and legs suddenly flew wild and frantic again. And while the three guys struggled to contain him, the squirming pig foamed at the mouth before calling us the C-word.

I don't know if the misogynistic slur held any real power to fuel me, but for some reason, the derogatory word that came out of his ugly pie whole, trying to make us feel dirty, didn't sit well. And yes, we were covered in dirt, mud, and bugs, and therefore by all standards, dirty we girls were, but I didn't like the implication. It was unwarranted. It was out of place.

Liam didn't seem to like the slur one bit either and dropped my hand almost instantly.

My breath hitched as I looked down at his fists. He had mentioned in the car that he played basketball and hoped a college scout would see him this year, and because I didn't want him to injure his hands, I pushed him forward. "Go. It's fine, Liam."

He grabbed my hand again and urged us to follow him down a single-file path, but all the while, I wanted so badly for someone to punch Ronnie in his face. We had just walked past Ronnie, and I'd nearly felt his body heat permeate off of him while he continued spewing offensive language. He reminded me of a possessed demon.

I let go of Liam's hand when Ronnie was on his one-hundredth repeat of yelling out the F-word, and I snapped.

My puny yet powerful fist made contact with Ronnie's ugly face, but my moment of triumph only lasted a second when a tinge of pain coursed through my middle finger and all the way up to my forearm. I had forgotten I was wearing my Aunt Liz's unique Christmas gift from last year—a handmade ring with a precious quarter-sized moonstone wrapped in bare copper around my middle finger. Though painful, my ring did its job.

With flashlights pointed in his direction, I watched in amazement as blood spewed and poured out of Ronnie's nose like a waterfall. I was pretty sure I'd broken the pig's nose. Ronnie's girlfriend stood near him and looked at me with eyes as wide as saucers. But I swear that little mouse had a pinch of a smile, like she'd suddenly been gifted a small piece of cheese.

But we didn't have time to gawk, as Ronnie punched one of the guys holding him and then head-butted another. He was coming for me.

Liam picked me up and threw me over his shoulder, yelling ahead to Heidi and Emily, "Run to the car, now!"

After thirty seconds of bouncing around on Liam's shoulders, I felt like a kid left too long inside a bouncy house after drinking an entire craft of Kool-Aid. "Liam," I asked, feeling sick to my stomach. "Can you put me down? I think I can run now."

"Fine," he said, standing me upright. "But you better stay behind me and keep up." We looked behind us and saw a large figure not too far behind, and Liam pushed me in front of him. "Run!"

One would think that when you were drunk, running was a near-impossible task, but when you had a bear chasing your tail, there was enough adrenaline coursing through your body to make you feel like you'd sprouted wings to fly.

My chest burned like wildfire when, at last, we reached Liam's car. He quickly unlocked the car doors, shouting, "Hurry, hurry!"

As Emily and Heidi jumped into the back, he shoved me into the front seat, and we heard people yelling. With the rustling of trees and branches breaking behind us, Ronnie was clearly only seconds away.

Our chauffeur drove, kicking up dirt behind us, just in time to see Ronnie's large frame almost reach the vehicle's back end.

"GO!!!!" Heidi and I screamed in unison.

~

No one spoke for a whole two minutes as Heidi looked out the back window. "They're not following us. I think we're good," she said, turning around to face us.

I tried to relax now that we were in the clear, but my entire body shook from either exhaustion, muscle fatigue, shock, or all three. My teeth chattered uncontrollably. "It's freezing in here," I said.

Liam's hand shook as he turned the heat on full blast. "Okay, I got the heat coming." He let out a long sigh of relief before his head fell back against his headrest. "I'm not gonna lie, but that was pure nuts." He looked through his rearview mirror at Heidi and Emily. "You know, you are all possibly borderline psychotic." He looked at me last and shook his head. "Especially *you*."

"Is that a bad thing?" I asked innocently.

"I haven't quite determined that yet, but being that you are a terrible dancer with an amazing right hook? At least no one will mess with you, Samantha Carey." Liam gave me a sideways glance again. "But really. What were you girls thinking? More importantly, what are you guys going to do now? Whose house should I drive you all to? Should we go to the hospital? Anything broken?"

"My middle finger hurts," I said, holding it up before the clock's fluorescent glow. But I didn't look closely at my finger when I caught the time on the dashboard. "Is that the time?" I blurted.

"Yes," he said mildly. "We could have left earlier to avoid whatever that was back there, but I couldn't find you guys when you vanished into the woods. I ran in your direction when I heard a Ronnie scream."

Emily spoke up, "That was when Samantha bit into Ronnie's stomach. I saw the whole thing with my good eye."

Liam's mouth dropped open for the second time that night, and Heidi laughed. "It was as if no one had fed her in years. I thought for sure she found his gallbladder or spleen."

"Nope. It was just some fatty tissue," I said. "But now that we are talking about food, Taco Bell sounds amazing."

"I would take you to Taco Bell right now, but should I remind you again it's 4:30 in the morning?"

"Oh. Yeah, that's not good."

"And why do you seem so calm?

"I guess I'm still drunk and don't care. I just want to eat, take the hottest shower, and sleep off whatever happened back there. But yeah, let's keep to the original plan and take me home first."

"Good idea," Heidi said. "We don't want you to get caught again. But if you do, you might want to fix your hair. Otherwise, you might have a hard time explaining your appearance."

I pushed the interior button light on and pulled the mirrored visor down. My eyes looked splotched and glazed over. My frizzed, curly hair stuck out like the four cardinal points on a map. And half the earth's floor covered my face, giving me the look of a scary cavewoman. I gasped, pulling out a small pinecone from my mangled hair. "Do I ... do I really look like this?"

"Just tell your parents you were kidnapped or something. It looks believable," Heidi suggested.

"Why do I have this feeling you're half serious?" I said, touching my face. "Although hideous, my face feels fine. I think it might all be just mud?" I wiped a chunk of dirt off my nose. "Yeah, it's just dirt."

Emily gently pushed me to the side and leaned over the seat to look at herself. "Yeah, *you* may only have mud on your face, but I'm the one with the shiner." She gently dabbed the corner of her eye, which was the color of plum pudding, and sucked in air between her teeth. "How am I going to explain *this* to my parents?"

"You'll think of something," Heidi said.

"Em, I feel so bad. Does it hurt a ton?" I asked her. "And what kind of guy kicks a girl in the face?"

Heidi grabbed the shoulders of the back of my seat and gave it a fierce shake. "A psychopath. That's who. God, I'm so mad about that creep."

"Same," I said.

Heidi released her grip on my seat but stayed at the edge of her seat. "But I think Ronnie learned his lesson."

"And what's that exactly?" I asked.

I looked back at Heidi just as she sat back in her seat. She crossed her arms as a villainy smile crept across her face. "Don't mess with chicks. *Duh.*"

Chapter 22

Sam 2003

It was another Friday, and precisely two weeks had passed since my first-ever fight with a dude. And I hoped it was the last. I blamed the alcohol as I stood naked in front of my bedroom mirror and looked myself over for the millionth time. It was like watching paint dry, but my wounds and bruises had finally healed, and quite nicely at that. The black and blue on my arms and legs were now a dull, pale yellow—barely visible. For a while, I'd wondered if the bruises would ever go away. Because the following day after the fight, and when the alcohol had thoroughly and painfully worn off, my entire body had hurt as if someone had hit me with a fifty-ton Mack Truck. I'd thought Ronnie had broken my back.

I turned around to look at the backside of my body to find that my rear end appeared the worst. The left and right sides of my butt cheeks looked like an over-ripe peach that had been dropped on the floor too many times. I knew it would all eventually heal like the rest of my body, but I thought of Nikki. I hoped at least she'd had enough sense to get out of that relationship, because guys like Ronnie never changed.

And as for changing, a lot had happened in the two weeks since that night. It wasn't something someone would be proud of or brag about, but I had changed by becoming a professional sneaker-outer, and was possibly on the verge of becoming a serial drinker. I told Heidi that deep down, I was a little disgusted with myself, but she reminded me that our risky escapades were typical and that 'We have our whole adult years to be responsible, and you live only once, Sam.' I could now see why Caleb thought she was a bad influence. But she was my bad influence, and only I could say that about my friend.

My partners in crime still consisted of Heidi, Emily, and Liam. That was, until lunch that day.

"I just feel like you guys are leaving me out on purpose," Matt said, sitting beside me. We had finally decided the masses were no longer interested in us being more than best friends, so we were back to eating lunch together.

I shook my head. "Matt, listen. Emily and I barely made it out alive a few weeks ago. Our rival school doesn't particularly like our kind at their parties. Sure, they've since accepted Emily and me, but that's only because Heidi and Liam won't allow anyone to give us any more crap. Trust me, I would love for you to come, but it worries me."

"Oh, quit it," he said. "Just let me come tonight. I promise no one will care. What's one more?"

Part of me wanted to say yes, while the other part of me liked my alone time as I discovered this new me. But as Matt sat across from me at the table, with his damn piercing blue eyes fluttering for me to say yes, I finally caved. "Fine. You can come."

Emily clapped her hands. "The more the merrier. Plus, you have to meet Liam. I think you guys would be great friends."

Matt rolled his eyes. "*Liam, Liam, Liam*. He sounds *amazing* and *super uber* charming. I can't *wait*," he said sarcastically.

I tilted my head sideways. "Do I detect a bit of jealousy?"

"No. But should I be? He's all you guys talk about."

I crossed my arms. "No we don't. We talk about the actual parties. So what if he happens to be there?"

Emily smirked. "Sure, he might be super tall and cute, funny, sweet, athletic, and always makes sure we girls get home safely, but he has a girlfriend, Matt. I just found out last week that she's Trisena Madden, from our school."

"Wait, Trisena from my science class?" Matt asked.

"Probably the one," I said. "It's funny, but I never knew her until Emily pointed her out last week. I've never had a class with her, so I don't know anything about her. But I can see Liam's attraction to her. Liam mentioned they've been dating for four years."

"Wow," Matt said. "That's how long you and Caleb dated. Guess it's not so unheard of."

I looked over at Caleb a few tables down as he sat with his jock friends and his new arm candy. He had moved on to a girl a grade below us, and I was happy not to be his focus anymore. He seemed no longer mad at me, and it was refreshing to say hello in the halls without any more added drama. Maybe we could still be friends.

"The difference is, I don't think Liam and his girlfriend fight like Caleb and I did," I said.

Emily asked, "Did Liam say he was in love with her?"

I shrugged indifferently to her question. "I'm assuming. Otherwise, why stay with someone if you don't love them?"

Matt scratched his head. "Sam, if you're such a good friends with this Liam guy, why hasn't he introduced you to his girlfriend, who just *happens* to go to the same school as us?"

Emily snickered, "There's that sound of jealousy again."

Matt was about to bite into his apple but set it down instead. "Really. I'm not jealous."

"Sounds like it," I said. "But to answer your question, she doesn't go to these parties, and Liam doesn't attend this school. So when would Liam have the opportunity to introduce her to me?"

Matt laughed. "Good point, but gosh, Sam, she literally goes to *our* school. You *could* just walk up to her, introduce yourself, and say, 'Hey, I'm Samantha, the one hanging out with your boyfriend every Friday night. Nice to meet you.'" At this, Matt took a large bite of his apple and gave me a cheeky grin.

He had a point, but I could only blink back at him a few times while giving him my best unamused stare. "Well, yes. I suppose I could introduce myself," I finally said. "But still, that's a little weird."

"Now that you mention it, Matt," Emily said, "I don't think it's our place to bring it up. And maybe there's a reason he hasn't mentioned us to her."

"Thank you, Emily," I added before looking at Matt. "Plus, everyone at the school already thinks I'm a cheating hussy because of you, so excuse me if I don't want to add the rumor that I'm a boyfriend stealer when I'm not." I sat back in my chair, satisfied with my answer, but when Matt gave me a skeptical look, I added, "We're all just friends!"

"Okay. If you all are just friends, how about you girls let me come with you guys tonight, and then Sam, you can prove you're just friends."

"You are so immature," I said, glaring at him. "But fine. I'll take your stupid challenge. But if you do come, Matt, then you have to prove to me *you're* not jealous."

Matt threw his hand out to me. "Deal."

~

I desperately sifted through my closet that night, only to find I had nothing new to wear. Party clothes had never been on my list of needs until now. But not wanting to spend my paycheck on anything other than a car, I stooped so low as to rummage through my little sister's closet.

After looking through everything she had for the third time, I slammed her door shut and yelled, "Mom! When can you buy me some new clothes?" She didn't answer from the living room, but I knew she'd heard me. I had just heard her hang up the phone after talking to her new long-lost daughter from New York, who had suddenly become her best friend. I was happy for my mother, but I still couldn't get over how she'd kept her little secret from me for so long. Plus, I was mad I still had to sneak out at all. Guess I had secrets too.

"MOM!" I yelled again while walking out of my sister's room in a huff. "*Oh*," I said, almost bumping into her. "You're right here."

A look of annoyance flashed across my mother's face. "That I am. Now, you wanna tell me what you are yelling about?"

"I need more clothes," I whined.

"Sam, you're grounded another week, so I don't think you deserve clothes right now. And second, it's the middle of May. With school out in June, I'd rather buy you warmer clothes in September before school starts. It's pointless to buy them now. And also," she smiled, "with the little cash we have right now, I would love to use it to fly out and meet my daughter."

I threw my hands in the air and stormed over to my closet, throwing it open. "But look. I literally have nothing. Is it so bad that I want to look like a *normal* person for the last few weeks of school?"

She crossed her arms and leaned against the doorjamb like she didn't care. "So, none of your clothes make you feel normal? You're being melodramatic."

"You would freak out too if you had to constantly rotate outfits to save face from looking like Oliver Twist at school. And can't we, for once, shop anywhere but the stupid thrift store?"

"That's a hurtful thing to say, Samantha. Please don't insinuate we're poor when you have everything you need. And Oliver Twist was an orphan. *You* are not." She squinted laser-focused eyes at me. "And when did you become so ... so snobby, wanting name-brand clothes?"

"Since I have a life now." I realized my mistake that I wouldn't necessarily have a life when still grounded. "What I mean is, I'd like to wear nicer clothes before school is out. Is that so hard to understand?"

"You know, you may not have designer clothes or top-of-the-line shoes, but Samantha, you are well cared for. Don't mistake that."

The minute I rolled my eyes, I knew it was a mistake.

"Well," she scoffed, "if I was going to take you shopping, I'm certainly not anymore. You have had the worst attitude lately." She turned to walk away but stopped short before turning to look at me. "I really don't know what has gotten into you lately, but you have been rude more often than not. Like the other day, you almost punched your sister over something stupid. It had us all baffled." She tilted her head. "Where is this anger and aggression coming from? This isn't you."

I hadn't realized my attitude was as terrible as my mother made it sound. My sister and I fought all the time, so to me, I was still the same Samantha Carey. But I made an excuse anyway, "I guess I'm just tired and overloaded with school and work. Last week I got my first C in English, so yeah, maybe I'm on edge because I'm trying to remedy that, but I swear my teacher is out to get me. He hates me. And as for work, you know Jane can be a real pill." The truth was, Jane's attitude and moods had been better than ever. I sat in the middle of my bed and pouted. "So you just don't get it. But whatever. I just thought it would be nice if you could splurge this once and take me to the mall for one lousy little outfit."

"I'm sorry you are having trouble at work and school. Really, I am. But Sam, you're not the only one with problems. If you can't understand the strains your father and I are in with our financial situation, then I don't know what else to tell you. Life isn't perfect. Besides, you have a job." She walked out of my room with her words trailing behind her, "You're an adult now. So, go buy yourself some new and better clothes if it bothers you that much."

I jumped off the bed and yelled out through my doorway. "I can't waste my money on clothes, *Mother*. I desperately need the money for a car, Remember?" When she didn't respond, I raised my voice louder,

"Might I remind you I am the last person on earth without a vehicle? I'll never be able to leave this God-forsaken town of nobodies."

My mother yelled from the living room, "I'm ignoring you, Samantha! You're acting like an entitled little brat right now."

Just as I slammed my door shut, the phone rang in the kitchen. A minute later, my mother popped her head in. "You have a phone call."

"I thought I was grounded?" I said matter-of-factly.

She glared at me and hissed, "*It's Jane.*" I looked dumbfounded, and she added, "You know, your employer?"

"Yeah. I know who Jane is; it's just odd. I mean, why would she be calling me after I just left her house?"

My mother met me with sarcasm, "Well, we could sit here all night and contemplate the many scenarios on why she is calling you, or you could just pick up the dang phone and not keep her waiting any longer."

"*Geez.* Okay, I'm coming."

Jane never called me. If she needed something, Charles was the one she called. I glanced at the clock on the wall, which showed it was nearly 9 p.m. As I made my way down the hall, I wondered if she was calling to tell me that the dinner I'd made her was not up to par. Or worse, I'd forgotten one of her pills. But I couldn't think of anything wrong. Not when she and I were getting along so well.

I picked up the phone in the kitchen. "Hello?"

"Samantha, this is Jane."

"Oh, hi."

"I won't keep you, but I was calling to inquire about hiring your services for a few more hours a week."

"More than Monday through Friday?"

"Yes, I know you already work for me five days a week, and the weekend is your only time for a break, and I know this may be a stretch to ask, but I wondered if you would like to come to work on Saturdays and Sundays as well? Make a little extra cash for that car you eagerly need. It would only be for a few weeks."

Sure, I desperately needed a car, but the thought of working seven days a week made my insides fold into themselves. I asked Jane, "I thought Charles came to help you on the weekends. Is he not okay?"

I heard a sharp intake of breath on the other end. "Sam, that's none of your business."

Her tone caught me off-guard, and she must have sensed it because her voice was softer when she said, "What I mean is, it's no concern of yours. It's a personal matter. But until I can find someone else to work the weekends, I was hoping you could fill in?"

A few weekends didn't sound terrible, but I still hesitated. "So just a few weeks?"

"Yes, just until I can find another worker to fill in."

I rubbed the back of my neck. "I guess I can do it."

"Great. I'll see you tomorrow morning at 7 a.m. sharp, the same time as the weekdays."

She didn't wait for me to reply before hanging up, and I stood there staring at the phone in my hand.

My mother came around the corner. "What was that about?"

I finally hung up the phone on the wall and looked at her. "For some reason, Jane's son can't take care of her on the weekends, so until she finds a replacement, I told her I would do it."

"Seven days a week?"

"Exactly. With school, on top of work, and now my weekends? That's a lot. I'll miss out on my favorite pastime—sleeping in." I didn't tell my mother I needed at least eleven hours of sleep after every Friday night.

"On the bright side, now you have more money to buy the nicer clothes you *so desperately* need," she said, batting her eyes.

"I guess so," I said, rolling mine.

I walked back to my room with a devilish smile, knowing I would pull a fast one over my mother in three hours. It served her right.

~

At the stroke of midnight, my friends were waiting for me down the road. I gave a wave when I saw Liam leaning against his car. "Hey."

"Hey yourself."

"You look snazzy wearing all black," I said. "What's the occasion?"

He winked under the street light while holding the car door open for me. "These are my mourning clothes when someone dies."

"Oh, no. Who died?"

He laughed, "No one died. I'm just unable to join you guys on Friday nights. Tonight is my last hurrah."

I tried not to sound disappointed, "Oh? Why?"

"My girlfriend signed us up to host late-night bunco, which happens to be on Fridays."

"You sound thrilled," I said.

Liam shrugged. "Boyfriend duties."

"Well, I'm slightly jealous of this bunco. Sure, you never drink with us at these parties, but you always make us laugh. And wait, who will make sure we drink water when I've had too much to drink? I mean, Liam, you always take that job seriously."

"True. I doubt Heidi will take over that job. Maybe Emily?"

"She'll have to," I laughed. "Well, you will be missed." I looked to Heidi in the back seat as she applied lipstick. "You look cute tonight too," I said. Under the car's dome light, I could see she wore a bright pink spring shirt with a choker and a short black pleated skirt to match her black combat boots. Her socks had kittens all over them. "And I'm loving the socks too."

She smiled. "I'm trying to talk the veterinarian into selling animal socks. You know, buy a pair to help save strays from being euthanized."

"I would definitely buy a pair," I said, sliding into the front seat. "But I kind of feel underdressed with you two," I said. I had settled on wearing the same low-cut ripped jeans with a light blue V-necked t-shirt to match my eyes and a pair of old Converse shoes that were more off-white than white anymore. But because the ensemble wasn't anything special, I'd taken extra care perfecting my makeup and my long, wavy curls.

Liam started the car, and Heidi laughed, "Samantha. You could wear a piñata on your head and still look amazing."

"Thanks," I said before turning around to find Emily missing. "Wait. Where's Em?"

"She forgot her parents were out of town and she had to babysit," Heidi said.

"Yep," Liam added, "just us three originals."

"About that," I said with a thin smile. "I sort of invited Matt to come tonight. Emily was supposed to give him the address to meet us all."

"Matt?" Liam asked. He turned off my road and went south. "The best friend you sort of kissed once?"

There was something in his tone that I couldn't quite place, but I answered, "Yes, that one. We still haven't figured out what that kiss meant, mainly because I've been grounded. Anyway, I was nervous about him joining us tonight since our schools hate each other so much."

"I'll introduce him to everyone and make sure no one has a problem," Heidi offered.

Liam and Heidi didn't know that Matt and I had stupid bets going, and since Emily wasn't there, I thought it best to keep that secret.

~

Once again, the streets lined up with cars, but I didn't see Matt's truck anywhere. The party inside was just as wild as the first party I'd attended—standing room only, with the room vaguely smelling like the song that played loudly over a boombox—Teen Spirit.

Heidi stopped mid-stride and hugged a few of her friends while Liam and I went to the crowded kitchen. Colorful Jell-O shots topped with whipped cream sat on the counter, and I laughed. "Finally, a drink I don't mind drinking. Or, I guess, maybe eating?" I picked a red one up. "I've never had one of these before."

Since alcohol wasn't Liam's thing, he picked up the bottle of whipped cream and sprayed a mouthful before swallowing. "Even if my Fridays are off-limits now, I'm sure I'll see you guys this summer."

"I hope," I said, trying to loosen the Jell-O from its container. "I'm finally ungrounded next week, so that's good. Can you believe I'm an adult who still gets grounded?"

"You know, you are the oldest junior around. What, you'll be like twenty by the time we all graduate?"

"Very funny. *Haha*. I'll be nineteen, mind you. And that's what happens when your mother doesn't start you in kindergarten until you're six years old, and then the school holds you back in the first grade because you're socially awkward."

"You've come a long way, mute girl. Can't stop talking now."

I tried wrestling him for the can of whipped cream, but he had a good grip. "Boy, you better listen to your elder and give me that."

"You older women are feisty," Liam said. His finger accidentally nudged the nozzle, and when some cold cream hit my face, he swiped a finger across my nose and licked it. "More for me." The humor left his face when someone bumped into me roughly.

I turned around to find Matt wearing an amused, gloating expression. Too much gloating for my liking.

I wiped any evidence of the whipped cream off my face. "Liam, this is Matt. Matt, this is Liam." They nodded in greeting, but I hated the awkward silence that followed. "Here," I said, thrusting a blue Jell-O cup into Matt's hand.

He downed the shot in one gulp before resting his arm heavily on my shoulder.

"How's it going?" Liam asked. "Samantha told me a lot of good things about you."

It was a lie, since I hardly remembered talking about Matt, but I smiled at Liam for making an effort.

"Really? That's weird. I haven't heard anything about you." I gave Matt the death stare, and he gave me a smile that didn't reach his eyes. "Just kidding. The girls talk a lot about you and Heidi and all the fun parties and all the drinking." He noticed Liam holding the can of whipped cream. "Oh wait, that's right. You don't drink."

Liam shrugged. "I still have a good time without all that."

"That's cool, I guess. But ..." Matt gave me a shot of Jell-O, "I need to catch up with Sammy here."

"Guess we're doing this?" I said hesitantly.

"Yep. Bottoms up."

My eyes met Liam's, and I wondered if I shouldn't have invited Matt.

"Wait!" Heidi yelled as she came rushing forward from across the room. She bumped into Matt. "What about me?"

He topped two shots with whipped cream and passed them to Heidi. "Sam and I had already had a few, so catch up."

"You must be Sam's Matt," she said.

He clinked his mini-cup to hers. "Yep, in the flesh."

"Cute." She looked him up and down with critiquing eyes and nodded. "I can see the appeal."

My eyes widened, and my face flushed.

While Heidi downed her Jell-O shots, Matt lined up four cups before grabbing a tequila bottle from the counter. "This seems more appealing."

"Whoa," I said as he filled the cups almost halfway.

He stopped at the fourth cup and didn't pour anything in it. "Well, appealing to all except Liam, who doesn't drink." He pointed the one empty cup at Liam. "Liam ... No fun."

Mortified, I gave Liam an open mouth full of silent apologies, all the while wondering if Matt had already had a few drinks before arriving. Either way, I wanted to block out my predicament, so I plugged my nose and chugged part of my drink down before any of them lifted theirs.

When they finished their cups, Heidi gasped for air, "Matt, you are going to fit *right* in." She grabbed his arm like they were the best of chums. "Let me introduce you to some of my peeps."

Matt beamed as if he had just won the coolest-new-kid-at-the-party trophy. "Sounds like a plan, boss. But one more drink," he said.

He threw back another tall shot of tequila and followed it with a manly growl before slamming his cup down with such force, some of its contents spilled all over my left forearm. He hadn't even been there five whole minutes, and he'd already drank half the bottle of tequila himself. I had never seen him act like this, and I didn't know what he was trying to prove by acting so macho.

And if I wasn't already embarrassed, I definitely was after he said seductively, "*Oops*. Did I get you wet, Sam?" I further died when he grabbed my arm and slowly sucked the spilled droplets clean off my flesh.

He was definitely drunk.

I looked down at my arm shining with his slobber and blinked several times. "*Okey-dokey*." I hurriedly shoved him towards Heidi. "I'm begging you. *Please* take him to meet your friends before he forgets everyone's name, including mine."

Heidi laughed and whisked him away, leaving me immobile as I stared down at my wet arm for God knew how long.

"Samantha?" I heard a voice call.

A face slowly inched its way into my peripheral vision, settling directly in front of me. His eyes twinkled with humor, and I shook my head. "Liam. I'm not even sure what just happened." When his hand flew up to cover his mouth, holding in a laugh that would not have held much longer, I threw my empty red solo cup at his head. "Laugh, and I will have to kill you."

"Okay, okay," he said, coughing down a deep-throated chuckle. "Here," he said, handing me a napkin with a pink flamingo on it. When I looked at it, as if it were a foreign object, Liam took charge and wiped my arm for me.

"Look, Liam," I said, "that guy you just met wasn't *my* Matt. I'm not sure who or what that was just then."

"I can tell you what that was."

"What?" I asked.

"He's threatened by me and our proximity." Liam balled the napkin up and threw it across the room to make a perfect basket. "He's simply staking his claim, is all. I get it."

My mouth dropped open. "Well, I don't want anyone staking their claim on me. I'm my own individual, and I belong to me and only me. I'm nobody's for the claiming." Once the defensive words left my mouth, I knew the alcohol was kicking in. My tongue was already heavy.

"I hear you, and I'm not a claim-staking-kind-of-guy, but all I'm saying is that who wouldn't want to make it known that you're off the market? You are the most gorgeous girl here, and not just in this room."

No one had ever given me such a display of words wrapped in a pretty bouquet. Not even my ex of four years.

"What's with that look?" Liam asked as I stood awkwardly. "What did I say wrong? I mean, you have to know, right?"

"I ...*ah*—"

"*Stop*. Are you telling me no one has ever told you you're absolutely gorgeous? Is this some silly joke?"

I looked down at my hands, realizing two things: One, my hands were becoming fuzzy and blurry, and two, my heart raced with an acceleration like that of a ticking time bomb. And neither issue had anything to do with the other. It was like my heart was its own entity, controlling every cell in my body. I tried to focus past its sporadic rhythm that surely made my face red as the solo cup.

I finally caved, "I mean, besides the typical, 'Your eyes are pretty' or that my mother always said I was beautiful."

"Yeah, but that's your mom. What about Matt? Or your ex?"

I shook my head, no, and Liam looked practically angry. "If your ex never complimented you, then one, he was threatened you'd leave him for someone better looking, or two, he assumed you already knew you were a gem, or three, he didn't want you to have a big head. Oh, and four, he took you for granted. Either way, good riddance to that guy."

I crossed my arms and tried to defend myself. "Or maybe he knew I didn't do well with compliments. You know, they do make me uncomfortable." *Especially from a guy like you*, I wanted to say.

"If you say so. But, Samantha, if that's the case, you've got to get over being shy about it. Just accept you're beautiful, inside and out. Own it."

I laughed. "What do you want from me? Do you want me to say I'm like a twenty, and everyone else is a ten? Is that what you want me to say?" I took hold of my head with both hands as if it weighed a ton. "Now look what you made me do. You gave me a big head. How am I to hold this thing up all night while drunk?"

Liam laughed. "Well, you did have quite a few drinks in less than twenty minutes, so maybe we quit while we're ahead?"

"My fingers do feel numb."

"Do you want me to get you some water?"

"Sure, water boy."

"Water is for sissies!" Matt shouted, popping up behind me.

"Did you make new friends at school?" I asked him, patting him on the head, almost forgetting why he'd annoyed me earlier.

Heidi came up and swung her arm around his shoulders. "Matt here just beat Blake Molly in Civil War! They want him to come back next Friday for a big-pot money-challenge."

"What's Civil War?" I asked.

Liam took the cap off a bottled water and handed it to me. "It's your classic beer pong game."

I went to drink the water, but Matt snatched the bottle from my hands. "Liam, this lady needs a real drink, you know, something to put hair on her chest."

I frowned and covered my chest. "I don't want hair there."

Liam grabbed another water off the counter. "Chill. It's just water."

"Alright, boys," Heidi said, grabbing the water from Liam before handing it to me, "this isn't the civil war I had in mind." She looked at Liam. "By the way, Blake wants you to play poker with him."

"Yeah, Liam. Poker is calling," Matt said.

I was disappointed when he said, "Alright, kids, have fun," and walked away. He glanced back at me once, and I gave him a friendly, reassuring wave that it was all good. I was sure I'd see him later that night, since it was his last night with us all.

But the remainder of the night, with Heidi and Matt as my companions, became a game of 'Who Can Get Sam Wasted the Most.' And as the night came and went in a blur of fazed and faded faces, and the shots went down without so much a burn, and the alcohol zinged through my bloodstream, leaving me in a hum of contentment, I finally found a quiet place to lie down before succumbing to the dark abyss that awaited me. I didn't see Liam the rest of the night but vaguely remembered falling asleep blissfully to someone saying, 'Goodnight, gorgeous.'

Chapter 23

Sam 2003

"Sam. Samantha!"

My eyes were void of all moisture, but I found enough energy to peel open one eye where I found Heidi standing above me.

Her red-splotched, fearful eyes looked into mine as she shook my shoulder again. "Girlfriend, wake the heck up!"

Disoriented, I shook my head. "What. What is it?" My words came out scratchy, and my mouth was drier than the Sahara Desert. Swallowing was a chore. I attempted to sit upright and half laughed, "I feel like SpongeBob in that episode Tree at the Tea Dome. W.A.T.E.R," I dragged out. "Seriously, is there any water?"

"Sam, get up! This isn't funny, and there's no time for water. We passed out!"

I tried to stand but immediately regretted the movement. My head pounded something fierce. I held it with two hands. "Wait, where am I?"

"You idiot, we're still at Jesse Keller's house. And *crap*, you're still drunk. *Great*."

I looked around. "Who?" Even with blurred vision, I could see an array of beer bottles and red solo cups that decorated the room. Heidi moved out of my way as I stepped over a pile of crushed Doritos.

"Sam. We have to go."

I squinted to find a clock but couldn't see one. "What time is it?"

Heidi squeaked, "It's almost nine-thirty." Heidi watched me count the hours on my fingers and clarified, "Nine-thirty, Sam. As in THE MORNING."

The memories of last night came pieced together all at once, and my heart dropped to the floor next to a slice of half-eaten pizza. "*NO*," I said with dread.

"*YES*."

The waves of drunkenness didn't help as I made my way to a door—any door that would get me home as fast as possible.

"Samantha. That's the closet door. The other way." Heidi pointed behind me.

I darted across the room as she attempted to wake Matt, who still slept sprawled across a small loveseat with drool dripping down his chin. Both his shoes were missing. He was hugging an empty Dorito bag in one hand and holding a hair brush in the other. I vaguely remembered him laughing and brushing my hair at some point, so I turned to look at myself in the hallway mirror and found that the gel that had once held my locks in place was no longer. I looked like I had stuck my finger in an electrical socket.

Heidi found one of Matt's shoes and put it on for him while explaining our situation. "But where is Scott? He was supposed to take us home," he groaned.

"Liam was supposed to take us home," I said.

"Matt sat up wobbly. "I found, *uh* ... Scott, our new DD, so I told Liam to leave."

"Who is Scott?" Heidi and I said in unison.

"*Uh* ... I don't remember."

I nearly cried when bending down to grab the other shoe I assumed was Matt's. It didn't match the one Heidi put on him, but when his keys fell out, I thrust them into his hands. "You have to take us home *NOW*."

While Matt took forever putting on a shoe that clearly didn't fit, I opened my pager to find at least fifty 911 alerts from my mother. I begged him, "*Please*, can you hurry?"

I didn't even care when Matt drove us home tipsy. I pressed my palm against my head, knowing how royally screwed I was. My days of running back and forth to parties were over. I wasn't even ungrounded to be grounded again.

IDIOT, IDIOT, STUPID IDIOT, SAM!

When we neared my house, Heidi sounded guilty. "Want us to drop you off at the stop sign?"

"Don't bother," I said, staring blankly out the truck's window. "What's the point? Plus, I can't walk straight; I'm still drunk."

Matt didn't say a word as he reluctantly pulled into my driveway.

I swung the passenger door open but barely got one foot on the ground before throwing up.

"Sam," I heard Matt say in sympathy, "I think I have a bottled water somewhere in the back."

"I think it's too late for that," Heidi said.

After emptying the entire contents of last night's festivities onto the gravel, I stood and wiped my mouth with the bottom of my shirt. "See you never," I said before closing Matt's door while the front door to my house opened.

I didn't even blame Matt when he peeled out. The wrath on my parent's faces said it all. And as I looked on with envy at Matt's fleeing vehicle, along with Heidi looking painfully out the back with her palm flat against the rear windshield in a sad farewell, I wished more than ever for my own car to escape what came next.

My mother was the first to reach me. "Where in God's name have you been, Samantha?"

I was too ill to even come up with a decent excuse. "I messed up. I fell asleep at a friend's house." It sorta wasn't a lie.

My father pointed an angry thumb down the road. "Was that Matt? Is he the one you spent the night with?"

It looked like my parents wanted to hash out our family crisis in the front yard, and I glanced behind me at our neighbor's windows. "Can we *please* go inside and not do this on the front lawn?" I begged them.

"*Oh*, I think it's a little too late to feel embarrassed," my dad said. "And quite frankly, I don't give a damn who's watching."

"Dear God, Samantha," my mother said, waving her hand over her nose. "You smell like you drank a whole bottle of rum." She stepped forward, peering closer to me, and then glared. "Are you still drunk?"

Having nothing to hold onto, I couldn't stop the slight sway of my wilting body. "Please, can you guys just ... I don't know ... just let me *be* for once?"

My mother shook her head. "Let you be what? An irresponsible adult? I cannot even talk to you right now. Look, if you want to go ahead and experiment, well, that's fine. But not if it hurts the people around you."

"Who am I hurting by going out and having fun with my friends?"

"*Wow*. It's like you don't even see it." I didn't expect her to start crying, but she did, and added through her tears, "You're playing with fire, Samantha. What if you drank too much and got alcohol poisoning or something? What if someone drove you home drunk? What if someone raped you because you're too drunk to defend yourself? Don't you care about anything? Don't you care about us or how we'd feel if something bad ever happened to you? I've told you before that alcoholism and depression run deep in our blood. Did you ever think that this was something you could become highly addicted to?"

I couldn't watch the look of despair cross on her face and stared down at the top of my white Converse. Except they weren't white anymore. Speckles of brown and yellow—remnants from barfing a minute ago—now painted my left foot. I swallowed and the lie that came too easy: "I have never gotten into a car with someone drunk."

When neither of them said anything, I looked up to find my father's face a shade of purple and his neck veins near bulging. "Do you know what today is, Samantha?"

At this, my mother walked towards the house, seeming disgusted and done with me. When she quietly shut the door behind her, I squeezed the sides of my head; it hurt too much to think. "*Um* ... today is Saturday?" My mind reeled with why a Saturday would be so important. And then it hit me. "Oh my God, I was supposed to work for Jane this morning."

"Yes, and it's already nearly ten in the morning. Your mother was just leaving the house to go tend to her until you showed. But what else is today? I'll remind you since you obviously can't remember. Today is your mother's birthday."

My eyes grew wide, and my mouth wider.

How could I have forgotten my mother's birthday?

I was the worst daughter on the planet, and nothing I did or said could fix the damage I'd caused. But I tried anyway. "Dad, I'm sorry. I forgot." I swallowed hard to keep the bile from rising again.

"At this point, I don't want to hear your apologies. Not only did you ruin this day for your mother, but your stupidity and lack of consideration for anyone but yourself are alarming. You've worried us, and you've let Jane down. But do you know what the worst part is? You're acting like someone we don't even know anymore. Your mother and I have noticed a big change in you. We thought the changes were from your breakup with Caleb and possibly being grounded and bored at home, but now all the pieces are coming together. It all makes sense."

I crossed my arms around my middle and looked down at a rock I nudged forward with my shoe. "I don't know what to say."

"Say you want more for yourself. Say you'll stop whatever is changing you for the worse. What you're doing to your body and mind is disgusting and disheartening to everyone who loves you." My father motioned me to follow him to his truck. "I'd like to continue this, but we'll have to discuss your punishment later, because Jane has called three times. The poor woman has not eaten breakfast or had her pills."

My father didn't speak another word as he drove me to work, and it was just as well. My head and stomach felt worse than any flu I had ever experienced. Not only did I want to put a bag over my head to drown out the light and suffocate myself, but death seemed the best option over the guilt that consumed me—my mother's birthday of all days. And Jane. She probably wanted to murder me.

Between the guilt crashing about in my head and my stomach rolling to and fro like an ocean tide from the truck's movements, I couldn't take it anymore. "Dad, can you please pull over."

"Why?"

"I think I'm going to hurl."

"Serves you right." When he pulled over, I didn't even make it out the door in time as some of the vomit slid down the side of his truck. "*Great*," he said. "Just making a mess of everything, aren't you."

"I think I'm done," I said weakly before shutting the door.

My father got in last dig before taking off. "I bet you'll have a *great* day working for Jane. Make sure you don't let her know you're drunk. I mean, how *very* unprofessional."

~

I opened Jane's front door and found her sitting on the portable toilet. "Sorry," I said, looking away. "I'll just wait in the kitchen until you finish your business."

"You just do that," she said in a clipped tone. While I stood by the fridge, her voice continued, "You know what? If you had shown up on time, I would have gone to the bathroom before you arrived. I always plan it that way. My privacy is important. But being that you are over three hours late, I don't see how I can plan these things, Samantha."

The kitchen was the perfect hiding spot as my body sweated profusely. The walk from the truck to her house had been taxing.

Leaning against the cupboard for support, I slid down to the floor like a wilted flower without any water and prayed for a miracle recovery.

"Samantha, tell me *why* you are so late? We had an agreement. Seven o'clock, remember?"

I called out, "Jane, I truly apologize. I overslept and forgot about our arrangement."

"If it's one thing I hate the most, it's lying. So why don't you tell me the truth? Because I called your house when you were an hour late, and your mother conveyed her shock when she found you were not home. She said it looked like you'd snuck out again. I pegged you for smarter than that."

"Okay, yes. That *is* what happened."

I could almost envision Jane's expression from where I stood as she scolded me from her toilet, "I'm going to need a few more minutes, so why don't you at least start my breakfast while you're in the kitchen. Or is that too much to ask?" She didn't let me answer. "And I'll take oatmeal. Do you realize I'm also three hours past taking my medications? I need to take them with food, you know. Do you know what it's like to feel this pain without my medication?"

"No," I answered shamefully.

"What did you say?"

I spoke louder, even though it hurt my head. "No. No, I don't know what it feels like to be you. I'm sorry."

"Then let me tell you. The mornings are the worst, especially after a long, insufferable night. So, it would have been nice if you arrived on time for me to take these meds. And tell me why you would do such a thing to your parents? Because they seem like nice folks, who don't deserve such an insufferable daughter as yourself."

"Yes, ma'am. I agree."

"Don't *ma'am* me now when you've never ma'amed me before."

"Okay," I said, totally giving up on pacifying her.

It was a chore not to gag as I cooked thick, mushy oatmeal, but an even bigger struggle as I contemplated taking one of Jane's little white pills to help ease the headache that split me in half.

The idea came and passed just as Jane called out, "Sam, you may come in now. I'm finished in here."

I delivered Jane's food tray with her medications and placed it on her bed. "Here you go."

She made a *tsking* sound. "You young adults nowadays. When are you ever going to learn, *huh*?"

Before Jane could say another word, I changed the subject. "What chores does Charles usually do on Saturdays for you?"

"For starters, the pisser."

The weight of a thirty-pound crap bucket made the blood behind my eyes almost explode, and I had to set it back into its slot when I blinked away the white spots that danced in front of me.

"What's the hold-up?" Jane asked.

"Nothing. I'm going," I said, attempting to lift the pot again.

My shriveled and dehydrated veins seemed unable to handle my overly thick blood as it pushed its way through my veins and arteries, so every step to the bathroom caused my temples to pulsate in protest. And because I nearly went blind as I bent down to set the heavy bucket on the bathroom floor, my foot caught the bathroom linoleum. I cussed out loud, falling forward, and completely spilled half the contents across the toilet and all over the floor.

My right shoe now matched the other foot I had barfed on earlier.

"Royal shi—" I said when an onslaught of smells hit my overly sensitive nostrils. I covered my mouth and nose as my stomach recoiled at the murder scene around me, and I couldn't stop myself as I turned to the tub and vomited for the third time that day.

"Samantha? Did I just hear the bucket drop?"

I didn't answer as I held a death grip around the bathtub.

"Are you throwing up?"

I still couldn't answer.

"Samantha, answer me. What is heaven's sake is happening?"

There was nothing left to throw up. My eyes watered with a mix of tears—tears for feeling sorry for myself and tears from all the exertion. I blindly searched behind me for toilet paper to wipe my mouth before finding my voice too high and chirpy, "Everything's fine here, Jane. All good. Just a little spill." I couldn't lie to her again, so I tried the truth, hoping she could handle it. "And yes, I did throw up, but it went right into the tub, so no worries."

My head spun from having to yell from so far away, and it hurt equally to hear Jane's backlash, "For the love of Pete! Get it together today."

Squeezing the sides of my head, I cringed as I yelled again, "I *am*, Jane; I'm trying here. *Really*, I am. Just not feeling myself today is all."

"I can only imagine why you're not feeling well. My guess tells me you were drinking last night." I remained silent, biting my knuckles as Jane stretched on, "This is me being completely honest, but you may be the worst caretaker I have ever had."

I couldn't take it anymore. With a lack of sleep, dehydration, feeling sick, and a migraine the size of Mount Rainer, I couldn't hold my tongue and snapped, "Well, thank you very much for your honesty. But, right now, can you PLEASE allow me to clean this mess without you yelling at me from all the way out there?"

Jane's silence was music to my ears as I contemplated how to remedy and clean the worst crime scene imaginable. The only miracle was when Jane didn't comment as I barfed two more times while dealing with the sloppy mess that took thirty more minutes to clean.

I stood before Jane with a face of ashen white and greenish hue, and said, "All done," as if nothing terrible had just happened.

Jane didn't congratulate me nor instruct me further. Instead, she opted to give me a silent treatment for the longest minute. She finally caved, "You know what? I wasn't going to say this, but you're just like every other kid—messing up your life and not giving a damn about what happens next. Have you not learned anything from my stories?"

Her question came as a shock. "What are you talking about?"

"I'll tell you what I'm talking about. It's called regrets. I ruined my life and the lives around me with my substance abuse, Samantha. And what about my daughter's story? Haven't you learned that sneaking out will only get you knocked up at fifteen?"

"I am not fifteen," I said, confused.

"It's beside the point. You come to work late, mess up almost everything you touch, and now you have proven to me that you are a sloppy drunk. Who knows if this is all you're dabbling with? Are you on anything now?"

I couldn't control my cold and sobering voice. "What do you mean 'am I on anything?' I'm *not* on drugs, if that is what you're insinuating. I am *NOT* you with a whole family to mess up. I'm eighteen and drank too much. Why is everyone making this a big deal? And the only thing you've taught me is that there's absolutely no pleasing you. I come to work and try my hardest, but you always seem to have something to complain about. You'll never be happy, no matter how hard I try."

Jane's eyes rounded wide before they downsized to slits. "I told you this once, and I'll tell it to you again. When you ignore the little things in life, everything will spill over into everything else. And then all you have left is crap. You will screw it all up, girl, and don't come crying to me when you have nothing left for yourself."

I couldn't understand Jane and why she was acting so high and mighty, and I couldn't stop defending myself. "I had a few drinks, Jane; big flippin' deal. And as for me ignoring the little things, well, I may *suck* at cooking, but I do almost everything you ask of me. Look, I'm here today doing you a favor, am I not? And where's your son anyway? Why isn't he doing this instead of me? None of this would have happened if Charles was here."

Jane's nostrils flared. "It's none of your business, like I told you."

It took me a moment as I tried to piece it all together.

Jane didn't fire people. They left.

"You pushed him away, didn't you?" I quizzed her.

"I don't know what you are talking about," she said as her eyes shifted out the window.

She was lying.

"Really? You once told me you fired all your past helpers because they didn't do a good job, but I found out from the state's coordinator that they all quit. You push people away. And maybe you pushed your son away, like you're doing with me right now."

"What do you care?" She glared at me.

It was true. I was past caring. "What I'm getting at is maybe it isn't just *me* who can't please you. Maybe *you're* the difficult one."

Jane's chest heaved up and down before she finally threw out, "You don't know what you're talking about."

"Then help me understand."

"You couldn't understand. You're just an ignorant child. You know nothing about the real world. All you care about is getting a stupid car and leaving home, all because you're what—you're bored? Well, guess what? You can't just pick up and leave the people who love you. There are bigger problems in the world than yours."

I threw my hands in the air. "If you remember, *you* wanted to run away from home once too. But the difference is you push people away because you can't handle being a disappointment, and you can't handle people disappointing you. But people have flaws, Jane." I picked up my purse. "Here you sit and judge *me* for being imperfect, but you are *far* from perfect. You, yourself, destroyed your family. And maybe because of that, you can't forgive yourself, which means you can't forgive anyone else either."

"You don't know a *damn thing*, and you don't understand. You're just some silly girl who's screwing up her life like ... like—"

"Like who, Jane? Like you? Well, guess what? I am NOT you! So stop trying to save me." I walked to the door before looking back. "I can't do this anymore, Jane. You'll have to call the agency and find a replacement immediately. I'm sorry, but I'm done."

~

I forgot to use Jane's phone to call my father to pick me up and the walk home was almost more than I could bear. The sidewalks welcomed my tears, and every other bush accepted my donation of mistakes—particularly tequila, beer, and Jell-O shots. A homeowner who looked like he was about to call the cops when he saw me behind a tree. I waved with sweat dripping down my face. "You're welcome. That's free fertilization."

After stopping to rest so many times, it took me over an hour to drag myself home. My parents were waiting for me in the living room, but I avoided my mother's eyes when my father spoke. "You look terrible."

The hallway mirror showed my face white as chalk, and my lips cracked from dehydration. "Can I go lie down before you start yelling?"

"In a minute. This won't take long. Your mother got off the phone with Jane almost an hour ago, and we are beyond disappointed that you quit on her."

I lifted my head to face them both. "But I had to! She—"

My father raised his hand in the air. "Don't speak. Just listen. Your mother has offered to make Jane's dinner tonight and prepare her pills until the agency or Charles takes over tomorrow."

I looked at my mother, horrified that this was what her birthday had come to. "Mom, I didn't want this to happen. I'm so sorry."

"If you're so sorry, then do it yourself," she said.

"I ... I can't be around that woman. Jane's—"

My father cut me off again, "Don't want to hear it. Whatever your excuse, Sam, it doesn't matter now. But this does prove what we feared."

"What's that?" I asked.

"How much you've changed in a short amount of time. The girl in front of us isn't someone we know, or even like, for that matter. You are self-centered, ungrateful, entitled, selfish, and seriously headed down the wrong path. That's why we just got off the phone making plans for you to attend a mission trip that helps those in need."

"A what trip?"

"You heard me. It's exactly what it sounds like. Helping people experiencing poverty is a way to better yourself and your views on life by focusing on something greater than yourself. We spoke to the coordinator that runs the mission program for teens, and they have made an exception to have you join them. You'll be gone for over a week."

My jaw hung open as he continued, "The little amount of money we had in savings was supposed to be your mother's birthday gift, for her to fly out and meet her daughter. So you better appreciate this time away from home and turn your life around. You leave for Tijuana, Mexico, a few days after school gets out for the summer."

I finally found my voice. "I feel like this is a joke. Tijuana? Mexico? Mom?" She didn't even look at me, and I turned to my father again and stuttered, "Dad, I ... I don't even know anyone going to this. Can't you just ground me like a normal parent?"

"Oh, because that worked out so well before, right? This trip is exactly what you need, Samantha. This is your shot to show us that you can act like this so-called adult you claim to be."

Chapter 24

Sam 2003

School had ended five days ago, with the hottest and most promising summer to follow; that is, for everyone but me. For the first time in my life, I'd longed for school to stretch another week just to avoid the inevitable. While everyone at school talked about their summer plans, mine would start with a twenty-hour bus ride to Tijuana, Mexico. I'd always complained about having the means to escape my small town, but this wasn't what I'd had in mind.

And dreading such an adventure was an overstatement. Sure, I had become accustomed to riding inside hideously large, yellow vehicles since my family owned one, but by five o'clock in the evening, when I stepped onto that yellow school bus that stunk of sweaty gym socks and peanuts, I wished for my boring life back.

As my already hot legs stuck to the freshly greased vinyl seats, I heard a girl's voice behind me. "No air conditioning?"

"They couldn't fix it in time," someone replied.

I tried not to have a panic attack. Without air conditioning, we would surely die from a lack of oxygen. The thought of no air circulation in such tight quarters brought on a claustrophobic meltdown, and I desperately looked out the windows in hopes my parents would pull me off the bus in time to say it was all a joke.

But they didn't.

A blond, brown-eyed girl named Laura with large boobs came and sat beside me. "Hi," she said. Even seated, she was at least two heads taller than me, with a body shaped like a linebacker.

I pointed to my name tag. "Hi. I go by Sam or Samantha."

To my right and across the aisle, a guy with shoulder-length brown wavy hair grabbed Laura's attention. He looked about my age, cute but nerdy, only because of the glasses he wore. His nametag read James. I counted a total of twenty-two high schoolers and five young adult leaders joining the crusade.

I realized no one knew me or why I was there, which relieved me. While they all actually wanted to be on the trip, I was only there to ride along to serve my penance.

A guy in his early late twenties stood tall at the front and introduced himself. "For those who don't know me, I'm Jeff, the head leader. Before we start this life-changing trip, it's customary that we set some ground rules going."

I immediately resolved that Jeff was no fun.

"Now, I know nobody likes rules," he continued, "but they're in place for your safety and well-being."

While he read off the rules and expectations for the rest of our trip, the other four leaders walked up down the aisleways, pretending to be flight attendants as they relayed Jeff's message. It took everything in me not to roll my eyes at their exaggerated game of charades. This was already becoming the worst trip of my life.

Jeff explained our primary goal for the trip. "And so, it will be our job to bring hope and blessings by building houses for the poor."

Hearing we were to build homes, I almost laughed out loud. They would regret giving me tools. The only thing I had ever built was a house made of graham crackers, marshmallows, and chocolate bars. I looked out the window again and tuned them all out while longing for a s'more. I thought of Liam and my friends and wondered what they were doing this whole summer.

I returned to the conversation when Jeff announced, "Before we take off, let's take roll call, because I think we're still missing someone."

The bus door swung open; perfect timing for whoever was running late. I could only see the top of someone's dark unruly, and curly hair, but that voice I knew all too well, and I gasped.

"Sorry I'm late. I had to make a pitstop for some gummy bears."

"You must be Matt, our extremely last-minute guest. Glad you could join us. Were you able to fill out the forms, and did you come up with the money in time?"

My best friend took the last three steps up the bus stairs. "Yep," he said, handing over a thick envelope.

I almost squealed like a pig on feeding day, but instead, I remained cool, calm, and collected. Matt looked around, and couldn't miss me. Not when I stood in a crowd of sitters, waving my hands like an SOS in crisis.

He smiled big-like and began his way down the aisle carrying a pillow and a plastic bag from Chevron.

"Laura," I said, looking at my current seat partner, "do you mind if I sit with my friend who just showed up?"

"Sure. No problem," she said, moving across the aisle.

Matt came face-to-face with me. "Care if I sit here a while?"

I grabbed the front of his shirt and yanked us both down to sit before giving him a massive bear hug. "What in the H. E. double L, Matt? What are you doing here? And how did you know I was leaving?"

"I called your house and asked for your sister Stephanie instead of you. She was able to give me the run-down of your punishment, and well, I couldn't let you suffer this trip alone, especially since part of the reason you're here is my fault. Liam was your DD that night, and I ruined it."

I shook my head. "I can't believe it."

"What can't you believe? That I'm the bestest friend ever?"

"You mean 'just' friends. You said a while ago you wanted us to be 'just' friends so that it wouldn't be weird for me to kiss my 'best' friend."

"That's the other reason why I'm here," he said, leaning back comfortably in a seat before throwing an arm over my shoulder. "How can we ever know where this leads if I can never see you this summer?"

With one of his fingers hanging just below my clavicle, I lifted it *and* his arm over my head. "You completely missed the ground rules a minute ago, when our leader Jeff said no fraternizing with the opposite sex."

"That's a stupid rule."

"Maybe," I laughed. "But you forget our company." I looked around, widening my eyes for him to take notice. "No one's journey here is to discover their relationship status. We are not Lewis and Clark in the wilderness alone. We are in a territory of watchful eyes, and now that you're here, I really don't want them to find a reason to separate us."

"Fine," Matt said. "But how about we lay some ground rules of our own? I'll go first."

I shifted, facing, and crossed my arms. "Oh *yes*. *Please*, let's hear it," I said sarcastically.

"Okay. Rule number one: try not to make any googly eyes at me. That would definitely alert the masses that you are madly in love with me."

"*Lordy*."

"Rule number two: no pet names. I can't have you calling me honey buns and sugar plum. That would start something I couldn't control."

I slowly slid my hand down my face and stopped it at my mouth, mumbling, "Continue."

"Don't worry; this is the last one. Whatever you do, don't touch the soft, fleshy part of my elbows."

I looked at him funny. "What? Why?"

"It's not funny, and it's quite the opposite of funny. If you touch me there," Matt said, pointing to his elbow, "I get this tingling feeling in other places you wouldn't believe. It's right about her—"

"Stop. Okay. Enough. You're done making rules. How about *my* one and only one rule."

"I have a feeling your rule is going to suck."

"You know me so well, so here it is: if anyone asks, we're back to being best friends, and I think we should act like it."

"No. I want to go back to being 'just' friends. How am I supposed to kiss you on this trip if you're my best friend?"

"That's the thing. This trip isn't for that. My parents said I'm supposed to, quote unquote, 'come back a better and grateful you.' Meaning, me."

"What is that even supposed to mean?"

"Heck if I know. My parents think this trip is the key to self-discovery, where I'll magically find purpose and meaning in my life. Anyway, just ... just chill out and be the good ole' Matty boy I know you can be. But it doesn't mean we can't have fun. Because before you showed up, I didn't think fun would ever be on the menu."

"Glad I can oblige in the fun department. But on a side note, you really are a killer of hopes and dreams."

"Speaking of hopes and dreams, I hope you brought another pillow. I forgot mine."

"You expect me to share my pillow without a single kiss from you?"

"How can I take naps without a pillow?"

Matt patted the tops of his knees and wiggled his eyebrows up and down suggestively.

"No," I immediately said. "Just no." I squeezed his shoulder to see how hard it was. "Your shoulder will do just fine," I succumbed.

~

With Matt now on the trip with me, I thought I could handle anything that came my way. But it wasn't even twenty minutes into driving when the entire bus began to sing camp songs. It didn't help when Matt pretended to blend in with the group by slapping his hands to the song's beat on the back of our seats.

I whispered in his ear, "You know you look ridiculous right now, jamming out while biting your bottom lip like that."

"So you're noticing my lips, *huh*? Wanna take back rule number one?"

"No."

I had a feeling I would be telling Matt 'no' plenty more times on this trip. And the first time came four hours later, after the leaders passed out our itineraries. I stared down at the paper in my hand. "Are you kidding me?" I said. "Do we have to sleep on the bus the whole trip?"

Matt read the fine print. "It says not every night. Just every *other*. We sleep on the bus tonight, but once we arrive in California, we get to stay at a university where they have dorms." Matt fluffed his pillow. "Looks like we better get comfy."

When he pointed to his lap again, I crossed my arms, irritated at the whole mess. "No. And no. How does anyone sleep upright *and* on a bus, for that matter?"

Matt shrugged. "I'm not going to lie, but I'm excited to have the night alone with you." He placed his pillow under his neck and joked, "Where's your pillow again?"

"Funny."

"Did you have any problems packing?" he asked, offering me a piece of gum. "Because I didn't know what to pack."

"I know, me neither." I opened the Juicy Fruit wrapper and folded the paper into tiny squares. "They gave me a list of suggestions, but I didn't have some of the items listed."

"Same. I'm sort of coming on this trip with short notice, remember?"

I smiled and tried to relax. "If I forget to tell you later, thank you for coming, Matt."

"You're welcome. And I won't give you any more crap about the pillow." He fluffed it up and put half of it on his shoulder. "You get half, and I get half."

"Deal," I said.

~

I was skeptical about the whole sleeping ordeal but was surprised to have fallen asleep so quickly when night fell. But I woke to find I'd barely slept—it was still dark, not fully morning yet. I tried to shut my eyes to fall asleep again, only to find it pointless when I jolted awake from a bad dream twenty minutes later.

While staring out the window with my thoughts running alongside the wheat fields just as the rose-pink of dawn spouted its head over the hills, I wondered if dreams held any meaning. It was the same reoccurring dream that had come to me for the third time that week, one with Jane in it. I held the unfinished book we were reading together, but no words would come out of my mouth. It seemed glued shut. And when I looked up to find Jane's face pained in disappointment, I tried again to make her happy, but the dream always ended without us finishing our story.

Somewhere between thinking of my mother and Jane and watching the sunrise through the windows on the bus, I must have fallen back asleep for a few more minutes, until Matt's voice came within an inch of my ear, startling me. "I see you found a better pillow," he said.

I opened my eyes, looked down at what was supposed to be his pillow, and found my head resting on his chest. Jerking upright rather quickly, I stammered, "Yikes, sorry about that." For someone who was supposed to have some feelings for her best friend, I couldn't place why I wanted to run from the intimacy and closeness of him.

"It's fine," he laughed. "I've always wondered why I was given these magnificent pecs, so you're most welcome."

I smiled and sat upright while patting his chest. "Well, for what it's worth, they're softer than any pillow I've ever used. My neck would be a lot worse without them, so thank you."

My eyes grew wide when I noticed the drool I'd left on Matt's shirt, and I contemplated whether to tell him. But because drooling, crying, and throwing up, as of late, made me feel like a complete and utter disappointment, I opted not to tell him.

"Why the sad face?" he asked me.

I knew deep down I was partly to blame for what had happened with Jane, and that I kept pushing the guilt out of my mind as my way of avoiding the truth. The truth that maybe I, too, couldn't handle being a disappointment to the people I cared for. And even though I controlled the outcome to my own story, I didn't know how to remedy any of it.

I wasn't ready to talk about my fight with Jane yet, so I asked Matt instead, "Matt, how do you stop doing something you don't want to stop? Everyone wants me to stop drinking, but if I do, I'm back to the same bored and suffocating Samantha Carey."

"So you're saying that drinking is your only way to have fun?"

"No. Well, maybe. But drinking has also helped me escape from my problems at home. Like with all the fighting, you know? And it's been nice to block out all the drama at school. So, if I'm being completely honest, I think I might like alcohol a little too much. I even crave it now."

"Do you think you drink as an escape mechanism to avoid conflict?"

"I'm not avoiding anything. Do I feel guilty I've disappointed some people? Yes. But I don't feel guilty for wanting to escape all the bullshit and have a little fun while I'm at it."

"Well, you can't have that kind of fun without hurting someone, so I guess it's all about your mindset, like positive thoughts over negative ones. If you're compounding a negative, like all the bullshit in your life, with another negative, as in drinking, then that's just a disaster waiting to happen. Plus, partying only makes a person temporarily happy. You can't drink your troubles away just because you're bored and unhappy."

I looked out the window again. "My parents' last words were, 'Change is good for you,' and 'Maybe you will come back a better and more grateful you.' I want to be that person for them, Matt, and perhaps I did lose sight of some apparent path that didn't involve drinking myself stupid, but I wish I didn't have to give up the partying. I've never had so much fun in my life. I'm depressed thinking about the fun ending."

"I know. But again, it's up to you to change that perspective. It's all in the mindset. You control the outcome with what fun means, right?" Matt bumped my shoulder and pointed outside our window to the shades of apricot and salmon lighting up the morning sky. "Look at those colors changing. See? Change isn't so bad."

~

We arrived in California at close to eight in the morning, and I wanted to scream out in relief. My butt throbbed from sitting overnight, my legs tingled from loss of circulation, and the sweat dripping down my back from the morning's rising heat was almost too much. "Get me off this bus before I break a window open," I groaned.

I didn't catch the name of the city or even the large university that loomed over us—old and worn, but I didn't care. Anything would have been better than the yellow nightmare of a thing that got us there. After everyone had collected their belongings from under the bus, we made our way inside the dorm.

"Do you think they'll let us be bedmates?" Matt asked.

"No," I laughed. "It was pretty self-explanatory when Jeff said boys in the left wing and girls in the right."

"This trip is turning out terrible."

"Positive thinking, Matt. Positive thinking."

"Whatever. Wish me luck while I go find a room buddy."

While Matt went to find a sleeping partner, Laura looked my way and asked, "Wanna be roomies?"

"Sure," I said as we both practically ran to our room with the promise of real beds.

We dropped our bags and plopped heavily onto our twin beds, breathing in the cool air conditioning before Laura said, "I just need to shut my eyes for a minute."

I barely mumbled, "A nap sounds splendid."

It was noon when we woke. The itineraries under our door said we were free to do whatever we wanted until 8 p.m., so Laura, James, Matt, and I had fun walking around town sightseeing before eating dinner. But by eight o'clock, when we met up for the activities our leaders prepared for us, it all seemed over the top and juvenile.

Matt nudged me playfully when I refused to join in on the ridiculousness. "Why are you so stiff-like?"

"I'm eighteen, Matt. Seems a little immature. No?"

He raised his hands and mimicked the red and green light commands. "Of course it is, but that's the point. It's okay to geek out once in a while. Mindset, Sam. Once you relax, you'll have fun."

I wanted to tell him I needed a few shots of Patrón to relax, but didn't. I laughed with envy at the effortless way Matt enjoyed playing the stupid games. He always made everything look painless. And maybe he was right that I needed to change my negative thoughts. Besides, if I continued to act aloof, I was more noticeable for not participating.

Blend in, Sam. Stop being a big baby.

Matt saw my baby steps in an attempt to partake, and he kindly made it easier for me to blend in by placing his body slightly in front of mine. He had everyone laughing when it was our turn to grab a balloon and place it between our chests to pop.

"Sam, put your back into it," he said, slamming me to him. "We can't let the other team win!"

"I'm trying," I laughed. "I swear our balloon doesn't have enough air to pop. Wait. Lay on your stomach. Hurry."

Matt did as I asked, and I placed the balloon on his back before I sat down hard on it. It popped, but so did his back. He groaned. "You broke me. I can't move."

I laughed, helping him stand. "You said we had to beat them. It was a sacrifice I was willing to make."

"Fine," he said, rubbing his back. "But next time, you're on the bottom."

By the night's end, I hated to admit it, but I was having fun.

We were back on the bus before we knew it. And by day two, every single one of us loathed that damn bus. It was another night when we had to sleep on the bus, so Matt positioned his pillow between us again. "Thanks," I said, laying my head next to his. "You up for some pillow talk? Because it's probably going to take me forever to fall asleep."

"There it is again. Negative thinking."

"Okay. Pillow talk with me before I fall fast fast asleep."

"Better," Matt said.

I moved my hair out of my eyes. "I still can't believe you came and my sister helped you."

"Me either. You always make Stephanie sound like the devil, but she was really sweet and helpful on the phone."

"You also don't live with her," I laughed.

Matt shrugged. "I think it's just an age thing. My sisters annoy me too, but since the oldest moved out, she's nicer."

"I've always wanted an older sister." I paused before laughing. "Well, actually, I've just recently acquired one."

"What?" Matt looked at me oddly.

I sat upright. "I've been grounded, and a tad self-absorbed with partying, so I forgot to tell you about the new addition to my family."

After telling Matt all the details, he shook his head. "Holy crap."

"I know. My sister is twenty-one now."

"When do you get to meet this older sister?"

"Tina? She lives in New York, so with money being an issue, I'll probably never be able to fly out and meet her." I immediately thought of my mother, and my heart sank. "Now that I'm thinking about it, I feel terrible. If my mom didn't have to pay for me to go on this stupid mission trip, she would have been able to afford a flight out to see her daughter. I really am the worst person. Here I've been so focused on myself that I've kind of screwed everyone over."

"That's a hard pill to swallow."

"I'm an idiot. I'm so stupid for hurting my mom like that."

"You can still make up for it."

"How?"

"Just work on yourself. Try and not be so self-absorbed, I guess?"

We were silent for a while before I spoke again. "My sister sounded pretty cool when she called the first time. It should be fun to get to know her eventually. But, as I said, it's a little surreal."

"Yeah, it is crazy."

"Maybe I could find a good-paying job again and help my mom get a ticket to fly out to New York."

"See? You're already changing on this trip, and we haven't even arrived in Mexico yet." Matt yawned and stuffed his fallen pillow under our necks a little better. "That's the thing about relationships; if you invest your time in them, only good things can come. But you have to put the effort in first."

"For a guy who's almost all jokester, you have really good advice."

"It helps that my mother is a psychiatrist. After listening to all her psycho-babble, you learn a few things. But you know, she gets paid for advice, so instead of me charging you for all this free therapy, I'd settle for a kiss about now."

I looked over to see Laura and James still awake. "No."

"Like I said, killer of dreams, you are."

~

We must have reached a pit stop when Matt nudged me. "Wakey, wakey. We're in Mexico and not far from the camp."

I rubbed the sleep from my eyes and took in the early morning light. "Then why did we stop?" I asked, hearing everyone's excitement hit at once when the bus door opened with a relieved hiss.

It was hard to see our surroundings through the dirty windows, but Matt pointed out a tire and a dirty convenience store whose outer shell of paint looked severely chipped from years of harsh weather and neglect. "They said we can grab some treats before we hit the campsite."

I didn't know what to expect stepping off the bus, but they weren't kidding when they said we were there to help the poorest of towns in Tijuana. Even the few trees and bushes staggered about were dying of hunger and thirst. I instantly missed my home and its lush greenery.

We stood impatiently outside, waiting for Jeff to finish his speech. "Please buy at least one item to show our support and appreciation for this struggling community. Our group's purchases here today might help the owner feed his or her family for an entire year. So feel free to spend whatever amount you wish, knowing it's for a good cause."

Everyone itched to go inside, but another leader held her hand up. "Oh, and we're strictly warned not to drink the water in Mexico, unless you want a permanent toilet attached to your rear. It's not safe."

Once inside, we met a stout, red-cheeked man in his thirties who greeted us cheerfully and walked us through the few aisles filled with a limited selection of goods. When the gentleman found his way to me, he held up a package of what looked like vanilla cookies of some sort. "Sí?" he asked. I nodded yes, and after I grabbed a few extra, his face cracked with gratitude before bowing graciously before me. "Gracias, señorita. Gracias."

Matt found me looking for chocolate and tugged at my sleeve. "Sam, this has to be the saddest place ever."

I looked over to see his wife in the corner crying happy tears, along with their barefoot children cheerfully ringing up items at the register. "I know. That's why I'm looking for some chocolate. I need chocolate when I get emotional."

A little girl in the dirtiest tattered clothes approached Matt and me, holding a box of gum called Chiclets. Matt looked at me and whispered, "Shouldn't these kids be in school?"

"Sadly, I don't think there is a school around here," I said.

Matt reached down and smiled as he took ten packages, but when the little girl smiled in return, he changed his mind, grabbing them all.

We left with as many snacks as we could carry, leaving behind the owner and his wife, who looked like they would break their wrists from waving goodbye so jubilantly. And for the next twenty-five minutes on the bus, the only noise was that of candied wrappers crinkling.

Matt shook his head. "I don't know how long it'll take me to finish this box of gum."

I looked at the entire box and laughed. "It will take you less time if you give me one."

~

When we finally reached our final destination, and after the dust settled all around us, we found ourselves in a dried-up, flat field that was our campground for the next five days.

"Guess this is home," Matt said, coughing the dust away.

We stood outside under the bus's shade as the leaders gave everyone their assigned jobs, setting up tents and doing daily chores for the duration of our stay at the campsite.

I opened a folded piece of paper, reading what chore they'd assigned to me. "Mine is washing dishes after dinner each night and setting up the morning breakfast."

Matt groaned. "I have the job of cleaning the Sani-cans."

"Finally, the tables have turned, and it's someone else's turn to clean the toilet."

Immediately, I thought of Jane, and my stomach dropped.

"What's the matter?" Matt asked.

I updated Matt about my quitting on Jane and all that had transpired. "Sorry I didn't tell you on the bus, but I wasn't ready to talk about it. I'm still bitter about it. Anyway, as much as I hate how things ended with Jane, I miss her in some weird way. I don't miss her yapping at me or the chore of cleaning her toilet twice a day, but I miss the newest and good parts of her. Like the part where we were becoming friends."

"I feel bad. You'd still have your job if I didn't mess up our ride home that night."

"It's just as much my fault for drinking too much and blacking out, Matt. Anyway, a few days before we boarded the bus to Mexico, my mom informed me that Jane now resides in a nursing home. I'm not sure if her son refused to work with her, which wouldn't surprise me, or if she was sick of going through so many caretakers. But ... "

"But you feel guilty."

"Yeah. Knowing I had a large part in it all makes me sick to my stomach. Jane always said a nursing home would be the death of her."

"Could you fix it?"

I looked up at Tijuana's blazing sky, so bright, it blinded me. "I think that bridge has burned. Plus, no one can fix Jane Nelson."

Chapter 25

Sam 2003

The next day in Mexico proved to be a learning day. The leaders gave us numbers in a hat before separating us into five groups. The first four groups would build houses, and the fifth would interact with the community.

I wasn't happy that they separated Matt and me, so he gave me a reassuring squeeze on the arm when I got the job of building houses. "Don't cry. You wanted to build a better you, and you don't need me there to do that."

"I'm not crying, you weirdo. It's called pouting. Anyway, look at this mini blueprint. I thought we were building a standard-sized home. These houses are only thirteen by ten-foot shacks—no bigger than my living room at home."

Laura heard me and leaned in. "Yeah. The organization could only raise just enough money for twenty small dwellings. Plus, since it's a teen program, they knew there was no way we could build real houses in under a week."

"Oh," I said. "So, an entire family would live in one of these miniature-sized houses? They look like shacks."

"Essentially, yes. The organization wanted to help as many homeless families as possible, so the budget was best used to build many smaller ones rather than one large one." She must have read my mind and explained further. "Even though these homes are simple and small, it's better than living on the streets without shelter from the harsh weather. A single mother might be able to shade her baby from the scorching sun and even lock her door at night from human predators."

I nodded, finally understanding as Jeff, our leader, announced, "It should take each group one day to complete one home, making it so that we hit twenty houses on the nose in four days. So let's get to work."

There was a lot to learn that day: how to set up our tents, cook and clean up after each meal, and read all the building instructions for efficiency the next day. So after everyone showered, and after the evening's motivational speeches, and after singing every annoying camp song they could come up with, it didn't come as a surprise that sleep came easy.

But it was on my second day, after driving twenty minutes to an area designated for shelter building, that my leader Jeff told me exactly what my job entailed, "Sam, your main purpose is roof duties after we get the foundation and sides set up." He laid a set of paper plans on top of a makeshift table. "Your job is to hammer all the nails into the shingles to secure them to the roof. But while you wait for them to build the main parts, you can make yourself useful by walking around to see if anyone needs help. Sound easy?"

"*Uh*, sure," I said.

Because Matt and Laura were assigned to go with the group that was going into town to visit the community, James was the only person I knew in my group.

I found him struggling to saw a sheet of plywood and hurried to help him by holding the other end to stabilize the table better. "Thanks," he said. "You know, before my dad died from cancer, we built things together all the time. But now that he's gone, I wish I would have paid more attention. He always made building look easy."

"I'm sorry you lost your father."

"It's all right. It helps to talk about him. That's why I came on the trip. Kinda to remember him since he loved building so much."

"What was he like?" I asked.

After James spoke about his fond memories and growing up with his father, he asked, "Do you do things with your dad like that?"

I took a deep breath before exhaling. "Not really. Especially lately. He works fairly hard and doesn't have much time for us. But I suppose it's partly my fault too. I've been a little selfish lately with my own needs. I wish we were closer, but my family is complicated."

"Well, take it from me. It's easy to take each other for granted while we're all still here. Just don't wait till it's too late."

I thought of my parents and their disappointment in me before I left and how I had so much to make up for. "You're right, James. I'll take that advice home with me for sure. And for what it's worth," I said, "you look to be doing a good job building. Your dad would be proud."

"Thanks."

We worked side by side for half the day until he handed me a box of nails and a hammer. "Okay, I think we're ready for the roof now."

It had to be two hundred degrees outside by the time I climbed on top of the scorching hot roof. I wiped the bullets of sweat off my brow a few hours later and looked to James, who stood on the ladder handing me more nails. "Now I know how hard my father's job is and why he's grumpy all the time after work," I said. "How much longer do you think we have out here? I'm melting."

"My guess is we have two more hours."

"No!" I groaned. "How do people work in these conditions every day?" I asked, hammering another nail into the black sandpaper that dug into my knees.

"I don't know, and I don't envy them."

"Well, if I die from a heat stroke out here, can you tell my parents I'm really sorry?"

"Sorry about what?"

"Everything, James. Just everything."

It took our group seven hours to complete our first home, and as we stood back to admire our hard work, our leader congratulated us. "Guys," Jeff said, "this looks great. Really amazing."

I looked at the simple structure without windows, without a sink, without running water, and without a toilet. "James," I said, "I wish we had more money to help these people, but I guess we should be proud of this little accomplishment."

"Exactly. And not bad for a bunch of amateurs."

Wholly sweaty, exhausted, and with a pinch in my lower back, I high-fived James. "Yeah, who knew I was so handy with tools," I smirked.

Once we got back to the camp, I stood under the cold water of a makeshift shower and closed my eyes, reveling in such luxury. Being that my bloodline was almost half Norwegian, I'd underestimated the sun and its effect on me. If it hadn't been for my stomach growing with the hopes our dinner was an all-you-can-eat buffet, I could have fallen fast asleep in my tent for an entire week.

Matt came to fetch me in my tent, and I groaned in protest. "No. Leave me be. I can't move."

"It's Italian night."

His mention of food forced me out of a wishful slumber. "Fine, but can you carry me?"

"Okay. A piggyback it is."

I didn't hold back from filling my plate, piling it high with spaghetti and garlic bread. And after we joined the others at the tables who looked just as tired, I asked Matt, "How was your day?"

He seemed to lack the sluggish look that most of us builders carried and answered, "It was super fun in the village. I mean, it wasn't fun seeing how many people came to sign up for free food and a free house; that part was sad, but it was fun keeping the kids occupied as they determined who was most in need of a house."

I stuffed my mouth with a second piece of bread, and thought about using a napkin when the garlic butter dribbled down my chin, but with my arms feeling like rubber, I settled for licking the mess clean with my tongue instead. "That's cool," I said. "My day was productive. Our group finished our first house. But, if I'm being honest, it's *way* too hot on top of the roof. I don't envy anyone who works for a living in such heat."

"That sucks. We were lucky enough to have a little shade from a nearby tree." Matt took a swig from his bottled water. "Your forehead looks a little burnt. Make sure you put some aloe vera on that before our meeting tonight."

My heavily lidded gaze met his. "First of all, I doubt anyone brought aloe, and second, we have a meeting?"

"I'm sure the meeting is about more motivational speaking and songs. If you're not going to make it past sundown," he laughed and took my empty plate, "I can do your chores tonight and cover for you so you can go to bed. Any requests in songs to put you to sleep?"

"The song Hallelujah," I said. "Because once again, you are saving the day. Thanks, Matt. I'm exhausted."

"No problem. It's funny, but it feels like we have a role reversal going on here; I'm the mom taking care of the kids, and you're the dad going to work." Matt leaned in and whispered in my ear, "Except, our marriage comes without all the good stuff. We have a million tents here if you wanna go find one," he joked. When I nearly choked on my water, he continued to laugh, even after turning his head to ask James a question.

I don't know why my heart hammered out of my chest or why the thought of going past the kissing stage with Matt freaked me the heck out, but it hit me all at once. And hard.

Could I go past the kissing stage with my best friend?

Why had I never thought of this before?

Lips were one thing, but his hand on a boob, or worse?

My eyes grew wider at the images in my mind of what it would be like together, *together*, and I panicked. I stood, accidentally knocking my chair down behind me. "Okay. I need to go to bed, like now. Goodnight, everyone," I said, nearly running to my tent.

Sleep didn't come like I had hoped, not when racing thoughts of Matt consumed my mind. We didn't make sense together. No matter how hard I tried to spin it, I couldn't get past the next stage. And who wanted a relationship of forever kisses with nothing to follow? I couldn't make us work. I loved him, but not like that. I could not see past the camouflage of what I wasn't, or couldn't ever be, for Matt.

I rolled over to my side, giving my makeshift pillow made of sweatpants a punch, and tried not to cry. I was so sick of hurting those who loved me and being everyone's disappointment, especially someone who'd loved me since the seventh grade. And my heart nearly broke wide open from the clarity and truth of what would become of us. I fell asleep in my warm tent to the sound of crickets singing Hallelujah while wondering how I'd gotten myself into this mess with my best friend.

~

The fifth day building houses started horribly—with a freak accident.

They sent James to the hospital when he nearly sawed off one of his fingers. There was so much blood that I was shocked he didn't cry. The scary incident left everyone's mood in shambles, and it didn't help mine either, not when my mind was on so many things just as my hammer slipped, causing me to crush my thumb with a heavy blunted thwack.

So between my thumb throbbing, my mind stinging with thoughts of James, and my heart hurting with the devastating news I still had to give my best friend, well, there were too many aches to go around. I wanted to toss in the towel and hitchhike home at that point.

I was relieved when our leader called it an early day.

Matt came back to camp early and saw me exit the first-aid tent. "Sam. We heard about James. That's so scary. Did you see it happen?"

"It was awful," I said. "I was hammering on the roof when I heard James scream from below. They have to fly him home as soon as possible for surgery." I caught Matt looking perturbed by my thumb in a bag of ice. "Oh, and then, like an idiot, I hammered my stupid thumb," I added.

"You gonna be okay?"

"Yes," I said. "Just really sore."

He frowned and took my hand in his. "I can fix it," he said, kissing my thumb with his soft, sensual lips.

And there it was again, that creeping flutter in my belly, except this time, it wasn't the one with butterflies from a lover's kiss. "Thanks," I said. "I think it feels better."

It didn't, and if anything, my heart hurt more.

God, I hated my life.

Matt let go of my hand. "I have an idea. I'll ask my group's leader if you could join us in our group tomorrow. I think you need a break from building. You look all out of sorts."

"You could say that."

~

My leader found me packing everyone's water bottles under the bus the following day. "Sam. Here," he said, handing me a clown outfit. "I heard you need a change of scenery, so you'll be joining Matt and Laura's group for the day."

"Thank you. But what are these clothes for exactly?"

"Today, your group will perform a small carnival function for the kids. Songs, games, face-painting."

I held up the outfit made for a person ten times my size. "Okay. But this looks like it belongs to the guy who ate the elephant at the circus."

"Would you rather come back and work on the roof again?"

Anything beat melting on top of a two-hundred-degree roof, so I quickly replied, "I will make this work."

"Good. And oh," Jeff said, reaching inside his pocket. "Here's your red nose to go with the ensemble. See you later, Bozo," he laughed before yelling orders for everyone to board the buses.

I hurried and changed into my ridiculous costume just before Matt flagged me down. "Love the outfit," he laughed, almost in tears.

We headed towards the bus, and I pulled at the sides of my pant legs, extending them out a good two feet from my thighs. "Can you believe this thing?"

"The kids will love it. The goofier, the better."

"Then I bet they love you the most. You're the goofiest person they'll ever meet."

"Why, thank you. Now shut up and get on the bus."

Thirty minutes later, we found the heart of a community village, consisting of tiny dwellings, shacks, and homesteads—all neatly lined in a row down a remote and unpaved street. I was shocked to see how most of the huts—made of various materials like planks, metal siding, and even plastic tarps—housed an entire family. Accenting the area was mismatched clothing strung across plastic lines, side yards with chicken coops, and pots, pans and plastic tubs adorning front porches. But even in such tight quarters, it seemed everyone had a system of organization.

"How do these people live like this?" I said to Matt, whose expression matched mine.

"I know. Pretty sad. Even though I've been here four times, seeing such poverty is still shocking."

Our group of six stepped off the bus to find thirty or more dirty but joyful faces of little children and their parents. I smiled nervously and waved to each kid, making sure not to forget to play the part. If this was what their lives consisted of, I had to try my best to bring some joy to this impoverished town.

A tiny thing of a boy grabbed my hand as if he had known me forever, and I looked down at him with a warm smile. "Hello," I said. He appeared to be around three years old, with a small, rounded head of hair closely shaven to his scalp. Every bit of him was dirty, except his face, which glowed and looked freshly cleaned, just like the smile he displayed for me.

I squatted, lowering myself to his height. "Hey, buddy. Wanna tell me your name?"

He continued to smile, showing perfectly white teeth, and I wondered how long before they would rot out from a lack of nutrients and dental care. When the boy didn't answer me for the second time, I looked at Laura, who spoke perfect Spanish. I pointed to my chest like I had seen in the Tarzan movies. "*Sam*," I said to the little man.

He giggled and pointed the tiniest thumbs at himself. "Vicor."

He must have been trying to say Victor, but he left out the 't.' "You're cute, Victor. Should we go over there?" I said, pointing to our group, which had made its way over to a shaded courtyard with the only tree in the entire village. I'd already begun to sweat in my forty-pound suit, and I didn't think I could last all day without shade.

After Victor found a spot on my lap to sit, I grabbed Laura's attention. "Hey, I don't know how to communicate. I wish I knew Spanish like you."

"You don't need to know Spanish. What is the most common language the entire world can understand without using words?"

It took me a second before I understood. "Love?"

Laura gave me a reassuring smile. "Bingo."

I thought of Laura's words before picking up a small rock in my right hand. Placing my fists in front of Victor on my lap as the audience waited, I asked him, "Can you guess which hand it's in?"

Victor knew the game immediately and crinkled his nose in careful consideration. He tapped the hand where he thought the rock resided, but after I opened the empty hand he'd chosen, I tickled his ribcage in consequence. The hysterical fits of laughter that emanated from his miniature-sized body were as if a million butterflies tickled his insides, and I couldn't help but laugh alongside him.

And by round ten, others began to cheer Victor on. They were just as excited to see if Victor would guess wrong, because nothing was better than hearing the endearing and contagious bubbles that burst out from him like a waterfall. I didn't know how many children took turns on my lap to play the torturous game, but I was happy when we moved on to face painting. My cheeks were hurting from all the laughing.

Victor never left my side as we worked together to make a humble Mexican spread for the community, and after we finished, Matt sat next to us to eat. "You know, kids look good on you," Matt said, chewing on his lunch. "When do you think we should start our family?"

I looked down at Victor, who was eating as if it were his first meal, and hurried to change the topic. "I heard one of the leaders say that almost fifty percent of children in Mexico live in poverty. If they don't already have serious side effects from malnutrition, most will likely turn to selling drugs, using drugs, or partaking in other illegal acts just to eat. And the little girls often choose prostitution over starvation—as a way to escape poverty. Isn't that horrible?"

"*Geez*, Sam," he said, skipping his last bite. "I was having a good day until now."

"Sorry."

I watched Victor devour his last bite of beans and rice and tapped his nose playfully before sighing. "I hope Victor won't fall into any of those categories. He seems smart enough to choose right over wrong. Don't you think? And if he knows he's loved by something greater than himself, maybe that will be enough."

"I hope so," Matt said. "But don't think about that. You have to stay positive for the kids. Clowns aren't supposed to frown."

"You're right," I said. "On a good note, this day is my favorite so far." Victor burped, making us all laugh, and I smiled. "This little boy has earned a special spot in my heart. Do you think we can keep him?"

"Our first child together?"

Again, I wanted to laugh, but it broke my heart that Matt was in a headspace I could no longer partake in. "Hey," I said, "is all the gum you bought still on the bus? It might be on the soft side, but—"

"You thinking what I'm thinking?"

"Yeah."

After Matt passed out gum to all, our leader collected our trash from lunch. "All right, crew, help your kids find their parents, and let's meet on the buses in ten."

Most of the children had found their parents, but not Victor. He raised his hands to indicate he wanted me to hold him. He looked tired, and I wondered where his parents had gone and why no one had come to check in on him for the entire day.

I picked his small form up to hold him to me before asking, "Laura, where should I take Victor? No one's come to claim him yet."

"His parents are probably around here somewhere."

"Aren't they worried someone might take him?" I looked down at Victor as he rested his sweet head on my shoulder, his eyelids too heavy to stay open. "I mean, anyone could just grab him and disappear."

"But our bus is leaving any minute, Sam."

"Well, I'm not leaving him. He's just a little boy. What am I supposed to do, leave him on the ground all by himself?"

Just before I took Victor with me on the bus, a young woman made her way over to us. She smiled, reaching out to take Victor from my arms. For a moment, I hesitated. Finally I gave in, but only because I saw the resemblance between mother and son did I reluctantly hand him over to his so-called mother.

Matt pulled at my arm. "He'll be fine, Sam."

I stood firm, watching the lady enter a tiny tent before finally feeling it was okay to leave him. "Well, if I don't see him tomorrow when we come back, at least I can point out to authorities the home she took him to. There is such a thing as human trafficking, you know."

~

On our last day in the village, we did the same routine. I was relieved to find Victor waiting for me again. After we danced and played while he pretended he knew everything I said, it was lunchtime again, and I had to confess to Matt, "If I could, Matt, I'd steal him onto our bus and take him back to Washington state with us."

"You'd take him from his mom?"

"She could come too," I laughed. "The funny part is I didn't even know I liked kids."

"Well, good. Because I want at least two someday."

I bit the inside of my cheek. Matt would make a great husband and father one day, but it broke my heart that I didn't see him as the one for me. I wanted it to be him so badly, but I knew forcing something didn't work. With a stitch in my side, I asked Matt, "Which family will get one of the houses we built for them?"

"I'm not sure. But only twenty families will get one."

I looked around. There were over a hundred tents and makeshift dwellings, with each one holding at least four to seven family members. I said a small prayer that Victor's family would get one of the homes we'd built, as his house was only a tent. I didn't think it would hold if the slightest dust storm rolled into town.

"Sam, you're quite attached, aren't you?" he asked me as I tied a piece of yellow yarn around Victor's ankle—a friendship bracelet, matching the one I wore.

I looked down at the little creature, watching him eat his watermelon like it was corn on the cob. "Yes," I said, my throat tightening with thoughts of leaving so soon.

Matt rested her hand on my knee. "Look on the bright side; today, we say goodbye to the village, and tomorrow before we leave, twenty families will have new homes."

"Yeah. That's pretty cool, I guess." I couldn't take my eyes off Matt's hand on my leg. "Hey Victor? Let's clap and sing a song. Like this," I said, standing.

When the time came to say goodbye and the songs ended, Victor didn't understand that I wouldn't be there to greet him the next day. I squatted down to memorize his large hazel eyes, the color of liquid gold that could melt the coldest of hearts, and waved my hand goodbye while pointing to the bus. "I have to go bye-bye, Victor. I will miss you," I said, making a sad face.

He understood this and jumped into my arms, squeezing me tight. For a little tyke, he was strong. I gave a little tickle under his chin to hear his sweet laughter one last time—to never forget him.

There was no door to his tent to knock on, so I called out, "Hola?"

Victor was on my hip when his mother opened the flap. "Sí?" she asked, greeting me.

I gave her a sad, thin smile while pointing to the bus down the road. "*Um*, I have to go now."

She smiled warmly, saying something to Victor, and I watched his face light up in understanding just before he happily took off the tiny colorful beaded bracelet from his wrist and handed it to me.

"Oh, no, I can't," I said, shaking my head. But when he nodded yes, with the biggest of smiles, I couldn't stop my chin from quivering as I kissed his cheek. "Okay. Thank you. Gracias, little señor. Gracias."

I couldn't believe this little boy was giving me something that was possibly the only materialistic thing that had value to him, so I struggled to hand him over to his mother for the last time before waving a heart wrenching goodbye. The walk to the bus was the most sobering moment in my life, and I prayed that if there were a God, He would protect this little guy who had done a number on me.

It was our last day of Tijuana heat. After we packed up our entire camp to leave, our group celebrated by presenting twenty families with a small home. As the children jumped up and down like it was Christmas morning, and the parents beamed ear to ear, I spoke to Matt under my breath. "There are seven people in that one family alone. How can they all fit in that tiny box?"

"I have no idea, but it sure makes me appreciate our lives."

"Yeah. I'm realizing I have it pretty good back home."

Matt grabbed my hand. "I'm glad I came. This feels good."

There were so many reasons for the heaviness in my chest. But I still needed my best friend's support, so I held onto his hand for comfort, just not in the way he probably meant it to be. I swallowed a hard lump as we returned to the bus and left for good. "Even though I will probably never see Victor or any of these people ever again," I said, "I think we will always have a connection to this place in some small way."

"Agree. We made some pretty cool memories in such a short time."

"That we did."

The entire bus ride back to Washington was a time for reflection. So when by nightfall, when everyone fell asleep but me and Matt, we kept talking.

Matt leaned his head next to mine and whispered, "How crazy different are our lives compared to these families in Mexico?"

"It's so true. I mean, they have little to nothing." I looked down at the simple bracelet Victor had given me. "I feel so guilty for complaining so much about not having enough, especially when so many people suffer. I don't think I'll ever complain again about not having a car or enough name-brand clothes."

"Same," Matt said. "But what surprises me the most is how their community is one big happy family, always helping each other despite all their bad luck. Family is important here."

I shook my head. "I wish my family were more like that. We can't even co-exist, let alone be in the same room without irritating each other. I guess it doesn't help that I compounded my own issues with my parents' already existing ones. Anyway, this trip has been eye-opening," I said. "When I get home, I need to be more thoughtful and grateful for what I already have, which is so much compared to others. Happiness isn't about money and having more things."

Matt nodded. "It's true what they say, 'If you can't find joy in the little things, no amount of money in the world will bring you happiness.'" Matt turned and faced me. "Anything else that you'll take with you from this trip?"

I nudged him smiling. "I'll take how lucky I am that my best friend came on this trip for me. You really are a great friend, Matt."

Matt bumped me back. "*Aw, shucks.* Thanks."

Reaching inside my pocket for the cinnamon-flavored gum Matt had given me earlier, I gave him a piece. After a minute of thoughtful pondering, I said, "You know what? For a long time, I was unhappy and felt out-of-sorts with myself, thinking I had to leave our small town to find whatever was missing. But I realized something."

"What's that?"

"I was stuck in a relationship that never allowed time for fun or time for my friends. But once I got out and adventured a bit, it wasn't all the drinking that made everything so fun and exciting; it was me just missing my friends and doing fun things again."

Matt laughed. "Well, drinking does add an element of fun, but yeah, it's whom you spend your time with that makes a person happy."

"Exactly. I mean, look at Liam. He's always having fun and seems happy without ever drinking. And as you said, it's all about the mindset."

"So, no more parties for Sam?"

"I might still go to hang out with my friends, but maybe I'd be more like Liam and not drink. I think alcohol makes me someone I don't necessarily want to be. I ... I regret some thing."

"Like what?"

"For starters, days after drinking, I always felt sluggish, tired, and grumpy, and I ended up treating my family like crap because of it. They didn't deserve that. But my biggest regret is Jane. I know she's cranky as all-get-out, but I regret how I handled things with her. If I wasn't so hungover that morning after partying, I don't think I would have said the things I said." I swallowed back my tears of guilt. "And now she's in a nursing home because of me. I royally screwed up."

"I wasn't there, Sam, but I wouldn't hold all that guilt on yourself."

"I don't know about that. But I feel terrible. I was just starting to really like her. I miss her stories."

"Well, at least you're going in the right direction by admitting to yourself all your wrongs. And again, who knows, maybe you guys can work it out?"

"Maybe." I gave Matt a thin smile. "I have a lot to fix when I get home. But on a good note, another big takeaway on this trip that surprised me was how much I like helping others. It's refreshing to focus on others rather than myself for once. I see myself doing more of it."

"Yeah. I could tell you really took the whole philanthropy approach seriously. I even got jealous of Victor a few times when your focus wasn't on me."

The tightness in my chest hurt, and I looked up at the ceiling to hold in the tears. "Matt, about that."

"I know, I know. This trip wasn't about us."

I turned my body to face him and swallowed. "Yes, true in part, but Matt, in a sense, this trip with you showed me some other truths about us."

"And?"

"Remember when you said you didn't want that night to be our first last kiss?" I watched Matt's eyes take in my somber ones, and his shoulders slumped.

He knew.

Hating myself for what I had to do next, I covered my face with my hands. I was so damn tired of letting people down. "Matt, that night you kissed me, it surprised me." I dropped my hands and looked at him. "It had been a long time since someone kissed me like that. So, yes, it made me feel things for you. But this trip with you made me realize I like us being just us—the us we have always been. You're like my favorite song on the radio, but play it on repeat forever and a lifetime? It loses its meaning. Trust me, I would do anything to see you smile, Matt, just not at the expense of ignoring my gut."

When Matt began to pull on the front of his shirt, twisting it in anguished grips, I asked him, "What the heck are you doing?"

"Pulling the knife out of my heart. It hurts, *dammit*."

I knew he was trying to make light of the situation, but I also knew him well enough to know he hurt. "Let me know when the knife is out," I said, wishing to take the hurt for him.

He crossed his arms. "Sorry. Continue. You were saying you don't want to be with me and *blah blah blah*. So why don't we work?"

I let my head fall back against the tall seat and squeezed my eyes shut. And after a minute passed, I felt his finger run across my cheek to wipe the mess I had tried so hard to avoid. "I don't know why," I finally said. "There's no reason why you shouldn't be the one. The only way I can explain it is that I don't feel the pull or whatever magic it is that people should feel when in love. Something is missing. But Matt, trust me," I said, looking at him, "I wanted that magic to be you so badly. I wanted you to be my forever. But loving you in parts where some pieces fit and others don't, isn't enough for me, you, or anyone."

Matt seemed to soak in my words before taking a long, drawn-out breath, "Number one, I'm not gonna force you to feel any certain way for me when you don't. I was hoping you'd feel the pull like I did for you, but in a sense, Sam, you didn't even give us a shot. We had one kiss."

"I know, I know. And I'm sorry. Really. But maybe I didn't give us a chance because I subconsciously knew we wouldn't work like that deep down."

Matt crossed his arms. "You know for absolute certainty that you don't feel anything for me?"

"I love you, will all of my heart, but not in that way. Well, I think so anyway."

"You aren't very convincing, you know."

"Well, I'm ninety percent certain of how I feel."

"Okay. How about we settle that remaining ten percent?"

"What do you mean?"

"I'm going to kiss you right here, right now, and how about afterward? Then you can truly decide our fate. At least give me that. As I said, I don't want that one night to be our first last kiss."

I looked at Matt hesitantly while wiping my face dry. I knew what he asked of me was only fair. And what could it hurt settling things once in for all? I took a huge breath in before releasing it. "Okay," I said, finally giving in.

"Okay?"

"Okay."

Matt took his gum out of his mouth and placed it under his seat, and I followed suit. "Ready?" he asked.

I looked around, ensuring everyone still slept, before facing him. I swallowed the last of my nerves and said, "Ready as I can be." While I shut my eyes and waited for the kiss, I decided I'd let him be the one to pull away to prove he'd given it his best shot. He deserved at least that much from me, and so much more.

When my best friend's lips met mine, soft, slow, and sweet, with a hint of spicy, I shut my mind off to see if the magic pull existed. But when I felt his hands on my face pulling me in further, and his tongue touched mine, making tender swirls and enticing teasers, all I could think of was yeah, there was no denying my best friend was a stellar kisser. Whoever's heart belonged to my best friend one day, damn, she was one lucky girl.

Matt pulled away finally after one last tender peck. "Well," he said, "that's all I have. Did you feel anything this time?"

I mustered a smile. "It was really good, Matt. Actually, spectacular."

His shoulder slumped for the second time that night. "But?"

"But for all the wishes in the world, I wished it were you."

He let out one quiet, sad laugh. "God, girl, me too. Me too."

It was me now who tried to make light of the situation. "Where did you learn to kiss like that?"

"My sister." When I gave him an appalled look, he laughed, "Just kidding. "I'm a natural-born kisser, I guess."

"Maybe you should become a lifeguard this summer. Save lives with those lips. I mean, your techniques are on point and life-saving-worthy."

"But it didn't bring *you* to life."

"No, but almost. I mean, super close."

Matt let out the loudest groan, shocking us both, and we quickly slumped down into our seats before anyone saw where the loud noise had come from. "Sorry," he whispered. I just really wanted us to work."

Our faces were inches from each other, and I kissed his cheek. "I know; me too. Are you mad?"

"Mad? No. Just bummed. Imagine hoping to drive that Mercedes Benz you've always dreamed of, only to be told you can never drive it. And then you realize the car was never yours to begin with and that my dream car is probably a minivan."

"First, I can't believe you're comparing me to a car. Second, you're selling yourself short with the minivan. You're more like a classy badass 1970 Boss 429."

"A what?"

"It's a rare Mustang. It's like my dad's dream car. He has a poster of it in his garage. But it's a cool car, trust me. And thirdly, your girl is out there, Matt. She'll be the one where you won't have to keep a secret that you love her. Really," I said, nudging his shoulder. "Whoever she is, Matt, she will be lucky to have you."

"Maybe. But whoever *he* is for you? I'm going to hate him."

"Really?"

"No. I'm kidding. I'll always support whoever you choose. And for what it's worth, Sam, I want you to be happy. Even if it's not with me."

"Best friends for life?" I asked.

"Always."

"Good. Because I can never replace you."

~

I knew we'd arrived back in Washington when the night's fresh, clean, and cool air reached our faces. I closed my eyes and took a cleansing breath, letting the air wrap its love around my heart—feeling at peace to be home again.

When we pulled into the church's parking lot late Saturday night, I laughed. "I can't believe I'm saying this, but I'm glad to be home."

"Same. Do you think you'll be grounded all summer?"

"I don't know. I hope not."

After Matt and I made our rounds, saying goodbye to everyone, he asked me, "Do you need a ride home?"

"Story of my life," I laughed, "but no. I see my mother here already."

Before Matt turned away, I grabbed him and hugged him fiercely. "Thank you again for coming. Just know, I wouldn't have wanted it to be anyone else."

He tousled my hair, which needed a good shower. "Whatever you say, heartbreaker. Now get out of here before you make me all weepy. And call me this summer if you're not grounded."

I walked toward my mother, who stood waiting outside our sizable yellow submarine. By the look on her anxious face, she was probably worried I hated her for sending me away. But as she waved a tentative hand in greeting, I couldn't hold back the sheepish grin to ease her worries—letting her know all at once that mothers were right about everything. I was still Samantha Carey, just a better version this time around.

Chapter 26

Sam 2003

The sentencing had eased.

A few weeks after my trip, my parents had decided Mexico was punishment enough. So because my current behavior demonstrated that of a refined modeled citizen, they allowed me one phone call a day, along with one outing a week. The old me would have argued, but it was a self-defeating cause and not worth fighting. Especially since the new me now saw a bigger picture: I was eighteen-year-old without a job who still lived at home and had one more year in school before college. So, I took my punishment like a champ and smiled through it all.

I looked down at my very adult to-do list, which prioritized the important stuff.

To-Do List (for the new Sam)

No more drinking. Fun is what you make of it.
Focus on family first before friends.
Write a letter to your new sister.
Possibly make up with Jane.
Get a new job and pay for Mom's flight to see Tina.
Don't sweat the little or big stuff. Life is too short.

I marked off numbers one through three and contemplated avoiding number four altogether. I still didn't know what to say to Jane or if I could even fix us. I mostly worried she wouldn't receive me at all, and because I never took rejection well, I dialed Matt for my one phone call for the day.

He must have seen my last name pop on his caller ID, because he answered, "So you're not grounded now?"

"No, and yes," I laughed. "I have freedom once a week and a phone call once a day, which is better than a lifetime of prison."

"And you're calling little ol' me for your one phone call?"

"Yep."

"I feel so special."

"You are, but don't get a big head. Anyway, I called to see what you're up to. As hot as it is outside today, maybe or possibly you were already headed to the peninsula?"

"I'm down to go to the lake with my Mexico buddy. Want me to call Emily and Heidi?"

"Yes, please."

The overly crowded peninsula was a long, thin strip of the smallest islands on the lake. It could only fit a large tree next to a volleyball net, which resided in the middle and only left ten feet on each side of the net before your feet touched water.

We placed our towels down onto the grass a few feet from the ends of the net—the only few spots left to lay out to tan. "I guess this is what we get when arriving too late. All the good spots are taken," I said.

"At least it's not near the snack shop and bathrooms." Matt cracked his knuckles. "Swim, tan, or volleyball first?"

"The water looks tempting," I said, walking the few feet over to the water's edge to dip a toe. "*Holy, no!*" I laughed, yanking my foot out from the chill. I sat down on my towel and adjusted my sunglasses. "It hasn't fully warmed up, and probably won't until the end of July. Which sucks because it's so hot out today."

"You're not going to swim at all?" Matt asked, sounding like a two-year-old.

I still wore my shorts and tank top over my black bikini. "I will, but I'm not hot enough yet. Volleyball first?"

Without Emily or Heidi to join us, I didn't leave Matt's side as we stood waiting for our turn to play. I hated the feeling of wanting a few shots of alcohol to ease the social anxiety, but I forced myself to stand in line to wait our turn to play. The new Sam would try and find fun with or without alcohol.

Our friend Adam from school came out from the shade of a massive tree and walked over to us. "Matt," he said, giving him a few rounds of secret slaps, tugs, and a long series of brotherhood handshakes before nodding to me. "Sam."

They went into a round of intense horseplay, consisting of noogies and crotch wars, and I rolled my eyes before stepping out of their way and into the shade of a tree. I bumped into a tall figure leaning against its trunk and turned to look up. "Hey," I said, taking a double take.

"Hey yourself."

"What are you doing in our neck of the woods?" I asked.

"He's with me," Adam said in a struggling whisper, still captured in Matt's headlock.

It had been over a month since I had seen Liam. His hair had lightened from the sun, and his bare chest was already a golden tan. Clearly, he had been enjoying the summer, unlike my albino self.

He leaned in and frowned. "Heidi told me what happened after the party that night. I should've stayed and taken you all home. I'm sorry you got in trouble."

Matt dropped his chokehold on Adam and doubled over with his hands on his knees, trying to catch a breath. "It's my fault," Matt said to Liam. "I was being a dick that night and clearly shouldn't have been in charge of finding us rides home when you had insisted multiple times."

That must have been all Matt needed to say, as I watched Liam nod to Matt in understanding. But I hurried to fill in the awkward silence that followed, "So, Liam, how do you know Adam?"

"Our girlfriends are friends. You just missed her; otherwise, I would've introduced you."

Adam pointed to the entrance. "Looks like your favorite person is here, Sam."

I looked to where he pointed. "Oh great."

"What?" Liam asked.

Adam and Matt laughed. "That's Jay Erin," Adam said. "Sam's special buddy in our history class."

"He's not my special buddy. He's more like an annoying gnat." I looked at Liam, whose eyes clearly said he wanted to hear the story, so I obliged. "How the class clown managed to be in at least one class of mine every single year for the last five years," I said, "*and* sits directly behind me throwing spitballs? I'll never know."

Matt chimed in, "You've been a good sport. I would have already clobbered him by now if it were me."

"Samantha does have a great right hook," Liam replied. "She could take him."

"No, I'm not going to hit him," I laughed. "Jay is a complete spaz but totally harmless. I normally ignore him."

Liam cocked his head. "Sounds like this pest of yours likes you, and that's why he messes with you."

Matt added, "Yeah, I second Liam; Jay probably likes you. It's a clear sign when someone continually messes with you. But hey, since you *are* single, I think I should give Jay your number?"

I caught a puzzled look cross Liam's face for a split second before I threatened Matt. "Is that so? Do that, and I'll give *your* number to Veronica Snell."

Matt shuddered. "Okay. Fine."

"Maybe today's the day you get Jay back, Sam?" Adam suggested. "Five years of spitballs? I think it's time."

As we all watched Jay laugh hysterically after slyly tripping an unexpected passerby, I suddenly had a sobering thought. I didn't want to be someone who needed a few shots to let loose to have fun. I crossed my arms. "It would be nice to get the twerp back. Who wants to help?"

Matt backed up with his hands in the air. "Hey, I'm not getting involved. My lady bits down below took a good beating," he said, glaring at Adam. "But I would *love* to watch all this go down. So, carry on."

"Adam, you in?" Liam asked.

"*Nah*. This looks like a job for two. I'd just be a third wheel."

"Okay, Sam, looks like it's just you and me," Liam offered. "What do you have in mind?"

There was a gleam in Liam's eye as he waited for me to answer him, but my mind went blank after a minute. "Dang, I got nothing," I said. "But whatever we do, it'll have to be playful—a harmless prank. I don't want to do anything too extreme."

Liam's face lit up. "We have an empty cooler of ice?" He rubbed his hands together, waiting for me to give the go-ahead.

A mischievous smile spread across my face, replacing any remaining anxiety. "Who am I to stop a bit of revenge fun?"

~

As I watched Liam walk over to fetch us his cooler full of ice, two girls from my school, who were behind me in line for volleyball, whispered. "God, he's cute."

I followed their line of vision—zeroing in on Liam. Even from a distance, it was clear why they thought so. Liam was taller than most, athletic, and had an air of confidence in his walk, along with a likable and yet unexplainable easiness about him. Anyone could see he was good-looking. But it was his caring personality that completed the package.

Liam returned with the cooler a few minutes later. "Here's the ice you ordered," he said. "Oh, and I added some water to give him more of that 'drowned-rat look.'"

"Fabulous," I said. My fingertips brushed against Liam's cool ones, sending a cascade of goosebumps over me. But due to the wet condensation that coated the container, I struggled to grip the handles firmly and nearly dropped it all at my feet. "This is heavier than I thought."

Liam took the cooler from my slippery hands. "Girl, you need to take some weightlifting classes," he joked.

"Maybe the gym would help. The last time I carried a bucket was for my boss. It was full of not-so-good stuff, and I spilled that as well. It was kind of the worst day of my life."

"Now I'm intrigued with what was in that bucket."

"You don't want to know."

As we walked toward my victim, I reminded Liam, "You know, it's kind of right that you should be helping me, after you ditched us all at the party. My parents sent me to Mexico for my punishment."

"Mexico?" he said, looking at me sideways. "Before you tell me about that, let me explain. Matt is, or excuse me, he *was* your boyfriend or something at the time, so when he told me to get lost, I did."

"Matt and I aren't anything now, but anyway, at the party he was also super drunk. And it's not like we are your responsibility, but you were the only responsible one there."

"True. But he said he found someone else to take you guys home, and I trusted him because you trusted him."

"Nope. Matt dropped the ball on that one."

"Well, I'm sorry you got in trouble again. Was Mexico fun, at least?"

"Try building houses for the poor in 110 degrees ," I said.

"So you built houses, and yet, your puny muscles stayed the same?"

I tilted the cooler towards Liam, threatening, "Not too puny that I can't trade my victim in for the likes of you."

He laughed. "You'll have to tell me about this Mexico trip."

"Okay. But after we get Jay."

Jay's back was facing away from us—perfect. My heart began to race, and I whispered in Liam's ear, "Maybe we should reevaluate this?"

"Don't chicken out *now*. You got this."

Liam looked down at me, waiting for my approval, and so with a determined nod, I gave him the red light.

He smiled and silently mouthed a countdown, '*One, two, three.*'

The avalanche of water and ice did its job. Jay's dark head of fluffy curls fell flat instantly, making him look, in fact, like a drowned rat.

Jay gasped in shock, "What the hell?" before turning around to see me standing wide-eyed and smiling.

But when his eyes narrowed in on mine, I didn't wait to talk. Instinct compelled me to drop the cooler and run.

"Sam Carey!" I heard from behind me. "Oh, it's on!"

My eyes flew wide with fear as I hunted for something to hide behind. I found Matt near the volleyball court and hid behind him.

He laughed, "I don't think so," he said, pulling me out from behind him. "Don't think you can hide behind me, missy."

Shocked at such betrayal, I whined, "What? But Matt!"

"I want no part. Plus, you always told me you could take care of yourself. So, let's see what you got."

"Traitor," I hissed.

Jay dripped with retaliation only a few yards away, and I nearly fainted until Liam came to my aide. "By the looks of it, Jay's coming for you and *only* you. But hurry," he said, thrusting me to stand behind him.

Not wasting a second, I scrambled behind Liam's tall frame, all the while wondering why I'd detoured from my theory that 'ignoring the idiot' was the best policy.

Liam barked orders to Adam, and they quickly blocked me in like a protected, caged bird.

But it didn't stop Jay from confidently encircling me like a playful panther toying with his prey. He tried to poke me through the open spots between the shirtless bodies that encased me, calling out, "Come out, come out, Sammy. Can't hide forever."

I felt like a trapped animal and squeaked, "Jay, I had to!"

"Is that so?"

"Yeah, you spit-balled me all semester. And the year prior, and the year before that."

He poked a finger and barely missed my shoulder. "And?"

"And, yeah, well ... you had it coming?"

He crossed his arms—as if ready to give up. "Well, since you have an army protecting you right now, perhaps I'll just wait and come back when you least expect it."

"Or we call in a truce?" I begged, sticking a pinkie out.

He laughed, walking backward. "Dream on, Sammy girl." He locked a promising gaze with mine while holding two fingers to his bright blue eyes. "I'll be watching you."

Adam groaned in disappointment, "*Bummer.* I was looking forward to a little fun. The twerp gave up too easily."

"Good job, Sam," Matt said, holding up a hive-five for me. "You stayed alive—*for now.*"

I poked my head out of my human fort. "I'm not talking to you, traitor," I said, bypassing his upheld congratulating hand.

He dropped his hand with a sour face. "Fine. But since it looks like you won't be dying just *yet*, are you playing volleyball with me or not?"

I noticed how Matt looked at me as I hid behind Liam and thought I saw a hint of jealousy. But his face quickly changed, hiding it well. It would take a little while for him to move on.

Since Jay was no longer an immediate threat, Liam turned to face me and patted me on my head. "I think you're safe for now. We can all play volleyball. And if it makes you feel better, I'll try to keep an eye out for you in the meantime."

We walked onto the volleyball's grassy court together before I admitted, "That was sorta scary. Thanks for saving me, unlike *this* so-called friend," I joked loud enough for Matt to hear.

Matt positioned himself diagonally to me on the court and threw the ball at me. "Must I remind you that it was me who saved you from going on that Mexico trip all by yourself?"

"*Fine*," I said, throwing the ball to Liam, "I guess I owe you both."

I stripped down to my bikini and threw my clothes to the side of the net. "I'm just warning everyone," I said. "I'm not good at this." When Liam gave me an expressionless look, I suddenly felt naked under his blank stare. "What? I asked him.

I watched his Adam's apple bob before he cleared his throat. "Nothing. I'm umm ... I'm just thinking that you should switch spots with me.

He gently pushed me behind him. "Good. Yeah, you're safer behind me."

"But how can you watch out for Jay for me if I'm behind you?" I asked as he stretched a long arm over and behind his head to prepare for the game. I had to look away and anywhere else but at his toned, bronzed, and tightened back.

"Maybe just don't let your guard down," Liam suggested.

I looked around me, losing sight of Jay's location. "Right. Eyes behind my head. Got it."

~

We played a solid forty minutes of volleyball before everyone found I sucked. With little to no game to bring to the table, I pointed to the lake after someone spiked the ball at my head. "I'll just watch you guys from the sidelines and get my feet wet."

As the sun blazed high above without a cloud in the sky, my toes curled with relief at the water's edge. I didn't know how long I collected rocks, but as I noticed another pretty stone with a hint of green, I heard my name called from across the water. I didn't have time to look up when someone's large hands took hold of my midsection and hauled me up and over their shoulder.

Startled, I let out a scream, "What the—"

Feeling like a rag doll, I yelled, "Jay, let's talk about this." He ignored my pleas, allowing the tension to build as he walked back and forth along the water's edge, pretending to find the right spot to dump me. I panicked. "Okay, okay! I'm sorry. Is that what you want to hear?" My feet kicked behind me endlessly, and I tried to cover my bikinied backside with a free hand while my other hand fisted and hit his bony back. "Jay, come on, let me go. Uncle! *U.N.C.L.E!*"

"Nope," Jay said calmly, clearly enjoying his triumphant moment.

"Truce. White flag. I'll do your homework for a week. Anything!"

"Nope. And school's out, Sam, in case you didn't hear."

My whine came in gasps now, "I'm sorry. It was just so hot out. I thought you needed some cooling off, that's all."

Jay finally stopped pacing. "Have a nice swim!"

"Wait, no—"

Jay's strength surprised me when he hoisted me high and paused dramatically before thrusting me forward into the icy waters.

A small scream escaped from my lips while my arms and legs took a pathetic grasp at who knows what. I was sure I looked like a flailing fish when my body landed awkwardly sideways into the lake, making a big, whale-like splash.

I barely had time to adjust from the cold shock when lake water came rushing into my nose—burning something fierce. When my head broke through the surface, just before I ungracefully sputtered, spat, and coughed up half the lake.

Jay's laugh came from somewhere behind me. "Looks like you forgot to plug your nose, silly girl."

A crowd of laughter followed Jay's, but I couldn't see who partook as I blindly wiped the water from my eyes. When I finally opened them, I found a pair of hazel ones—with gold specks—looking intently at mine. I yelped at Liam's proximity and closeness before coughing, "Hey."

His laughter emerged as deep as the lake while he lazily floated on a pink floaty. "Hey yourself."

"Really?" I said, dipping my messy mane of hair into the water behind me. I emerged from the surface while smoothing my long hair back with my hands. "And you couldn't have warned me as you watched from out here?" I sputtered the last word while ensuring my swimsuit was covering all the right places.

"You were too far away to hear me yell. But I *did* try to warn you. You need eyes in the back of your head."

"Yes, that would have helped," I said, shaking the water from my ear. "I decided I don't like pranks anymore."

"Quitting before the fun ends?"

"I could get him back, Liam, but that would mean an endless war of pranks that would most likely last too long for my liking. Too stressful and not worth it."

"Yeah. A summer of endless pranks could get old, real quick."

Liam offered me the opposite end of his floaty when he noticed my doggie paddling skills had left me tired.

"Thanks," I said, pulling the front half of my body.

He waited for me to catch my breath before asking, "So, Samantha, you always find yourself in deep waters?"

As we faced each other, his words played over in my mind before my honesty spilled out without shame. "More or less. Trouble could have been my middle name these last few months. But as of late, and after my humbling experience on a mission trip to Tijuana, I think I am finally on my way to a more ... hmm, let's say, solid ground?" I shrugged. "Don't you ever find yourself in trouble?"

"No, I'm pretty solid. Almost perfect." His voice held no gloat, and his easy smile carried a shimmer of innocence.

I pretended to pull something out of the water and handed him the imaginary item. "Here. You dropped this," I said. He looked at my empty wet hand, perplexed. "It's your halo," I said. "You dropped it."

"Very funny."

"No, but really. You can't be perfect."

"Perfect? No. But I have a confession if you want something to hold over my head. But you can't judge me."

"Okay. What is this confession?"

"There is this girl here today. She's sort of hard not to notice."

I don't know why it irritated me, but I looked over my shoulder. "Who?" I asked. "Does she go to your school or my school?"

"She's the one wearing all black."

Liam laughed when I couldn't find anyone walking around wearing all black. "You are ridiculous. Samantha."

"What?" I said, annoyed. It was so unlike Liam's character to check out someone when he already had a girlfriend.

His eyes narrowed in on mine with a playful light in them. "What color are *you* wearing?"

I looked down at my bikini of all black. "*Oh*," I said, my face growing hotter than the sun.

"Sorry. I probably shouldn't have said that. But there you have it. I'm not perfect." He laughed playfully again, "Stop looking at me like that. You're telling me you never admired someone, even when you were with your ex?"

I thought of our school's quarterback, Sam Johnson, and how everyone admired him. "I guess I have."

"See? We're only human. But truthfully, the last time I got into trouble was when I forgot to close the gate to the house at night, and our dog Moose got loose."

I stared at him as if he were an alien, but I was happy we were off the subject of me. "*Wow*. You really are nearly perfect." My toes accidentally touched his under the water, and I quickly pulled them behind me. "Sorry."

"It could have been a fish."

Looking cautiously at the water, I asked, "What kind of fish?"

"My dad and I fish here sometimes. We've seen a few bass, perch, tiger muskies, and little minnows."

"I've never heard of tiger muskies. What do they look like?"

"They have long slimy bodies, scales like tiger stripes, with relatively sharp teeth."

Pulling my feet closer to the top of the raft, I panicked. "Wait, what? You're lying."

"No, I'm serious. But don't worry; tiger muskies don't bite."

"How do you know? And why would someone put a fish with teeth in a man-made lake?"

"To scare little girls like you."

"Touché. I don't like lakes where I can't see the bottom."

Liam nodded his head towards the volleyball game in progress. "So, are you and Matt not an item anymore? You two seemed pretty close that one night. I mean, at one point, he was brushing your hair."

I laughed, "I barely remember that or anything else that happened that night." We floated aimlessly and watched Matt play from afar. "But no, Matt's been my best friend since the seventh grade, and I realized I'd like to keep it that way. It's too complicated." I didn't want to talk about myself, so I asked him, "How are you and ... Trisena, right?"

"Sena for short. We've been together since the eighth grade, and I suppose, like most relationships, it's complicated."

"I get it. I was with my ex for just as long, but it didn't work out."

"Caleb?"

"Yeah. You know him?"

"I know *of* him in the sports world, but not personally. Anyway, if I'm being honest, you two don't seem like the right fit."

"No. It's okay; a lot of people said we didn't fit. It just took a long time for me to see that and a long time to finally pull the plug."

"Relationships are hard."

"And complicated," I added. We watched Matt dive into the water and swim effortlessly to us. He shook his head like a wet dog—spraying water in my face. "Thanks, brat," I said.

"So I hate to do this, but I gotta cut our lake fun short today. I forgot I have a family function in a few hours. I need to head home and get ready. You know my mom; prompt and proper."

"Oh, okay," I said. Being that it was my first day out for weeks, it was times like this that I wished for my own car.

Matt sensed my hesitation. "Do you want to stay longer? I'm sure Liam or someone could give you a ride home?"

It was an olive branch to Liam, but I didn't want to inconvenience him. "I'll just go with you now, Matt."

"I can take you home," Liam offered. "I'll probably stay for two hours or so." He looked at me. "Is two hours too long?"

I was so tired of charity rides everywhere, but I shrugged. "I've got nothing else to do today, so sure. Thanks."

"Then it's settled." Matt winked. "Call me later," he said, before swimming away.

"Wait," I said, looking at Liam. "Just making sure, but, your girlfriend wouldn't be upset if you took me home later? Caleb always got mad when Matt took me home."

"Sena has a ton of guy friends, and I have a lot of girls as friends too. We're both mature about it. This is harmless."

"If you say so."

~

I was a tad embarrassed when Liam pulled up to my house three hours later. I knew I shouldn't have cared about my meager home, but from our talks earlier at the lake, I knew Liam was an only child, his parents paid for his red Mustang, he didn't have to work, and he had a giant pool in his backyard. In Washington, no one had pools. A flashback from my Mexico trip came to mind of Victor's little tent, and suddenly, humbling thoughts revived me. My family's financial status didn't matter in the scheme of the bigger picture. Plus, Liam didn't seem like the type who pitied anyone based on their class or status.

Liam gave me his phone number. "Seriously, call anytime you need a ride. It sucks not having a car. Especially when it's summertime."

"Tell me about it," I said, taking the piece of paper he'd written it on. "And thanks again for the ride." Before I shut his door, I laughed, "Also, it was nice meeting you officially sober today."

"Yeah, it was fun getting to know the real you."

"You don't think drunk Sam is way more fun than this Sam?"

"I like all sides of Samantha Carey. But Sober Sam? Don't go changing her."

Just as Liam waved out his window and drove off, Sarah Hansen happened to drive by right behind him, on her way home from the lake too. I wanted to put it behind me that she'd made the last few months of school hard for me when Caleb and I broke up, so I threw an olive branch in her direction, waving hello to her just as she passed me by. The new me wanted a fresh start. And who knew? Maybe Sarah and I could be friends.

Chapter 27

Sam 2003

There comes a point in time when you decide the person you want to be. I wanted to be a person without regrets. So, I decided to tackle item number three off my grown-up to-do list—Jane.

But being that it was a Thursday with both my parents working, once again, I found myself without a ride.

My sister Stephanie asked me, "Why the bummed look?"

We sat on opposite ends of the couch, watching afternoon reruns of *Sabrina The Teenage Witch* with me on my second bowl of Doritos.

I offered the rest of the bag to Stephanie. "I need a ride to Jane's nursing home."

She declined the bag. "I'm watching my figure. And why do you want to see Jane? I thought you hated her?"

"I don't *hate* her," I said, licking the orangey cheesy goodness off my fingers. "I just don't like how she treats me sometimes."

"Gotcha. Just go see her another day when Mom's home to take you."

"I kind of want to make amends *today*. Otherwise, I may lose my last nerve."

"Call Matt."

"Tried. He's on a family trip. I called Heidi, too, but she has a second summer job now. And Emily's stuck watching her little brother, like always. So, I'm crap out of luck."

"Call Caleb."

I looked at my sister as if she had two heads. "Out of the question."

"Yeah, probably for the best not to get involved or bring those old feelings back." Stephanie grabbed the tanning lotion off the counter. "Well, good luck with that. I'll be on the roof tanning."

A minute passed before I remembered Liam's offer for future rides. I found the paper he'd given me with his number and hesitated before calling. I didn't know if he'd been serious, but it was now or never, before I lost my nerve.

I cringed before finally dialing his number.

"Hello?" he answered.

"Hey."

"Hey, yourself."

"This is Sam, Sam Carey?"

"I know who this is, you weirdo. That's why I replied, 'Hey yourself.' It's kind of our thing. Plus, I think I know your voice by now."

"True," I laughed.

"You know, I tried calling you a few days ago; I got your number from Adam. I was checking to see if you needed a ride to the lake."

"You did? I didn't know you called."

"I think your sister answered and said you were still sleeping and that you were still grounded or something."

"Yeah, I was still caged in then. But Sunday was my last day, so I'm a free bird now."

"Well, that's good news."

I was uncomfortable coming out of the gate asking for a favor, so I made a small talk first. After a few minutes, I finally caved. "Well, there is a reason why I called. Remember when you offered to take me anywhere if I needed a ride?"

"Yeah. And I meant it."

"Well ... today would be a perfect time to take me somewhere IF you aren't too busy? It's only fifteen minutes from my house."

He laughed. "Sure. Where to?"

"Really? Okay. So, I need to go to this nursing home, but my parents are at work. And everyone I know who has a car is unavailable."

"So, you're finally ungrounded and choose to go to a nursing home as your first go-to? And did you just say I was your last choice for a ride?"

"Well, I feel bad even asking you, which is *why* you were my last choice. Liam, we've only hung out a handful of times, and here I'm already asking you for favors? How pathetic I must seem to you."

"You're not pathetic, and I would love to help you. I can come by in thirty minutes?"

"You're the best. Thank you."

Before Liam hung up, he asked, "So do you have a grandparent there you're visiting?"

"Jane's my ex-boss. We're not related. But I do feel connected to her in some way, even if she seems more like an evil step-grandmother of some sort. Anyway, we kind of ended on bad terms, and I'm trying to make it right. It's a long story. I can tell you all about it in the car when you pick me up?"

"Sounds good. I'll see you in thirty."

I fidgeted with Victor's bracelet the whole way to Jane's as I explained my weird and complicated relationship with my boss to Liam. He seemed to understand my need to make things right. "Yeah, regrets are something I wouldn't want either." He glanced at the red mark I'd made on my wrist. "You're nervous about talking to her, aren't you?"

I didn't tell Liam it wasn't just Jane who made me nervous. Even though his statement about me at the lake seemed innocent enough, I felt the urge to cover my kneecap with my hand after I noticed I'd forgotten to shave that area. "Nervous is an understatement. I have no idea how Jane will receive me. She probably hates me for putting her in this place."

"What's your favorite ice cream?"

"Ice cream? I don't particularly like the stuff."

Liam lightly tapped on his brakes, as if threatening to stop the car. "What? You're kidding."

"It's weird, I know. But my teeth are sensitive to the cold. Also, I kind of need to crunch on something when I'm eating. And I'm not too fond of popsicles, either. They're too sour."

"I don't think we can be friends," he joked.

I laughed. "It's not that I hate it. It's just not my favorite go-to treat. But if I had to pick an ice cream, maybe rocky road? There's a bit of crunch and chewing involved. And you can never go wrong with chocolate. What's your favorite?" I asked in return, knowing quite well he was trying to distract me from feeling anxious.

"Hands down, cookies and cream and or a root beer float."

"I'm more a killer of all pastries. Give me donuts, cookies, pies, cake, or my fave, cornbread with butter and honey, and I feel like I'm riding a magical unicorn on its way to Disney."

"Well, I guess you're redeemed, because Disney unicorns rock."

~

I didn't know what to expect when we pulled into Jane's nursing home. The place looked like a sad afterthought. The one-story beige building deemed itself dingy with a capital D, along with a few shrubberies in front that needed a good watering—which Jane would have never allowed. And with the roof missing a few shingles and the welcome sign sitting crooked, it did the opposite in making one feel welcomed.

We walked together toward the entrance, and I whispered to Liam, "This place reminds me of one of those old run-down inns on the side of a highway—always vacant—never full."

"Yeah. It does look a little depressing. But hey, maybe the inside is better?" But once Liam walked me inside and past the electronic doors, he looked around like I did at the drabby décor and whispered back, "Guess not. Looks like a horror movie from the 1970s." He pointed to a few chairs the color of dull maroon with muted tones of green swirls. "I'll just wait in this lobby while you do you."

He sat down next to a cute, aging bald man in a wheelchair with a few grey hairs on his freckled round head, who looked at Liam with piercing blue eyes and a toothless smile. "Hello, young man," he said.

Liam stuck out a hand. "Hello to you, good sir."

The older man seemed charmed to have someone pay him attention, and even as I walked away to sign in at the front desk, I could hear their voices carry, with the senior chuckling in response to something Liam said. It warmed my heart and annoyed me that Liam might be perfect after all.

"Which room and which way do I go to see Jane Nelson?" I asked the front desk lady after signing in.

The directions down the winding halls to Jane's room left my stomach twisting at each turn. With the distinct smell of urine, mothballs, and or something else that permeated the narrow hallways, I ignored the urge to cover my nose. Instead, I politely smiled as I passed a multitude of tired residents in their wheelchairs, all looking bored, staring off into space.

When a little older woman the size of a small child dozed in her chair with her chin resting in a low, uncomfortable spot on her chest, I wondered why someone didn't put her in her bed, where she could sleep more comfortably. The poor woman looked as if she would fall out of her wheelchair at any given moment, and I automatically rubbed the back of my neck, knowing she would have a sore neck when she woke.

Feeling lost, I made a guess and turned a corner to find the numbers on the wall were correct. And after walking past four more doors, I hesitated just outside Jane's room—number thirty-three. I'd made it this far, but my feet stuck like glue—refusing to move me past the threshold. Just before I gained my nerve and took a step forward, an older fellow behind me at the end of the hall shrieked, making the hairs on my arms rise in response.

With loud, incoherent wailing sounds like that of an ambulance siren singing higher and higher, I looked around to see who would help him. But no one came to his aid, even after he started to thrashed and banged his hands on his armrests.

I covered my ears as his wails grew louder and I frantically searched for a nurse. A nurse came out from a nearby room, and I quickly grabbed her attention, "Ma'am? Excuse me?"

"Yes?" she said, turning around, looking flushed and tired.

"I think the gentleman around the corner needs help?"

"That would be Kenny."

"Okay, well ... Kenny is hitting his arms on the wheelchair."

"He does that all the time. He's just bored. Don't worry."

"*Oh*. Okay," I said, feeling no better.

The nurse walked away without adding anything else, and I helplessly gave up before turning back to Jane's room with even heavier steps.

I loathed myself—fully aware of what Jane's new home represented. It reminded me of a place where someone discarded worn, broken, lost, and forgotten toys that had once had the purpose of bringing joy to many. My mother was right—nursing homes were a living hell, a place where one goes to rot away and wait for a wishful early death. And as much as Jane had made me angry with her harsh expectations, no one deserved to live out the remainder of their lives in such a sad, decrepit, and lonely place.

Guilt squeezed my heart, and I wiped away a remorseful tear that stung my eyes just before entering room thirty-three.

Here it goes.

Jane's bed sat closest to the door. And although she lay flat on her back, arms crossed, and her eyes closed as if napping, I wondered how anyone could rest with all of Kenny's siren calls down the hall. I noticed Jane's wrist was wrapped in a medical brace of some sort and wondered what the heck had happened to her.

Her roommate had not seen me enter yet as she continued to stare out the window to a dry and deserted courtyard with one lone birch tree. Judging her age from her side profile, the woman appeared taller and older than Jane. With white braided hair as thick as rope cascading past her hips, she reminded me of a sturdy senior Rapunzel—one who still hoped for her knight in shining armor to rescue her from the prison in which she now dwelled.

And I didn't blame her.

I looked around Jane's room with its bare essentials. The woman was already a minimalist, but the space reminded me of a small college dormitory, except without the personal touches and memories that some proudly displayed. I regretted not bringing flowers to add the slightest color to such a drab and depressing room. And even though she had her favorite African violets sitting on the side desk, they weren't yet in bloom. I presumed she probably hadn't been able to bring the rest of her prized plants because there was no room for such things.

I swallowed before leaning in, and whispered close enough not to startle her, "Jane?"

She flinched at the sound of my voice and adjusted her glasses to see who greeted her. I watched the recognition hit my old boss, and just as fast, Jane laid her head back down, closing her eyes—as if pretending she didn't see or hear me.

Typical Jane.

"Jane?" I braved again.

Eyes still closed, she responded with a clipped tone, "What do you want, kid?"

My legs were too weak to stand on their own, so I slid my jellied body into the chair next to Jane's bed—very unladylike. I glanced over at Jane's roommate and found her smiling at me kindly. I smiled back, but my words were for Jane and Jane only. "Jane?" I said again. "I came to talk, if that's alright?"

Jane finally opened her eyes but stared at the wall ahead as she dryly introduced me to her roommate with a surprisingly loud voice. "Alice, this is Samantha! Samantha, this is Alice!" Jane finally looked at me.

"Sam, you have to talk loud because Alice is deaf in one ear and nearly the other."

"*Oh*," I said, understanding. I faced Alice. "NICE TO MEET YOU, ALICE!"

"Not *that* loud," Jane barked.

Alice laughed. "Very nice to meet you, love."

Jane's mouth formed a thin line. "Alice calls everyone soul and love, so don't think you're anything special."

Alice's right arm hung angled inside a sling, and she cradled it with care. "Do they call you Sam for short?" she asked me.

"Yes, ma'am."

"And how do you know the enjoyable Ms. Jane here?"

The sarcasm in Alice's voice did not go unnoticed, and Jane gave a disapproving *hmph* sound.

"I used to take care of her," I replied.

"*Pshh,*" Jane huffed under her breath, sounding unimpressed.

Alice buffed back, "I can only *imagine* that must have been a difficult job for you, yes?"

Jane interrupted, "Alice, I'll take it from here. *Thank you*."

"All right. But please be nice to this here young lady, Ms. Jane. Don't want to be scaring her off." At that, Alice stood up. "I'll just go now and make myself scarce—see if I can trouble one of the nurses for some extra pudding. It's the only decent dessert here. You two want any?"

"No. I'm fine," I said. "Thank you, Alice."

Before Alice shuffled out the door wearing pink slippers, she looked back at me and winked before exciting, as if to say, 'Good luck, kid.'

And I did need all the luck I could get.

Jane struggled to sit up more comfortably before shaking her head disdainfully. "Alice is here only temporarily until her right shoulder heals. She's here for physical therapy for a few months before heading home. The rest of us—not so lucky."

The sting of her last words bit into my soft flesh, and my own words stuck in my throat, just like in my dreams. "*Um* ... so, how are you, Jane?"

"That's a stupid question. How does it look like I'm doing?"

"Not good. What happened to your hand?"

Jane held up her arm. "Sprained a week ago. A new lousy nurse's aide did this to me. He tried to make me eat my meals in the dining hall instead of allowing me to eat in the comfort of my bed. The aide wouldn't listen when I told him they couldn't pick me up every day, as my bones are too brittle for all that manhandling. But no, the idiot lifted me into the wheelchair and damned near broke my wrist. Now I just point to the board if they give me any lip." Jane pointed to a whiteboard above her bed where it read:

Resident with severe arthritis.
Bones fragile.
All meals in bed.
DO NOT LIFT!

"That's terrible, Jane," I said, looking back at her strained face. "I'm sorry that happened to you."

"Yeah, well, this place is a crock, which is what I expected when Charles couldn't find anything decent left with a vacancy. I suppose this is what you get for being a stay-at-home mother who never saved up enough for retirement. And with only having the state's Medicaid insurance, we could only afford this crap-hole. So, here I am. Twenty-four-hour care. Or they should call it twenty-four-hour neglect."

We stared at each other for a long quiet moment before I got to the point, my words coming out in a rambling torrent. "Jane, I came today to say I'm sorry about everything that happened between us. I was not at my best that day and acted unprofessionally. When everything quickly got out of hand, I lost my temper and said things I didn't mean. But I'm mostly sorry I quit on you. That was wrong of me. I didn't give us a chance to make amends or see if we could have made it work somehow. I regret that. Especially after seeing this awful place."

My apology might have shocked Jane Nelson, but I didn't know, not when her expressionless face camouflaged any and all emotions. She stared silently at the blank wall for what seemed like forever. It gave me hope when her shoulders finally relaxed. "I'm not going to lie, kid; you get my goat most of the time. I know I was hard on you at times, but that was me wanting to prepare you for the world. I didn't want you to make the same mistakes I made." Jane scratched under her bandaged wrist. "Some of my actions are just part of who I am. Do you think I want to be this angry person all the time?" she said defensively.

It was a rhetorical question, but I answered anyhow. "No."

"It's not like I woke up one day and thought, 'I want to be a bitter old shrew. I know my temperament gets the best of me more often than not, so I'll admit that much. And maybe what you said was right, how I push people away. I would like to change that, but changing who we are isn't always easy."

Jane's *almost* apology was better than I had expected. All the built-up tension left my body, and I nodded. "Change is hard," I said, agreeing with her. "I've been trying to change for the better, and you're right; it's not easy. And I suppose if I were in your condition—suffering in pain every day—I would be more than irritable too. So, I understand. My only wish is that I could have been more understanding at the time."

"Well, yes, since you put it that way, my pain does make me testy. You mentioned that you're trying to change. Does that mean you're not poisoning your body with all that drinking? It would be such a shame to waste a perfectly healthy body. And as I said, that day when you left, I only wanted to ensure you didn't make the same mistakes as I did."

"Yes, I see that was your point that day. Again, I was too angry and maybe not in the right head space to see where you were coming from. But yes, I stopped drinking. And the change feels good."

I went into detail to catch Jane up on my trip to Mexico and could tell she was genuinely happy for me. "Sounds like you had a wonderful life-changing experience. And you're right; we must be thankful for even the littlest things. It's hard to remember that. I regret not having seen or done more things when I had the chance, before my disease took hold."

"Jane," I said, looking down at my ripped shorts, playing with the fringe-tattered holes. "I feel responsible for you being in here. This place is ... it's awful."

"You're right about this place being awful. But no. Charles made it clear that I'm the sole reason I'm here today. He's right in some ways. So I take full responsibility. Who knows, maybe it all happened for a reason."

"What do you mean? You want to be here in this place?"

"No, of course not. No one in their right mind wants to be in this hell hole. What I mean is, while I've been here, I can see a little clearer now. My roommate Alice made me see things differently. Alice is in the Godly way, if you know what I mean." Jane said, placing her hands in prayer and looking up at the ceiling. "She showed me that everyone has to make mistakes before learning the ins and outs of life. Mistakes are what makes us *us*, I guess."

"This makes sense."

Jane shook her head. "I guess I still have much to learn, even at my age. Anyway, Alice gave me no choice but to see my errors, as you had tried to make me see as well. You are not me, and you have your own path of mistakes to make. I shouldn't begrudge you life experiences that will ultimately shape you."

"Alice seems like a very wise woman."

"Yes. Alice is good and decent. When Charles visits me on the weekend, he tends to visit with her more. Everyone loves Alice. You would love her, because she's nothing like me," Jane laughed.

"I'm happy you and your son are okay now."

"Charles and I still have a long way to go to mend our relationship, but we're making strides."

"Family issues are no fun. I wish my family didn't always fight."

"Every family has its issues; that much is true. But for me, my family troubles stem from something deeper. You could dig as far as China, and I would have still wanted to keep those secrets buried. But I've recently learned that some secrets might need to surface. I know I'm to blame for everything, but I will eventually need to come clean with my son about why our family was the way we were. He still doesn't know anything about his father and the depths that that man went to ruin all our lives."

Jane looked at me with her head tilted. "You've never met Charles, have you?"

"No."

"Charles has always sided with his father. Maybe I'm to blame for sheltering him from all the bad and keeping him in the dark about everything that went on under our roof, but the worst part is, sometimes, I can't even look at my child. He's the spitting image of the *one person* I hate with every fiber in my body. Could you imagine such a thing for a mother to feel? For her own child?"

"No," I said sadly.

"It hurts me to say this, but my boy is a constant reminder of something that burns deep inside—hotter than this crippling arthritis that runs through my bones. And I know none of it is Charles's fault. None of it." Jane's head hung low in defeat, and when her eyes met mine again, it broke me to see the unbearable pain behind them. "The real reason I pushed Charles away for so many years is that Charles is the lucky one. He's the one who got away without any scars—scars that never healed in our family. And I envy him for that. But I know it's the memories of what my husband did that truly feed my envy and starve me of a full life."

I had no idea why Jane trusted me enough to tell me about her pained past, but I owed it to her to listen. I touched my fingers lightly to her trembling shoulders and encouraged her to let out whatever pasts held her hostage.

Jane closed her eyes. "It's as if he kept pulling me underwater. And each time I died, unable to find the surface, everything that lived and breathed so effortlessly became a constant reminder of the life he stole from me."

Chapter 28

Jane 1972

After coming home from the psych ward with plans to kill my husband, I took my first hot shower without being watched and monitored. As the water washed over me, I thought of Kathleen and my soon-to-be grandchild. It's funny what your mind can think up when you harbor so much hatred for someone. I was so consumed with it that I forgot the most important thing.

What good was I to my daughter and her child if I ended up in jail?

I slid to the shower floor and closed my eyes in defeat.

I couldn't go through with murdering my husband. My possessed thoughts were reckless at best. Again, I had lost sight of what was important. I stepped out of the shower with a new focus. The days of playing make-believe were over for me. I needed to lay those fantasies to rest for good, because Kathleen and my first grandchild had to be my only thought from then on forward.

But plans are fickle things.

The day I tried to salvage the broken in our family? Never happened. Like a shipwreck after a storm, the damage was too great, and what little hope I had left came crashing to an end. I often asked myself, where exactly did I go wrong? When did the storm first begin? Could I have stopped it if I had recognized the warning signs?

I think the storm started with my husband's billowing betrayal of affairs. And after that, the shipwreck that followed had to be the pills that carried me away. Without even realizing how far I had drifted, that was when I gave up. It may not have been intentional, but the pills made me lose sight of everything important, and salvaging anything after that felt hopeless.

~

I knew Friday night was my chance to talk alone with Kathleen. Charles had already left for the weekend to stay at his friend's house, and Daniel had left for the night shift at work. I only prayed my daughter would forgive me for my past choices so we could start fresh. I wanted to tell her that she could trust me to help take care of this baby, even though Daniel had made me look crazy by overdosing me and sending me to that terrible mental facility.

Entering my daughter's room that night, I found her covered with a blanket, lying on the bed, napping, or pretending to be. I sat down at the foot of her bed, wondering how much the baby had grown and if she had yet to feel the baby kick. "Kathleen?" I said.

When she didn't answer me, I tried again, "Please look at me. I have so many questions. Can you please talk to me about this?" She continued to ignore me, but I forged on. "Look. I know I haven't been there for you for quite some time. But I'm here now."

When Kathleen remained unmoved to my touch, I silently observed my daughter's bedroom. Pink and green were her colors. Drawings, poems, quotes, and a few Beatles posters covered her wall, along with miniature purses and colorful scarves draped over a chair.

When had she started accessorizing?

I was a lousy mother for not knowing.

The cream dresser beside her bed sat adorned with a music box, which lay open, with trinkets inside—bracelets, ribbons, and hair ties. A brush and a handheld mirror lay next to the box, along with a white vase of artificial daisies. A record player sat in the corner with a few records splayed onto the floor, as if she couldn't decide which to play first.

I didn't even know what kind of music she liked.

And near the corner of her bed, Kathleen had lined up old baby dolls and stuffed animals—a reminder that she'd been little once. Even as a little girl, she had always wanted to be a momma one day. But now my baby girl was pregnant at fifteen.

A baby having a baby.

My hand smoothed over her floral comforter, and I took a deep breath before pushing on. "I have not been here for you these last couple of years when you needed me the most, Kathleen. And I can't tell you how sorry I am about that. I know you are unhappy with who I have become, and I don't blame you. But if you give me a chance, I want to show you I have changed. I stopped all the pills, honest I have."

Kathleen rolled her body towards me and jerked herself upright, a loathing expression on her face. "Change? You can't change. You're the most selfish person I know, Mother. You have always only cared about one person. Yourself. You lock yourself away each day and never give a damn about your kids, and now you say you've changed? Well, it's a little too late for that."

Her anger towards me was warranted, but I couldn't give up as easily as before. "It's not too late," I cried out. "And I do care, Kathleen. I love you both *very much*." My hand reached for her, but she flinched away as if I had burned her. "Please, Kathleen, I know I don't say it enough, but I do; I love you. And I know I've been absent. I wanted to care more about what was going on before; I swear I did. This is not an excuse, but all those damn pills the doctors gave me, they ruined everything. I couldn't think or see straight, let alone be the decent mother you kids deserved."

A few tears rolled down her cheeks and onto the comforter. She whispered something under her breath, but I didn't quite hear her.

"What? I didn't hear you, Kathleen. Speak up. I want to fix this."

"If you love me so much, why did you force him to take me to that place? Why? How could you?"

"What place?"

Her nostrils flared before the lashing, "You don't care about me, *Mother*, or you wouldn't have told him to do this to me!"

"Do what?"

My daughter's face reddened. "You can't even admit it as we speak."

"Admit to what? That your dad cheated on me? That I live with a man whom I no longer know? Or that I took pills to wake and pills to sleep? That I became lost and was drowning little by little? Well, I admit to all of that. And yes, I was not myself for quite some time, but I want to make it right. I just hope it's not too late for us."

"Mother! Just *stop*! You pretend you don't know, but you do. He told me. He said you forced him to take me to that awful place to end it."

"End what? And who is him?"

Kathleen's voice broke, "Daddy."

I shook my head, not entirely following. "Kathleen. What in God's name are you saying?"

Tears spilled from my child's eyes as she choked out the unfathomable, "You told Daddy to take me to that doctor's house. I thought he was only checking on the baby, but he got rid of my baby like *you* wanted. I bled so much that Daddy had to take me to the hospital to repair the damage. I was there for almost a week, Mother. But you know this because you planned it from the beginning."

The room seemed to shrink smaller and smaller, taking my daughter's words far away from me. But just before an endless black hole sucked me in and dry, I returned with the sound of Kathleen's forced laugh. "By the look on your face, I'm assuming you didn't know I ended up in the hospital or what happened next." She gave me a grimacing face full of hate and disgust. "Thanks to *you*, I can never have children. I will never be a mother. But it's just as well, because if I ever turned out like you, I wouldn't want to be born either."

No other words could split me wide open. With skin flayed inside out and exposed, I covered my ears. "*No, no, no. Please* don't say that. Kathleen. *No.*"

I stood up too fast and held onto the bedpost for support, seeing black spots. Even as my child's face twisted in anguish, I wanted to believe she was lying, only to hurt me for not being there for her. But I gravely asked, "Tell me you're making this up. Tell me you're lying."

When Kathleen got out of bed and ripped the covers off, it was then that I saw the flatness of her belly through her thin t-shirt.

No more did a belly hold my grandchild.

No more did my hope of holding a babe in my arms.

No more were the songs I would sing to him or her.

She came two inches from my face, jabbing a finger into my chest. "You're the one lying, and you *KNOW* what I'm talking about. Don't act like you're surprised, Mother. You may not have known I had to go to the hospital, but you told Daddy to take me to get rid of my baby in the first place."

Her sharp, jagged words pushed me back a step, and my heart bled out. There were no lies in my daughter's truth, but how I wished there were. I stood immobile and shaken to my core with the sickening thoughts of what Daniel had done to our baby and the baby that once was. My perception of the depths my husband would go to make his life easier had not even been close.

A tsunami of my mistakes came rushing in and swallowed me whole, and once again, I found myself in murky waters. Except this time, the currents surrounding me now held a monster unlike anything I could ever imagine. And no amount of swimming could save me from my husband's claws, which continued to pull me under. I thought my husband would only hurt me, but I was wrong. Now both mother and daughter were drowning in storm and sorrow.

I desperately grabbed my child by her shoulders and shook her hard. "You have to believe me, Kathleen. I didn't know. This is all your father's sick doing." My hands shook as I reached up and grabbed my sweet baby girl's face. "Look at me. Kathleen, look at me!" She looked into my wild eyes as I pleaded with every fiber of my being, "I swear to the Lord above," I cried, "Kathleen, I promise with everything in me, I *would NEVER* have allowed such a thing." I begged my daughter again, "You have to believe me. Please, God. You have to believe me."

Kathleen broke and fell to the floor, sobbing, "I ... I don't believe you."

If I had a knife, I would have killed myself right then.

I deserved it.

The unraveling sorrows tore at me, and I doubled over. The unfathomable nightmares my child would have to carry for the rest of her life were unbearable for any fifteen-year-old, and I could never erase the mistakes that had brought us to this point. My child was no longer a child but a broken product of her parents, and I hated myself. But I hated *him* more for letting him ruin all of our lives. We lived with a monster, and I was to blame for not protecting her.

With hands clenched at my sides, my eyes took a scathing glance around my child's bedroom at everything that would remind her of her loss. I panicked, threw her dolls into the closet, and shut the door behind me, fearing they would haunt us. But it wasn't enough.

I wanted to burn the whole house to the ground.

Running to the bedroom I was forced to share with Daniel, I grabbed everything and anything in sight and imagined it was him that broke into a million pieces. Glass figurines shattered everywhere; pictures and lamps I demolished instantly; blankets flew off the bed, and sheets ripped and tore as I shredded them with my bare hands. Nothing was left but a million scattered pieces of heartbreak.

An inaudible muffled sound came from behind me, like words formulating underwater. I finally snapped back into the moment—

finding Kathleen's voice bubbling to the surface, "Mother, STOP. Stop, please," she cried. I turned to face her and found her hand cradling her empty belly, as if hoping it was all a bad dream. She whispered the only vital words that could heal part of me: "I ... I believe you."

Relief flooded me, and I fell to my knees, weeping at her feet. I looked up into those hardened eyes that had softened just barely enough to let me in, "Thank you," I cried. "Thank you for believing me. I'd rather die a thousand times than have you think I would *allow* such a thing. I didn't know, baby girl. I didn't know. And I can never be sorry enough for not being here to save you from him."

Kathleen bent down to help me stand, and once I stood on unsteady feet, she motioned for us to sit on my empty bed that I had just destroyed. And for a long time, we held each other, crying for all we had lost over the years. But we both knew it was my Kathleen who had lost the most.

Our foreheads still touched. "I didn't know anything. If I did, I would have taken us away from all of it, Kathleen. I wanted you to keep the baby," I cried. "I wanted my grandchild."

As I wiped Kathleen's wet cheeks, she said, "I wish you never left me here."

I pulled away to look into my child's eyes. "That's the other thing I have to tell you. It wasn't my fault when they took me away. I can never prove it, but Kathleen, I think your father put the leftover medication I had stopped using into my coffee that morning the ambulance took me. I think all along he wanted to—" I couldn't say the words out loud and nodded to her stomach instead. "He knew I would have *never* agreed. That's why I think it was his plan to put me away in that mental hospital so he could take care of things here at home."

"You think he poisoned you?"

"I am almost one hundred percent certain. And there is something else you should know. I only ever took pills to sleep and wake up because I was in complete depression when I found out your father had been cheating on me our entire marriage. I wanted to leave him, but he wouldn't let me. He threatened to take you kids away from me for good. But it was my fault for seeing too late that the pills would eventually take me away from you kids, regardless of my husband's threats."

My daughter absorbed my words before nodding. "I believe you."

Of course, she would know. She saw firsthand the depths her father had taken to destroy not only her life but the child she'd once carried.

I laid my head on my pillow, exhausted, but I couldn't stop thinking of that sick, lying bastard. I nearly cried all over again. "If I could only go back to the beginning where it all went wrong, Kathleen, I would."

My daughter lay beside me and cried. "I missed you," she said.

Her words killed me for the second time that night. My child lost a mother when she'd needed one the most, and she'd lost more than that too. But I wasn't going anywhere anymore. My mind was clear, and I would do anything to save what had been lost. In the bed I shared with Daniel, Kathleen fell asleep in my arms. And for the first time in a long time, I protected her.

~

Sometime in the middle of the night, the sounds of my husband coming home awoke me. My heart pounded in my chest as my hands slowly fisted at my sides, and my nails nearly broke through to the skin as I thought of all the reasons I hated him. And I wanted him to suffer as we had. I wanted him to pay for his sins. The hurt stopped here.

I quietly climbed out of our bed without waking my daughter and headed to the bedroom door to listen. While recollecting all the terrible memories and hurts Daniel had brought me over the years, and now, with him destroying my babies, I walked to the opposite end of our bedroom and pulled my father's thirty-inch Winchester shotgun off the wall.

I couldn't remember if the gun was loaded, so I grabbed the extra bullets from the drawer. In my rush and haste, I accidentally dropped the box of shells, which made a loud *thud* when they hit the floor. I froze and prayed Daniel hadn't heard the noise from the kitchen, and I was even more surprised Kathleen slept through it. The poor girl was exhausted.

I tip-toed back to sit at the edge of my bed and waited in the dark.

He must have heard the noise, because it wasn't long before our bedroom door handle creaked with an unlatching turn. When the sick bastard came slithering into our bedroom, I had to swallow the bile at what I was about to do.

The moonless night left our bedroom a sea of pitch black, but my eyes had already adjusted to the darkness, while his had not. He couldn't see me waiting for him with a shotgun aimed right at him, and he couldn't see the wicked smile across my face.

"Jane. Did you hear that?"

When Daniel nearly reached the side of the bed, that's when I cocked the gun. My husband stopped dead in his tracks at the bullet clicking into place, and the sharp intake of his breath satisfied me more than I could imagine. I had not killed him yet, but my voice was just as deadly. "Stop right there."

Kathleen woke with a jolt from a dead sleep while Daniel quickly turned around and slapped the light on. As light flooded the room, I'll never forget his surprised, shocked look as he registered the chaos and what was left of the room I had destroyed.

I stood up, aiming that gun right at his heart. "I'm glad you turned the light on. It helps to see the devil more clearly." He stepped forward, and I threatened, "Take one step closer. I dare you." The snarl and grimace on my face should have said it all. "It's over."

"Mother?" Kathleen questioned.

"You have to trust me, baby," I said, without taking my eyes off my target. "He won't be hurting anyone else ever again." I wasn't ever really going to kill him. I only wanted to scare him enough to leave us for good.

Daniel stared at the barrel aimed at him and dared a glance over at Kathleen, but I shook the gun at him, screaming, "Don't you *dare* look at her! You look right at me and only me because *this* is the face I want you to see before I kill you!"

Daniel backed up with his hands in the air. "Now, calm down, Jane." He assessed the room while trying to exert his authority over us. "Just calm down and tell me what the hell is happening here?" He ignored my warning. "Kathleen?" he questioned her again.

I shook the gun and screamed at him again, "Shut up! Don't you speak to her. You don't get to speak to her after what you did to her."

"I don't know what she told you, Jane, but you've gone crazy again. Look at this room. Are you not taking your pills? Maybe I should call the doctor right now," he said, backing up.

The laugh I made sounded like a cackle coming straight from the mouth of a crazy person, but I was the most sane one there. "Go ahead and call them so I can tell them it's *you* who is crazy," I said, waving the gun. "Because what kind of father would scheme to such levels? I'll tell you. A sick, thieving father who takes away his daughter's choices and then destroys her future of ever having children. *You* will *never* hurt any of us anymore. Whatever game you are playing to have your control over us, it's over, Daniel!"

My finger wanted to pull the trigger, but I hesitated when Daniel's face lost its composure. "Look, I'm not perfect," he said, with his chest rising in waves. "But I love you both. Can't you see that? I had to do what was best for everyone."

"You sick bastard. *This—*" I said, circling the gun around his sickly body aura, "this isn't love. You are the opposite of love. Love didn't give you the right to choose what's best for us. You destroyed my life and your daughter's life just so you could continue a life of whoring around. You only do what's best for you. You don't know the meaning of love. And it ends here."

"Fine," he said bitterly. "You want me gone? You want to blame me for all of it and the cheating? Go right ahead. But I might as well tell you. All my cheating started because deep down, I knew you would have chosen that idiot soldier boy over me. After everything I did to prove I loved you, you still would have picked him. I knew in my gut you were pining over him. Even after he died, you *still* pined over him. Do you know how that made me feel, to be second best? To have my wife love another man?" Daniel gave me a smug look. "That's why I had to do what I did. I will always get what I want, Jane. And the poor kid didn't even see it coming."

"What the hell are you talking about?" I asked with a sickening feeling.

"Even with my daddy's fists beating it into my head, saying I would never amount to anything, he was wrong. Because he taught me two things: never lose a fight, and know how to fix a car. You were mine, Jane, and I wasn't going to let him win if I could help it."

The gun in my hand feverishly shook when I finally understood. "Clint didn't crash his car because he was drunk, did he?"

"That's the thing about brakes, *Janey*. Sometimes they work, and sometimes they don't."

Daniel's words came with a sickening knowledge that scraped and scratched at my skull like hell fury. "No!" I screamed, not wanting to believe it. "*Noooo!*" I envisioned Clint's face then, my sweet Clint, and thought of the poem he had written me, 'Without you, I wouldn't exist.' But the truth was, if I had never brought Daniel into the equation, Clint would still exist today.

It was all my fault.

"My God," I cried out as angry tears poured from my broken soul. "You are sicker than I ever imagined. God above me, I wish I had never met you, Daniel Foley. You do not deserve to live."

It was clear that Daniel regretted speaking his mind, because the smug look on his face quickly vanished. "Jane. Wait. Stop."

"No! This is for Clint. This is for all your cheating lies and forcing me to stay a prisoner in my own home. This is for putting me in that place where you tried to make me forget, and this is for our little girl and our grandchild who never had a chance!"

With steady hands, I gave him one last look before pulling the trigger.

But not a second before my finger made his world black like his heart, Kathleen's hand cautiously covered mine. She stared at me like someone helping a lost soul down from a ledge and gently removed the gun from my grasp.

"Kathleen. *No,*" I said. "Please," I begged her. "Let me do this."

Daniel quickly saw his chance and coaxed her, "That's a good girl Kathleen. Now listen to me. Slowly hand me the gun so no one gets hurt, alright?"

Kathleen stood tall and surprised us both when she braced her footing and pointed the gun at her father.

For the second time that night, I enjoyed seeing the shocked look on his face.

With firm conviction in her voice, she faced our monster. We faced our monster. "No, Daddy. You are right about one thing—no one will get hurt anymore. It's over."

"Okay. *Okay*. I hear you," Daniel pleaded with a fearful look.

"No! You lied to me. You said you were taking me to a good doctor to look at me, and after what he ... after he killed my baby, you lied. You said it was Mother's idea all along." Tears slid down her precious face, but she held her ground. "*You* are the liar. I believe you never meant for me to ruin my chances of having children ever again, but there is no going back. You hurt me, and I can never forgive you."

"Kathleen. Listen, baby."

"No." Kathleen's eyes blazed with pain as she screamed, "Mother told me everything! And now, what's this about you killing someone named Clint? Don't you think you've done enough to us? Please, Daddy. *Please.* Please, just go."

The heavy gun became unpredictable as she trembled, and Daniel pleaded again, backing up, "Kathleen."

"I won't put this gun down until you leave this house. Leave now. I'll call the police and tell them everything myself. Is that what you want? I swear I'll tell them, Daddy."

For a moment, my husband's face held one last daring look, and I welcomed the chance. In my mind, I mentally willed him to make a move. I wanted justice served; for me, for Kathleen, for the baby, and for the man who had to be my forever. Clint.

But just when his shoulders dropped, I knew he'd given up the fight. And without a word, Daniel Foley turned and left our lives forever.

"It's done, baby," I said, gripping my daughter to me for dear life.

She dropped the gun to the floor, and for once, we were safe. Safe but forever broken and damaged.

Chapter 29

Sam 2003

"Taking all that medication back then and losing my reality caused a ripple effect—an unexpected downpour, Samantha. And like a shipwreck after a storm, exhausted and without direction or purpose, you just give up, and allow the current and waves to carry you without a care. Some may end up on a calm, safe beach where second chances exist, but others, like myself, risked landing near rougher and rockier destinations, one that cut me deep, leaving me with a lifetime of scars and fears.

"I just didn't know that what lay beneath the currents was *far* more dangerous than any storm. Because if I have learned anything from surviving my mistakes, it's that you must *never* give up on what is important. I should have kept swimming with absolute determination, never losing sight of what was at risk and what can be lost when giving in to the storms of life.

"And now you know. My past is the reason I am who I am today. I can never escape from these memories. I'm *angry* at the world for giving me nothing but pain and tears. My life was supposed to be filled with love and beautiful memories, but it only left me with nightmares." Janes's story haunted my thoughts, and I wished to find the words to ease her pain, but she carried on. "I was a mother who was supposed to protect her child. Choosing to love Daniel was the beginning to the end, and I hate myself for being so blind and naïve."

"You didn't know what kind of man Daniel was, or who he would become, Jane."

"It doesn't change anything, does it? I will forever be sickened that Kathleen should have had a father to trust rather than the one who stole her future. I am saddened and angry that cancer stripped Kathleen of whatever was left of her spirit at the age of twenty-nine. And I am disgusted at myself for the resentment I have towards my son. He still knows nothing and still blames me for his father leaving, and yet, at the same time, I blame him for being the spitting image of the very man I hate. But my biggest regret is not pulling the trigger myself."

"Oh, Jane, don't say that."

"Why? All that's left of me is anger, hatred, sickness, sadness, resentment, and regrets. I sit here every day, suffering not just from my disease but from scars in my heart that never healed. All the while, a horrible man lived and breathed without ever enduring a single consequence. He never had to suffer from his choices or pay for the lives he obliterated."

Knowing that Jane was not a murderer after all, and only wished she had the chance at one time, I asked her, "Why didn't you turn your husband in? He should have gone to jail for what he did to Kathleen, for poisoning you and for killing Clint."

"I had no proof of what Daniel did to Clint. It happened so long ago. As for Kathleen, her father had already told the hospital that the young man who got her pregnant was the one who took her to that back-alley doctor. And even though Daniel almost killed our daughter in the process, Kathleen didn't have enough courage to go to the police. As much as her father hurt her, she still loved him. I know that sounds sick, but love is complicated. Plus, how were we to turn someone over to the authorities if we never knew where he went?"

"You never saw him again?" I asked.

"No. That's why Charles hates me so much. He blames me for his father leaving without even a word of goodbye. He blames me for destroying our family."

"Why didn't you and Kathleen just tell him everything?"

"Because he was already disappointed in his mother, so why cause him anymore hurt to know his father was the worst possible human being? There was already too much hurt to go around. Why make it worse?" Jane shook her head. "I should have pulled the trigger and buried him when I had the chance. Every day I think that's why my hands have stiffened with the disease. It's my karma for not having a pliable finger to pull that trigger."

"You already blame yourself for so much, Jane. Killing your husband would have just left your children without a mother. I truly believe that Daniel will get what's coming to him one day in hell. That is *his* karma. But having all this anger and all this hate bottle up inside you doesn't help you heal, Jane. It hurts me to see you like this."

"Fine then," she said, wiping a tear. "I wish that if there is such thing as hell, karma hits him so hard it sends him straight to the deepest pits."

I patted her hand and added, "Me too. Me too."

"Sometimes, I welcome my disease. I feel I deserve it for all the wrong choices I've made. It's like my own form of punishment."

"Your disease is not a punishment. It's just ... it's just beyond unfortunate, is all. It's unfair, if anything."

Jane stared up at the ceiling. "Everything I touch ends up destroyed."

"Jane, I don't know why some are given fairytales and happily-ever-afters while others are given sad and unfair lives, but I know you didn't deserve any of the horrible things that happened to you, Kathleen, and Clint. And you didn't destroy anything. Daniel did."

I looked at Jane and hoped she took my words as true. "You know, in a way, I look up to you and your daughter for fighting and loving and never quitting when it counted. You two were like women warriors, fighting battles worse than grown men experience, and yet, you lived through it all. If I were Kathleen, I'd be honored to call you my mother."

Jane let out a small sob, and I hurried to gently hold her broken frame as she poured out fifty years of heartbreak and betrayal. I now understood the who, what, and why Jane was the woman she had become. Like pieces of a puzzle, it all made sense. The warrior in Jane was tired, weary, and beaten. I would be mad at the world too.

She wiped her eyes with a tissue I handed her. "Your words are too kind, Samantha, and I don't deserve them. But if you say I am this woman warrior, my only wish is to lay this sword down and finally be with my sweet Kathleen. And my Clint, if he will still have me. I'm just so tired of this life, and I'm ready to move on to the next."

I nodded in understanding, but thought of something I had recently learned about disappointing people and disappointing even yourself. "Jane, maybe the past wouldn't hurt so much if you forgave yourself? If those you love were still here today, I know they would truly and wholeheartedly want you to forgive yourself. No one blames you."

Jane's chin wobbled in doubt. "I don't know if I can do that."

"You have to *try*," I said. "It begins with you understanding that some things are out of our control, and what happened to you was not something you did on purpose. The mistakes you made are forgivable. Please try and forgive yourself."

Jane looked up to the ceiling as if conjuring all the loved ones she had lost before her. "I suppose I could try. For them, I'll try."

"You should. Because at some point, we must accept the unfairness of life and move forward. Forgiveness might not erase the past, but could allow the soul to move forward."

Maybe it was the light playing tricks on me, but I could have sworn the furrowed lines on Jane's forehead smoothed a little, like a crumbled love letter pulled from the trash, reopened, and given a second thought. And her eyes that had once held so much bitterness and sorrow finally softened in what looked like acceptance, forgiveness, or both.

Because I now understood the woman behind the hard shell, I told Jane I would come back every week to visit her, as she had grown on me like a wart that I could possibly live with and learn to love. And maybe that was the key to life, I thought, as I headed back to find Liam. Life was about learning to love others, beginning with yourself first.

~

Liam was not in the lobby where I had left him. I looked at my watch and cringed. "*Crap*." I'd been with Jane for over an hour. I didn't blame him for leaving.

The receptionist behind the counter grabbed my attention. "Miss?"

"Yes?" I answered.

"If you're looking for the younger gentleman, he wanted me to tell you that he's in the dining hall. It's down the next hall and to the left."

"*Oh*. Thank you."

Not wanting Liam to wait any longer, I rushed to the mess hall to find him playing some game with Jane's roommate, Alice. As I approached the pair, Liam's eyes met mine, and I searched his face for any indication that he was irritated with me for leaving him for such a long spell. After all, it was his summer, and hanging out with a bunch of geriatrics probably wasn't at the top of any high-schooler's list.

But the corners of Liam's lips curved upward. "Hey, he said, seeming happy and content.

"Hey yourself," I laughed.

"How did it go?"

"Surprisingly amazing," I beamed. "So, what are you guys playing?" I asked loudly enough for Alice to hear.

Alice moved a tiny plastic peg into a hole inside an odd wooden board. "It's a card game called cribbage," she said.

Liam moved a peg into a slot. "You ever play?"

"No. Can't say I have ever heard of cribbage."

Liam stood up and motioned for me to sit. "Here. Take my spot, and I'll show you." After he explained the rules, he laughed. "Oh, and I should warn you. Alice here likes to cheat and move extra spaces if you're not watching closely." He pointed a playful finger at her. "She says she's a Christian, but watch this one."

Alice chuckled in an agreeable nod, as if cheating was a notable quality. "Game on," she said with a mischievous smirk.

After Alice beat me by a landslide in only twenty minutes of playing, Liam cocked his head in wonder. "*Uh* ... wow, Samantha. I don't think I've ever seen anyone get such a bad hand of cards. Don't be going to Vegas anytime soon," he joked.

"Oh, quit; it's my first time."

Alice spoke to Liam through the side of her mouth, "Hey, you can bring her anytime. She's an easy beat, and I didn't even have to cheat."

I stood and laughed. "It was very nice meeting you, Alice. I'm sure I'll see you next week. And thank you for letting me play."

~

After I bought Liam a thank-you-for-taking-me burger, we ate in his car with the windows down. My legs were sticking to the seat as I told Liam all about my session with Jane, but I didn't care. I was a million pounds lighter.

"I'm happy for you both, then. Sounds like a good day all around."

"Yeah. It wasn't something off my summer bucket list, but it feels better than that." I turned toward him and pointed a fry at him. "Now, as for that game you showed me? It involves adding, and I suck at adding."

Liam nearly choked on his burger. "What? It's simply adding anything that equals fifteen; nine plus six, eight plus seven, five plus—"

"No, I get it, but ... can I tell you a secret?"

"Sure."

"I never memorized my addition." Liam squinted one quizzical eye at me, not fully believing me. "No, really," I said. "I still have to use my fingers. That's how my first-grade teacher taught us, and I guess I've been too lazy to sit and memorize it all. Plus, I have the worst memory when it comes to math. I do, however, excel in English. But don't get it twisted; I've memorized all my multiplications, FYI."

"Really? But addition is the easiest to memorize," he teased. He set his burger down and faced me. "Quick, what's eight plus five without using your fingers?"

I did the finger counting in my head. "Thirteen."

"*Samantha*. That took you almost three seconds to answer. Ask me any addition problem with double digits, and I'll give you the answer in less than half a second."

I flattened the Don's Drive-in paper bag and passed it to him along with a fry as a makeshift pen. "*Wow*. A number wizard. Can I please have your autograph?"

"Haha. If it makes you feel any better, English is my worst subject. Guess we excel in only the things that interest us because I will probably never pick up a book if I don't have to. That's how much I hate English. But I like stories read to me."

"Crap," I said, reaching down to the floorboard. "Speaking of books, if Jane forgave me today, I was supposed to ask if she liked this genre."

Liam grabbed the book for me. "Do all romance covers have these pictures on them?"

"How else will we know if the character is hot?" I said, laughing.

He shook his head. "You girls and your fantasies." He put the book on top of the dash. "Well, since we are on the subject of fantasies and summer bucket lists, I have an idea."

~

We drove around town for ten minutes before parking. "Oh. This is a Decoursey park," I said, recognizing it. "When my sister and me were little, my mother used to take us here to feed the ducks."

Liam took the book from off the dash. "Ready?"

We walked a bit before coming to a beautiful creek with a few ducks floating about. Liam stopped after we went under a little bridge to get to the other side. "Do you trust me?"

I gave him a wary look with only one eye open. "I think so?"

"Good. We have to walk through and then across this creek to sort of go onto someone's private property. But, I think it will be worth it." We waded across the cool and refreshing creek, and as the water closed in over my knees, Liam held out his hand. "Here. The rocks are slippery right here."

The moment I took his smooth hand in mine, a live wire beneath my skin shot its way up to my cheeks.

"So, how did you happen upon this spot?" I asked, feeling the sudden need to talk.

"I brought my dog here once. After he took off to chase the ducks, I found him in this yard I want to show you. You'll see."

The sun's rays sparkled over the water's slow current like gemmed crystal, allowing me to see the mossy veins of vegetation that waved over the rocks beneath our feet. The hair of moss looked as if it belonged to a green goddess mermaid swimming, and I smiled in awe. "This has to be the prettiest creek ever," I said.

"That's what I thought the first time I saw it too."

We reached the opposite end, where a few homes sat far back from their lawns that butted up to the creek's edge.

And then I saw it. A few yards away was the largest of weeping willows. The massive tree bent its body halfway over the creek, with its graceful long arms sweeping delicately and playfully into the wandering stream below.

"It's beautiful," I whispered.

"It is. Beautiful meets beautiful." He held out the book to me. "You said you wished to find the biggest weeping willow so you could read under it. So bucket list, check," he said.

I let go of his hand and took the book without trying to reveal the glow of my cheeks. I knew Liam was trying to get me to be more receptive when someone gave me compliments, but I wasn't sure I would ever get used to it. His compliments sat with me for too long.

We made our way over to the tree, and I gave a worried look at the house a ways back. "Do you think we'll get in trouble for being on their property? I'm not interested in another trip to Mexico."

"The tree's branches with leaves are long enough. I'm pretty sure they won't see us sitting underneath it. We're good."

I crouched under the tree's long limbs and found a log to sit on before opening the book. A fresh sprig of lavender nestled itself between two pages, and I smiled, wondering when Liam had time to sneak it in there.

Liam found a massive rock halfway in the water and sat, dangling his feet across from me. "Well, go ahead and read it to me," he said.

"What?" I laughed. "You expect me to read to you a romance novel? No. That is not happening."

With the sun behind his head, it gave him a glowing halo. "The whole novel can't be that ... that dirty. Just find a few pages without all the mushy parts."

I skimmed over the first chapter before deeming it safe. "Alright. This page looks innocent enough."

I read the first two sentences to Liam and suddenly hated my voice. And while the story continued about a modern woman who was left crying at a church until suddenly a gorgeous knight from the 1500s came to her rescue, I couldn't help but feel Liam's eyes watching me. It was one thing reading to Jane from time to time but reading to Liam, under the shade of the tree with the sound of the creek bubbling, I wanted to hide my bare feet under the rocks for some reason. Eventually, I had no clue about the words coming from my mouth, so I shut the book after the second chapter. "So?" I said. "You like?"

Liam scratched the back of his neck and blinked. "The book?"

"Yeah. What else?"

He gave a half laugh before reaching down to find a rock in the stream to fidget with. "What are the odds those two fall in love?" he asked, not meeting my eyes.

I didn't know if it was his rhetorical question that made me laugh or if it was the way his face flushed. "They may be complete opposites, but I'm betting the odds are high," I said. "Although I'm not sure how a relationship can exist when one of them lives in the future and the other is from the past."

"Time travel at its finest." Liam's eyes finally met mine. "You'll have to tell me how their future ends."

"Sure. But I am almost certain it ends with kissing."

Liam stood and skipped his rock. "Speaking of the future, a bunch of us are going bowling tomorrow night. You're welcome to join since you're done with parties."

"You saw how well I played volleyball last week. I suck at bowling and *all* sports, for that matter. But sure, why not add some more fun and torture."

"No one will throw a bowling ball at your head. You'll be fine. Just call me around ten tonight. I still have to find out the exact details from Adam, who's planning it."

"Alright. Sounds fun. Do you know what time?"

"It's called Midnight Bowl, so I would probably have to pick you up close to 11 p.m. since it starts at midnight exactly."

"Oh, that's pretty late. I'll let you know if my parents say yes or not."

"I thought they ungrounded you."

"They might be leery about the time. I'm not to be trusted at the stroke of midnight. Also, if I forget to say it, thank you for showing me this amazing tree and taking me to see Jane today."

"I'm happy you two made amends. Maybe next time you'll introduce me to her?"

"She'd like that. But beware; she might flirt with you."

He laughed. "I'm not married, so I might flirt back."

My parents surprised me when they said yes to bowling so late. Apparently, I was a fully redeemed adult after I told them I went to see Jane to apologize. While I sat on our couch waiting for Liam to pick me up, I yawned and hoped I could stay awake long enough past two in the morning. The night prior, after I'd called Liam to get the details for bowling, we'd lost track of time and stayed up almost til dawn talking. It seemed we both had diarrhea of the mouth, and talked about our lives—beginning, middle and current. I felt nearly whole when speaking of how my troubles were behind me, and stuck didn't feel so bad after all.

The knock on the door pulled me out of my dazed thoughts at the same time my mother came out of the kitchen.

"Bye, Mom," I said before she came any further.

My mother stopped me. "I need to meet this new guy of yours."

"Really? Can't you meet him another time? And Liam is just a friend. Nothing more."

"Sam, we just want to know who to call if you go missing again."

"Fine. But please don't embarrass me."

"What? But that's what parents are for."

Twenty minutes later, Liam was laughing.

"What's so funny," I asked, as he drove us.

"I can see where you get your sense of humor."

"Well, I'm just glad she didn't search your body for a hidden flask of alcohol. She may have forgiven me for everything, but she hasn't forgotten just yet."

"Do you think she believed me when I said *I* didn't drink?"

"I think so. You seem the honest and reliable type."

When I yawned for the third time, Liam looked at me and frowned. "You're tired already? We're not even there yet."

"Hey, you're the one who kept me up late last night talking. Which, by the way, is weird. Considering we have zero in common."

"Well, yeah, that's what makes our conversations so interesting. Having a friend who's my complete opposite makes me a well-rounded individual. And here I thought I couldn't get any better."

"Wow. My compliment that you're nearly perfect has gone to your head. Just put the halo down already."

I pointed to the large sign when we pulled into the back parking lot. "They should have named it Tulip Bowl instead of Daffodil Bowl. Tulips are my favorite."

"Roses aren't your favorite?"

"Nope. Hate 'em."

"You're so weird."

"Thank you."

"Okay, so since you love tulips, here's a fun fact—and I only know this answer because my mother always buys tulips at Van Lierop's bulb farm half a mile down the road. I guess Puyallup and Sumner valley farmlands used to be the nation's largest producers of daffodils and tulips. I bet they almost did name it Tulip Bowl."

"Wow. Reliable and knowledgeable—a rarity. Your parents must be so proud," I teased.

"The rarest. Want to hear a tulip joke?"

"And you say I'm weird."

The minute Liam opened the door to a vast dimly lit, smoke-filled room, rock music blasted us along with a strong dose of cigarette smoke. "I wish they would make it illegal to smoke here," he said, the neon décor making the whites of his eyes and teeth glow. "Every time I leave here, I have to convince my parents I don't smoke."

I looked at the bar with its row of beer-drinking chain smokers buying colorful pull tabs lined up against the wall. "Too bad I didn't know that. I just washed my hair."

While loud video games lined the walls to our right and the sounds of bowlers and pins crashed down lanes to our left, Liam pointed to a group of six on lanes twelve and thirteen waiting for us. I immediately recognized Adam and his girlfriend, along with two of Liam's basketball friends I'd met at the lake. And after a few high fives, Liam loudly introduced me to two girls, one of them being Liam's girlfriend.

I waved an awkward hand up. "Hey."

She was pretty, with a small, athletic body, straight black hair, and kind green eyes. If she was worried about Liam driving me here alone, she didn't let on as we made small talk. Plus, I remembered Liam mentioning they both were used to having friends of the opposite sex.

After talking for a bit and adding names onto the screens above our lanes, we all separated to find individual bowling balls. I was alone when I spotted a bright pink one clear across the room, and just as I bent down to retrieve it, I heard Liam's voice a few feet away.

"Sena, it's not a big deal."

They couldn't see me squatting, but I heard his girlfriend loud and clear. "Why did you bring *her*?"

"What's the big deal? It's not like you don't talk on the phone and hang out with guy friends all the time. It's innocent, okay? Samantha's cool. Give her a chance."

"But since when do you pick girls up and drive them places?"

"I'm just trying to be nice, okay? She needed a ride, and meeting new people would be good for her. Look, why are you acting like the jealous type? You've never cared before. Why *now*?"

"I don't know. I'm Sorry. Let's just find a ball and play. I don't want to fight."

Only when the coast was clear did I stand up and hug my pink ball to my body. Great. I was an unwanted third wheel. I immediately wanted to go home, knowing Sena had probably only pretended to befriend me for Liam's sake, but I couldn't find a good excuse. My parents were already in bed, and asking Liam to take me home seemed unfair. So instead, I slowly returned to our assigned bowling lane, all the while giving myself a pep talk that I could handle a few awkward hours.

I passed by the lane just before ours, recognizing a few people from school—Sarah Hansen being one of them. When she saw me, I waved hello, but her returning smile came the same as always—disingenuous. I wanted to ask her for a ride home since she lived just down the road from me, but I opted out. I didn't think I could handle even one car ride with someone who gave me the vibe that she wanted me dead so she could wear my skin all over town.

The rest of the night went by with fake smiles, meaningless conversation, and a not-so-stellar bowling score, so I was more than ready to leave when Liam took me home at two in the morning.

Liam parked in front of my house and shut off his engine before facing me. "Are you alright? You seemed ... off tonight. Not really your perky self."

"Sorry about that."

"Was it too weird that my girlfriend was there? I should have told you she was coming."

"No, Sena was nice. But that's not why I was off." That last part was a lie, but I didn't want to cause drama, so I told him the partial truth. "I'm just tired, is all. That's two nights in a row that you've kept me up late."

"Would you be too tired to help me pick out some basketball shoes later today?" With Sena's words playing heavily on my mind, I almost declined until Liam pointed out, "You know, you kind of owe me for all the car rides."

"How can I forget?" I turned to face him. "Why don't you ask your girlfriend to help you?"

"She has prior engagements. Plus, you're a girl. You love shopping."

"Actually, I rather loathe shopping."

The lack of light in the car made him look dark and mysterious, but the tone in his voice came sweet and innocent. "Pretty pretty, please?"

Liam was right when he'd told Sena we were just friends, and he was right that I also owed him for so many things. Like how he always made sure I was safe when drinking at parties, especially by hauling me away when Ronnie could have murdered me, or how he made me laugh when helping me prank Jay at the lake, and how nice he was to drive me to see Jane when I had no one else, and how sweet it was of him to help me mark something off my bucket list.

"Sure. What time?" I said, caving.

"Is 9 a.m. okay?"

I blinked my heavy eyelids just once. "That's ... less than seven hours from now, Liam."

"So?"

"So, it's summer, you freak. Don't you want to sleep in till noon like the rest of us?"

"Yes, I get that Saturdays are for sleeping in, but I have to leave today around noon. I entered a weekend basketball tournament called Spokane Hoop Fest. I needed basketball shoes like yesterday, but I didn't go shopping at that time because I had to take a special 'someone' I know to a nursing home."

"I see. I see. Fine. But after this, we're even." I looked down at my watch before shutting my door. "I'll see you at the crack of dawn."

Chapter 30

Sam 2003

"These shoes are cute. No?" I said six hours later, showing Liam a pair of red Nikes at the mall. "You could even match your car. How snazzy would that be?"

"No offense, but *cute* is not the word I'm looking for."

"What are you looking for then, exactly?"

He flipped over a shoe on display to check the price before looking at me. "I'm looking for something to admire, yes, but more importantly, I also need something with stability and longevity. You know, durable—to last forever."

"Well, they don't make shoes that last forever."

"They might if I take good care of them."

We had been shoe shopping for over an hour, and Liam seemed not to care that I had zero knowledge about basketball shoes and, more importantly, how much I hated shopping. I wasn't your typical girl who would drop everything to tackle such a tedious task. Maybe because money was always tight, and shopping for me had been more about bargaining diligently to match whatever was in my wallet, but I longed for my bed over shopping any day.

"What about these?" I suggested pointing to a pair of white ones. Liam was a little too picky for my liking, especially so early in the morning. And with little sleep, my patience began to run thin.

He wrinkled his nose in distaste. "Huh, no. They remind me of those doctor shoes at the hospitals."

I ran a hand slowly down my face in frustration. "Why would you buy a brand-new pair of shoes right before a full weekend of basketball anyway? Won't your feet hurt? Most people have to break into their new shoes beforehand to avoid a million blisters."

He shrugged. "I once had shoes die on me during a game, and we lost because I had to sit out."

"Fine." I held up a pair of shiny black ones. "What about these? These specifically say, 'court shoes' right on the display sticker. Perfect for the occasion."

"I don't know ... the sides don't seem long enough. They need to be a little higher so I don't sprain my ankles."

Throwing my hands in the air, I exhaled, "I give up," before dropping my butt onto the bench in defeat.

"You're quite the irritable one this morning," Liam said as if reading me for the first time.

My words came playfully but with a hint of truth, "And *you,* Mr., are picky." I waved my hand at the millions of shoes in front of us. "Let's choose a pair already. I'm not getting any younger here."

"Now I feel horrible asking you to come so early. You're obviously still tired from the last few nights."

"Sorry. You were so patient waiting for me when I was with Jane. The least I could do is act like this is fun."

"Did you not eat breakfast?"

Feeling light-headed since I hadn't eaten for sixteen hours, I crossed my arms and pouted, "No."

"That explains everything. You're tired *and* hungry—a bad combo. Forget about the stupid shoes. I'll have to take you to the food court before your head starts spinning."

I laid down and closed my eyes while curling up on the bench like a cat. "It's fine. I'll just lay on this bench while you find what you're looking for."

Liam grabbed hold of my arm and hoisted me up. "Nope. Get up. Let's go before they kick us out thinking we're homeless."

~

Liam didn't order anything for himself but watched me eat as if I were a science project gone wrong. Usually, I wouldn't approve of someone staring at me while I ate, but I didn't care as I scarfed down my veggie breakfast burrito.

"I'm a little worried," Liam said, tilting his chair back with his hands behind his head.

With a mouthful, I asked, "Why's that?"

"I don't know the Heimlich. Do you ever chew your food before swallowing?"

I suppressed a smile after finishing my breakfast in record-breaking time. "Sometimes."

"Don't get me wrong," he laughed, "you may be gorgeous, but you eat like a trucker."

I laughed. "I've been told that before. I guess I mean serious business when I eat. I do have a fast metabolism and am a little anemic. My iron levels get low if I don't eat every so often."

"Then remind me never to take you anywhere until you've eaten. You had me scared back there at the Nike store."

His response made me laugh again, "Sorry. I'm in a better mood now. If you want, I can continue helping you shop. But wait." I tilted my chin up and gave him a wide toothy grin. "Is there any spinach in my teeth?"

Liam came close to my face for a thorough inspection. "Nope. Everything is perfect."

~

It was nearly one in the afternoon when Liam finally dropped me off before having to drive four hours to Spokane. I didn't even reach the front door of my house before my mother called my name from behind a bush, "Sam. Just in time to help me pull weeds."

All I wanted to do was climb into my cozy bed and sleep the rest of the weekend away, but after looking at all the trimmed bushes in the yard and the sweat matted to her head, it was clear my mother had been working outside for quite some time. The old me would have brushed her off with excuses, but I liked the new me, and decided to help her for the next few hours.

When my mother returned from inside the house with a glass of iced tea, she handed it to me. "Thank you for helping." She looked around. "It's shaping up quite nicely out here."

"It is. I can see your roses now."

"Speaking of other things shaping up nicely, I wanted to say again how proud I am of you for going to see Jane yesterday."

"Me too. Except, Jane still has to stay in that horrible place. And Charles isn't moving her back to her duplex, so that means I still need to find a job."

"I'll take you to see Jane as often as you like so she doesn't feel so lonely there, and as for a job, you'll find something. Don't worry." My mother sat beside me and placed one of our new cordless handsets beside her. "I miss my antique phone, but these cordless ones are so convenient. Your sister is supposed to call me to pick her up later."

"Yeah, I like these modern phones way better. We're finally like normal people," I joked. "The other night, I got to lay in bed for hours talking without being stuck in the kitchen. It's a nice change."

"I thought I heard someone's voice talking at around three in the morning when I got up to use the restroom. Who were you talking to?"

"Oh, that was Liam. I didn't even know how late it was."

"Your new friend seems really nice."

"He is," I said, smiling. "He is so different than most guys I know."

"And very handsome."

"It's not like that," I said. "He has a girlfriend, and I had Matt to think about for a while, so I've never thought anything past a friendship."

"Well, I'm happy you seem happier. You seemed down for a while there, especially after everything with Caleb and Matt."

I picked at the grass and let it fall through my fingers. "People calling me a cheater, with the whole Matt and Caleb drama, wasn't the best of times, no. I really thought I would have to transfer schools at one point," I laughed. "But lately, people have been nice again, and I feel good. Even without a job or a car, I can honestly say I'm happy. I'm in a good place."

"Good. That makes me happy to know you're happy. I have a good feeling about your senior year. Things are going to be amazing."

The phone rang, and my mother grabbed it. "That's probably your sister." She got up to leave but stopped and turned around, handing me the phone instead. "Sure, Matt. She's right here."

She winked before handing me the phone.

I walked inside, where it was slightly cooler. "Hey, Matt. How was your mini family vacay?"

"It was fine. But hey, I'm not calling to talk about me. Don't freak out, but I wanted you to hear it from me before hearing it elsewhere."

"Heard what?"

"I don't even know how to say this."

My heart raced when hearing the worry in his voice. "Matt, spit it out, will you?"

"Adam just called. He said his girlfriend got a call from Sarah Hansen, and apparently, she's calling around telling people that ..." I took a large swig of the tea at the mention of Sarah's name, and just before Matt finally blurted, "Liam slept over at your place after bowling?"

I choked and spat out my tea. "What?"

"Samantha, I know. I didn't believe it."

"Matt, you mean like people will think we slept together?"

"Yes. Like Liam slept over, and you two slept together or *something* along those lines."

"Matt, you know that is not true. I would never."

"I believe you."

I chewed on the inside of my cheek. "Why would Sarah start something like this?"

"Hell if I know. Maybe Caleb started it?"

"He wouldn't be *that* mean. Would he?"

"I don't know. Either way, the news is making the rounds now, so don't be surprised if you get a phone call from a few people. I'm really sorry. I knew it was a lie as soon as I heard it."

My stomach turned over on itself. "Why is it the moment you say you're happy and life is good, that's when it all goes to shit!" I wanted to cry. "Matt, a rumor like this is going to ruin what little reputation I had. I might as well go live in a nunnery!"

"I know. I know. But calm down. It's going to be okay. Look, I'm sorry to be the bearer of bad news, but remember, just like last time, when the bad news hits the masses, after a while, it dies down. You'll find a way to clear your name, and if not—"

I didn't let Matt finish whatever he was about to say. "Thank you for giving me a heads up, but I need to call Liam immediately."

"All right. But call me later when you figure it all out. Let me know if I need to beat someone up."

"Sure," I said.

~

I pinched the bridge of my nose, trying to figure out how to stop the storm from wiping me out and almost dialed Liam's cell number until realizing the news would ruin his weekend tournament.

Sarah-freakin-Hansen. WHY?

I knew I had to go straight to the source.

After punching her number in a little too hard and starting over, she answered on the first ring, letting me know she was probably already on the phone to half the world with my name loosely on her lips.

I barked or maybe growled, "Sarah!"

"Who is this?"

"It's Samantha Carey." I didn't waste time making pleasantries. "*Please* tell me why you're saying Liam spent the night?"

"Okay, listen, before you freak out—"

"Nope. That's already happening," I said, pacing the kitchen.

"Fine, but *you're* the one ruining your own reputation, so don't pin your problems on me."

"What? You are the only problem, Sarah."

"Really? You know Liam has a girlfriend, right, Sam? I can't help what I saw this morning."

I clenched my jaw and gripped the phone. "Please, Sarah, enlighten me on what exactly you saw. Did you see Liam and I sleep together? Was he braiding my hair while I painted his toes? Please, what truths did you see? I'd like to know."

"No, I didn't see you two physically do anything. But it's a telltale sign of what happened since I saw that he stayed overnight."

"Sarah, he did no such thing! Why are you lying, and what kind of game are you playing here?"

"I'm not playing games. I saw what I saw. Liam's car was there late last night after bowling. I went bowling late, too, remember? So, on my way home, I saw his car. But he never left. His car was still there when my mom and I drove by for Sunday church this morning. No one else has a red Mustang. Everyone knows Liam's car."

I wanted to reach through the phone and choke her to death. "ARE YOU KIDDING ME?"

"What? I saw what I saw!"

"What you *saw, Sarah,* was Liam dropping me off after we bowled, and then he came BACK to pick me up in the morning to take me to the mall to help him pick out a pair of basketball shoes. We are just friends. My God, you misread everything, Sarah. He left and came BACK!"

"Well, excuse me. It looked like he spent the night."

"You have singlehandedly ruined my reputation, and I doubt you even care that people will call me a slut and a homewrecker. What you should have learned at church this morning was that you don't go around assuming things you don't know and then gossip about it the first chance you get. How hard was it to call me and ask me?"

"Whatever. It was an oversight. And I only told a few people."

Her apology wasn't even an apology. "With the few you've told today, it has already reached Matt, and it's only been like, what? Four hours since you started this rumor? I swear I have had this conversation with you before. Come to me *first* the next time you think the worst of me. No, I take that back; there will never be a next time, because if I ever catch you dropping my name in any pool again, I will personally drown you myself!"

I slammed our new phone down, nearly breaking it. There was no remedy to the dark stains on my reputation, because, like always, people loved believing lies over the truth. My summer, my senior year, my life was officially over.

~

My wish to sleep the weekend away came true. I never left my room. And by the time Liam called me late Sunday night after his trip, I tried to keep the hurt hidden but couldn't. Not when my nose was stuffy, and I sounded like I had been crying.

"Sam, I don't know what to say. I feel awful. All I can say is that people are jerks."

"Yes. Yes they are. How'd your girlfriend take it? From what I hear—not well."

"Yeah. We sort of had a big fight before I called you." Liam took a deep breath before pausing. "She doesn't want us to be friends. She's totally paranoid even after I told her whoever started that rumor is an idiot and a complete liar."

"The biggest liar."

"Look. My girlfriend believes we didn't spend the night together, but only because my parents confirmed to her parents that I was indeed at home sleeping after we bowled. I hate that Sena's parents are so close to mine, and they call each other about everything."

I controlled myself from hyperventilating into panic mode but couldn't control the sarcasm. "Oh *great*. Your parents and her parents are involved? This is rich. It's super great Sena believes you, Liam, really. And I'm happy for you. But *I* am the one who got a million phone calls yesterday from people inquiring whether or not we slept together. And I can tell them it's not true until I am blue in the face, but let's face it, people want to believe what they want. And now, apparently, the word is out that I'm a boyfriend-stealing cheating slut." I knew none of it was Liam's fault, but the unfairness that I would get the brunt of the abuse gave me a heaviness I couldn't shake.

"I'll tell everyone the truth, Samantha. I'll make the calls today and fix everything."

"The damage is done. I'm the villain once again. I was already an outcast with the whole breaking up with Caleb thing, then just when I thought it had almost all died down, I'm back in this unforgiving and negative light where I can't see my way out."

"I am so, so sorry about all of this, Samantha. It's my fault. None of this would have happened if I hadn't asked you to the mall or bowling. At the time, I didn't see the harm in our friendship."

"Your girlfriend's right about one thing: friends or not, you shouldn't be taking me places. It doesn't look good, especially for me." Swallowing my tears never tasted worse and it physically hurt to say the following words. "I ... I can't see any other way around it. We can't be friends. The rumors are too much." I wiped a runaway tear, bitter that it got loose at all. I didn't know why saying goodbye to Liam hurt more than my breakup with my ex of four years and worse than telling Matt he wasn't my forever. And I'd mostly never imagined my friendship with Liam, which somehow made me feel whole, would end with me splitting in half with a goodbye. "I can't see you again. I'm sorry, Liam."

Liam sat quietly on the other end for far too long, and I wanted him to hurry and end the call before I had a full-on cry-sesh. "Samantha, I don't want to stop being friends. I have had so much fun getting to know you. You've become ... you've become my favorite person lately. *No one*, not even my girlfriend, can tell me who I can hang out with or who I can't be friends with."

He was brave, sweet, and kind for standing his ground, but I had nothing to stand on. The ground beneath me swallowed me whole, and once again, I wanted to leave town for good this time. "*I'm* telling you, *I* can't see you again. The gossip will only stop when *we* stop. I need to save face. I needed to leave the country, like two days ago. And as much as I hate it, we just can't be friends."

I knew Liam's silence meant he was trying to find a way for us to remain friends, but there was no easy out, and he knew it. His voice came low—almost inaudible, "You sure you want this?"

I lied, holding back a sob, "Yes. I'm sorry. Goodbye, Liam."

Chapter 31

Sam 2003

They say not to let people determine your worth, and that the only way to stay above the water is to ignore the naysayers. But that advice seemed only appropriate for the courageous and sturdy types. Not for me. I was like a thin branch that broke with the slightest of winds.

"It's been nearly three weeks of hiding. You're missing the rest of your summer," my mother said. "Stop being a hermit and go do something already." When I didn't move from the couch and continued to surf through a few more channels mindlessly, she clapped her hands at me. "Come on, Samantha. Just call someone and go outside today. It's a beautiful sunny day. Call Matt, Heidi, Emily, or even Liam if you want."

My stomach dropped at the mention of his name, followed by the hurt and loss all over again. I didn't even know what the hell was even wrong with me or why I still cared so much. "I'm fine alone."

"Do you want to go see Jane again today? I can take you."

I had seen Jane nearly every week as promised. Now that I no longer worked for her, the expectations had disappeared, and we got along great. We talked about everything under the sun, except my issues. I didn't want to bum her out with my current sad and pathetic life; it was hard enough for the woman who lived in a joyless coffin that served only green jello. But because no one's heart broke more than Jane Nelson, misery loved company. "Fine," I said, getting up from the couch. "Let's go."

"Do you want to brush your hair first? You look a little wild."

"Jane doesn't care."

~

"Should we begin where we left off last week?" I asked Jane, sitting in my usual chair beside her. We were halfway through the same romance novel I had first read with Liam, under the willow tree. As I looked down at its cover, with the title *A Knight and Shining Armor* by Jude Deveraux, I knew I would never get the chance to tell him the book ended.

"I think we left off where Douglass had to transport Nicholas to his time period before he died," Jane said loudly enough for Alice to hear.

Jane and I had agreed to skip the few sex-fluffed parts for Alice's sake —she'd almost choked on a biscuit when I'd read a sentence containing, 'his hand on her thigh.'

Jane shook her head. "I'm not sure how Douglass will convince Nick they were once in love. He has no memory of anything that happened in the future and thinks she's a crazy mad woman."

Alice pulled up a chair and sat next to me. "I have faith in them," she said, pointing a finger in the air. "Their strength in their love will be proven. Nicholas has *got* to remember her. We can't give up hope. Men can be idiots, but you'll see. Go on, Sam, keep reading."

After reading four chapters, and with my audience grossly invested in the next scene, I paused to drink from my water bottle before asking, "Do you two think it's possible that in this decade, a few hotties on horses could just come rescue us already? Like, take us far away from all this meaningless nothing?"

Jane coughed and wiped her nose. "I think you have a better shot, girl. At least you can climb up on his horse." She coughed again. "I can't seem to shake this cold, sorry."

I didn't want to say it, but she looked terrible. She had been sick for over two weeks, and the doctor was finally coming later that day.

"Horses are overrated anyway," Alice said. "I'd be just fine with someone pulling up on a big yacht. Take me out to the sea, and let's travel the world by boat."

Jane cocked her head to one side. "I didn't wanna say anything, but you seem morose today. And last week, you seemed off too. But as I said, I didn't wanna say anything. Do you want to tell me what's gotten into that mind of yours?" she asked me.

I shut the book closed. "I don't know. It's just that this book is supposed to make me happy, but all it is doing is reminding me that fairy-tales don't exist, do they?"

"I thought the same thing years after losing Clint and learning what a monster I married. But deep down, I believe that if I had never been persuaded to look any further beyond Clint, I would have found that fairytales exist. Samantha, you have nothing to worry about. You have your whole life ahead of you to choose the path you want to take. That special someone is out there, and when the time comes, you'll know he's the one and *only* one."

"How? How will I know he won't be a creep like Daniel?"

"Oh, I know the answer to that," Alice said, clutching her hands to her heart. She looked up to the ceiling. "He'll be the one who consumes your mind and thoughts. He will be the one who makes your heart ache with longing and your body ache to be held, and you'll never want him to let go. But remember, he should be someone who will fight for you. That's very important."

I didn't know if Alice was talking about God or an earthly man or if she secretly read romance novels, but I laughed. "Wow, Alice. He sounds perfect. It sounds like you once had a fairytale ending."

She looked at me with such seriousness that I knew there were many stories to be told behind those light blue eyes. "I did once," she said. "That was forever moons ago, though."

"Well, if you two say fairytales are possible, then maybe there's still hope for me," I said.

"Good," Jane said. "Now stop worrying about finding love, and let's get to the next good part of the story, because I'm not getting any younger here."

"I second that," Alice said.

~

Another week had come and gone. Typically my Saturdays on a hot summer day would consist of enjoying my time at the lake with my friends, but instead, I insisted on joining my mother with the morning grocery shopping. But when we arrived home, I saw Matt's truck in my driveway, along with Heidi's and Emily's cars.

"Mom," I said. "What the heck is everyone doing here?"

"I hope you don't mind, and please don't be angry with me," my mother said, "but I called in the reinforcements."

"I wish you wouldn't have."

"Look. Your friends have been calling you for weeks. Stop pushing everyone away. It's time to come back and join society."

I couldn't argue with her, not when I walked into my house to find my friends sitting on the couch waiting for me.

"Well, well," Heidi said. "What's this? We don't even exist anymore? Am I right, Emily?"

"Yeah," Emily said before looking at me. "We're worried."

Matt held our Chinese pug Ollie on his lap. "It's time for an intervention—knock some sense into you. You can't hide forever."

I snatched my dog from him. "I can stay here forever if I choose to. A girl just needs her home and her dog, and everything will be fine."

"You don't look fine," Heidi said. "So this is your solution?"

"Actually, yes. That and I should especially stay clear of all men. I'm thinking that this September, instead of going to school, maybe I join a nunnery and give my heart to the One and Only. Seems the safer choice."

"Funny," Matt said. "Look, this is stupid." He stood and grabbed the dog back from me. "For one, you're scaring the dog, and two, you sound like a crazy person. Have you been taking your vitamin D? Because that's what happens to crazy people when you stay secluded indoors too long without sunshine."

With the thought of having to face my adversaries for one more year in high school, I gave Matt a sarcastic look. "Fine. Skip the nunnery. Maybe I should go to a different school for my senior year."

"Now you're being ridiculous," he said. "So what if a stupid rumor is going around? You're above it."

I scoffed. "Don't you get it? It's different for us opposite-sexers. Guys aren't held to the same standards as we are. The ramifications for a woman, especially when rumors float about saying she's a whore, are completely different than they are for men. If you were called a whore, you would most likely relish in it, and every one of your friends would high-five you as you become the most popular guy in school."

"I get that, and yes, it's totally unfair how everyone is viewing you right now, but Sam, some things may never change. And then what?"

Emily cleared her throat. "I think what Matt is trying to say is that you shouldn't stop living your life just because of some social norm."

I sat down with a thud. "Everything was going so beautifully for a while, and boom, in an instant, I was robbed of a new identity. And you know what, you guys? I finally loved the new me. It's like having a new colorful flying kite, and you're minding your own business—living your life high in the sky, happily and free, and when suddenly, someone steals your colorful kite and returns it completely trashed. I looked outside. "Trust me, I want to fly a kite again, but you have no idea what it's like to feel torn and ripped with no wind in sight."

"I'm not saying your situation doesn't totally suck," Heidi said. "And we wish we all could fix it for you. But at some point, the show must go on. Wave your freak flag and forget them all!"

"Just come hang out at the lake with us," Matt added. "If you keep hiding, the more they'll think the rumors are true." Matt let the dog down, and Ollie jumped to lick my face. "See? Even the dog agrees."

"Also," Emily said, "we miss you."

"I know. But I'm not ready to see anyone."

"Have you talked to Liam?" Heidi asked me.

A tightness gripped my chest. "No."

"Well, I have," she said. "And that guy is just as miserable."

I thought of Liam more times than not, wondering how he was faring. Surprisingly, I still missed him, even weeks later.

"And what do you want me to do about it?"

"Call him," Heidi said.

My eyes felt wet. "I can't."

Matt looked at Heidi before he looked at me. "What Heidi really wants to say is, we don't know exactly what's going on except ... well, we may know you better than you know yourself. We think you might kind of like him, Sammy. And we also think he likes you too."

My jaw dropped. "What? No, you guys. He has a girlfriend."

Heidi shrugged. "We might be totally wrong here, but we think there may be something between you two, whether he has a girlfriend or not."

"I—"

"Wait, just hear us out, please," Heidi said. "We've seen the way you two look at each other—as if no one else is in the room. And there are other telltale signs, like your body language. If he leans left, you naturally lean in that direction too. If you turn to walk away, he watches you go. And when either one of yous talks about each other to any of us, there is a light in both your eyes and a sweetness in those smiles. So yes, you may be blind to it all, but we're not. And you might not want to fully admit it yet, but something exists there."

I couldn't stop the jackhammering in my chest. "Just to make it clear, I am *not* that girl who steals other people's boyfriends. This kind of talk isn't helping anything, you guys."

"Sam, don't get so mad," Emily said. "We're not here to judge. Just answer this one question. Would you see Liam differently if he didn't have a girlfriend?"

"You know what? I've never thought of that scenario, so I don't have an answer for you guys, or whatever it is you're looking to stir up." I set the dog on the ground. "What is going on, you guys?"

Emily scratched her head. "Can you at least be honest with yourself and tell us how you felt after you cut Liam out of your life?"

I looked down at my beaded bracelet for a long minute before facing them, angry they'd put me on the spot. "It felt like crap, okay? Is that what you wanted to hear? Are you all happy now? Yes, the rumors hurt, but I guess it hurts more that I can't be friends with someone I've grown to care for. I can't explain why I'm mad, angry, and depressed, and why the hell I miss someone I barely know." I wiped a tear that got loose. "But I can't think about him in any shape or form. All I need to do right now is keep my head low under the radar and focus on somehow getting through another stupid year of high school. And then, I'm out of here."

Matt let out an exasperated breath, "Always wanting to run away when things get sticky."

"Yeah? So what," I said bitterly. "Looks like the new me isn't so new after all. Same ol' Sam—stuck where nothing ever changes."

Emily's voice was quiet when she stood to look down at me. "Sam, if you want things to change, then prove to everyone that you don't care. Come with us today to the lake. Because hiding and being bitter and angry won't help." She sounded like me when I'd told Jane her bitterness and anger did nothing for her mental well-being. Guess it was easier to give advice than to take it.

"She's right," Heidi said. "Summer is wasting away, and we won't let you become a hostage in your own home. We're putting our foot down."

Matt stood up with the rest of them. "Guess what. There's a nice breeze outside. You'll never know if you can fly that kite of yours if you don't at least try."

Even though my friends had hit a nerve with something I wasn't ready to admit or face, I looked at them with both annoyance and admiration for their determination to help me. I knew I was having a pity party for myself, but they were right. As much as I hated it, they were right. I couldn't hide forever and needed to fly at some point. As for the other things they'd said, I couldn't think about him.

"Fine," I said. "I'll go. But only because you three are relentless."

Emily swung her arm around and through mine, pulling me up. "Don't worry. We won't leave your side today. We promise."

"Good," I said when they all hugged me, "because I have no idea which way the wind will be blowing when I get there."

~

"They all can suck it," Heidi said once we arrived at the lake.

By the looks on people's faces, the rumors had *not* subsided. My heart plummeted as stares and glares reached my peripheral vision. Even a couple of girls who'd been pleasant acquaintances merely weeks ago now gave me the stink eye, and the other few pretended not to see me at all.

When Heidi glared, hoping to scare them, it only made it worse. Their heads came together in low whispers, clearly painting me an outcast.

"Ignore them," Matt said, handing me a bottle of sunscreen.

I took the bottle. "I don't think this will help. I feel like I'm burning from the inside out, and I wish you guys hadn't forced me to come." I glanced over at the volleyball court and nearly panicked. "I can't do this. Liam is ... he's right over there."

Liam stood by the net, oblivious to the game in progress once he noticed us, until someone on the court called his name. "Hey, Liam. Your one-nighter is here."

A few people laughed, and I watched Emily's eyes grow wide at the same time as Matt stood up, holding his fists to his sides.

But before Matt could even take a step, Liam bolted toward the guy who'd made the hurtful comment and grabbed him by the shirt. "Shut your mouth, or I'll shut it for you, Joel."

I didn't know who Joel was, but I assumed he was from Liam's school. "Great," I said. "I have two schools partaking in my misery." I couldn't stay to watch and quickly stood. "Guys, I'll be right back."

"Where are you going?" Emily asked.

"To the bathroom."

Heidi stood. "We'll come with you."

"No. Please stay here. I can go potty by myself. I'll be okay," I lied.

I walked briskly to the restrooms before they could follow me and before anyone saw my meltdown. But with the bathrooms seeming a mile away, I made a bee-line detour into the forest by the cars and cursed when a few tears broke free. I was so sick of crying like a baby.

Stupid, stupid, stupid, Sam! Why did you come?

I'd barely reached the safety of a canopy of trees to hyperventilate when someone gently tapped my shoulder from behind. "Hey."

I turned to the voice I hadn't heard for weeks and faced him.

He stood bare-chested, except for the white towel that drooped downward around his shoulders, just like the sad smile that dipped low upon his face. His cheeks flushed with red blotches that cascaded down to his neck, and I wondered if it was from the hot day, the fight he'd nearly had, or from running the distance to get to me. Probably all three.

"Hey yourself," I said, failing to wipe away the evidence of tears fast enough. "Shouldn't you be with your girlfriend right now? Don't want to make a big awful scene." My anger wasn't at him directly, but more at the unfairness of it all.

"Samantha. I don't care if we make a scene," he said, throwing a hand toward the crowds across the lake. "I don't care about those people."

"*I care,*" I whispered.

"You shouldn't." Liam handed me his towel to wipe my wet face.

"Thanks."

"I hate seeing you this way, and it's partly my fault."

"You didn't do anything wrong, Liam."

Liam squeezed his hazel eyes shut, denying me access to read him better. "I don't know about that."

"What do you mean?" I asked.

When he opened his eyes, I saw the hurt behind them. He hurt just as much as I did. He ran a trembling hand through his wet hair, causing a few strands to stand up, making him look more beautiful than before. "Sam, I was wrong to let you think we were better off saying goodbye. Ever since the day you told me not to contact you, I can't stop thinking about you and everything that happened. It consumes me. I drove by your house a hundred times, hoping to catch you coming outside. I've been to the lake every other day, hoping you'd show up. And even though you hate shopping, I went to the mall, chancing my luck that I'd bump into you. I've kept my word not to contact you like you asked me, but Sam, I don't want to follow that rule anymore. Some rules are meant to be broken."

I shook my head. "But at whose expense, Liam? I'm the one they're all taking a huge bite out of, and I don't think I have much left."

"Maybe for a while, it will hurt you more than me, but in the end, I'm hoping it's worth it. Because would it be so bad if the rumors were true?"

"What?"

"I mean, yes, we've done nothing wrong, but, Sam, I'm not completely mad about these lies and rumors everyone created. Not when they put into motion the existence and the possibility of something real."

I swallowed. "What... what is real exactly?"

"Real is something tangible. Something you can trust and hold onto. It's something worth fighting for. Look, we're not guilty of anything. They're the ones who set the tone," he said, looking behind him. "But maybe they also set something beautiful into existence. I hate them for hurting you, Sam, but I love them for forcing me to see the realness of what you mean to me now." When Liam closed the space between us, it felt as if the air's particles made room for him. "*This*, this between us?" he said. "This real. The existence of us together, *we* are real."

Not wanting to meet the intensity of his eyes, which confessed such an array of hopeful, dangerous words, I found myself mesmerized by the droplets of water that clung to the tips of his hair instead.

"Sam," he continued. "Will you please just look at me? I need to you hear this. I need to know."

I forced my eyes away from that one droplet and took him all in as he spoke. "I may have fallen for you the moment I heard your laughter across the crowded room that first night we met. I think you were attempting the running man," he said with a shaky laugh. "Maybe I didn't see it before like I'm seeing it all now, but I'm in love with you. And by the look on your face, I know what I'm saying scares you. So, tell me you don't feel anything, and I'll walk away right now. I care about you too much to make this any harder for you."

My mind and heart raced alongside the truths of his words, and I wanted to lie, saying I felt nothing. But standing so close to him made it hard to remember what the problem was in the first place, or why our problems existed at all.

Until I remembered his girlfriend of four years.

"You forget the biggest problem," I said, taking a gut-wrenching step back. "You have a girlfriend, remember? How ... how could you think I'd be that person? *This—*" I said, waving a finger back and forth between us, "this can't happen. It complicates everything by a million."

"I *know* you're not that kind of person. That's why my girlfriend and I agreed to go our separate ways two weeks ago. We had our doubts before I ever met you. We didn't break up because of you; we broke up because we had run out of excuses on why we should stay together."

Liam's words hit me full force, and every cell in my body rushed to my skin's surface, as if waiting for permission to break through every pore in my body. But my old fears held them firmly in place, suffocating them in the process. "How does that fix anything? We just met. How can you know you feel this way about me?"

Liam reached a tentative hand out towards me, but tucked it under his arm instead, looking pained by the action. "I know it sounds crazy since we've only known each other for a short time. But I just know, Samantha. I know what I feel, and it's different this time. I know because I'm scared you don't feel the same way. And I'm terrified of losing the only thing that makes complete and utter sense in my life."

Frustrated that nothing ever came easy, I blurted, "Even if I admitted I felt the same way as you, it doesn't help *me*, Liam. I can't go anywhere without being criticized. If we were to explore what was *real*, it would all just be tainted with what everyone thinks of us. It would confirm what everyone thought. And how can I ever be happy knowing what people think of me? Or think of us?"

Liam gave in and reached a hand out to brush a fallen tear down my cheek. "In the end, does it truly matter, Samantha? In one year, we'll be graduating and everyone will be gone making lives for themselves. But what about you? Will you still care about what *they* all thought or said years after? Will you still want to pack up and leave this place to find whatever happiness you think you'll find? Or could you possibly stay forever if you found the right person?"

"I ... I don't know," I said.

"What are you so scared of?" Liam asked me.

I didn't answer him for almost a whole minute. "I'm ... I'm scared of the future, okay? I'm scared of choosing wrong and every decision I make might lead me to a hopeless fate I'll regret. I don't want to be a disappointment if it doesn't work out and I'm scared I don't know where home is for me."

"I know you're scared, and so am I. But fate isn't something hopeless. Fate is knowing you're exactly where you're meant to be." Liam shook his head. "It's as if your mind doesn't have a wide enough angle to see the bigger picture. Because, Sam, I truly think you wouldn't care where you lived or went, not when 'home' is always with the people you love."

I wanted *so* badly to give in and throw away my cares. I wanted to throw my arms around his shoulders and kiss those lips that had never looked more tempting. I truly wanted to live in the now without the what-ifs and without any doubts. But I couldn't. "Liam, I ... I want this to be real, but what if this isn't what we thought, and we just imagined it all? How could we ever know if what we want and what we feel is fake or real? How can we know this for sure?"

My friends came up behind him and joined us just as Liam was about to say something. "Sam?" Emily said. "Is everything okay?"

Maybe it was a bad habit that I always ran away from my fears rather than faced them head-on. Matt always knew me best; I was too chicken to take the next step. I handed Liam his towel, and he took it as his cue not to press me. I'm sure all the fears in my eyes told him that much.

Before Liam turned away, he left me with one more thought. "There will always be too many 'what ifs' in life. But sometimes you have to have a to take the shot. And ... and I hope you take the chance with me."

Chapter 32

Sam 2003

The events at the lake left me overheated, overwhelmed and overstimulated. My parents could never afford air conditioning, so I tried laying my cheek flat against the cool, smooth wooded grains of our old kitchen table. With my arms hanging lifeless to my sides, I was jealous of that table. Its only job was to welcome us to eat, without any expectations. It had taken a beating throughout the years and yet, it never seemed to mind the abuse or harsh words spoken when our family had had enough of each other. It just was.

I shut my eyes as my mind and heart battled each other over Liam's words, 'I hope you take the chance.' My mind told me that even if we took our friendship slowly and to the next level, people at school would assume even more that the rumors were true. But there was no ignoring or denying what my heart felt. My friends were right. My heart gravitated towards him like a force of nature—impelling, inevitable, and with unexplainable purpose. Was it fate? I didn't know.

I heard the front door open and with one eye open, I watched my mother's feet make their way to me. "I know this house is smoldering hot. Want a cold sandwich to help?"

"No," I said.

"You're passing up food? Does this mean the lake didn't go so well?"

"More or less."

My mother dropped her keys on the table and sat in the chair next to me. "What happened? I'm a good listener and might be able to help."

I lifted my head off the table. "You are a good listener, Mom. But this time, you can't fix this."

I cried then as I explained how I felt torn in two. "I ... I didn't realize how much I liked him, Mom. But I do. Why do I feel sick without him? It makes no sense. But it could never work out between us. It's already too complicated and already a disaster, when nothing has even started yet. I feel like this small, lost dwarf planet floating aimlessly without any direction—not knowing where to land. Don't you think falling in love shouldn't be this hard?"

She picked up the piece of paper on the table with Liam's number on it and smoothed over its corners. "When a friendship suddenly changes and catches fire, that kind of love can seem scary at first. No one wants to get burned. But sometimes, the best love stories come from the ones who took the greatest risks. And yes, Sam, you're right; I can't fix this for you. I can only promise you this much: all those kids gossiping, it's not forever, sweetheart. This, too, shall pass. *You* know you didn't do anything wrong. All that matters is what you think, and what you know is the truth."

"And as for Liam," she continued, "I can see why you like him. He sounds smart with a good head on his shoulders. He seems to have a good sense of knowing what's important, and he is willing to fight for that. Those are good qualities. So, my advice is to take it slow, one day at a time. What do you have to lose? It will all fall into place if it's meant to be. And he's right; you'll never know if you don't take the chance. Regrets can last a lifetime, my Sammy girl. Some risks are worth taking."

The telephone rang, and I shook my head left and right. "You answer it. Please? I just can't right now."

"Hello?" my mother answered. "Yes, this is Sam's mother, Julie." I gave my mother a perplexed look as the lines on her face drew downward, just before she gasped, "*Oh no*. I am so sorry. Yes, this is terribly sad."

The pained look in my mother's eyes made my heart thrash against my chest. "Mom?" I mouthed, "Who is it?"

She held up a finger. "Yes, thank you for calling. I will inform Samantha right now. And again, I am so very sorry."

She hung up, and I slapped a hand over my erratic heart to slow it down. "*Mom*. Who was that? What's wrong?"

"Honey. It's Jane."

~

We rushed to the nursing home immediately after my mother explained how Jane's cold had taken a turn for the worse. Her son thought she had only a few days and had kindly offered me a chance to say goodbye before it was too late. As much as it scared me, *this* I couldn't run away from.

I blamed myself and the nursing home the whole drive there. "She needed to see a doctor sooner, but like always, they're too busy or shorthanded." I slammed my palms against the side of my head. "This is all my fault. If I had been taking care of her, maybe she wouldn't have gotten sick in the first place."

"Oh, Sam, honey. Don't put that guilt on yourself. It will do neither you nor her any good." My mother pulled up to the front doors and asked, "Do you want me to come inside with you?"

"No," I said. "I need to do this alone."

"Okay, sweetie. I'll be back in an hour. I love you. Stay strong."

I choked back a sob. "I'll try. And I love you too, Mom."

I ran to Jane's room, not wanting to miss saying goodbye. She needed to know how much she meant to me. She needed to know how much I had grown to care for her. Because through all the good and bad, our friendship had turned into its own kind of love story—one that came with great risks. And even though we were burned a few times, the chance to get to know Jane Nelson had been worth all the fires.

A heavy somberness hung in room number thirty-three as Jane's son sat quietly by her side. And Jane's roommate, Alice, sat in bed, rocking back and forth—murmuring prayers from her Bible. I crossed the threshold and looked bravely at my friend's small frame under a thin white sheet. Her eyes were closed, and I panicked.

I was too late!

Charles turned to see me standing there with my hand over my gaping mouth, and his anguished expression quickly resolved. "No, no, Sam," he said standing. "She's just resting right now. Hospice gave her a little morphine to help her rest easier."

"Oh, thank God," I said, feeling some weight lift. "I thought I was too late."

He offered me his chair. "Come sit. And thank you for coming, Samantha. She talks a lot about you."

I folded into the chair. "What happened?" I said, looking down at her, hoping she would wake up soon to see me there.

"It's pneumonia. The doctor said she needed to go to the hospital immediately, but you know my mother—stubborn to the end. She refused any further help."

"But why?"

Charles looked down at his mother and hung his head. "She's simply too tired, Samantha. She *wants* to go. And I have to follow her wishes."

The day Jane and I made peace with one another, she said she wanted to leave this place. She said she wanted to be with those who'd left her behind. It looked like she would finally get her wish. And though it was hard to accept, I tried to take comfort in knowing she wanted this. But I asked anyway, "Isn't there any way she'll get better or pull through this?"

"Unfortunately, no. Jane's body is too frail to fight off the cold. We're told it's not much longer."

Obliterated went my brave front as I quietly cried into my hands.

Alice appeared at my side and handed me a tissue. "There there, dear soul. It will be okay."

"I hate to say this," Charles said, "but there is a good even in the bad." He looked over at his mother and reached a hand over hers. "The good being, no more suffering, Mom. No more suffering."

I agreed for the most part, but in my heart, I wished Jane could stay a little while longer, for at least my sake. She didn't know how much I needed her, especially now. I wanted to tell her about Liam, and I needed her wisdom. I needed her to stay.

Charles moved to the door. "I thought you might want some privacy to say goodbye, so I'll just be in the dining hall to get some coffee."

"Okay. Thank you," I said.

Alice added, "I think I'll join you in the mess hall, Charles. They may need a reminder to make a fresh pot of coffee." Alice gave me an affectionate squeeze on my shoulder with her good arm before leaving. "God will take good care of her, love. Angels are waiting as we speak."

In a sense, I'd met two seniors that I had fallen in love with, and I stood and turned to face Alice. "I'll see you around, Alice?"

"You betcha. I'll finish the story I was telling you."

"I'd like that very much," I said before hugging her tightly for a good long while.

Once alone, I hesitantly covered Jane's hand with mine. Her face looked tired and worn out, and her breathing labored unevenly in stretches. I had difficulty catching my breath every time she struggled for air. Jane wasn't lying when she said she always felt as if she were drowning from her sorrows. Even now, on her deathbed, she was doing just that. But this time, it was from natural causes and not from the evilness of our world.

I looked around her meager room and zeroed in on the top of her dresser at the end of her feet. One of her cherished potted plants—once vibrant—sat looking tired and worn-out, like its owner. But the blooms of dark iridescent purple surprisingly still flourished. I remembered Jane's words: 'If you don't care about the little things, it will all spill over into the most important things,' so I stood and reached over to dip my finger into the soil. Someone had forgotten to water it. It was bone dry.

With Jane's knowledge about houseplants, I'd learned a lot about caring for them, especially this delicate African violet I now held in my hand. African violets liked moist soil but could never be over-watered or sit in water for too long; otherwise, they would drown. African violets preferred indirect light; otherwise, they burned. They were highly sensitive to the cold, and their leaves and blooms did not like to be touched. But with the proper care, they could flourish and had been known to live up to fifty years. And in a way, Jane was like an African violet—delicate, sensitive, and temperamental.

Even though the houseplant was traditionally given to mothers and daughters worldwide for its feminine symbolism of loyalty, strength, courage, and the deepest depths of love, I felt it should be given to friends too. Because even though I had only just learned how to care for my friend properly, our relationship had grown and flourished into something rare and beautiful—between the young and old, everlasting and strong. My mother was right. Maybe it was the most challenging relationships that were worth fighting for and worth the heartaches. They were the ones we grew the most with, and for the better.

After pouring a small amount of water into the plant, careful not to drip any onto its wilted leaves, I looked over at Jane, wishing in all the worlds of magic spells that I could have poured a little more life into my friend. I reached out again and gently rubbed the top of her hand, watching her skin's thin, delicate layers roll back and forth like an ocean wave, and softly hummed a tune my grandmother and mother used to sing to me when I was a little girl.

I was on the second verse of "I Walk Through the Garden" when Jane's eyes fluttered like a butterfly opening its wings for the first time. I thought she would fall back into a deep slumber momentarily, but she surprised me and opened her eyes as if coming out of a heavy fog.

"Jane? Jane?" I said, hoping she could focus in on me.

She turned her head towards me, smiling sweetly—the morphine doing its job—but her smile did not last long before a cough took hold and attacked its victim with a vengeance. I panicked and tried to reach a hand behind her back, but she couldn't sit up for me to do so. I looked at the door and debated finding Charles, but Jane squeezed my hand surprisingly hard and firmly shook her head 'No.'

As I watched her struggle, I mentally created an imaginary burst of air from my lungs, willing it through her body to expel whatever she choked on, and finally, after the whole episode, when her cough eased enough to allow her the precious air she needed, I collapsed into a heaping pile of tears at her side.

It took Jane a full minute to regain her composure before straining a whisper. "Sing that tune again. I know it."

My voice was unsteady at first, but I eventually sang the tune evenly and softly, just loud enough for the two of us to hear. Jane's smile was like a warm sunset, but I worried that like all fleeting sunsets, they faded behind mountains in a blink of an eye. And because I didn't know how much time I had with her, I choked up on the second verse before having a good cry into the thin folds of her bedsheets.

I felt her hand comfort my back, before I muffled an apology, "I'm so sorry, Jane."

Her voice labored. "You know this is life's cycle." She coughed but continued, "I am ready. I'm not scared, sweetheart. Please, please don't cry for me."

"I know you're not scared. I just don't want you to go, is all. I don't know what to do without you. There's so much to say still."

Jane caressed my wet face that still rested beside her. "We *have* been having a swell time, haven't we?"

I looked up at her. "Yes," I said with a sniffle.

She patted my hand. "You're a good girl, Samantha. You're a good girl. Can you do me a favor?"

I nodded yes, happy that the morphine had worn off a little, enough that she could be coherent with me one last time.

"Come back and check in on Alice. She could use a friend here before she heads home in a few weeks."

"Sure, Jane. I'd love to visit Alice."

"Good." Jane pointed to a tape player on top of her dresser. "There's a cassette sitting there. It says Benny Goodman and Peggy Lee on it."

I picked up the cassette and asked, "This one?"

She nodded. "Go ahead and put it in that tape player. It's the band that Clint and I danced to that first night."

Pushing the tape into its slot, I pressed play. Immediately the room filled with the sounds of an orchestra and band music playing from an era long ago.

"I forgot to tell you about the night Clint died," Jane said. "It was around 3 a.m. when this *very* song came on the radio, next to my bed."

When Jane's cough came on strong, I was afraid she couldn't finish her story. I handed her a tissue just in time for her to spit thick, greenish-yellow, bloodied mucus into it, temporarily relieving her. Once she seemed calm again, Jane continued speaking with a little more ease. "I swear to this day, that radio was off when I fell asleep. This was, of course, before I knew about Clint's accident. That devastating news didn't reach me until much later that morning. But it was 3 a.m. when I woke from a dead sleep to hear this tune on the radio. Of all the darnedest things."

Jane pointed a finger in the air. "You gotta wait almost a minute before Peggy sings her part. Listen carefully."

Jane and I sat together, listening to the crackle of an old band playing an enchanting song. And when the singer finally made her entrance, her smooth voice sang:

'We'll meet again,
don't know where, don't know when,
but I know we'll meet again,
some sunny day.'
'Keep smilin' through,
just like you, always do,
till the blue skies drive the dark clouds far away.'

My eyes were wide at the meaningful words behind the song, and Jane asked me while the music played on, "Do you believe in fate?"

The word 'fate' hit a nerve inside me, making the hairs on my body stand on end. "I'd like to believe it exists," I said slowly. "But I don't know for sure."

Jane shook her head. "Normally, I wouldn't believe in such silly things either, but it wasn't until weeks after Clint passed that I remembered the radio playing that same song next to my bed the night he died. So, days later, and wanting to believe it was a sign from Clint, I inquired about what time he'd possibly died. Samantha, I was told he died around three in the morning—about the same time that song played and woke me from my sleep."

"That doesn't sound like a coincidence."

"No. It doesn't. I think Clint sent me a sign from above—a whisper saying how we would meet again. Fate has a way of finding you, don't you think? Even if the world interferes, in the end, it finds you in the smallest of whispers, letting you know nothing is forever lost."

I could only nod with my hand on my heart, afraid I'd cry again.

Jane nodded as well. "Yep. So there you have it. Don't get all bent out of shape. I'll be seeing my Clint, after all."

I smiled and squeezed her hand. "I believe you will, Jane. I believe it."

"She's awake," Charles proclaimed behind me.

I stood to allow Charles the little time he had left with his mother, and before leaving the room, I hugged my dear friend as tight as I could without breaking her. Our eyes met in understanding—a silent goodbye—but not forever.

Jane's eyes were tired and heavy again. "We will meet again, Samantha? Some sunny day?"

There was no stopping my tears or my answer, "Yes. Yes, we will, Jane. I'm sure of it."

Before leaving the room, I picked up the African violet off the floor to place it back on the dresser until Jane stopped me. "No. No, you take it. Take extra care of it."

I was grateful to have something to remember Jane by and smiled. "Thank you. And I promise not to over-water it."

A faint grin reached the corners of my friend's mouth. "Just remember, only a teaspoon of water every couple of days. It also needs fertilizing twice a year. And for Pete's sake, Samantha, don't get any water on the leaves."

Of course, Jane Nelson couldn't resist one last lecture. I kissed her forehead and whispered, "Do you ever give up, woman?"

"Never," she said with a wink.

I memorized her face at that moment like an etched tattoo inside my heart, never forgetting the immense impression she'd left on me, and walked out of room thirty-three with only half a heart.

~

While waiting for my mother to come back to pick me up, I found a chair in the lobby, where I closed my heavy eyes and imagined a world where my friend found peace.

A small piece of my grieving heart mended itself when I thought of Jane finally finding relief from all the suffering that had held her captive for far too long. With a body that failed her and haunting memories that stripped her of precious time, she deserved to find freedom and relief. So I imagined her at peace, at last.

And my heart eased a little more when I envisioned Jane leaving this world to find her daughter Kathleen, who'd long waited with wide-open arms for her mother. And alongside Kathleen would be her grandchild, who'd never taken his or her first breath but now stood whole, and all good things children were meant to be.

And lastly, I imagined Clint with his long-kept promise that he *would* see his girl one sunny day. The heavens would fill with sweet music, and Jane Nelson would take the hand of her a knight in shining armor and dance once again. That last vision comforted me the most, because as for the question of whether fate or choices determined our destiny, in the end, I believed it was a little of both.

So I stood tall, feeling more brave than ever before, and headed outside to see if my mother had arrived. When the doors slid open, and the sun came down brightly, blinding me, I shielded my eyes with Jane's African violet plant in hand to locate my mother's yellow beast of a car. But it wasn't there. Instead, a red one stood before me—one I had come to fondly recognize.

This time, my heart didn't race with uncertainty. It raced at the choice I had finally made. When the owner of the car walked toward me with an unsure step, and his concerned hazel eyes with golden specks met mine, I saw my fated future in them and smiled, taking the chance at last.

"Hey," I said.

He pulled me into his arms, exactly where I was always meant to be. "Hey yourself."

Acknowledgments and Words from the Author

When I first thought to write the trilogy, *The Caretaker of Secrets*, Fate, Faith, and Freed, about a young coming-of-age girl who would care for three senior women throughout her life, it sounded easy in theory. How difficult could it be to write a duality of stories about life, love, and heartbreak in different time periods and piece them together? Being that this is my first debut novel, it wasn't easy. Not in the least.

But I forged on, because my ultimate goal in this trilogy was for women readers to find themselves stronger and more determined when facing the never-ending challenges in life, like I did when writing this series. And although the series has been the hardest thing I've ever done, it also came easy at times, because the three women in these stories are *real* people, *real* women, whom I have cared for, all of whom have shaped and molded me in so many ways.

Anything is possible when you have the love of your three wise friends pushing your hand and pen forward. So, it is because of these three women I have learned that when life gets tough, and you feel you are drowning, that's when you keep swimming—never to give up. My sweet and wise friends have also taught me never to lose sight of my destiny, and they have taught me, *and* hopefully, **you**, that fate, faith, and the ability to find freedom within ourselves, is the ultimate goal in life.

And so, without further ado—to my women warriors, Jane in Fate, Alice in Faith, and Malaya in Freed, I thank you from the depths of my soul for the memories you shared with me and your life stories of love, heartbreak, and betrayal. You have no idea how much you have shaped and molded me into the woman I am today and how much I cherished your love and friendships. And as your caretaker of secrets, who kept some secrets hidden just between us, I hope I did you all justice in making parts of your memories stay alive forever in our hearts. Thank you, my dearest angels.

To my amazing beta readers, Terry Schweitzer, Emily Geiger, Marcy McCreary, April Bouchard, and Evelyn Cammon! This book would not have been what it is without your insightfulness. Your thoughts and ideas have furthered this book into something more than what it was at the beginning. I can never thank you enough for helping me complete this.

Much gratitude for my writers' club at the Bonney Lake senior center, thank you, Larry Krackle, for introducing me to the sweetest group known to humankind. Every single one of you in this club has touched my heart and has been beyond helpful in editing my very rougher-than-rough first drafts. I only wished some of you were still here to have read the finished product you took part in. Love you the most, sweet Norman. I'm letting my heart lead me, just as you told me.

Cheers to my bestest of friends—my encouraging tribe. There are too many of you to list, but you all know who you are. If it weren't for you all, who continued pushing me to think past all the negative, I wouldn't have finished this. There are no better words than to say y'all were in my corner from day one. And a special shout out to you, Erin Perkins. I can't thank you enough for showing me that I have a light inside me and that I need to shine it for all to see. Thank you for lighting me up, my soul sister. Fate brought us together for sure.

So. Much. Love to my family of women warriors. My rock, my mother, there are not enough words to describe the beautiful woman you are inside and out. Your journey in life and your stories alone have changed me. I hope you will write your story someday, because you are a light in this world and would bring people as much hope as you have shown me. Thank you for being my number-one cheerleader and pushing me to follow my dreams. And to my beautiful sisters, Audre and Christina; without your never-ending positivity and strength, I couldn't have done this. I look up to you in more ways than you will ever know. Thank you.

To my most cherished ones whom I took the chance with—my life, my soul, my everything—my husband Sean and my two children, Emily and Jackson. I feel bad for you guys the most because you had to endure the constant crying and the meltdowns of self-doubt. How you all handled all the many crazy sides of me, well, you guys are the truest of warriors.

Thank you for putting up with me and never giving up hope that I could one day finish this feat. I love you so much.

And lastly, to you, my readers who have read this far, thank you for giving me a chance. I hope you stick around for the long haul. But ultimately, I hope that through *The Caretaker of Secrets* trilogy, you find yourself better and whole in some ways because we are all women warriors young and old. So be kind to one another, cheer each other on, and brave on, my friends. Brave on.

Sneak Peek into The Caretaker of Secrets {Faith}

Prologue

The dark wet whorls of matted hair clung to her tiny head as curious dark blue eyes stared back into mine, as if daring me to choose her over him. Maybe some young mothers would look away, but I didn't dare. I memorized every finger and toe, embedding the fine, delicate details of her perfect little body into my soul. Skin soft like cream, a button nose, a pursed-lipped mouth of pink and white, and a soft mewled cry of a kitten.

How could I ever forget.

"It's a selfless act of love," he said, trying desperately to console the inconsolable.

I couldn't even bear to look at his face as my own became wet with anguished cries, mimicking that of my daughter's, whose face contorted in confusion, wondering why I couldn't give her what she needed—milk? A mother's love?

Already a blurred question.

My heart tore in two when the nurse took her from me with arms spread wide as my own now hung lifeless against the still-bloodied bedsheets.

It was the hardest decision I ever had to make.

A mistake never to mend itself.

Chapter 1

Sam 2005

The low evening sun hovered at eye level, blinding me as I drove north on Highway 167. I snapped the visor down to block its glare while taking a reluctant glance at the clock above the dash. Groaning, I bit the inside of my cheek, a habit that often left my skin raw. Not even a Bon Jovi song on the radio could help my mood.

While "Livin' On a Prayer" played, I couldn't help but relate to the lyrics. 'Gina works the diner all day working for her man, she brings home her pay, for love.'

Bless Gina.

Did she ever find the silver lining to her crappy life?

Was love enough?

Did fairytales exist even after the prince rescued you?

What happened to Gina!

Tired of living on a prayer from day to day, and with a million cars driving at a snail's pace, I flicked the radio off in a huff, gritting my teeth, while digging my nails into the steering wheel. The date finally dawned on me—Monday, October 31st—Halloween—explaining the traffic.

I imagined the troves of parents rushing to find the perfect neighborhood to appease their child's sugar cravings—"Trick-or-treat," the greedy buggers would say as they held out their saliva-stained candy-filled pillowcases—and my stomach moaned as an image of a candy bar tempted the forefront of my thoughts. I hadn't eaten for hours, and envied the little twerps as they stuffed their faces with fistfuls of Twix and Kit Kat.

Why had I wanted to grow up so fast? I'll never know. Because now, without the sweet treats and only left with tricks, the joke was on me—a struggling twenty-year-old full-time college student who worked evenings at a filthy restaurant and had little to no time for fun whatsoever.

I struggled to remind myself daily that I should be grateful to have a job that paid for my college and a place to sleep, even if I was still living with my parents. And I was lucky to have a boyfriend with whom I could see a forever future, one whose lips were still on my mind from the night before. But today it was hard to remember all the good. Not when Mondays were my night off from my perverted boss, and someone had called in sick, forcing me to cover for them. So yeah, I would give my left pinky to be young again without all the cares. Hell, I'd even give my right hand for a Twix.

I looked to my right, toward the exit, and wondered whether the backroads would be faster. I couldn't be late again, or I'd lose my job. The manager at the restaurant was a stickler for tardiness. Making a quick decision, I swerved my hard-earned first car—a 1990 teal-green Honda—onto the off-ramp and prayed for a miracle.

At the end of the exit, near the stop sign, an older homeless woman paced back and forth, holding up a bent piece of cardboard reading HELP ME, PLEASE. She wore a dirty, oversized, thinly tattered jacket and jeans that had seen better days. Clearly, she wasn't equipped for Washington state's cold and wet weather. Although the evening was rare and sunny, October's chill was crisp, and temps would drop to the mid-forties by nightfall.

With only two cars in front of me, I thought of the woman's dire situation and contemplated what to do. I didn't want my hard-earned money to go towards someone's addictions, but at the same time, I didn't want anyone to starve or freeze to death either.

And it wasn't like we could just ask them, 'Hey, mind telling me what you will spend this money on?' But I also knew from experience that after listening to people's backstories and hardships, it left little room for judgment. So, with only one car ahead of me now, and with the woman's pale blue pleading eyes connecting with mine, and noticing she didn't have any fingers on her right hand, fate and choice decided for me, and I reached inside my purse.

Once my car came within a few feet of her, I quickly rolled down my window, ready to give my money, but she couldn't grab the money fast enough. Not when her good hand still held the sign, and the wind picked up both our hopes and dreams, blowing it into a field behind her.

As she hobbled with a bummed knee, failing terribly to stop the wind from completely blowing our money further away, I cursed and pulled over to help her.

"Sorry," she said after I fetched and handed over the few dollars I could find. "I'm a veteran and haven't much mobility."

Up close now, I could see the woman's face was dirty, cracked, and worse, she grinned a wide toothless smile. No teeth typically meant a drug user. Guilt washed over me, and I imagined the lady shooting up and overdosing from her never-ending habit. A habit to which I'd now contributed. But it was too late. And I was also definitely now late for work.

"I hope you can have a warm meal tonight. Have a blessed evening," I said, running back to the car.

After turning the corner and getting off the freeway, my decision to take the backroads seemed to be the best choice. With no cars in front of me, I tried to compensate for lost time and pushed my car to sixty, ignoring the speed-limit sign that said thirty-five. After a quick glance in the rearview mirror at my face, I gasped in horror at a face that needed severe freshening up. I doubted the patrons at the restaurant would tip me well if I looked like the bag lady off the side of the road.

As a full-time college student in school from 7 a.m. to 3 p.m. and then at an evening shift at work starting at 4:30 and ending an hour before midnight, sometimes I didn't have time to do anything but a quick change of clothes. So, with one hand on the wheel, I wiped the black smudges from under my eyes and pulled out a stick of Maybelline's 'Sun-Kissed' from my purse.

Lipstick always made me feel better. It helped my lips appear more prominent and proportionate to my other sizable features. I blamed my father for my not-so-feminine nose that seemed to clash with the narrowness of my face. However, I was grateful my mother had given me two blue eyes that made me appear wide awake, no matter how tired I felt.

When a black hatchback pulled out in front of me, causing my hand to jerk upward, smearing the lipstick onto the tip of my nose, I slowed back down to the speed limit and hit the steering wheel with the palm of my hand before yelling, "Oh, come on."

While using the back of my hand to wipe it off, I cursed when some of it smudged onto the sleeve of my white uniform. Now I was tired, hungry, dirty, and as luck would have it, a headache began to form. I pinched the bridge of my nose and debated taking an Advil. The dull throb in my head was either from having no time to eat dinner or from my long, thick curly brown hair pulled too tightly into a severe ponytail on top of my head.

I growled in frustration as I freed my hair from its hair tie. With the restaurant only five minutes away, I carefully used my left knee to steer the wheel while attempting to braid my hair, and when I finished with both hands safely on the steering wheel, I looked into the rearview mirror to admire my handiwork. Not satisfied, I pulled down a few strands of hair to frame my face to give a wispy look. "There," I said, feeling better.

With my eyes reverted back to the road again, my heart lurched forward and launched straight out of my chest at the sight of the hatchback in front of me.

It had unexpectedly stopped, and there was no way to avoid the crash.

I gripped the steering wheel in terror while slamming my brakes to the floor with all my strength. And as the brake pedal vibrated violently, disagreeing beneath my feet, I knew it was inevitable as the black vehicle loomed all too fast before me. With my eyes tightly shut, I instinctively stiffened and waited for the hard impact.

The sick sound of metal on metal reached my ears at the same moment my entire body slammed forward with a quick whoosh. My head hit the steering wheel briefly before the seatbelt dug into my left shoulder, forcing me to slam back into my seat with a jolting thud.

It was over as fast as it started.

The only noise was that of the loud thrum deep within the canals of my ears as rapid adrenaline coursed through my veins. And the once-dormant headache I felt earlier now felt like an active volcano about to explode. With eyes still shut, the unsteadiness of my hand found its way to my forehead, where a small bump had begun to form at the hairline. I slowly opened my eyes to see if the presence of blood greeted my fingertips, but relief followed from its absence.

Before braving a look up to survey the damage I'd caused, I thought of Liam's last words to me the night before. He had pinned me against the wall, giving me his best kiss yet, leaving my lips wet and swollen.

"Knock em' dead tomorrow," he said, knowing I had a stressful test in the morning and a whole night's shift at work.

I didn't think his last words to me would come true. So I prayed no one was hurt. I prayed no one was dead.

Need Help From Abuse?

*If you or someone you know is suffering from violence, help is available. Call the National Domestic Violence Hotline at 1-800-799-7233.

Want To Help Our Seniors?

*Feeling a little charitable towards our seniors, young and old? The Blessing Movement is a non-profit organization that places senior high school students to work closely with our local senior citizens with disabilities or terminal illnesses that prevent them from maintaining their yards. Not only are special bonds made between the young and old, but donations to this organization go towards funding college scholarships and also providing materials needed to beautify yards. If you would like to donate, please visit this organization at https://blessingmovement.org/.

Or

Adopt A Senior!

The Adopt A Senior Organization is another non-profit that brings a personal touch to the forgotten seniors in nursing homes by directly providing them with some outside love and contact, as well as gifts, birthday cards, and holiday cards, to let them know they are not forgotten and are not alone.
https://www.adopt-a-senior.org/about_us

Book Club Discussion/Questions for The Caretaker of Secrets {Fate}

1. Do you believe in such a thing as fate? Why or why not?
2. Have you ever felt like you were drowning in the sea of life? How did you overcome these obstacles?
3. What was your first job, and did it mold you in any shape or form?
4. Have you ever had a job where you wanted to tell someone off but didn't?
5. Do you think Samantha was too harsh when she quit working for Jane?
6. Jane's trials and tribulations were from the late '60s and early '70s. Do you think she still would have felt trapped living at home with Daniel if her battles occurred in the present day and age?
7. Kathleen didn't go to the authorities. Do you understand her decision?
8. Jane and Samantha's relationship had a fifty-year age gap. Has someone younger or older in your life impacted you in a way that has changed you?
9. Did you ever have something dramatic happen in high school that, when looking back, it was merely trivial? Or was your feeling and emotions valid even then and even now?

10. How did Jane's drug addiction differ from Samantha's addiction to alcohol? Was there a difference?
11. What was Samantha's pivotal moment where she found growth? How about Jane's?
12. How did the character's views and personalities change throughout the story, and did your opinion of them change in the end?
13. If you could change the story's outcome, what would it be?

Printed in the USA
CPSIA information can be obtained
at www.ICGtesting.com
LVHW030738240923
759090LV00026B/278/J

9 781961 910027